In Good Times and Bad

A sequel to Always Faithful and True

Christian Romance Fiction

by Janet DiFabio

Always Faithful – Series:

† *Always Faithful and True*   (book one)
ISBN 978-0-578-45394-1

† *In Good Times and Bad*   (book two)
ISBN 978-0-578-47555-4
(Both books can be read as a stand-alone.)

Other books by Janet DiFabio

† *All for the Good*
ISBN 979-8-218-06579-9

In Good Times and Bad

A sequel to Always Faithful and True

"Rejoice in hope, endure in affliction, persevere in prayer. Romans" 12:12

By
Janet DiFabio

StarWolf Communications, LLC
New Jersey

In Good Times and Bad

ISBN: 978-0-578-47555-4
Library of Congress Control Number: 2019936559
StarWolf Communications, LLC
Ingram Spark and KDP Distribution

Acknowledgements

I wish to personally thank the following people for their contributions toward this book. Their knowledge, feedback, and inspiration made it happen.

To my family, for your continued patience and support. You put up with me while I wrote my first novel, *Always Faithful and True*, and encouraged me to finish this sequel. I know it's been a long, difficult journey, especially for having to tolerate my moodiness during the writing process. I appreciate your understanding.

To my critique partner and husband, Mike, for reading my drafts more times than you wanted. You helped me to think outside the box, enabling me to write with more depth. Your suggestions gave me ambition and determination. Without those, I'd be back on page one.

To my sister, Laura, for sharing your EMT experience, which was especially helpful in this specific story.

To Virginia, my copyeditor, for your professional advice and assistance in polishing my manuscript. No words can express my gratitude for your expertise.

To my readers, thank you for choosing my book for your reading entertainment. If it weren't for you, I'd have no reason to publish. I hope, if anything, my stories inspire you to stay strong through life's tribulations and to help you find comfort knowing that God is *Always Faithful and True*, even *In Good Times and Bad*.

To StarWolf, for bringing my story to print.

And most of all, thank you Almighty God for the gift of life, your guidance, and endless love.   *Janet*

Dedication

In memory of my two angel babies:
4/5/05 and 2/7/16

"An angel in the book of life wrote down my baby's birth. Then whispered as she closed the book, 'too beautiful for earth'."

~Author Unknown

✝

"I prayed for this child, and the Lord has granted me what I asked of him. So now, I give him to the Lord."

1 Samuel 1:27-28

Chapter One

What happens next. Gianna reflected as she gazed out the oval-shaped airplane window at the white, pillow-like clouds floating by. If only it was possible to relax, she might feel better. Although the plane reached altitude, her stomach was still queasy, and her head continued to pound. She shifted in her seat, trying to get comfortable, but the rhythmic thumps to her backside from the youth sitting behind her made it impossible. She thought about calling him on it but figured it was useless. His plugged-up ears couldn't hear her anyway. Gianna, a middle school teacher, thought she had more tolerance, but this brat proved her wrong.

She reached into her purse and checked the time on her cell phone. It had only been forty minutes since she and her bridegroom boarded the New York bound plane. *How am I going to handle another eight hours of this?* She reclined her seat, closed her eyes, and took in a soothing breath. *Lord, please bring us home safely. Thank you.*

"You ok?" Danny asked, reaching for her hand.

She opened her eyes and met his gaze. His soft blue eyes seemed to reach into her soul. "Yeah, but I wish we didn't have to leave Italy. It was fun."

"I think we covered a lot of ground in two weeks," he said.

"I suppose." She turned her head away pretending to be more interested in watching the blanket of clouds soar past her window.

Danny brushed a few strands of chestnut brown hair out of her face. "Babe, this isn't about leaving Italy, is it? You're not ready to face going home."

She blinked back the moisture in her eyes, and then looked at his ruggedly, handsome face. *Golly, he knows me like a book.* She shook her head. "I wish we were going home—to Montana. I felt safe there."

Danny's tough cowboy features grew somber. "I know, but your life is in Manhattan with me. Chad can't hurt you anymore."

She gave him a reassuring smile. "I know."

Although Chad Garrett was behind bars, she still feared returning to Danny's home, where the assault had taken place just twelve weeks ago. Since the incident, she'd been coping well; living at home in Montana with her parents and siblings and receiving professional therapy. However, the reality of returning to New York was beginning to rear its ugly head.

She leaned on Danny's shoulder and breathed in his bold scent of Drakkar cologne and leather. As she inhaled deeply, she could smell a hint of Irish Spring soap. Just having him near calmed her anxieties.

Hours later, the flight reached its destination at JFK International Airport. Gianna, unable to stomach chaos, confusion, or rude people, latched onto Danny's arm as they shuffled their way out of the plane. As they weaved through the crazed airport crowd, mindless people continuously bumped into her petite frame as though she were invisible. After she and Danny claimed their luggage, they worked their way outside the airport's main entrance to meet their close friends and neighbors, Troy and Tracy Evans.

As Gianna exited the airport, she winced at the blast of muggy, dense air that slapped her in the face. Dressed in a sleeveless blouse and pencil skirt, her frozen air-conditioned body quickly defrosted. Within minutes, her neck, exposed by her ponytail, burned from the intense August sun.

She glanced up at her new husband, who looked hot in more ways than one. His solid black t-shirt, tucked neatly into the waist of his boot-cut jeans, clung against his well-muscled torso and powerful biceps. She wondered how he tolerated the heat dressed in black from head to toe. She watched in awe as he put on his sunglasses and adjusted his cowboy hat to shade himself from the blazing sun.

Outside the noisy airport lobby, Gianna bounced on her tippy-toes and searched for Troy and Tracy.

"They should be here already," she shouted over the roar of the jet engines.

"There's Troy now," Danny said, pointing straight ahead toward a crowd of people.

Gianna laughed. "Easy for you to say, you're six- foot."

When the group of people parted, Gianna caught a glimpse of Troy. "My stars! How did I miss him wearing that lime green polo shirt?"

The color was stunning on him, complementing his bronze complexion. Even out of police uniform, Troy was well dressed.

Danny waved his arms. "Hey, bud, over here!"

Troy raised his hand to his forehead to shield his eyes from the glittering sun. Once he spotted them, he waved, then sprinted down the sidewalk toward them.

"Hey, cowboy!" Troy said. "Hello, Gianna!" He reached for her carry-on bags. "Here, let me help you with those."

"Thank you," she said, scanning the crowd for Tracy. "Didn't Tracy come with you?"

"No, she's at home fixing an early lunch for us."

Gianna put her hand to her chest. "Oh, you guys...that's so sweet, thank you."

She smiled thinking about how incredibly thoughtful and caring her neighbors were. Tracy had a kind heart and always went out of her way to do something nice.

On the drive home, Gianna sat quietly in the back seat. She rested her right elbow on the door panel with her fist under her chin and stared out the window at the mad rush of vehicles whizzing by. She wondered where everyone was going in such a hurry.

Danny sat up front and gushed to Troy about their trip to Italy. She wanted so badly to share in his enthusiasm, but she couldn't take her mind off, *'what happens next.'* Was

Chad's evil grin going to welcome her home? Her stomach twisted as that rotten image entered her mind. She sucked on her bottom lip and tried to refocus on her honeymoon memories.

Just a few miles from home, traffic came to a sudden halt. A nauseating smell of burning rubber clogged the air. The faint sound of ear-piercing sirens rapidly grew louder as an emergency vehicle elbowed its way to the curb.

"Darn!" Troy smacked the steering wheel. "It looks like we're going to be sitting here for a while. I would need my patrol car to get through this mess."

"Traffic, what a shocker," Danny said with sarcasm. He reclined his seat and stretched out his long legs.

"Welcome to New York City," Gianna mumbled.

Her stomach became tight with uneasiness as the crazy action-packed streets unfolded before her eyes. Buses weaved in and out of lanes, horns honked, and people exchanged obscene sign language. *What did I ever see in this city that was so appealing?*

Gianna rested her head against the seat and closed her eyes, allowing her mind to wander back seven years, to when she was fresh out of high school. She knew exactly what she wanted to do with her life, and when a prestigious university accepted her on a scholarship, she knew that New York City was the place to be. She couldn't wait to be there. But why? Back then she wanted her independence from her parents and her four brothers. But now, she realized that she was young and naïve and had no clue about the real world.

Sighing heavily, she reached into her purse for her cell phone. She texted her parents to let them know the plane had landed safely. It had been two weeks since she'd spoken to them, and she missed them terribly.

An hour later, Troy, Danny, and Gianna reached the private tree-lined street called home. Her heart raced as their car passed by the familiar cluster of four-story brownstone buildings. She was getting closer to finding out, *'what happens next.'*

Troy pulled his hunter green sedan into the gated lot and parked it in his assigned spot right next to Danny's polished black Ford pickup.

Danny eyed his truck. "Hey, it's still in one piece."

"Of course, cowboy. It's in a secure lot," Troy said. "Besides, you know the streets that *I* patrol are safe." He glanced into the rearview mirror at Gianna. "You can head inside. We'll get the bags."

Gianna faked a smile and said, "Ok."

Reality struck. She was home where the assault took place. She hadn't been there in three months. Would Chad be waiting for her? She shook her head trying to snap herself out of her outlandish thoughts. Chad was in prison and couldn't harm her anymore. *Everything's going to be all right.*

Gianna's trembling hand reached for the door handle, but before she could pull it, the door opened. She jumped in her seat.

"Babe, I am so sorry I startled you," Danny said.

She took a deep breath. "I'm ok."

She reached up and clutched his hand. As she exited the car, she took another deep breath, almost choking on the stuffy, smog-filled air.

"Are you sure you're ok?" he asked.

"I'm good," she gasped. "I guess I'm not used to this fine quality air."

He looked at her with staid calmness.

"No worries," she said, caressing his cheek. She loved the sandy texture of his designer shadow against her smooth hands. "I'll wait for you two in the lobby."

"Ok," he said and gave her a kiss.

Gianna started down the concrete sidewalk toward their end unit. As she slowly climbed the steps, she eyed the two shabby shrubs on both sides of the porch. That was it for green space. She had forgotten how compact everything was compared to the open land in Sheridan, Montana. She missed her father's cattle ranch already.

She swiped her key pass to unlock the lobby door. As she entered the building, a sudden light-headedness came over her. The queasiness in her stomach grew more intense, too. Feeling unstable, she took a seat in the lobby and rested her eyes.

The lobby was so peaceful, unlike the chaotic airport and hectic city streets. The trickling sound of water cascading down the rocks in the garden fountain lessened her woes.

She opened her eyes and looked up at the exposed ductwork, then scanned the whitewashed brick walls. She admired the industrial feel of a city building.

She gazed at the ivory marble floor and recalled the first time Danny invited her there and how he succeeded in impressing her. She smiled at the happy memory, realizing she was now home.

"Hello Gianna and congrats," a deeply distinguished voice called out, echoing through the lobby.

She looked up and saw Kurt, one of the security officers, waving at her. "Thank you, sir," she said.

She carefully rose from her chair and gracefully walked to the front desk to greet him. During their chat, he informed her that she had a stack of letters and a large package waiting for her. She thanked him, then stepped away from the counter to retrieve her mail.

While Gianna was unlocking the mailbox, she spotted Danny and Troy wheeling in the luggage. As she thumbed through the envelopes, weeding out the junk, she listened to Danny rave to Kurt about their exciting honeymoon. She smiled inside, so happy that Italy was everything he dreamed it would be.

She stuffed the pile of mail into her purse before crouching down to pick up the oversized box. When she tried to lift it, her legs went numb, her head felt woozy, and the conversation around her became muffled. She caught a glimpse of Kurt's troubled expression prior to her vision blurring and her stumbling backward.

"Whoa there!" Danny yelled, catching her fall.

"I'm ok," she insisted. She rubbed her eyes and attempted to stand up unassisted.

"And just how many drinks did you have on the plane, Gianna?" Troy teased.

"Funny, Troy! You know I don't drink," she snapped. "I haven't eaten in a while, that's all." She rubbed her eyes again. When she regained control over her balance, she wiggled out of Danny's embrace.

Staring at the floor, Danny ran his fingers through his thick hair. "How long have you been having these dizzy spells?"

She shrugged dismissively. "The box was just awkward—I lost my balance. Forget it."

"Hold on there," he said, reaching for her arm. "Are you sure you can walk? Maybe you should sit a spell."

"I'm fine, really. I've been sitting for hours already." She sensed the doctor's side of him surfacing and didn't want an evaluation.

Danny frowned. He opened his mouth, about to say something, but didn't. He just shook his head, picked up the bulky box, and directed her to the elevator. Troy, noticeably stunned, just followed behind with the luggage in tow.

As the three exited the elevator on the second floor, Tracy coincidently poked her head outside her front door. "Welcome home, Dr. and Mrs. Christiansen," she shouted as she sprinted down the hallway. Her silky, black hair bounced with each step, and her dazzling smile glowed with delight. "Oh, we missed you both," she cried, giving Gianna and Danny a hug. She eagerly reached for Gianna's arm. "Girl, you've got to tell me all about Italy!"

"Uh, honey," Troy interrupted. "Please take Gianna inside and get her something to eat. We'll be along in a minute."

Tracy nodded, reaching for Gianna's hand.

Troy prodded Danny. "Let's drop this stuff off at your place."

Before Tracy opened her front door, she turned to Gianna and asked, "What's going on?"

"Nothing," Gianna said with a weakened voice. She crossed her arms over her chest and looked over her shoulder. *I wish I could've stayed in Italy.*

Tracy touched Gianna's shoulder and attempted to make eye contact with her. "Talk to me, girlfriend. Is this about Chad?"

Gianna peered up at Tracy. "I just need to sit down."

Tracy opened the door and invited her inside.

At once, Gianna noticed the special homecoming brunch that Tracy had prepared. Her eyes filled with unshed tears. "This is beautiful. Thank you for thinking of us."

Tracy placed an arm around her and smiled. "My pleasure." She offered her a seat at the counter and handed her a plate and utensils. "Please, help yourself; and don't tell me you're dieting again."

"Nope; in fact, I probably gained ten pounds eating all that food in Italy," Gianna said, boldly.

"Oh, I know I gained, girlfriend," Tracy said. She reached into the cabinet for a glass. "I haven't stopped eating since your wedding."

"Oh please, you look fantastic!"

Gianna recalled the extensive hours the two of them had put in at the gym trying to get toned up for her wedding. It was strenuous work, but well worth it.

"Mmm, this is delicious," Gianna said, tasting the mini quiche.

"Thank you. Please...dig in," Tracy said, pointing to a plate of sausage links and pancakes.

Gianna nodded. "Thanks."

Gianna paced the hallway while Danny fumbled through his wad of keys to unlock the door to their unit. She paused when she heard the clicking sound of the key manipulating the lock. *How can I go back inside?* She had addressed that issue during her therapy sessions, but at the time, the answer seemed so simple.

Danny turned the doorknob and opened the door. He turned towards Gianna. "Welcome home, my beautiful wife," he said.

Gianna stepped back against the wall and slid to the floor. "I'm sorry, but I can't go back in there."

She recalled the night she returned home from the ER. Her body had ached all over from the struggle, and she had Chad's sweaty body odor all over her.

A somber look appeared on Danny's face. "It's going to be all right." He held out his hand. "Trust me."

She swallowed hard. "I trust you." She reached for him and rose to her feet.

When they entered the foyer, she looked around the space. A fresh coat of pumpkin butter paint covered the living room walls, adding warmth to the space, even more so than she remembered.

To her left was the kitchen and dining room combo. She hadn't set foot in there since Chad attacked her.

She froze, experiencing a horrific flashback. Chad's dark, evil eyes glared at her. She heard his devious laugh and ridiculing voice. *'You're going to like this.'*

Gianna squeezed her eyes closed, attempting to visualize a pleasant thought, like she'd learned in counseling. Then two firm hands touched her shoulders, breaking her concentration. Her body shuddered from the contact.

"You scared me!"

"I'm sorry, babe," Danny said, holding her. "Relax."

"I don't know if I can go back into that kitchen."

Danny sighed. "I'll help you through this."

She looked up at him and nodded. She trusted him with her life and knew the strong bond they shared could get her through any tribulation.

"Close your eyes and walk with me," he said.

"Ok," she said, determined to face her demon.

Danny wrapped his arm around her and guided her steps. "Remember at Christmastime when you were baking cookies?"

She smiled. "Oh, yeah. I made a huge mess."

Danny chuckled. "You smeared icing on my face, and I chased you around the kitchen island."

Gianna's body warmed up to the memory. "I slipped and took you down with me." She smiled bitterly. "I sprained my ankle badly that day."

"Well, nothing's perfect," he said, laughing.

With her eyes still closed, she felt her back brush up against the kitchen counter. She held onto him and relaxed against his protective body. She felt his smooth hand caress her cheek and his soft lips touch hers.

"You're in the kitchen," he whispered.

Cautiously, Gianna opened her eyes, afraid of what she might see. At once, her body quivered when she realized she was standing in the exact spot where Chad had cornered her.

"Baby, look at me," Danny urged. "I'm here and you're safe. Push him away."

Gianna focused on Danny's gentle eyes and encouraging voice. A comforting peace washed over her.

"You ok?" he asked.

"Yeah, thanks," she whispered.

Danny's eyes brimmed with patience and compassion. "Welcome home, *Mrs. Christiansen.*" He picked her up and set her down on the quartz countertop.

With complete confidence, Gianna said, "It's so good to be home." She reached for his hands and laced her fingers through his. "Now that we're married, how about we make a few new memories?"

"Hmm, I like the sound of that," Danny said.

Gianna leaned into him and brushed her mouth against his. His tongue rimmed her lips, then danced its way inside her mouth, sparking her passion.

She buried her face in the hollow of his neck and inhaled his masculine scent. Then, wrapping her legs around his torso, she clung to his powerful body. He lifted her up and carried her to the living room couch.

Chapter Two

Gianna sat down on an overturned laundry basket and watched the clothes tumble through the sudsy water with an intermittent thump and splat. She hated laundry duty but having the convenience of a washer and dryer in their home, even though it was just a closet in the hallway, made the grueling task more bearable.

"Are you sure you don't want to go with me?" Danny called from the kitchen.

"I'm sure," Gianna shouted over the sound of the washing machine changing cycles. She stood up and made her way to the kitchen where Danny was scribbling out a shopping list. "I still have to move my things out of the guest bedroom into your room."

Danny looked up from his notepad and flashed his mischievous grin. "You mean *our* room."

She returned the smirk. "Right, our room." She took the pen from him and jotted down a few more items that they needed. "You go ahead."

"Ok but take it easy. If you need me, call me. Oh, and Troy and Tracy are right next door if you need them."

"Ok, but really, I'm fine. I'm over Chad," she said, walking him to the front door.

Danny kissed her. "I'll hurry back." As he turned the doorknob, he said, "Make sure you lock up after I leave."

"I will."

Right away, Gianna secured the door, then plopped down on the couch. "I really should call Mom," she mumbled. She grabbed her phone off the coffee table and gave her mother a ring.

"Mom, hi. Did you get my text earlier?"

"Yes, honey. We were in church. I shipped your shower gifts. You should be getting them any day now."

"They arrived. Thank you."

There was a lot of background commotion, and her mother didn't respond right away.

"Mom, are you there?"

"Yes, I'm here. Sorry, honey, but Jessica and Matthew just arrived. They're taking us out to eat."

"Oh?" *Since when do you dine out?* "What's the occasion?"

"No reason," Mom said, still sounding a bit disengaged. "Honey, Jess just told me she'll call you tonight."

"Ok. Listen, Mom. Call me later. I love you."

"Love you, too, honey."

When Gianna ended the call, a stranded, left-behind feeling lingered in her heart, and jealousy consumed her thoughts like a killer migraine.

So, what if my best friend and my brother are going out to eat with Mom and Dad? Sure, it could've been me, but I made the choice to leave Montana and move to New York. I followed my dream to become a teacher, and I married the love of my life. Besides, I'm sure Jessica will tell me all the details when she calls later.

Gianna hopped off the couch and headed down the hallway. She needed to move her things into the master bedroom.

She unpacked the handmade photo quilt that her mother and Danny's godmother had made for them. She spread it out over the king-sized bed, admiring the intricate collage creation. She especially loved the precious newborn picture of Danny with his parents and the photo of his godparents, Dr. Joe and Evelyn Kendall, holding him beside the baptismal font at the church.

She smoothed her hand over the quilt, appreciating the effort that was put into it. She caught sight of a photo of her with her parents at her first holy communion and another one of her when she was eleven, aligned in chronological order with her four brothers in front of the Christmas tree. Her oldest brother, Matthew, and her younger brother Mark had the most jubilant smiles on their faces, each holding their favorite gift. Her youngest brothers John and Luke, the twins, were only eight months old at the time. They were sitting, contentedly playing with blocks.

As she reminisced, she smiled at the memories. Both her family and Danny's did so many activities together growing up. Over the years, they had gone camping, fishing, hiking, and horseback riding. Where had the time gone?

Tears clouded her vision. If only Danny's parents were still alive to share in the memories. Although the accident was a long time ago, she knew he still privately grieved. Losing both his parents to a drunk driver was something he'd never get over.

She knelt beside the bed and prayed. She prayed for his parents' souls and thanked God for blessing him with his devoted godparents.

Two hours later, Danny wrestled four canvas bags of groceries through the front door. "Hey, I'm back," he said, setting them down on the kitchen counter. "I have two more in the truck."

"Do you need help?"

"Nope," he said, rushing out the door.

Gianna eyed the bags on the counter. She wanted to help unpack the groceries, but her stomach gnawed at the idea of entering the kitchen alone. *I can do this.* She took a deep breath and stepped forward. She looked around. *I'm ok.*

She peeked inside one of the grocery bags. There was deli meats, cheese, and fresh Kaiser rolls. She unpacked another bag of fresh fruits, vegetables, and eggs. The next bag had a small oven-stuffer, sausage, and a roast. *Did he leave anything at the store?*

When Danny returned with the milk and orange juice, Gianna had most of the items put away.

"Wow, Danny! You really stocked the fridge!"

She turned to thank him for doing the shopping, but a spinning, dizziness in her head returned. Her consciousness began to diffuse, and Danny's face came in and out of focus.

"Whoa there!" he said, catching her in his arms. "Again, with these dizzy spells?"

She clung to his arms and uttered, "I think I just need to eat something."

"That's not what I asked," he said, assisting her to the living room couch.

"I don't know. It started this morning with that box."

Danny laid her down on the couch and knelt beside her. He brushed her hair back and looked into her eyes, his own eyes, sharp and assessing.

"What, what is it?" she asked, her voice trembling.

"Post-concussion syndrome?" Danny said with uncertainty. He rubbed his scruffy chin. "No, can't be. Symptoms usually occur within ten days and subside after three months." He stood up and said, "Wait here."

Danny left and returned with his medical bag.

Gianna rolled her eyes. "Is this really necessary?"

He narrowed his eyes. "You fainted. Humor me, ok?" He took out his blood pressure cuff and stethoscope. "BP is one-ten over sixty. Do you normally run low?"

Gianna gave a baffled shrug. "I don't know."

Danny took out his ophthalmoscope and examined her eyes. "Ok, now follow my finger."

She sighed. Keeping a straight face, she tracked his finger back and forth. "Find anything yet?"

"Not yet. Stand for me with your arms out. Now, touch your fingers to your nose."

"Come on, Danny. I'm not drunk."

Danny dropped his head. "Please, babe."

She touched her nose right on. "Happy now?" she asked, sitting back down. "So, what is it?"

He shook his head. "I'm not sure yet, and I don't want to guess. When was your last physical exam?"

"Last August when the school hired me."

"I mean your last *complete* physical exam."

"Never." Gianna swallowed hard. "I mean, aside from that ER visit after Chad..."

She quickly looked away. She had dreaded going to the doctor ever since she was a little kid, but it was ten times worse since that uncomfortable, horrifying experience in the ER.

She looked back at Danny nervously. "Oh no, I'm not going through *that* again," she protested.

He took her hands in his. "It's not like that. We'll start with blood work."

"Forget it. I hate needles." She turned away and mumbled, "I'll feel better after I eat something."

Danny touched her chin. "Hey, we can't let this go."

She swallowed hard.

"Come on. I'm here for you," he said.

"I trust you," she said, nodding.

Chapter Three

Sound asleep, Gianna lay curled up in bed under the warm covers. She squirmed when Danny's moist, tender lips tickled her neck.

"Baby, wake up," he said in his usual chipper voice.

"But I'm so tired," she groaned, snuggling deeper into her soft pillow.

"I know it's early. How're you feeling otherwise?"

Gianna groaned again, then carefully sat up. Her head pounded, her eyes ached, and her stomach felt bloated. "Much better," she said, dishonestly. "In fact, I'm going to report to Mr. Sterling this morning."

"Glad to hear it, but your boss can wait. Dr. Barton is in early on Mondays."

"But you just examined me last night."

"I want a second opinion," Danny said. He kissed her forehead, then slid out from underneath the covers.

Gianna held her tongue. She didn't feel well enough to argue with him anyway. Besides, she was barking up the wrong tree. The medical field was his turf, and it was a useless battle trying to win an argument with him.

Gingerly, she slipped out of bed and tottered her way to the bathroom. By the time she finished showering and getting dressed, Danny was already in the kitchen preparing breakfast.

"I'm not hungry," she mumbled.

"You need to eat something. How about some toast?"

"Fine," she grumbled.

Gianna wandered into the living room and gazed out the window. The early morning sky showed unbroken gray clouds. No doubt rain would fall at any moment. *Ugh! What a perfect gloomy day to have stayed in bed.*

"Breakfast is served," Danny called from the kitchen.

Gianna moseyed into the kitchen and sat down. "Thank you." She sipped her milk, and then took a few nibbles out of her toast. "Sorry, but I can't eat any more."

"Crackerjacks, Gianna! Even a city mouse eats more than you."

"I told you I wasn't hungry."

"Ok," he sighed. "It's almost time to leave anyway."

Gianna waited in the lobby of their condo complex while Danny pulled the truck around to the front entrance. By the time she climbed in, tiny drops of rain beaded on the windshield, just like she had predicted earlier.

It was a short drive to the medical practice. Danny pulled into the private lot, careful to avoid the potholes.

Gianna rubbed her bloated, cramped stomach. "I don't know if it's my nerves or this rutted parking lot."

"Sorry," he said, parking the truck in his privileged space. "They're repaving next week."

She glanced out the passenger window at the construction equipment parked in the back corner. *Anything to add to the chaos, but I'm sure it'll be nice when it's finished.* She looked up at the old brick building and noticed the new gold-lettered sign: Riverview Family Practice and OB. She recalled having only been there two times, once for an employee physical, and once for a sprained ankle.

Gianna's stomach felt like one gigantic knot. She wondered how Danny could work in an infectious, unfriendly environment every day. *To each his own, I guess.* She was certain he questioned how she could work in a classroom with rebellious, smart-mouthed preteens every day.

Danny touched her forearm. "Hey, I promise it's going to be ok."

Fear and uncertainty crept through her body.

"How do you know that? Last night, you told me you didn't know what was wrong and you didn't want to guess."

"Babe, stress can make you feel sick. Jet lag can cause your fatigue. Low blood sugar can make you dizzy. Nevertheless, a doctor can't properly diagnosis you without a thorough examination. You know, you lost a lot of weight a few months ago."

"Yeah, Danny, and I gained it all back, plus some," she retorted. She unlatched her seat belt and grumbled, "I get it. Let's just get this over with."

Danny helped her out of the truck. He took her hand and led her through the light drizzle to the main entrance and unlocked the door. "This place is going through some major renovations, both inside and out," he said, opening the door. He led her through the dark waiting room to his private office. He flipped the light switch. "Wait here. I'll be right back."

"Danny! Before you go." She grabbed his arm. "I'm sorry for being curt with you. It's the exam, Chad, and..."

"Whoa there! I understand. Your dad warned me about your Italian temper," he said with a smirk.

"Oh, no he didn't," she said, placing her hands on her hips. "Well, I get my hot blood from him."

Danny laughed. "If I remember correctly, you were always pretty feisty, and your brothers knew just how to push your buttons, but that's what I love about you."

"Oh, is that so?" she asked, laughing just a bit. "Go, do whatever you've got to do so I can get out of here," she ordered, prodding him along.

While Gianna waited for Danny's return, she sat down on a couch. She looked around his snug, little office. He was neat and organized, just like he was at home. His desk had a caddy filled with all his office supplies, a Montana coffee mug, and a rustic picture frame with a photo of the two of them posing in a gazebo at Matthew and Jessica's wedding.

She dropped onto the sofa and listened to the wall clock tick against the silence. It was only a few minutes after seven. *Where did he go? Who else is here?* Her hands fidgeted restlessly in her lap. Finally, after another five minutes, footsteps shuffled outside the office door.

"Sorry it took me so long," Danny said, sitting down beside her. "Maggie, our receptionist, isn't in yet, so I had to find the intake paperwork myself." He handed her a pen and a clipboard. He rubbed her back and said, "If you're ok, I'm going to see if Dr. Barton is in."

Dan left his office and headed down the corridor toward the kitchenette, where his colleague, Dr. Steven Ross, was reading the newspaper.

"Good morning, Steve. How's it going?"

Dr. Ross removed his glasses. "Hey, welcome back, Dan, and congrats!" He motioned for him to join him at the table.

Dan sat down with a hot cup of coffee and shared with Steve some memorable moments of his wedding and honeymoon. "It was great! Everything was perfect!"

"Must've been. The smile hasn't worn off your face yet," Steve joked.

Dan chuckled. "Yeah, but unfortunately, good things must come to an end."

"True." Steve cleared his throat. "So now that the fun is over, are you ready for a manic Monday?"

Dan raised his eyebrows. "Can today be *any* different than a normal day here in the office?"

"We're down one doc today. Dr. Barton was up all night delivering the Miller baby." Steve's face became a warning. "Dr. Stetson expects *you* to round at the hospital this morning, and then see office patients in the afternoon."

Dan rubbed his jaw ruefully. *Dr. Stetson's ugly mood is on duty.* "Where's the boss now?"

"Hospital meeting again."

Dan rubbed his eyes. Although he didn't mind the last-minute change in his schedule, he sensed it was going to be a long week. "Steve, can you do me a favor?"

"Sure. What is it?"

Dan explained how Gianna wasn't feeling well and hoped he might be able to examine her before their crazy day began. He briefed Steve on Gianna's history and her dislike for medical intervention.

"Bring your wife back to exam room four. I'll pull her ER records," Steve said.

"Thanks."

Dan returned to his office where he found Gianna curled up on the couch resting. "Baby, you ok?" he asked, sweeping her hair away from her face.

Gianna opened her eyes. "Yeah, I'm just tired."

"Dr. Ross will see you now."

Gianna carefully sat up. Her eyes looked stricken, her cheeks dead white. "Who's Dr. Ross? Where's Dr. Barton?"

"Dr. Barton's not in today, but Dr. Ross is a fine doctor, with excellent bedside manners. You'll like him."

"Him?" she asked, her voice trembling. "I don't want to see a male doctor."

"Trust me. I trust him."

"Fine," she said.

Gianna stood frozen in the doorway of the exam room. *Whoa!* It wasn't how she remembered it. The off-white scuffed walls were repainted a soothing blue. Artwork accented the room giving the space just a hint of energy. The old, dented cabinets were replaced with a row of whitewashed wood cabinets.

"Wow! I almost feel welcome here," she said.

"The boss had this place remodeled a little over a month ago," Danny said, handing her a mauve cloth gown. "My nurse usually sets up the room, but she's not in yet."

Gianna changed into the gown and hopped up on the exam table. She sat with her hands folded tightly in her lap and her feet dangling over the edge. "I'm freezing."

Danny nodded in agreement. "Yeah, the air conditioning works great in these rooms," he said, draping a white sheet over her lap.

"Much better, thank you."

Danny walked to the door. "Doctor Ross should be in any moment."

"Fantastic," Gianna said with sarcasm.

After the exam concluded, Gianna quickly changed out of her patient gown. *What a fuss I made. The exam was painless, and Dr. Ross is an understanding, sensitive professional. I am so grateful that Danny referred me to him.*

She stepped into her jeans and wiggled them up over her hips. As she zipped them up, there was a knock at the door. "Yes?" she answered.

The door opened slowly, and Nurse Amy poked her head in. "I'm back to draw labs. Are you ready?"

Gianna gave a weary nod. "I guess I have to be."

Amy nudged the door open with the lab cart and rolled it into the room. She pulled a tourniquet out of her box. "Which arm do you prefer?"

"Neither, but if I must, my left arm will have to do."

Amy smoothed her gloved finger over Gianna's vein. "This looks like a good one," she said. She tied the tourniquet and instructed her to make a fist. "You may want to look away. That helps with the queasiness."

Gianna turned her head. When she felt the cold, wet alcohol swab swipe the crook of her arm, she squeezed her eyes closed, expecting the worst.

"Ok, just a little pinch," Amy said.

Gianna gritted her teeth as the needle pricked her arm.

"You ok?"

"So far."

"Good," Amy said, releasing the tourniquet. "We're almost done here."

Gianna opened her eyes. "That wasn't so bad." She glanced over at the vial holder and noticed all the tubes of blood. She swallowed hard. "All that came from me?"

"Uh-huh, but actually, it's not that much."

Gianna's vision grayed. *Easy for you to say.* Her stomach became woozier than it was earlier.

"Sweetie, you look a little pale," Amy said as she pressed the cotton ball against her arm. "Are you still feeling ok?"

Gianna rubbed her sweaty forehead. "I don't know."

"Ok," Amy said, sticking the bandage on. "I want you to stay seated while I get you some juice. I'll be right back."

Moments later, Amy returned with a cup of juice.

Gianna took a sip. "Thank you. I feel much better."

"Good. Dr. Ross will be back in to speak with you. Would you like your husband to join you?"

"Yes, please."

"Ok," Amy said, pushing her lab cart out the door. "It was nice meeting you."

When the door closed, Gianna remained in her chair, bouncing her knee up and down. *Great! What does Dr. Ross have to tell me that he didn't already say during the exam?* "C'mon, Danny. I just want to go home," she uttered.

Danny entered the room. "You ready?"

"No. Dr. Ross wants to speak to me first."

"Oh, ok," Danny said nonchalantly as he took a seat beside her.

Gianna cautiously peered up at him, looking for an answer in his honest eyes. "Do you think he found something wrong?"

Danny hesitated for a moment, then seemed to choose his words carefully. "Let's not jump to conclusions."

Shortly thereafter, Dr. Ross returned to the exam room. "Ok!" he said, clapping his hands together. He rolled a stool out from beneath the counter and straddled it. "Gianna, the results of your blood work will be back in a couple of days. We'll notify you only if there is a problem."

"Ok..." she responded with hesitation. She cast a baffled look at him. "Then why do I feel so lousy?"

Dr. Ross's round face relaxed into a wide smile. He folded his fingers together and dropped them below his chin. "The result of your urine sample indicated traces of a hormone, HCG."

Gianna stiffened and her face grew tight. *Your fluent gibberish means nothing to me.* She looked at Danny. There was a certain energetic gleam in his eyes, and an all-knowing smile emerged sharply.

"Babe, what Steve is trying to say is...you're pregnant!"

Goose bumps erupted on her arms. "What?" Her mind refused to listen. *But my period is coming. I can feel it.* She rested her finger on her lips trying to grasp what he was saying. "A baby?" Her eyes pooled with tears.

"A baby," Danny said. His hands took her face and held it gently. "We're expecting!"

"Congratulations to you both," Dr. Ross said.

"Thank you," Danny said.

Still shaking, Gianna asked, "When...when am I due?"

Dr. Ross put on his gold-rimmed glasses. He picked up a pregnancy calculator wheel and referenced her medical chart. "April twentieth."

Gianna smiled weakly. "Thank you, Doctor."

Back in Danny's office, Gianna retreated to the couch. She felt the tightening and gnawing in her stomach again. She stared, stricken, at Matthew and Jessica's wedding photo. *They've been married nine months, and they aren't even pregnant yet.* She twirled her wedding band. *We've only been married two weeks. What did we do?*

Danny sat down beside her. "You ok?"

She unconvincingly nodded her head. Mixed feelings wove through her mind. She'd always wanted to be a mother, but not this soon.

She looked up at him and answered, "No, no, I'm not. In fact, I'm scared." She ran her fingers through her hair. "I mean...I teach this stuff in my classroom, but now it's for real. I know we talked about having a family someday, but now? I mean, the timing—"

"Is perfect," Danny said, completing her sentence. He kissed her hand. "Trust me." He stood up, walked behind his desk, and opened a filing cabinet. "Here," he said, handing her an information packet. "We give this to all our pregnant patients." He sat down beside her. He still had an ecstatic glow on his face like he'd won the lottery. He placed his hand on her stomach. "We're going to have a baby." He cradled her face in his hands and kissed her.

Gianna gazed into his reassuring eyes. *It'll be ok. He's ready to be a father.* "I love you," she whispered.

"Love you, too." Danny glanced up at the clock and patted her hand. "It's getting late, and I have hospital rounds." He stood up and put on his lab coat, then grabbed his keys and ID badge off the desk. "I need to visit a few postpartum patients. I won't be gone long. Would you like to go?"

"Ok."

Gianna slowly stood up. She felt bloated and crampy.

"Do you feel up to it?" he asked.

"I guess so. But it really doesn't matter because I still need to stop at the school."

"I can drive you, afterwards."

Riverbank Hospital was a tall brick building that was conveniently connected to the medical practice by a lengthy glass corridor. As Gianna and Danny walked through the long hallway, an ambulance with pulsating sirens screamed out of the parking lot. Gianna conceded that the hospital wasn't much different than the crowded city that loomed beyond its footprint.

The lobby, however, painted a different picture. It was extremely quiet, with only a few people waiting in the lounge area, tinkering with their smart phones.

Danny escorted Gianna to an employee elevator. When they reached the heavy security doors leading to the maternity-newborn wing, she felt her nerves scrambling in the pit of her stomach.

Danny swiped his security badge and the automated doors swooshed open. The sterile smell and authoritative atmosphere stirred up a mixture of apprehension, excitement, and fear in Gianna. She gripped his hand a little tighter.

"You ok?" he asked.

"I think so," she said, scanning the unit. It was quiet, unlike that crazy night in the ER after Chad had assaulted her. No longer feeling intimidated, she released her grasp on his hand. "I'm good. I'm ok."

"Dr. Dan the Man, you're here!" A reedy voice called out from behind the nurses' station. A plump, yet sprightly nurse leaped forward and nearly tackled him with a hug. "Ooh-ooh, the others are going to be thrilled to have our favorite charming doctor back."

Danny's complexion turned an intense scarlet. He quickly tucked his face in his shoulder and mumbled, "Uh, I don't think so."

"What do you mean you don't think so?" she asked, bobbing her head back and forth. "Now, don't try to be all bashful." She shook her finger at him. "Tsk, tsk, you know you're the preferred doc around here." She turned to Gianna and said, "Hi, I'm Sheila. I don't think we've met."

"I was getting around to that," Danny said, putting his arm around Gianna. "Meet my beautiful bride, and the mother of my unborn child."

Gianna's cheeks burned. She was almost embarrassed at how happy he made her feel. "Hi, I'm Gianna."

"Oh, girl!" Sheila placed her hand on her chest. "Congratulations! You are one lucky lady." She turned and looked at Danny. "That must've been one hot honeymoon." She fanned herself with her hand. "Ooh! Someone needs to jack up the air in here."

Danny rubbed the back of his neck and quickly changed the subject. "Do you have the files for rooms 610, 18, and 23?"

"Yes, right over there." Sheila pointed to the cart behind the nurses' station. "And while you're doing your thing, I'll be happy to give your wife a tour. Not much happening here now."

"That'd be great," Danny said. He kissed Gianna. "I won't be long."

Sheila took Gianna to an empty labor and delivery room. It looked like a regular hotel room decorated with a baby themed wall border. In addition, it had all the necessary medical equipment, a couch, table, and chair.

"Rooms are all set for labor, delivery, and postpartum," Sheila said. "And the OR is just down the hall, should it be needed. We encourage all moms to room-in with their newborns. Dads are welcome to stay overnight, too. Any questions?"

"No but thank you."

Although Gianna had plenty of time before she'd be a patient there, she thought the educational experience was perfect to incorporate into her health curriculum.

Sheila gestured Gianna to follow her. "I'll take you to the nursery window so you can see the babies."

"Oh, you can do that?"

"Girl, I'm the head nurse. I can do anything."

Sheila led her back to the main nurses' station where the nursery was and pulled the window blinds open.

"I must leave you now, but your husband should be along shortly. It was nice meeting you," Sheila said.

"Thank you."

Gianna peeked inside the nursery window. There were seventeen bassinets lined up in rows, each one with the iconic white blanket that had pink and blue striped edges, bundled inside. Two of the bundles were coming undone from their tiny bare feet kicking furiously.

Even through the thick glass, Gianna could hear the babies screaming in between breaths. *How can the others sleep through all that fussing?* Goose bumps pebbled her arms.

They're so precious. I wish I could hold one. She placed her hand on her belly. *God, I think I'm ready to be a mother. Thank you for blessing us with this pregnancy. Please help me to do everything right to ensure a healthy baby and guide us to be nurturing parents. Amen.*

"Hey, babe," Danny called.

Gianna turned and watched him approach her, all confident and full of life, carrying a smile of extreme bliss.

"They sure let you know when they're not happy," he said. He draped his arm around her. "You ready to go?"

"Sure." She tilted her head back and smiled. "Thank you for bringing me here."

"No problem. Just think, in nine months, we'll be here having our own baby."

The thought froze her brain. "Uh-huh."

"Don't worry. You'll do fine."

On the way to the school, something clicked in Gianna's mind. *I haven't been back here since Chad attacked me. What's it going to feel like stepping back into the past?* She hoped her joy for teaching would cast a shadow over her negative memories.

When she and Danny entered the red brick school building, a sudden surge of wooziness flooded her, and she had to fight to stand on her feet.

"Take it easy," he said, massaging her back.

"I just need a second," she said, holding onto him. "Maybe I should eat something."

"I still have time. Why don't we grab brunch now and I'll drive you back afterward?"

"No, I'll make this quick."

Gianna reached for Danny's hand and started walking again. As she turned the corner, her friend, Nick stepped out from behind the security desk.

"Hey, Gianna, welcome back!" he shouted. His voice echoed through the lobby entrance. "Hey, Doctor, nice to see you again," he said, shaking Danny's hand.

Gianna squeezed Danny's hand. "While you two chat, I'm going to speak to Mr. Sterling," she said, excusing herself from the conversation.

She knocked on Mr. Sterling's office door. When she heard his deeply distinguished voice invite her in, her nerves began to tremble. *It's all good,* she told herself.

She opened the door. Mr. Sterling looked up from the pile of papers on his desk. His usual tight expression relaxed into a contented smile. "Gianna, welcome! How've you been?"

"I'm fine, Mr. Sterling, thank you."

She sat down and briefly filled her boss in on her plans to return to work. During their discussion, she learned that the substitute who had replaced her during her absence didn't meet his expectations.

"I'm sorry to hear that," she said, although deep inside, she was flattered to know she was missed by the faculty, parents, and students.

"Gianna, you're to be commended for your outstanding work last year and especially for creating the curriculum for the 'family living' portion of the course."

She gave a pleased smile. "Thank you."

"And on such short notice," Mr. Sterling added.

Gianna nodded in appreciation for his recognition. She remembered last summer vividly. She crammed for three grueling weeks to complete those lesson plans. She swore she'd never do that again.

"Do you recall your former student, Rhonda Higgins?" he asked.

"Yes, I do."

Rhonda was a thirteen-year-old pregnant student in her class. She had left school in November to have her baby.

"Well, Gianna," Mr. Sterling said. "Since Rhonda, three more girls became pregnant."

He swiveled in his chair, stooped over, and rummaged through some boxes on the floor behind his desk. He grabbed a book and handed it to her.

Gianna glanced at the title, *Preventing Premature Pregnancy*. It was a teacher's manual about reaching out to teens with unplanned pregnancies.

"Gianna, parents feel that our school is lacking sufficient safe sex education. Therefore, the Board has agreed to alter the curriculum to cover the material outlined in this book. Do you think you can work your magic and develop fresh lesson plans to reflect the new material?" A probing query appeared in his eyes. "No pressure," he said with a hint of humor in his voice.

"I'll do my best, sir."

"I know you will."

Gianna left Mr. Sterling's office feeling less confident than when she arrived. *How am I supposed to create lesson plans in two and half weeks?* She wanted to go back and tell him that it was impossible for her to redo a curriculum on such short notice, especially since she wasn't feeling well, but she wasn't ready to unveil her own pregnancy yet. *What would he say if he knew?*

Gianna turned the corner toward the main entrance where Danny was waiting for her.

"Ready to go?" he asked.

"Yeah," she mumbled.

Danny took Gianna to a small café for lunch. They sat in a corner booth and reviewed the menu, trying to figure out what they were in the mood to eat.

"How about a pizza burger?" he asked.

Gianna shook her head. "I don't know."

He reached across the table and took her hand. His face grew serious. "Hey, I don't want you eating anything from street vendors, ok?"

She stared at him in bewilderment and half laughed. "I don't think you have to worry about that. I can't stomach anything at this point." She felt nauseous, yet hungry. "Earlier, I had a craving for something with tomato sauce, but now I'm turned off."

"I think you just miss your mom's Italian cooking," Danny said. "Why don't you try a sandwich instead?"

"Ok," she said, closing the menu.

While they waited for service, her brain obsessed over her conversation with Mr. Sterling. Her blood boiled with frustration just thinking about her challenging assignment.

"So, are you going to tell me, or do I have to pry? How did your meeting go?" Danny asked.

Gianna parted her lips in surprise. She declared that he could read her mind. "Mr. Sterling is insisting that I redo the curriculum because the parents feel their kids aren't educated enough on preventing pregnancy."

"Oh?" he asked.

"Yeah, but I disagree with him. I think the curriculum I developed last summer covered the basics of safe sex, contraception, and protection against STDs and HIV. I encouraged students that the best prevention is abstinence. What else can I do?"

"Well—" Danny couldn't get a word in edgewise as Gianna continued her rant.

"What these kids need today are morals and religious values, and I can't preach mine in a public school. It must come from their parents."

"Did you tell that to Mr. Sterling?"

"No," she sighed. "And I didn't mention *our* pregnancy either. He's going to flip when I tell him. I mean, how am I supposed to instruct kids not to get pregnant when I am? I'm not exactly a good role model."

Danny laughed. "Babe, you're a responsible, married adult. These kids are hardly teenagers. There's a significant difference. Trust me. Everything will work out."

Chapter Four

I t was early Tuesday morning when Gianna stirred to the touch of Danny's bristly goatee tickling her neck. The scent of his Drakkar cologne tantalized her senses. "Mmm," she moaned.

"Good morning, babe," he whispered, scattering butterfly kisses on her cheek, neck, and shoulders.

Gianna opened her eyes and gazed up at the crucifix that hung above the brick fireplace. *Wait. Where am I?* She rubbed her tired eyes. "Why am I on the couch?"

Danny's face broke into a wry grin. "I can't answer that, but when I came home last night, I thought I was back in Montana."

"Why?"

"I thought there was a bear snoring in our living room, but then I realized it was you."

Gianna's face burned. "I don't really snore, do I?"

Danny raised his eyebrows and smirked. "You looked so pretty, all cuddled up; I didn't want to disturb you." He leaned forward and kissed the top of her head. "How're you feeling this morning?"

Gianna pushed up on her elbows. "Refreshed. I think I'll go into school today to prepare my classroom."

"Ok but try to eat something before you go. I'm heading to the hospital now to meet two patients for scheduled inductions."

Gianna nodded, then carefully stood up and walked him to the door. "I wish we could both stay home and spend the day together."

Danny touched her chin. "Listen, if these two deliveries go quickly, I'll be home early."

Hours later, Gianna arrived at school. She unlocked her classroom door, flipped on the light, and stared at the disorganized space. *What on earth? Did a tornado touch down here?* All the students' desks were crammed in one corner, her teaching materials were stuffed into a plastic milk crate on the windowsill, and her office supplies had been heaved into a cardboard box on her desk with as much care as a child's unwanted ragdoll.

She examined the room and realized she'd have to straighten it up before she could even attempt to revise her lesson plans. She sighed. *It is what it is.* She tossed her keys and purse on her desk and went to work.

I may as well start with placing the desks in rows. She walked to the back of the classroom, grabbed the top edge of the first desk, and pushed it into position.

"Hey, you shouldn't be doing that," a low throaty voice called out. The man's gruff tone gripped her heart like a cold hand.

Gianna spun around to find herself in an old familiar scene. A young, muscular man who looked like a surfer dude from the west coast stood there dressed in gym shorts and a t-shirt.

"You shouldn't be lifting desks," he said, picking one up and placing it behind the first one. "It's the custodians' job."

"You're a custodian?" she asked.

"No, I'm the new gym teacher, Brandon Ryder." He smiled and held out his hand to greet her.

Horror crawled over her. *Oh no, not another Chad.* Apprehensively, she extended her trembling arm and shook his hand. "Hi, Brandon, I'm Mrs. Gianna Christiansen," she said, emphasizing the *Mrs.* "I'm the health and family living teacher."

"I know. Yesterday I saw your husband in the lobby talking to Nick."

Gianna felt the hair on her arms spike. *Ok, this is creepy. How does he know Danny? Is he stalking me?* "How do you—"

"Dr. Christiansen is my GP and my wife's OB."

Instant warmth returned to her body. She softened her posture and let down her guard. "Oh," she said.

"My wife is due with our son any day now."

"That's wonderful! Congratulations!"

"Thank you."

Brandon's exciting news made her want to tell him about her own pregnancy, but she decided against it. In due time, her baby bump would reveal itself.

"Now let me finish moving these desks for you," he insisted, "and then I'll get out of your hair."

Gianna spent the entire morning working diligently organizing her desk and decorating bulletin boards.

"Hey, girlfriend!" Tracy said, capturing her attention.

"Hi!" Gianna said, placing her stapler down on her desk. She rushed over to greet her with a hug. "I've got some exciting news!" Eagerly, she closed her classroom door and blurted out, "I'm pregnant!"

Tracy's eyes widened in astonishment. "Oh, my goodness! Congratulations," she said. She gave her another hug and said, "So am I!"

"What? Really?" Gianna asked. She glanced down at Tracy's canary-yellow empire-waist dress. "That's awesome!" An uncrushable enthusiasm filled her heart. "We can share this whole pregnancy experience together!"

"Hey, let's celebrate—my treat," Tracy said.

"Now?" Gianna scanned her half-organized classroom, then lifted her shoulder in a casual shrug. "Ok. I guess my work here can wait."

Tracy unfolded her cloth napkin and placed it on her lap. "When Troy and I found out we were expecting, we came here to celebrate. I'm now sixteen weeks along, due in January."

Quickly, Gianna calculated the weeks in her head. The result sent her pulse spinning. "Wow, so you knew at my wedding?"

Tracy blushed. "Yeah, we found out in May, but we vowed to keep it under wraps until we were sure."

Gianna reached across the table and took Tracy's hand. "I'm sure everything will be fine."

Tears glistened in Tracy's eyes. "We prayed a long time for this child."

"And God has blessed you."

Tracy was lost in her thoughts when, suddenly, her face lit up. "We heard the baby's heartbeat last week! My doctor says it's strong."

Gianna smiled. "See? No need to worry."

Tracy returned the smile. "Hey! After we eat, let's go shopping."

"Well, ok. I can always finish my classroom tomorrow."

Hours later, Gianna returned home, tired, light-headed, and hungry. She stood in the kitchen with the refrigerator door open, wondering what she could make for dinner. She didn't need to worry about feeding Danny because he had called earlier to say he was working late.

Gianna hard boiled an egg to make a sandwich. However, when she peeled it, the stinky sulfur smell made her nauseous. She threw her hand over her mouth and ran to the bathroom. When she felt better, she decided to soak in the tub.

Later, she changed into her pajamas and climbed into bed. *Ooh, I must call Mom.* She reached for her phone on the nightstand, and it started ringing.

She answered it. "Oh, Jess, hi! I'm sorry I missed your call the other night. I've been so tired, but I have great news to share."

"Me, too," Jessica said. Her voice lilted. "I'm pregnant!"

Goose bumps tickled Gianna's arms. "What? Really? That's awesome! Congratulations."

"I'm due in April," Jess said. "So...what's your news?"

"I'm pregnant, too!" Gianna said. "Oh, and so is Tracy! She's due in January!"

"Really? Wow!" Jessica said.

"Jess, I'm so excited...all three of us pregnant together." A girlish, tingly feeling fluttered through her body. "I must call Mom. I haven't told her yet."

"Mom is in the kitchen," Jessica said.

"Huh?" Gianna's mind whirled with confusion.

"I'm at your parents' house. Hold on. I'll get her."

Gianna clenched her teeth. *Jeepers! Did Jessica move in there?* That interior dig of jealousy raced through her again. She wished she were there, too, to tell her parents her great news in person.

"Hi, honey!" Mom said. "Did Jessica tell you I'm going to be a grandmother?" she asked, her voice bubbling with joy.

"Uh-huh, and guess what?" Without giving her mother a chance to speak, she blurted out, "I'm pregnant, too!"

Silence struck the phone line.

"Mom, are you still there?"

"Uh, yes, honey, I'm here. But are you sure?"

"Of course, I'm sure. Danny's a doctor, remember?" she asked, detecting a hint of censure in her mom's tone. "Mom, what's wrong? You don't sound excited."

"Oh, I am, honey. It's just...I miss you," Mom said.

"You think it's too soon, don't you?"

"No, honey, it's not that at all."

"What then?" Gianna asked. She bit down hard on her lower lip. *Spill it, already. What are you thinking?*

Mom sighed. "Honey, it's the city. Dad and I hoped you'd—"

"Mom, if you and Daddy saw where we live, you'd know we're in a relatively safe area." She swallowed hard, thinking about the assault that had taken place there. "I'm sorry, Mom. I guess I'm just...hormonal."

Mom laughed. "I understand. Pregnancy does that. Listen, get some rest, and give Daniel our love. And, honey, congratulations."

"Thanks. Love you, too, Mom."

Gianna placed her phone on the nightstand and picked up one of her pregnancy books. She read it until the words blurred on the page.

Hours later, Gianna stirred when Danny's warm body pressed up against her back. "Finally, you're home. I was starting to worry."

"Sorry. I had to do an emergency C-section."

"Oh, no! Is everything ok?"

"Yeah."

Gianna rolled over and rested her head on his chest. "You'll never guess."

"What's that?" he asked.

"Both Tracy and Jessica are pregnant."

Danny lifted his head off the pillow. "Really? That's awesome news."

"I told Mom about us, but she didn't seem happy. I guess it's because we live here in the city."

"Your parents want what's best for us and their grandchild. They'll come around."

"I suppose."

"Babe, don't fret about it." He kissed her forehead, then rolled over. "Try to get some sleep."

"Ok," she sighed. "Good night."

Gianna lay awake, listening to him breathe. She knew he was exhausted and didn't need to hear about her drama. Instead, she gathered her thoughts and gave them to God. *God, please forgive me for getting angry with my mother. Danny's right. Mom and Dad are concerned. Please guide us along your righteous path. Amen.*

Chapter Five

Gianna blew through the remainder of her summer break rewriting her lesson plans to cover the material in the new textbook. *Ugh, there's so much to do yet.* She tapped her pencil on the edge of the desk and studied the notes she had written. *This activity won't do. The kids will hate me for sure.* She crumbled up her paper and tossed it across the classroom, missing the wastebasket. She sighed. *Maybe they'd like to act out a skit instead. Oh, I don't know.* Her thoughts became foggy with exhaustion.

Drained of energy, her eyelids grew heavy. She leaned forward in her chair and laid her head on the desk. Just as she began drifting away on dream clouds, an unfamiliar hand touched her shoulder. Fear jolted her body like electricity. Instantly awake, she lifted her head and saw Brandon standing by her side.

"You ok, Gianna?"

"Oh, Brandon," she gasped. She put her hand to her chest. "Yeah, only tired. I'm not even a quarter of the way done with these lesson plans."

"Sorry I startled you. Forgive me for saying so, but you don't look well. Can I take you home?"

Gianna violently shook her head no. "I'm fine, really." *I don't need you or anyone to know where I live.*

Brandon spotted her cell phone on her desk. "Can I call your husband then? I don't take this pregnancy thing lightly."

Gianna's heart pounded inside her chest. "How'd you know?"

"Your husband told me last night. He delivered my son," Brandon said, proudly. "Mom and baby doing well."

Gianna's eyes welled up. "Oh, congratulations!"

Brandon pulled out his phone and thumbed through his pictures. "He's eight pounds, ten ounces. Twenty-one inches long."

"Aw, he's a cutie, Brandon. I'm so happy for you."

"Thanks. Well, I should get back to the hospital." He turned toward the door, then paused. "Are you sure you're going to be all right?"

Gianna smiled. "I'll be fine."

Not more than five minutes after Brandon left, Danny strolled in. "Hey, I just saw Mr. Ryder leaving, and he said you—"

"I'm fine!" Gianna insisted, before closing her eyes and exhaling. "No, that's not true." She rolled her chair out from the desk and stood up. "I'm sorry. I'm tired and my back is killing me from this stupid chair."

"Come here," he said, wrapping his arms around her. "You need to talk to your boss. His demands are unrealistic."

"Oh? And your job isn't?" she snapped.

"This isn't about me," Danny said, calmly. "I'm not the one who's pregnant."

"I'm sorry. You're right." She ran her hand through her hair. "School starts the day after tomorrow. This is as done as it's going to get." She turned and grabbed her purse from the drawer. "Let's go home."

That evening, Gianna and Danny relaxed together on the couch. Danny channel surfed while Gianna browsed her pregnancy books. She was fascinated with the miracle growing inside of her.

"Hey, look at this," she said, nudging him. She pointed to the page she was viewing. "This is what our baby looks like now at eight weeks."

She peered up at him, flaunting that big, boyish grin. His face was beaming.

"It's amazing. I mean, being a doctor, I share this joy with my patients, but this is *our* baby."

He clicked off the TV and took the book from her, placing both the remote and the book down on the coffee table. He cradled her in his arms and rubbed his cheek against the top of her head.

"Thank you," he whispered.

Gianna gazed at him, mystified. "For what?"

Danny exhaled a long sigh of contentment. "Thank you for letting me have *you*...and for giving *us* this baby."

She watched the play of emotions on his passionate face. His lingering smile and his dancing eyes told her how much he wanted this child.

"Babe, you've been blessed with a big, Italian family, and I've been fortunate to know all of you," he said. He stood up and walked toward the window. "Your brother Matt was the closest I had to a sibling."

Gianna nodded. "And you mean a lot to him, too."

Danny peeked through the slats in the blinds and went off topic. "There isn't a star in the sky."

"How can you tell with all the lights?"

He lifted his powerful shoulders in a casual shrug. He turned and said, "When I was five, my dad and I would gaze at the night sky waiting to see a shooting star. When I did, I wished for a baby brother or sister, but my wish never came true. Years later, my parents told me they couldn't—" He choked on his words. "Mom told me I was their miracle baby."

"Oh, Danny!" Gianna said, too stunned to cry.

"And now, I've lost them to that drunk driver."

A flash of anger betrayed his calm demeanor, and his eyes filled with tears. Feeling his pain, Gianna stood up, and in one forward motion, wrapped her arms around him.

"God, I miss them," he cried. His body shuddered as he drew in a sharp breath. "You're all I have."

Gianna caressed his cheek. "Look at me," she said, her own eyes filling with tears. "I love you, and you have Joe and Evelyn, and my family is your family, too."

Clinging to her, he said, "I love you, too." He lifted his chin from her head, then gently pulled away, holding her at arm's length. A spark of hope quickly ignited in his eyes. "Wait here. I have something for you."

When he returned, he handed her a huge yellow gift bag stuffed with tissue paper. "This is for you." A renewed smile tipped the corners of his mouth.

"What's this?"

"Check it out."

Gianna nodded and removed the pink and blue tissue paper from the bag. A warm, giddy feeling flowed through her as she reached inside and pulled out a personalized wooden picture frame engraved with *Love at first sight*. She stared wordlessly, her heart pounding.

"It's for the first ultrasound print," he said. "Go on. There's more."

Enormous anticipation filled her heart like a child waiting for Christmas. She peeked inside the bag and pulled out a body care gift set, made specifically for expectant mothers. It contained a bottle of lavender fragrance bubble bath, a jar of belly cream, and a tube of massage oil.

A hot jubilant tear trickled down her cheek. "This is so sweet. Thank you."

"You're welcome. I want your pregnancy to be memorable for both of us." He pointed to the bag with his eyes. "Hey, there's one more thing in there."

She noticed the sensuous flame in his eyes and dipped her hand back inside the bag. She felt a slippery, shiny textured fabric. *Oh, no! You didn't.* As she slowly retrieved the item, her face burned with embarrassment. She stared, speechless, at the flirty, red satin, maternity lingerie. *I didn't even have anything this sensual on our wedding night.*

Danny must've read her mind because the sparkle left his eyes. "You...don't...like...it," he said, spacing his words out evenly.

His suggestive gift left her too stunned to object.

"It's...very pretty," she said.

"You won't wear it, for me?"

A sense of inadequacy swept over her. *I'm going to look huge in a few months.* "I don't know, Danny. I..."

"Babe, you'll always look beautiful to me. I love you."

Chapter Six

*G*ianna, *you're fired!* Mr. Sterling's husky voice boomed inside her head. *But sir, I did my best on such short notice.*

Gianna sat up in bed, wide-eyed, mouth ready to scream. *What a nightmare!* She lay back down, perplexed over her bad dream. She glanced at the clock on the nightstand. It was only four thirty. She rolled to her side and stroked Danny's stubbly cheek.

"What is it?" he mumbled.

"I can't sleep. I'm nervous."

"Just lie here with me."

Danny rolled to his side and cradled her in his arms. Comforted by his warmth, she drifted back to sleep.

Three hours later, Gianna rushed around the bedroom like a chicken without a head, scrambling to get ready for work. "I can't believe I slept through the alarm on the first day of school!" When she opened the window blinds, she noticed it was a dreary, rain-spattered day. "No wonder I overslept."

"Slow down, babe. I'll drive you to work."

"I can't slow down. I'm supposed to be there in thirty minutes," she answered from the bathroom. As she pulled her wet hair back into a clip, she poked her head out of the doorway. "At least you have the day off."

"Not exactly. I have a ten o'clock board meeting at the hospital," he said in a dull, troubled voice. He leaned forward on the edge of the bed and pulled on his boots.

Gianna sensed his anxiety and recalled how edgy he had become before his last hospital meeting. She grabbed her purse and her flats from the closet and hurried to catch him before he left the room.

"You all right?" she asked, tugging his arm. When he turned around, she noticed an inexplicable look of withdrawal on his face.

"Yeah," he answered.

She saw the sullen frown set in his features.

"No, you're not. Talk to me."

She no longer cared that she was running late for work. It was more important that she understood his feelings.

He gestured to her to walk with him to the kitchen so they could grab a bite to eat before they left. As he poured a bowl of cereal for each of them, he started explaining. "Dr. Stetson, my boss, wants to expand the OB practice and..." his voice faded. He sucked in a shallow breath and jerked his gaze away. "It's complicated." He took her hand and gave it a confident squeeze. "Never mind. It's nothing to worry about."

"Ok," Gianna said. *If you say so, I believe you.*

Gianna arrived at school with five minutes to spare. She unlocked her classroom door, flipped on the light, and quickly settled in at her desk. She glanced at her student roster, recognizing most of the names. She pinpointed a few troublemakers, but most of her students were ones who, in the past, made an honest effort to succeed. Just like last year, she didn't have a homeroom class, but did have a full schedule.

She glanced up at the wall clock. *Good, I still have some time left.* Just then, Tracy strolled in wearing a super cute coral crepe dress.

"Tracy, you look fantastic. How're you feeling?"

"Wonderful, thank you," Tracy said, displaying her beautiful smile. "This morning, I felt the baby move for the first time." Her eyes sparkled with merriment. She was blissfully happy, and rightfully so. "So, how're you feeling, girlfriend?"

"Good. No morning sickness."

The homeroom bell rang.

"Darn, got to go," Tracy said, rushing to the door.

Gianna reviewed her roster again. Her first period class was a large group of eighth graders. *Oh, this is a class with six challenging boys.* She sighed. *I may have to separate their desks. Worst-case scenario, they'll be spending time with Mr. Sterling. I refuse to tolerate any shenanigans.*

When the first period bell rang, she stood in the doorway and greeted her students as they filed into the classroom like a cattle drive. She watched the six tough boys herd to the back corner of the classroom. *I'll give you boys one day, and then I'm moving you.* She closed the door, put on her happy face, and marched to the head of the class.

"Welcome back, eighth graders. It's so nice to see so many smiling faces on this dull, rainy day. For those of you who don't know me, I'm Mrs. Christiansen. Welcome to Health and Family Living."

As she turned toward her desk to grab her notes, a well-known boisterous preteen called out in a cocky voice. "Hey, *Miz* Christiansen...uh...wasn't your name *Miz* Stefano last year?"

Gianna put her hands on her hips. "Yes, Zack. I got married in July. Do you recall the lesson I covered last year on engagement and marriage?"

A few of Zack's friends snickered at his ignorance. Gianna folded her arms and waited for them to settle down before she continued her introduction. She handed out the class syllabus, then discussed her expectations for class participation and the requirements for earning a passing grade.

She barely made it through the period before her back started to hurt from standing too long. Desperate for a break, she returned to her chair and gave her students the privilege of conversing quietly before the period bell rang. While reviewing her lesson plans, she overheard Zack talking to his friend, Trevor.

"Dude, remember she left in May? Mr. Garrett hit on her. She got'm fired."

Gianna gave Zack an icy cold stare, letting him know she had heard him.

With a dumbfounded look on his face, he asked, "Well, isn't that what happened, Miz Stefano...uh, I mean, Christiansen?"

"Something like that, Zack," she said. She closed her eyes briefly and a clear image of Chad's craggy face appeared. She opened her eyes to shove the dreadful vision aside.

She should really set the story straight with her students to avoid rumors, but her feelings were still raw, and she did not want to reopen that wound. Fortunately, her response satisfied Zack.

When the period bell rang, her students jumped out of their seats, grabbed their books, and barreled out of the classroom.

The remainder of Gianna's day was uneventful. With only a few minutes left of class, she gave her students free time to socialize.

With her body feeling drained of all its vitality, she sat quietly at her desk. Although she did not intend to eavesdrop, she caught the tail end of a thirteen-year-old girl's conversation with another female classmate.

"What am I supposed to do, Tina? He won't even talk to me," the girl whispered. Her eyes seemed damp and overly bright.

"Who cares, Sophia? Wyatt treated you like dirt. He'd make a lousy father, anyway."

What? Gianna peered up at the two girls chatting. *Please, not another teen pregnancy.* She tuned in to their conversation, but it quickly ended when the dismissal bell rang.

Quickly, the two girls gathered up their belongings and left. Sophia, a size-zero frame, could barely carry an armful of books. It was hard to envision the possibility of her being pregnant.

After the room emptied, Gianna left a voice mail message with the school counselor. She returned to her desk and rubbed her forehead. *I can't believe this.* Sophia was an above-average student. She came from an affluent, stable family. *How can a brilliant girl compromise her future? I need to help her. But how?* She bowed her head and prayed.

Later that evening, Gianna and Danny cuddled on the living room couch and shared their day with each other. She told him about Sophia. "I doubt she has any prenatal care. Can you help her?"

"I will donate my services," he said.

"You can? I'll talk to her tomorrow." Eager warmth filled her heart. "Thank you, Danny," she said, touching his shoulder. "How'd your meeting go today?"

Danny's face turned pale white, and she knew it couldn't have gone well.

"Ok," he sighed.

"Danny, talk to me. What's wrong?"

He shook his head to dismiss the conversation. "Everything's fine. The owners of the practice are offering additional services to expand the clientele, and it's...stressful." He got up from the couch. "I'm beat. Let's just go to bed."

The next day, Gianna arrived at work early, geared up to speak with Sophia. She wanted her to know her rights to confidentiality, medical care, emotional support, and her options for continuing her education. But unfortunately, Sophia was absent from school.

It was Friday, late afternoon, and Gianna's last class arrived. She was thrilled to see that Sophia was present. As soon as the students quieted down, she assigned them a group project. She excused herself from the room and requested Sophia accompany her out into the hall.

"Sophia." Gianna placed her hand on the girl's shoulder. "Pardon me for prying, but the other day, I overheard you talking to Tina...about your pregnancy. I just want you to know that I can help you through this."

There wasn't the faintest flicker of interest in Sophia's eyes. "No, thank you, Mrs. Christiansen," her timid voice answered.

"But you're going to need prenatal care."

Sophia's face was impassive and unchanged. "No, ma'am." She glanced over her shoulder and muttered, "It's all good. I...uh...took care of it yesterday."

Gianna's heart sank, her body trembled, and suddenly she felt weak. Stunned by Sophia's resolution, she was speechless.

"Can I go back to my desk now?" Sophia asked in a low, diffident voice.

"Uh, certainly."

No glimmer of remorse showed on Sophia's face. Without another word, she rushed back to her seat. Her cool, aloof manner disturbed Gianna. *How could she terminate her pregnancy? She sounded relieved, not the least bit sorry for her actions.*

Gianna returned to her classroom. Sick to her stomach, she barely made it through the remainder of the class. When the bell rang, her spirited students blew out of the room like a tornado. Sophia followed her peers, taking her bubbly disposition with her.

Gianna covered her face with her hands. *If only I had confronted her two days ago, the outcome could have been different. Did her parents know? Who influenced her decision?* She rested her hand on her abdomen. *How can she deny her child life? Adoption was a viable option.*

She bowed her head and prayed. *Heavenly Father, please forgive Sophia for aborting her baby. Please allow this baby to live eternally with you. Amen.*

Chapter Seven

Flustered from a disturbing day, Gianna took advantage of the warm, summer-like weather and walked home, hoping to de-stress her body.

When she arrived home, she wiped the afternoon's incident out of her mind. *I'm going to take a warm, relaxing bath, dress in something comfortable, then cook a special supper for my love.*

But all too quickly, her plans changed, and her calm mood reverted to dismay. As she undressed in the bathroom, she noticed some spotting. She covered her mouth with her hand. *Oh no! This can't be happening.* In a panic, she quickly pulled on her clothes, grabbed her phone, and called Danny. "Please answer," she uttered. The call went to voice mail. *Where is he?* Without leaving a message, she ended the call.

Her fingers trembled as she hit the buttons for the central office. When Maggie, the receptionist, answered, Gianna nearly cried. "This is Gianna, Dr. Christiansen's wife. Is he available to speak with?"

"No. I'm sorry. Is something wrong?"

"Yes, I'm eight weeks pregnant, and I'm bleeding."

"Ok, Gianna. May I put you on hold a moment while I find a nurse to help you?"

"Yes," Gianna said, wiping her tears. She sat down on the bed. *How are they going to help me?*

"Gianna, this is Kelly, one of the nurses. Can you come in right now for an ultrasound?"

Gianna hesitated, trying to comprehend what she was hearing. She stood up and paced the bedroom floor. "You mean this isn't a miscarriage?"

"We won't know until we see what's going on. Do you feel well enough to come in?" Kelly asked.

"Yes, I'm on my way."

Gianna arrived at the doctor's office, and Kelly escorted her to the ultrasound room. "Jody, our technician, will take care of you," she said, handing her a gown. "Your husband is in with his last patient and will join you shortly."

"Ok, thank you."

Gianna's knees trembled as she changed into the gown. *It's freezing.* She hopped up on the table and cupped her hands over her face. *Please God, let our baby be ok.*

There was a knock at the door and Danny entered. "Babe, I just heard," he said, wrapping his arms around her.

"Oh, Danny, am I going to lose our baby?"

"Shh," he said. His fingers halted her moving lips, the touch firm, but gentle. "Not necessarily. Some women *do* experience bleeding during their pregnancy and go on to have a healthy baby."

Although he sounded so encouraging, doubt still hovered over her head like a dark storm cloud. "No. I just know something isn't right," she cried.

"Let's just see what the ultrasound tells us."

A few moments later, there was a knock on the door and Jody entered the room. After she introduced herself, she instructed Gianna to lie down on the table.

"Gianna, I'm going to do a transvaginal scan. This exam may seem intrusive, but this is the most accurate way to see what's going on," she said, draping a sheet over her hips.

Gianna nodded woodenly. *Whatever it takes.* She just wanted to hear that her baby was fine. She angled her head and took notice of Danny's melancholy frown. She reached for his hand. When the gel-coated probe slid inside her, she gasped, then squeezed his hand tighter.

"Just relax, babe," he uttered, kissing her forehead.

She took a deep breath and looked up at the monitor. A tiny image appeared. "Oh, wow, that's our baby!" she said with mounting excitement. She suddenly felt powerful and alive. *I'm already in love with this child.*

Jody glanced at Danny, then looked back at the monitor. "The embryo is only measuring six weeks, and I'm not getting—" Her words ended abruptly. She quickly stood up and excused herself from the room.

A spark of hope quickly extinguished. Gianna looked at Danny. His mouth dipped into an even deeper frown, and she could tell by his empty expression that it wasn't good news. "What's going on? I know you know."

"It's procedure for Jody to bring in Dr. Ross."

Gianna flinched at his reply. His words seemed worn, thin, and rehearsed, used so often by physicians—*It's procedure.* Those were the exact words the ER doctor had told her after Chad assaulted her.

She pleaded with him. "Please, Danny. Tell me."

He shook his head in dismay. In the corner of his eyes, tears began to glisten. In a grim voice, he said, "Our baby has no heartbeat."

Gianna's spirits sank. Bitter cold despair ripped through her soul. "No, no, that can't be," she cried.

"I'm sorry," Danny whispered.

A few moments later, Jody returned with Dr. Ross. Danny gave him *the look*, alerting him that she already knew.

Dr. Ross touched her shoulder. "I'm so sorry, Gianna. I wish there were something we could do."

When Gianna arrived home, she tossed her purse on the couch and continued down the hallway to their bedroom. She closed the door and plopped down on the bed. *Why me?*

Immediately, the door opened, and Danny walked in. "Can I get you anything?" he asked in a weakened voice.

She shook her head. "Why did this have to happen?"

Danny sat on the edge of the bed; his expression of knowledge was terribly serious. "It was Mother Nature. Something didn't develop properly. It's usually due to chromosomal abnormalities."

Angry and confused, Gianna's mind swirled with unanswered questions. "How long is this going to take? How do I know when it's over?"

"You'll know when it's over. The bleeding will get heavier, and you'll experience contractions," he said. He rubbed her back. "We'll follow up next week with another ultrasound to make sure it's complete."

"What if it's not?"

"Then we'll do a D&C. That's a surgical—"

"Stop!" She put her finger to his lips. "Please, spare me the details."

"Ok," he whispered, stroking her cheek. "I'm here for you. We'll get through this together, I promise."

"Oh, Danny, I really wanted this baby."

"I know, and I should've cautioned you about the possibility of a miscarriage, but I got caught up in the anticipation." Tears filled his eyes. "I welcomed this pregnancy, too."

"And you know what?" she asked. "Sophia had an abortion! She could've had a perfectly healthy baby, but she threw it away like yesterday's garbage!"

"What?!" Danny's mouth dropped open. His eyes had a burning, faraway look in them. When he finally spoke, his voice trembled. "Not everyone, especially a young teen like Sophia, sees God's gift of new life as a blessing. Too many see a choice and take it."

Gianna closed her eyes and sighed. *He's right. I wish there was something I could've done for her.* She peered up at him. "Let's pray for her and her unborn baby."

Danny nodded. "Ok."

They held hands and bowed their heads.

Gianna prayed, "Lord, have mercy on Sophia, and may her baby's soul have repose. Amen."

The next morning, Gianna woke to the delicious aroma of sizzling bacon and eggs and coffee brewing in the kitchen. *I guess it's time to get up.*

She wanted to go back to sleep, back to the wonderful dream she had. The scene came vividly to her eyes. It was a warm spring day; the birds were singing, and the flowers were blooming. She was sitting on her parents' porch swing rocking and cradling her newborn daughter.

But dawn found her, and so did reality. She gazed up at the crucifix that hung over her bed. *Lord, I accept your will. Please take care of our baby and heal our broken hearts. Thank you. Amen.*

She slid out from underneath the covers and ambled to the window. The sky was a gorgeous blue without a cloud in sight. She cracked open the window. A cold breeze blew, and her body shuddered from the chill. *This is SO not the weather I had in my dream.*

After she showered, she dressed in a black pair of leggings and a black three-quarter sleeve ribbed shirt.

When she ventured into the kitchen, Danny was standing at the stove scrambling an egg.

"Good morning," she said.

Danny turned to her. His eyes were gentle and understanding. "How're you feeling?"

"I'm ok." She spoke with quiet, but desperate, firmness. "The bleeding is heavier, but no cramping. I'm going to get through this."

"I know *we* will, but don't rush it." He set the spatula down on the counter, then walked to her and wrapped his arms around her midriff. "I love you."

"Love you, too." She withdrew from his embrace, then reached up into the cabinet for the plates.

"I've got this, babe. Please relax," he said.

Gianna nodded and sat down at the counter. Danny carried over the plates and sat next to her. As they ate their breakfast, they discussed their plans for the day.

"It looks gorgeous outside," she said, setting her fork down across her plate. "Maybe I'll go for a walk."

"I admire your strength, and walking is good, but I don't want you to overdo it."

"I won't. Will you join me?"

Danny reached for her hand and smiled. "I wouldn't have it any other way. Besides, the crisp autumn air will do us *both* good."

Dan drove Gianna to Central Park, arriving near the Jacqueline Kennedy Onassis Reservoir. They walked together along a paved path, taking in the views of the cherry trees, the cast iron bridges, and the great Manhattan skyline.

"Wow! It's a gorgeous fall day," Gianna said, gazing at the vibrant shades of yellow, red, and orange foliage. "I want to put this all behind me."

"I'm glad to see you smile," Dan said, leading her to a park bench. "Let's sit a spell."

Gianna sat down and stared off into the distance. For a moment, she didn't say a word, but then she uttered, "I miss Gray Wolf State Park. I wish we were home."

Oh, boy! Dan knew home meant Montana, and that topic was like opening a can of worms. He sighed. "Speaking of home, your parents called early this morning."

"Oh? Did you tell them?"

Dan lowered his eyes. "Yes." He cautiously peered up at her not knowing if her unstable emotions would explode. To his surprise, she nodded and smiled softly.

"What'd they say?"

"They said to tell you how sorry they were and... they're coming for a visit."

Gianna reached up and caressed his face. Teardrops filled her eyes. "Thank you for telling them. I couldn't have."

Dan nodded. "I understand."

Gianna's voice suddenly perked up. "But when are they coming? I've got to clean the house."

"Whoa there," he said, taking her hands. "Their plane arrives tomorrow afternoon at four."

Gianna's eyes lit up. "Ok, then let's go home."

It was as if a rush of adrenaline surged through her body. He hadn't seen her so full of life since they learned of their pregnancy. He was thrilled to see she was handling the miscarriage so well, but still, he wasn't going to let his guard down. He knew she hadn't experienced the extreme hormonal changes yet.

Early Sunday morning, a silver spike of pain jerked Gianna from the edge of sleep. It plunged deeply into her back and radiated to her stomach. "Oh, God! The pain," she cried as she curled into a fetal position.

Danny sprang awake. "I've got you," he said, cradling her in his arms. "Take a deep breath and blow it away."

"I can't," she cried. The wrenching pain overpowered her senses. "It hurts!"

"Easy, babe. Ride it out," he urged, rubbing her back. "Look at me and breathe."

She looked at him for the briefest moment, then shouted, "I can't!"

The contraction reached its peak, and then the pain suddenly subsided. Slowly, she released the tension in her body. "It's over. Oh, it's over," she exhaled.

"Relax," he whispered, continuing to rub her back.

Once she was sure the pain was over, she gently pulled away and scooted to the edge of the bed. She wobbled to the bathroom and closed the door.

She ambled to the toilet and sat down. She covered her face, afraid to look at what she would find. When she regained her composure, she looked down and saw a huge blood clot. *Please, God, no, not my baby.*

She cleaned herself up and then opened the door. She stood there shaken and numb. "Our baby's gone."

A tired sadness passed over Danny's features. "I'm so sorry." He wrapped his arms around her and rocked her back and forth. "We're going to get through this."

Chapter Eight

Dan woke up early Sunday morning and went for a two-mile jog. When he returned home, he checked in on Gianna. She was still sound asleep. *God, she's been through so much. Please heal her pain.*

He sat down on the edge of their bed and stroked her soft cheek. "How're you feeling?"

"Tired," she said, barely moving her lips.

"I'll be leaving shortly to pick up your parents at the airport. You stay here and rest."

"Thank you," she mumbled.

"Take it easy while I'm gone. And make sure you call me if you have contractions or start bleeding heavily again. We'll do another ultrasound in a few days to make sure the miscarriage is complete."

She sniffled, "Ok."

Dan gazed into her tired eyes. His own filled with tears. "Hey, when you're feeling better, we can always try again."

"Maybe," she said.

"I love you so much, and I'll wait for you."

"Love you, too," she cried.

Dan sifted through the airport crowd in search of his in-laws. There were so many people from a vast array of lifestyles, some friendly, some not so friendly, and others plain mixed up. He couldn't help but wonder what issues other people were facing and how easily problems can affect a person's behavior.

"Dan, over here!" a hearty voice called out.

Dan recognized Mr. Stefano's distinguished voice over the animated noise that surrounded him. He scanned the area, then caught a glimpse of Mrs. Stefano waving her hands in the air. Alongside her was her husband, with luggage strapped over both shoulders and two carry-on bags dangling on his forearms.

Dan raced forward to assist them.

"Ah, thank you, son," Mr. Stefano said, sighing in relief. "If I had to stand here any longer, I would've collapsed. Arianna thinks we're moving in."

"Oh, Daniel, don't let him fool you. Most of this is his," she argued.

Dan laughed. "I believe you, ma'am."

He knew his father-in-law was the type of man who'd take a frying pan and a camera when he went fishing, and he also knew his mother-in-law, a lovely woman, went for polished clothes with a keen sense of style. Hence, he knew they were both equally guilty of overpacking.

Dan gave an appreciative smile. "It's good to see you both. Thanks for coming on such short notice."

Mrs. Stefano reached up and gave him a hug. "We wanted to be here for both of you." She reached for his hands and held them warmly. Her brown eyes showed sincere compassion. "How are *you* doing?" she asked.

"I'm fine, Mom, really."

"How's my bella?" Mr. Stefano asked.

Dan sighed. "She had a difficult night. She's at home resting." He patted his father-in-law's shoulder. "Come on. I'll take you to her."

He led his in-laws through the parking garage. When he reached his truck, he clicked the remote to unlock it.

"Ah, so there's still a little country left in you," Mr. Stefano said, admiring the black Ford pickup.

"Yep, and there always will be," Dan said.

The highway traffic moved smoothly until they reached the Holland tunnel. It was then that the cars seemed to pause and purr with curious satisfaction.

"Ah, my *favorite* city...so glad to be back," Mr. Stefano said with full-blown sarcasm.

"Honey, you *could've* stayed home. Mark would've made the trip with me," Mrs. Stefano said.

"Nah, Mark's got school. Besides, somebody's got to straighten out my daughter," he replied haughtily.

"Pop, she's doing *surprisingly* well," Dan said.

As they exited the tunnel, Mr. Stefano sighed. "Have you given any thought to leaving this rat race of a city yet?"

"Nope. Not yet."

"What about your family?" Mr. Stefano asked, his tone, calmly disapproving.

"Vinnie, you're overstepping your bounds," Mrs. Stefano warned.

"It's ok, Mom," Dan said. "Pop, I know you hate the city. I get that. But a man must work, and this is what I need to do right now. I hope you can respect that. Joe and Evelyn understand."

"I suppose," Mr. Stefano mumbled.

Dan glanced in the rear-view mirror and caught Mrs. Stefano elbowing her husband's side.

There was an uneasy silence during the remainder of the drive home. Dan recalled the conversation he'd had with Gianna after she told her mother she was pregnant. He remembered telling her, *your parents want what's best for their grandchild and us.* He now understood her insecurities. It was clear as day that her parents objected to them living in the city.

Just a few blocks from home, Dan asked, "Mind if we stop at the pizzeria for take-out?"

"Daniel, I'll cook supper," Mrs. Stefano said.

"That won't be necessary, Mom. Relax!"

"Daniel, I did enough relaxing on the airplane."

"Son don't argue with your mother-in-law. Arianna will cook. Stop at that meat market on Ninth Street."

"Yes, sir." Dan gritted his teeth. He secretly wondered whom Gianna took after, her mother or father. Regardless, he was grateful to have generous, caring in-laws and a loving wife.

Gianna tidied up the house. Afterward, she relaxed on the couch while waiting for Danny to return home with her parents. She gazed up at the crucifix hanging over the fireplace. *God, thank you for my family.*

Moments later, keys jingled outside the front door. She stared intently as the door opened. When her father stepped inside, she carefully rose from the chair and greeted him with a hug.

"Daddy, I missed you."

"My *bella ragazza*," he said, kissing her cheeks.

Her heart melted just hearing her father call her bella ragazza, Italian for *beautiful girl.*

When Gianna saw her mother, she backed out of her father's embrace. "Oh, Mom. Thank you for coming."

"Honey, we're so sorry about the baby," she said.

"Thanks," Gianna sniffled. "But I'm ok now," she said, trying to sound confident. She didn't want her parents to worry about her. She wanted to enjoy their visit. She grabbed both her parents' hands. "Come with me." She led them down the hallway to the guest bedroom. "You can stay in my old room," she said, proudly showing them the space. "It's a full-size bed and there's a private bath."

"Honey, this is lovely. I never imagined a home like this in the city," Mom said.

"I told you, Mom," Gianna said, smiling. Those were her exact thoughts when Danny had first showed her his home.

That evening, Gianna's mother insisted on preparing a full-blown meal—a pasta dish with braciola.

"Mom, this really isn't necessary," Gianna said as she set the table. "We could've gone out to eat."

"Hogwash, honey. Why waste hard-earned money at an overpriced restaurant?" Mom asked, placing the dish on the dining room table. "Sit, and I'll tell the men it's time to eat."

Gianna dropped her hands to her sides. *Unbelievable. Even on vacation, Mom cooks a homemade meal. Who does that?* She pulled out her chair and sat down, letting her mind drift back to her childhood. Dinner was always on the table, the house was always tidy, and the family was always well taken care of.

She smiled, thinking about her mother inhabiting her kitchen today, then rolled her eyes. *Mom is just being Mom, and as always, is perfect at it.*

"They're coming," Mom said, returning to the room.

Gianna stood up and hugged her mother. "I love you, Mommy."

"Aw, I love you, too, honey," she said in a tear-smothered voice. "But what's this all about?"

Gianna opened her hands wide. "I just wanted to say thank you. Thank you for being you."

After supper, the four retreated to the living room. Gianna's mother shared photos Mark had taken at the church and wedding reception, and Gianna and Danny shared pictures of their honeymoon in Italy.

"I'm so glad you two enjoyed yourselves," Mom said, placing the photo album on the coffee table.

Gianna's father took his wife's hand. "It's time we visit Italy, see our hometown. What do you say?"

A reluctant smile tilted the corners of her mouth upward. "Oh, I don't know, honey. Jessica's due in April. I don't want to miss our grandbaby."

"I'm not asking you to move there," he said. "We'll go in the summer. What do you say?"

"I want to spend time with my grandchild."

"You'll have plenty of time for that."

"But they grow up so fast," she sniffled. She looked at Gianna and said, "Luke and John started high school."

Dad nodded. "Yep, freshman. They bring home tons of homework. Made them wise up in a hurry."

Gianna rolled her eyes. "Luke and John—grown up? Daddy, get serious." She exchanged a wary glance with Danny. He laughed and nearly choked on his coffee.

"Sorry, Pop, but I have to agree with your daughter," Danny said. "The odds of high school straightening those two out anytime soon are one in a million."

Gianna's parents turned to each other and shrugged.

"I thought their behavior improved," Mom said.

Dad raised his index finger and thumb and curled them. "Ok, maybe just a little," he said with an infectious laugh.

Gianna tapped her chin in deep thought. *Maybe Luke and John are better behaved only because I'm not there to tease.* Not that she didn't love her twin brothers, but they were rambunctious, mischievous, and immature. They always knew how to push her buttons. She recalled their last stunt when they tried to throw her in the swimming pool. She knocked John on his backside and socked Luke a good one right in the nose. Those two were always up to something, but she had to give them some credit. They were better behaved in school than her students, Zack and Trevor.

"Gianna, honey, are you ok?" Mom asked.

"Huh?" she asked, snapping out of her thoughts.

"Did you hear what I said about Mark?"

"No, I'm sorry. I was daydreaming."

Mom's voice perked up. "Mark doubled up his college classes this semester so that he could graduate sooner."

"Oh, that's awesome! Good for him."

Gianna wasn't surprised. Her brother Mark was an honors student. She knew how much he enjoyed photography and how eager he was to travel and use his skills and talents. She was pleased that he had found his niche.

Gianna fidgeted in her seat, trying to get comfortable. "So, Daddy, how's Matt doing? He must be overwhelmed taking care of the ranch."

Dad flipped his wrist. "Matt has everything under control. He is a hard worker, bella."

She smiled respectfully. "Yes, he is, Daddy."

Her oldest brother Matthew wore the name tag, 'Mr. Responsible' well. He was Daddy's sidekick when it came to the cattle ranch. Gianna felt the closest connection to him, perhaps because she was the second oldest or perhaps because he was Danny's best friend.

Gianna's mom shifted in the chair and gave an anxious little cough. "Jessica's, uh, feeling well. She's three months along in her pregnancy, and her morning sickness has ceased."

"Hey, that's wonderful news, Mom!" Danny said with a huge smile of approval. He turned to Gianna and gave her arm a nudge. "Isn't it, babe?"

"Uh, yeah," Gianna said. As the words began to flow, she gathered her strength. "I'm really excited for them." She looked at Danny and smiled. "Wow, I'm going to be an aunt!" A sense of hope came to her, and her despair lessened. She was genuinely happy for her brother and Jessica—so happy that she lost track of time. "Jeepers! It's late! I have work tomorrow."

Danny's mouth formed an O in surprise. "I thought you called in sick."

"No, I have a new lesson to teach. Besides, it'll keep my mind off..." Her voice withered as her determination faltered. She took a deep breath and said, "It's time I stop dwelling on what could've been."

"Bella, you need to rest," Dad said.

"I know, Daddy. That's why I'm turning in now."

She leaned over to Danny and kissed him. "Good night." She stood up and kissed her parents. "See you in the morning."

The next morning, Gianna groaned at the irritating buzz of the alarm. "Ugh! I hate Mondays." She reached for the snooze button and smacked it.

"You don't have to go," Danny mumbled.

"Yes, I do," she insisted, her tone a bit miffed.

"Babe, you're still hurting. I know because I am, too. You're not giving yourself enough time to grieve."

"Look, I cried for two days. I'm tired of crying. I need to keep busy, so I don't think about it anymore. Please, try to understand."

Danny rolled on his side and pulled her into his arms. He caressed her face and smiled gently. "Ok but take it easy today."

"I promise I won't overdo it."

A half an hour later, Gianna made her way into the kitchen. Her mother was already brewing coffee at the counter. She was right at home.

"Mom, you didn't come here to be a maid."

"Hogwash, honey. I know how hectic mornings can be. Remember, I had to get you, your four brothers, and your father motivated every morning."

Gianna glanced over her shoulder into the living room, wondering where her father was. "Is Daddy still sleeping?"

"*Your* father, asleep in *this* noisy city?" Mom asked sarcastically. "You know he's up when the rooster crows." She shook her head. "He went for a walk."

Danny entered the kitchen. "Good morning, Mom." He pulled out a stool and sat down at the counter.

Mom carried over a cup of coffee and set it in front of him. "Would you like some bacon and eggs?"

"That sounds good. Thank you, Mom," Danny said.

"Mom, stop!" Gianna scolded. "You're not a waitress. Besides, you're making me look bad."

"Shush, honey! I want to do this," she said. "Now sit! Your father should be back any minute with the bagels."

Gianna sat down beside Danny and ducked her head to hide her embarrassment. *Oh, mother! What am I going to do with you?* She peered up at Danny. The grin that lifted the corners of his mouth was more of a smirk than a smile. "What?" she asked.

"Your mother loves me," he said, playfully sticking his tongue out at her.

Gianna fought the urge to smile even though she found his humor both attractive and annoying.

The front door opened, and her dad walked in toting a brown bag. He grumbled under his breath, "You know my hungry cattle are friendlier than the stampede out there on the streets."

"Pop, it's Monday morning," Danny said. "People are in a rush."

"Monday morning? Heck, those people are no different on Christmas Day."

"Vinnie, relax," Mom said. "You're going to get your blood pressure up." She led him into the kitchen and sat him down next to Gianna. "Now, *mangiare.*"

Gianna arrived at school only fifteen minutes before the bell. She had planned to come in earlier to review her lessons, but her mother's grand breakfast had delayed her departure.

She sat down at her desk and bowed her head. She thanked God for giving her strength and determination. As she prayed, the squeaking sound of sneakers against the glossy tile floor broke her concentration. She lifted her head and saw Brandon standing in the doorway.

"Good morning, sunshine," he said.

"Oh, hey, Brandon. Happy Monday."

Brandon approached her desk and handed her an envelope. "I've been meaning to give you this to pass along to your husband."

"What is it?"

The homeroom bell rang.

"Shoot! I got to go!" As Brandon rushed out of the room, he called out, "See you at lunch."

Gianna watched him disappear from her sight. For a moment, she fixed her eyes on the colorful bulletin board that hung on the wall outside her door. She sighed. *There's never enough time to chat.*

She looked down at the envelope Brandon had placed in her hand. When she opened it, her eyes blurred with tears. It was a photo of Danny dressed in cobalt scrubs with a bandana on his head, crouched next to Brandon and his wife, holding their newborn son in his arms. The blissful smile on his face was priceless.

Pain squeezed her heart thinking of him. *He really wanted a child, and I failed him.* Overwhelmed with sadness, she dropped her head and cried. *Why did this happen, God?* She took a deep breath and muttered, "Come on, Gianna, keep it together."

Gianna managed to muddle through her morning classes without breaking down. During her prep period, she kept her mind preoccupied by grading her students' essay papers on drug and alcohol abuse.

"No, Zack!" she grumbled under her breath. "Wine coolers and beer are not safer to drink than hard liquor." She dropped her head into the palm of her hand. *Doesn't anything I teach this kid sink in?*

"Hey, girlfriend!" Tracy said, entering the classroom.

Gianna lifted her head. "Oh, hi. I hope my head banging against the desk didn't disturb you."

"That bad, huh?" Tracy asked. "I didn't see you all weekend. Thought I'd stop by to chat."

Gianna managed a faint smile even though she was crumbling inside. She set her pen down and said, "My parents are visiting."

Tracy placed her hands on her hips and shot her a blank look. In a shrill voice, she asked, "Your parents...here...in New York City? Then why're you here, girl?"

Grief and despair tore at Gianna's heart. She couldn't mask the pain any longer. She bowed her head and covered her face with her hands.

"Sweetie, what's wrong?" Tracy asked, crouching beside her. "C'mon, talk to me, girlfriend."

"I lost the baby," Gianna cried.

Tracy stared wide-eyed for two full seconds. "Oh, no!" She wrapped her arms around her and cried with her. "I'm so sorry. Do you want to talk about it?"

Gianna sniffled. In between tears, her trembling voice managed to tell her about her devastating miscarriage.

Tracy handed her a tissue. "This is my third pregnancy. I miscarried my first at six weeks and my second at eight. That's why Troy and I kept this one a secret."

"I'm so sorry; I had no idea," Gianna said, taking Tracy's hand. "Thank you for telling me."

Tracy nodded. She walked over to the wall phone. "I'm calling the office to arrange a sub for you. You need to go home and be with your family."

Gianna nodded. "Thanks."

Once her substitute teacher arrived, Gianna left. When she stepped outside the school building, the heat of the September sun thawed her air-conditioned body.

She refused a cab, thinking the brisk walk home would help clear her head. However, the sidewalks seemed overly congested with baby strollers, reminding her of what could've been. Avoiding eye contact, she walked with her head down, dodging the colorful blobs of chewing gum that enhanced the gray concrete like an abstract piece of art. Mixed smells of soft pretzels, hot dogs, and pollution left a stale taste in her mouth.

By the time she arrived home, she was relieved to have reached the air-conditioned building. The scalding sun beating down on her had only added to her misery. She was tired and irritable, feeling much resentment toward society.

When she opened the front door to her suite, the delicious aroma of Italian sausage and lasagna wafted through the living room. Her mother was at it again.

Frustration overrode Gianna's good manners. She walked into the dining room where her mother was setting the table. "Mom, quit it! You're not our personal chef!"

Mom looked up; eyes widened with surprise. "Honey, I didn't expect you home so early."

"Obviously not!" she shouted.

"Honey, I just—"

"I'm sorry," Gianna said, lowering her head in shame.

She slid her purse and satchel straps down her arm, dropping them to the floor.

Mom's face etched with empathy. "I know. It hurts."

Gianna raised her hands to her head. "I can't take it! Everyone and everything reminds me..."

Too distraught to explain, she rushed to her room and closed the door. She dropped onto the bed and buried her face in her pillow. *Why me?*

Moments later, a gentle hand massaged her shoulder.

"It's ok to cry, honey," Mom said.

Gianna picked her head up. She looked at her mother through her tear-clouded eyes and exploded. "It's not fair! Why do terrible things always happen to me? First, it was Chad, now this. How much more do I have to take?"

Tears of frustration streamed down her face.

"Shh, I know you've been through a lot these past few months, but things are going to get better."

Gianna glared at her mother. "How do you know that? You won't even be here!" she shouted. "You'll be home with Matt and Jessica's baby."

"Oh, honey," Mom said, reaching for her hand.

Gianna pulled away. "Just go! Go back to Sheridan!"

A melancholy frown flitted across her mother's features. "Honey, please. Let me—"

"Just go, Mom," she repeated, pointing to the door.

When her mother left, Gianna dropped back on the bed and cried. It wasn't until the door shut that she realized how hurtful her words were. *What's wrong with me?*

Meanwhile, Dan arrived home. As he parked his truck, he noticed Mr. Stefano strolling along the sidewalk carrying a grocery bag.

"Hey, Pop! Wait up," he called as he hurried to meet up with his father-in-law. "I see you're enjoying this fine city on this beautiful afternoon."

Mr. Stefano stopped midstride and tossed him a *'you're crazy'* look. "I can't get enough of this prosciutto from Alfonso's Meat Market." He shook a finger at him. "How come you, uh, home early?"

"It's my afternoon off," Dan said. He patted Mr. Stefano's shoulder. "Let Gianna and I take you and Mom out to dinner this evening."

"No, save your money, son. Arianna will cook supper for all of us."

Dan smiled, shaking his head. Now he knew where Gianna got her stubbornness.

When Dan opened the front door, he noticed Mrs. Stefano straightening up the kitchen. "Mom, please relax. You are not our housekeeper." When she turned, he caught a glimpse of her sullen face. He knew in an instant that something was wrong. "Mom, everything ok?"

Mrs. Stefano gave a weak smile, but there was a distinct sadness in her eyes.

"Arianna, what's wrong?" Mr. Stefano asked. He set his paper bag down on the counter and wrapped his arm around her. He led her into the living room and gestured for her to sit down on the couch. "What happened?"

"It's Gianna. We had a little argument."

Dan entered the living room. "She's home?"

Mrs. Stefano lifted her eyes. In a weakened voice, she answered him. "Yes, Daniel. She came home early."

Oh, man! Dan knew this phase of Gianna's miscarriage would eventually come, but he expected her to fire her crude emotions at him. "I'll talk to her."

"No, Daniel. Please, don't fight with her. You two have been through too much. I understand my daughter, and I know she is hurting."

"Yes, Mom, but that doesn't entitle her to be rude."

"Son, my bella didn't mean anything by it," Mr. Stefano said.

Dan shook his head. He knew Mr. Stefano had a forgiving heart, especially for his baby girl. "I'll talk to her," he said before leaving the room.

Dan knocked on the bedroom door and opened it. Gianna was laying there curled up on the bed with her back facing him and a pillow embraced in her arms.

"Tough day?" he asked. He sat down beside her and rubbed circles in the middle of her back. "Do you want to talk about it?"

Gianna rolled over to face him. Her eyes were red and swollen, and her face was soaking wet. "I lost it." She sat up and cried. "I was so nasty to my mother. I need to apologize to her."

"She understands," he said, taking her hand.

"But I was so hateful. What's wrong with me?"

"Your hormones are crashing. You have a valid reason to be upset, but it's how you deal with it." He patted her hand. "Everywhere you go, you're going to see reminders. This is a joyful time for Tracy and Jessica, and sometimes they're going to forget that you're grieving. I know you won't believe this now, but one day you *will* feel happy again."

Gianna's face clouded with uneasiness. "Oh, Danny, I don't know. I can't see past today."

"I know your heart is filled with uncertainty, but trust me, you will," he whispered. "Remember the rainbow we saw in Italy?"

Gianna nodded.

"God promised that you won't have to walk through life's storms alone. Go to your parents, Gianna," he urged. "They're hurting, too, and they love you."

Gianna entered the living room where her parents were waiting. She approached them with her hands clasped tightly together. "Excuse me, Mom. Can we talk?"

Her mother answered with a nod of her head.

"I'm so sorry for being disrespectful and immature. My words to you were hurtful. I know that you wouldn't be here if you didn't care. I hope you can forgive me."

"Oh, honey," Mom sniffled. She gave a tiny smile, then wiped her tears. "I understand the pain you feel. It's ok to be angry and sad."

"I let jealousy eat at me, and I took it out on you."

"Jealousy is a natural feeling. It doesn't make you a bad person, just human," Mom said.

Dad reached out, gesturing for her to sit with them. "Take it one day at a time, bella."

Gianna nodded and gave them a hug. "I love you both."

It was Friday, and Gianna's parents had an early morning flight home to Montana. Danny had an overnight emergency at the hospital and couldn't be there to see them off.

Gianna helped her parents carry the luggage downstairs to the lobby. "You know, I can drive you to the airport."

"Bella, don't worry. That's what a taxi is for."

While Gianna and her parents waited for the cab to arrive, she thought about how refreshing it had been having them there, and how she missed living near them.

"Thank you for coming."

"Bella, you take care," Dad said.

"You too, Daddy."

Gianna hugged him and then her mother.

"Thanks for everything, Mom. Tell everyone I said hi."

"We will," Mom said.

Gianna waved good-bye as the taxi pulled away. She stood on the front step and watched until the car disappeared from her sight. She thought about the next time she would see them. It would be Thanksgiving. A sudden burst of joy rippled through her. *I can't wait!*

Back inside, she straightened up the guest room. While she changed the linens on the bed, she noticed the Bible on the nightstand. She picked it up and smoothed her hand over the leather cover. When she opened it to the bookmarked page, a folded piece of floral stationery sailed to the floor. She picked it up and read the handwritten note.

My Dearest Gianna,

May you find comfort in these words from John 16:33. "I have told you this so that you might have peace in me. In the world, you will have trouble, but take courage, I have conquered the world."

Gianna, please know that God hears your cries and feels your pain. He understands and is with you in your deepest grief. Trust in Him.

Love, Mom

Gianna held the paper against her heart. *Thank you, Mom, for helping me find peace.*

That evening, Gianna met Danny at the office for her follow-up ultrasound. As she lay frigidly on the unfriendly table, she gripped his hand like a vise. *God, please get me through this.*

Jody performed the exam.

"The miscarriage is complete," she said.

"So, I don't need a D&C?"

"No, there isn't any more tissue matter present."

The news twisted and turned inside Gianna like a ship lost at sea. Although hearing Jody's words was excruciating, it was a reality she was ready to accept. It was the closure she needed to end this tragic chapter of her life.

Danny swept her hair away from her face. "You ok?"

"Yeah," she said, tears rolling down her cheeks. "This was the funeral."

Chapter Nine

Bright and early Saturday morning, Gianna stood in front of the refrigerator door contemplating breakfast. *What do I want to eat?* Usually, she'd make bacon, eggs, and toast on weekends if Danny were home, but last night, the hospital had called him in for an emergency. She closed the refrigerator door and moseyed over to the pantry. She peered inside at her options, still unsure as to what she wanted to eat.

"You're up early this morning."

Danny's masculine voice rumbled from out of nowhere, sending gooseflesh rippling up her back.

"Jeepers!" she yelled. "Where'd you come from?"

"I just got in. Didn't you hear me unlock the door?"

"No, I didn't."

Danny's gentle hand took her face and held it tenderly. "I'm sorry." He brushed a few strands of her hair back and tucked them behind her ear.

Gianna's vision fogged with a scene from the past. She recalled that horrific moment when Chad leaned into her and smoothed her hair. His intruding voice thundered inside her head, *'Your hair looks pretty all pulled up.'*

"Don't touch me!" she screamed, stumbling backward into the counter.

Danny held up both hands in a classic gesture of surrender. "Baby, what's wrong?"

Gianna closed her eyes and drew in a slow, calming breath. "I'm so sorry." She put her hand up to her forehead and mumbled, "God, what's wrong with me?" She peered up at Danny. "I don't know what's real anymore."

"No, I'm sorry. I didn't mean to scare you," he said. He held his arms open, inviting her into his loving embrace.

Cradled in his strong arms, she felt small, feminine, and safe. His strength tamed her rapid breathing and pounding heart, erasing all the negative tension in her body.

"I'm ok now," she breathed.

"Good," he said, kissing the top of her head. "Did you eat already? I brought home bagels."

Gianna lifted her head from his shoulder and spotted two brown bags on the counter. "Yum! Perfect."

Danny guided her to the counter and helped her onto a stool. "I'll get the plates."

"Ok," she said, grabbing one of the bags. She reached inside and pulled out a box of pregnancy tests. Her face grew hot, and her body tingled. "What the..."

Danny turned around. "The other bag."

"Wait; explain this first."

"I brought them home from the office."

"Why?"

"Just in case," he answered easily. His face was full of strength, shining with a steadfast and serene peace.

"Oh." *Wow, he really wants a baby.* A crazy mixture of hope and apprehension swirled in her mind. *But I can't deal with another miscarriage.* She gave her head a shake, and then took a bagel.

"Now, what's that look?" Danny asked.

Gianna shrugged. "I just have a lot on my mind."

"Ok, talk to me," he said, taking her hand in his.

"How long do we have to wait to try again?"

"One or two cycles, but it's more important that you're emotionally ready." Hope and anticipation left his face. "Why? Are you ok?"

She cracked a tiny smile. "Yeah, I was just wondering." She bit into her bagel. "Mmm, these are fresh."

A shadow of alarm settled on his face.

"Something else is bothering you?" he asked.

She shook her head. "I'm fine."

"Babe, what is it?"

She peered up at him. "I need to see Chad."

"What?" There was an edge to Danny's voice. His eyes studied her with intense curiosity. "Why?"

"I need to forgive him so I can heal."

For a moment, Danny sat there in silence. He clenched his fists and replied sharply, "Baby, I can't forgive him. I caught him in the act."

Gianna clutched one of his hands. "Danny, *we* can forgive others because Christ forgave us."

Danny's coolness was evidence that he wasn't thrilled with the idea. He ran his hand through his hair. "I don't know if I can do it."

"Then pray about it. Ask the Holy Spirit to pour God's love into your heart." She hopped off the stool and stood behind him, locking her arms around his torso. "Please, Danny," she pleaded. "I can't hold onto this anger any longer. Forgiving is not forgetting. It's letting go of anger and your right to revenge. It's offering it up to God and leaving the justice to Him."

"That's fine, but you don't have to *tell* that snake." Danny shook his head and sighed. "If you must, then I'm going with you," he said with a possessive desperation in his voice. He rubbed his bloodshot eyes and added, "But first, I'm going to sleep."

It wasn't until late afternoon when Gianna and Danny left to meet Chad. According to Troy's directions, the halfway house was about thirty-five minutes outside of Manhattan.

Gianna rested her head against the seat and closed her eyes. Again, she glimpsed inside a world she was trying hard to forget. *I can't believe Chad is out of prison already. Troy said he had admitted his guilt, so they released him on good behavior.* She recalled a Bible verse, Ephesians 4:32: 'Be kind to one another, compassionate, forgiving one another as God has forgiven you in Christ.' She sighed. *Who am I to judge?*

Danny's gentle hand patted her knee. "Babe, you're quiet. You ok?"

She lifted her head and touched his forearm. "Uh-huh," she said. She turned and looked out the truck window at the easy-flowing traffic. Hoping her visit with Chad would go just as smoothly, she folded her hands in her lap and prayed. *God, please give me the courage to forgive Chad. Deliver me from resentment and grudges. Allow me to move forward and live a grace-filled life. Thank you. Amen.*

Danny exited the highway and made a quick left and then a right. Out of nowhere, the town seemed to spring up. It looked like a quiet, innocent little suburb.

Two blocks later, Danny pulled his truck into a small parking lot alongside a neat, two-story house with green shrubbery closely banked around a huge wraparound porch. The front yard looked like a golfing green and fit in well with the neighboring manicured lawns.

"Are you sure this is the right place?" Gianna asked, hesitant to unbuckle her seat belt. "This is a prosperous-looking neighborhood."

"Yeah, it is. Troy said this community holds grand expectations. Only low-risk cases are transferred here."

"Chad is low risk?" she asked, taking an angry breath. "He threatened to kill me."

"I know, but Chad plea-bargained. They don't feel he's a danger to society."

Gianna frowned.

"Baby, I'm not agreeing with them."

"I know, but it just makes me so angry."

Danny rubbed the bridge of his nose. "Look, are you sure you want to go through with this? There's no guarantee that you're going to have closure. Chad may blame you again, causing you more pain."

Gianna looked Danny straight in the eyes.

"Yes, I have to do this."

"Fine, but don't expect much from him," he said, as he hopped out of the truck. He walked around to her side and opened the door. "I support your decision."

"Thank you," she said.

Danny pulled her close to his side and walked her to the front entrance. He rang the doorbell and waited.

The front door opened, and a strong whiff of fried onions escaped. A lanky, bug-eyed man dressed in staff uniform and an apron greeted them.

"You're here for Chad, right?" the man asked.

"Yes, sir," Danny said, tipping his cowboy hat.

"I'm Earl. We spoke on the phone." He offered a handshake and said, "Come inside. I'll get him."

"Thanks," Danny said.

Gianna held Danny's hand and followed Earl into the 1960s retro living room with dark paneled walls and green shag carpet. She sat down next to Danny on a crate-style couch and was immediately drawn to the exquisite saltwater aquarium that took up the entire wall across from them. The humming noise of the fish tank's pump and the bubbling water prompted her memory of a visit to the dentist when she needed a tooth drilled.

I think I'd prefer another filling than to see Chad again. She pulled on a hangnail. *What am I going to say? Please, God, help me find the right words.*

Danny nudged her arm. She looked up at him, and his eyes motioned for her to look through the French doors that separated the living room from the dining area. Chad was standing there speaking with Earl and a big biker dude.

Chad's once muscular physique looked carelessly flung together. A heavy growth of bristle added harshness to his features, and his body had grown soft and weak looking. Obviously, four months in prison aged him ten years.

His tall shape turned and entered through the French doors. As he approached the sitting area, he paused and openly studied Gianna. His hazel eyes held a cold stare that made her shiver.

Gianna flinched as visions of the assault attacked her mind. She grasped Danny's hand tighter, and then slowly rose to her feet.

A tense silence filled the room.

"What're you doing here?" Chad asked.

His hostile tone chiseled away at her confidence.

"I...uh." She looked at the floor and drew in a deep breath, forbidding herself to panic. *God, help me get through this.* At that moment, Danny's protective arm reeled her in. His warm touch reassured her. With restored confidence, she looked up at Chad. She folded her arms across her chest and said, "Chad, I came here to forgive you. What you did hurt me. I won't forget it, but I won't hold it against you. That's all I have to say."

Chad's ill-shaven, sunken-looking face appeared confused. He stepped backward, then reached into his pocket and pulled out a compact Bible. Between the pages was a slip of paper. He took it out and handed it to her.

Gianna read it aloud. "1 John 1:9, 'If we confess our sins, He is faithful and righteous to forgive us our sins and to cleanse us from all unrighteousness.'"

She nodded and returned the paper.

A glint of hope appeared in Chad's eyes. "I prayed for your forgiveness. I'm sorry that I let temptation get the best of me. I not only disrespected you and caused you pain, but I destroyed my life and my career, too." He held the Bible to his chest and dropped his head. "Even after my probation, I can never work in a school again."

Gianna stared wordlessly, her heart pounding. *I can't believe he confessed.* She almost felt sorry for him. She took in a quick breath and uttered, "Chad, just pray. The Lord will guide you." She reached for his Bible and opened it to Psalm 25:4, which she read aloud. "'Make known to me your ways, Lord; teach me your paths.'" She handed the Bible back to him then looked up at Danny and said, "Let's go."

Danny tipped his hat. "Good luck, Chad."

He put his hand on Gianna's shoulder in a possessive gesture and guided her to the front door.

Chad called out, "Thank you, brown eyes."

Danny turned the key in the ignition. "Well, that went better than I expected."

Gianna nodded. "It sure did."

"How do you feel?"

"Like my soul has suddenly been unchained. I'm no longer a prisoner of pain. Thank you for bringing me here."

Chapter Ten

Six weeks passed, and it was mid-October. The autumn temperatures were balmy during the day and crisp at night. Gianna took advantage of the pleasant weather and continued to walk to school every day. She made an effort to take care of herself by moderately exercising, eating healthy, and keeping a positive outlook for her future. Her career was satisfying, and life was good.

Meanwhile, Danny continued to work ridiculous hours, and Gianna became concerned for his well-being. It appeared to her that he was no longer enjoying the highs and lows of being a doctor. Many nights, he came home looking drained, and the pleasure of life seemed to fade from his eyes. Whenever she questioned him, he told her he was only tired.

It was another gloomy Monday morning. Dan woke to the patter of rain against the window. After he rubbed his weary eyes, he peered at the clock. It was six forty-three. He sat up and nudged Gianna's shoulder. "Babe, it's late. I must go."

"Again?" she grumbled. "You worked all weekend."

"I'm sorry." He kissed her forehead, then slipped out from underneath the covers.

Dan showered and dressed, then bolted out the door without breakfast. He deftly tooled his truck through the city traffic as a rippling film of rain rolled down his windshield. By the grace of God, he arrived at the hospital in time for another all-important staff meeting.

What brilliant scheme does Dr. Stetson have to present this time? The question edged upon his mind as he hurried through the corridor to the conference room.

Dan pulled the door open and stepped inside. He carefully guided the door shut, not wanting to make a scene, but at the last minute, it closed with a thud. All heads turned, and he grimaced. "Sorry, folks."

He quickly grabbed a pastry and a cup of coffee and carried them over to the last unoccupied seat next to Dr. Ross. As he rolled the chair into place, he banged his knee on the crossbar underneath the table, nearly spilling his coffee.

He gritted his teeth to stifle his profanity. *Dang! Can this day get any worse?* He massaged his knee, trying to drive out the sharp sting. After the throbbing pain subsided, his heart resumed something of its normal rhythm.

"Dr. Christiansen," Dr. Stetson called out.

Dan looked up and noticed Dr. Stetson's muddy brown eyes flaunting her arrogance. "Good morning," he said.

"It's so nice of you to join us," she said.

Dan returned a small, bitter smile. "Sorry, ma'am."

He glanced at Steve and they both exchanged mutual expressions of discontent.

Dr. Stetson pulled a white lab coat over her form-fitting minidress then paraded her overly slender figure up to the podium. She cleared her throat and began her opening speech.

"Welcome, doctors. I speak to all of you on behalf of Dr. Collins and Dr. Browne. Unfortunately, due to an emergency, they can't be here this morning. With that said, let me first recap the old business. As you know, we signed the lease for the suite next door and approved the architectural plans to incorporate the new space with our existing office. So far, this has been a smooth process."

The doctors nodded and clapped. Dr. Stetson took a sip of her water, then continued her speech. "I called this meeting because the state has offered us a substantial amount of funding to perform abortions at Riverview."

Dan pinched the bridge of his nose. *No, this isn't right.* There was a sudden tightness in his chest. *There must be a better way to expand the business.* He peered up at his nine colleagues. Their heads bobbed as they jotted down notes. They all seemed in tune with Dr. Stetson's pitch.

"This is an opportunity for our practice to expand our clientele." Dr. Stetson's mouth grew sure and all knowing. "Plus, line our pockets," she added, smiling with perfect poise. She further explained the details, the financial benefits, and the scheduled in-services offered to the OB surgeons. "Does anyone have any questions?"

All hands around the table eagerly rose, and Dr. Stetson was flooded with queries. The feedback from Dan's coworkers, including the four GP's, was shockingly positive. Dan shook his head. *No.* He doodled on his notepad and wondered sourly, *Am I the only antiabortionist here?*

After the two-hour punishing meeting adjourned, he privately approached Dr. Stetson regarding his concerns.

"Doctor, I'm afraid I can't participate due to my religious beliefs," he said.

Dr. Stetson gestured to him to sit down, and then took a seat across from him. She removed her glasses and replied, "Dr. Christiansen, you are *only* one of six OBs practicing in this clinic. To get state funding, 100 percent participation is crucial."

"But, Doctor, I'm not willing to compromise my faith."

Dr. Stetson straightened her posture, pushed her shoulders back, and flipped her hair. She took a quick, sharp breath, and then poured her derision on him like syrup. "You need to let go of your backwoods' morals. This is New York City. Our duty as physicians is to provide a service to our patients." She waved her pen. "Women should have a right to choose. It's their body."

"What about the rights of the unborn? I became a physician to protect and preserve life, not end it. Life begins at conception. Abortion is murder."

"We all have our beliefs. Look, Dan, you're an excellent surgeon with pleasant bedside manners. It would be advantageous for both of us to resolve our disagreement."

"And how do you propose we do that?"

An eager hunger flared in her eyes. "How about we discuss this matter further over dinner?" she suggested, placing her hand over his.

Dan's skin prickled as though he was holding a live wire. Dr. Stetson's undertone of meaning was unmistakable. "I don't think so." He whipped his hand away and stood up. His temples pounded thickly, and his throat was tight. "This conversation is over."

"Dr. Christiansen, I thought we could handle this like two mature professionals, but evidently not. I represent seventy-five percent ownership of Riverview, and since you're not part owner of this clinic, and you are not on board with progress, I suggest you find alternative employment by the first of the year." In a haughty manner, she grabbed her briefcase and turned on her heel. "Now, if you'll excuse me, I have another meeting to attend."

Kimberly's voice was intimidating, even sinister sounding, but Dan refused to let her pressure him. As she strode out the door in a huff, he mumbled, "Don't let me keep you from being physician of the year."

Dan was so angry that tears dampened his eyes, and that made him angrier still. *Unbelievable!* It had always been evident that their personalities clashed, but that witch had threatened his employment. Even though Kimberly didn't have legal grounds to fire him, it'd be awkward to stay. *Now what do I do? She threw me both ends of the rope.* He sighed, then bowed his head. *God, I really didn't need this.*

He left the conference room, his mind still simmering about the meeting. How did his fellow OB docs really feel about the mandatory participation? Was he the only one who didn't agree?

Hours later, after countless patient appointments, Dan managed to get a break. He stopped by Dr. Ross's office to chat. "Steve, what're your thoughts about this morning's meeting?"

Dr. Ross looked up from his charts. He set down his pen and said, "I don't agree, but it doesn't matter. I resigned."

Dan widened his eyes. "What? Oh, wow! Where...where're you going?"

"New Jersey. My wife's parents are getting up in age, so I'm moving my family back there and starting my own practice. What about you?"

Dan shook his head. "Looking for another job, I guess."

"I can always use a good doctor if you don't mind relocating," he said. "It's not Montana, but it's rural." He shook his finger to make a point. "You, my friend, the Lone Ranger, will fit right in."

Dan's mood lifted. "Thanks, I'll keep that in mind."

Later that evening, Gianna was at home preparing a special supper for Danny. She made filet mignon with two side dishes, then set the dining table with an ivory linen tablecloth, a floral centerpiece, and two red candles.

Now, to get ready. She quickly showered. Afterward, she slipped on a flirty, cranberry-red baby doll dress. She curled her hair and styled it down, the way Danny liked it. Afterward, she spritzed her neckline with a sweet fragrance.

Gianna took one last look at herself in the mirror. *I'm ready.* Her heart pounded and her pulse raced thinking about Danny. It had been weeks since they'd had a romantic evening together, and her body ached to feel his love.

She returned to the kitchen to double check dinner. "Perfect, if I do say so myself." She lit the candles, flicked on the gas fireplace, and dimmed the lights. She retreated to the couch and anxiously awaited his arrival, her body tingling with anticipated pleasure in the evening ahead.

She looked up at the crucifix that hung above the fireplace. *God, I miss him. I'm so worried about him. He's wiped out. Please help me make this evening special for him, and please strengthen our marriage. Thank you. Amen.*

At once, she heard keys jingling as they manipulated the lock. The door opened and Danny entered.

"Welcome home, sweetheart," she said with a cheerful smile.

Danny returned a drained smile. "Thanks," he said, setting down his laptop bag. He pulled off his leather jacket and hat and tossed them on the recliner. "I'm going to take a shower," he grumbled. Oblivious to supper, he walked down the hall and turned into the bedroom.

Gianna frowned. *Poor guy.* She hated seeing him so depressed. In lonely silence, she closed her eyes. *What can I do, God?*

She rose to her feet. *Please help me find the right words to say.* When she stepped forward, she eyed Danny's jacket lying on the chair. As she grabbed it, a slip of paper fell out of the pocket. *What's this?* She reached down and picked it up. It was a note written like chicken scratch.

Dan,
We need to talk. I don't want to lose you.
Kimberly

Cold fear gripped Gianna's heart. Her muscles tightened as a mixture of anger, jealousy, and betrayal attacked her. *He's having an affair.* Her worst nightmare was coming true before her eyes.

"Excuse me?!" she roared.

She crumpled the paper into a ball. *So much for romance.* She stomped into the dining room and blew out the candles. With her body quivering on the edge of hysteria, she marched down the hallway to the master bath. When she opened the door, a rush of steam escaped.

"Who's Kimberly?" she shouted.

Danny turned off the shower and slid the curtain open. "My boss...why?" he asked nonchalantly. His tone was smooth, his expression blank.

"What's this?" she snapped. With her trembling hands, she held out the scrunched-up paper.

Danny shrugged his shoulders, then grabbed his towel. After he wrapped it around his waist, he took the paper from her. "Where'd you find this?"

His cool, aloof manner irked her, making her even hotter under the collar. "It fell out of your jacket pocket," she shouted.

Danny shook his head. "I swear I never saw this before." There was a long, brittle silence as he read the paper. The muscles in his jaw tightened. "This isn't what you think," he said, stepping out of the tub.

"Then what?" A pulsing knot within her demanded more. "You have a lot of explaining to do."

Danny nodded, then walked out of the bathroom into their bedroom.

Gianna followed him out. "What's this about then?" The tight knot within her begged for release.

Danny sat down on the bed. "I handed in my resignation today."

"What? Why?" When he didn't answer right away, she pleaded, "Please, look at me. Talk to me. What's going on?"

He reached for her hands. "It's over."

"What's over?"

"Remember all those meetings?"

"Yeah, and..."

"Well, my boss accepted state funding to perform abortions, and she's demanding all OBs participate."

"You're not going to do this are you?"

"No!" he shouted. "That's why I quit."

"Have you *ever* performed an abortion before?"

Danny's eyebrows shot up in surprise. "No! I did my residency at a Catholic hospital." He lowered his eyes and in a calm voice whispered, "I'm sorry. Let's not argue."

"I'm sorry, too, but—" Gianna crushed her mouth to his lips and kissed him zealously. Her heart smiled, not because he'd quit his job, but because she was relieved that it wasn't their relationship causing him misery.

Between kisses, Danny murmured, "I've missed you too, but what's—"

"Shh." She put her finger to his lips. "Let me say something first. I thought you had other female interests, and when I found that note—"

"No, never," he interrupted. His eyes clung to hers. "Gianna, I love you and *only* you."

Tears clouded her vision. "Forgive me for doubting you."

"Hey." He held her face in his hands. "I can see how it must've looked. My boss has a knack for causing trouble." He took her left hand and manipulated her wedding ring. "I'll *always* be faithful to you."

"I'm really sorry for not trusting you."

He shook his head. "Forget it." He glanced up at the bedroom door. "Hey, isn't supper getting cold?"

"Let's have dessert first."

"Hmm, sounds good to me," he said, stroking her hair. His eyes skimmed her body and beamed with approval. "You look so sexy in that dress."

"Now you notice?" She rolled her eyes. "Oh, you!" She palmed his shoulder and pushed him back on the bed. She straddled him and leaned into his warm, steamy body. The contact ignited a fire that spread through her veins. She hungered for his masculine taste.

Her mouth all but consumed him in a rush of frantic kisses. She kissed him with all the pent-up stress of the past weeks, scattering kisses on his chin and neck. His freshly showered body teased her senses. "I want you," she whispered in his ear.

Danny moaned, urging her to continue.

Her lips followed the path of her hands, sprinkling wet kisses down his shoulders to his hair-roughened chest. She lowered herself onto the floor in a kneeling position and loosened his towel. Her seductive stroking stirred his passion. His body hummed and throbbed from the desire she created.

Danny sat up and whispered, "Come here. Let me hold you." He pulled her onto his lap and kissed her. His mouth never left hers, not even when he unzipped her dress. "I missed you," he breathed. He lifted her dress over her head and tossed it on the floor.

He laid her on the bed and opened his mouth to her neck. He placed soft, wet love bites here and there, leaving a trail of kisses along the edge of her collarbone.

Shivers rushed through her. "I need to feel you now," she breathed, raking her fingers through his wet hair. A hot tear slipped down her cheek.

Danny lowered himself over her. His warm body against hers felt as if an electrical current pulsed beneath her skin. As the heat of their bodies fused together, an amazing sense of completeness filled her soul. She felt more content than ever before.

Chapter Eleven

Early the next morning, Gianna was in the kitchen making a pumpkin and granola parfait for breakfast. As she opened a new package of granola, she split the bag, dumping half of the contents onto the counter. *Oh, sugar! What am I doing?* Last night's romance had left her brain somewhere out in the ozone.

"Good morning babe," Danny said, walking into the kitchen. "Ooh, that looks delicious," he said, watching her top the bowl with blueberries and sliced strawberries.

"There's plenty," she said, grabbing another bowl out of the cabinet.

As the two of them ate their breakfast, Danny touched her forearm. "Have you given any thought to Dr. Ross's offer and moving to New Jersey?"

Gianna smiled. "I haven't thought much about anything other than you and our amazing evening last night," she said, feeling the flush rise in her cheeks.

Danny pulled at his collar. "Yeah, that *was* good."

She sipped her orange juice. "In all seriousness, living rural again has its appeal, but I'd like to visit the area first."

"But are you comfortable with leaving your job?"

Gianna nodded. "I can get certified to teach in New Jersey." She propped her chin in the palm of her hand. "Honestly, I'm tired of the rat race."

Danny's face glowed with eagerness. "Then it's settled. Let's get a realtor out here."

"What about that note from your boss?"

"Don't worry. I'll handle Kimberly."

With her elbow resting on the table, Gianna dropped her forehead into the palm of her hand. "Yeah, that's what I'm afraid of."

"Don't worry." Danny sipped his coffee. "I think this is the right thing to do, and Doc Kendall agrees, too."

"Oh, you spoke to your folks already?"

"Yeah, and Matt too—yesterday afternoon."

"Oh, horse manure! Mom must know then."

"Relax," he said, taking her hand. "Let's pray for guidance."

It was midday and Gianna was in her prep period. *Ooh, I need to call Mom.* She picked up her phone and hit the call button. What was her mother going to say about moving to New Jersey?

Mom answered. "Gianna, how are you?"

The sound of her mom's voice made her pulse skip.

"I'm good, Mom." She leaned back in her chair and put her hand to her pounding heart. It seemed a bit calmer now. "I can't talk long because I'm at work, but I wanted to give you a heads up before you hear the news from Matt."

"Oh? Is everything all right between you and Daniel?"

Gianna rolled her eyes. "Yes, Mom."

She took a deep breath, gathered her thoughts, and told her mother about the changes in Danny's career and their new adventure.

"Tell Daniel, congratulations! It'll be less hectic for him and more peaceful for you both. You'll enjoy the open space and fresh air."

"I'm sure, Mom. Look, I do need to go, but I wanted to share our news with you. Oh, and tell Jessica I'll try to call her tonight."

When Gianna ended the call, she dropped her head on the desk. *Thank you, God. That went better than I expected.*

She set her phone aside and pulled a stack of test papers out of her desk organizer. She'd barely finished grading one paper when her cell phone sang a country love song. The distinct tune was a text from Danny.

Had some free time. Met with Realtor. Open house, Sunday. I'll give you the details later. Luv you.

Tears stung her eyes. She liked her job, and she loved their home and neighbors. She was uncertain about moving. She covered her face with her hands and prayed.

Oh, God, what're we doing? Everything is happening so fast. Please show us the way. Amen.

The period bell rang, and it was lunchtime. Gianna put her head down on the desk. She wasn't hungry, nor did she feel like socializing. She squeezed her eyes shut to keep from crying.

"Hey, girlfriend. Ready for lunch?" Tracy asked.

Gianna lifted her head and quickly grabbed a tissue to dab her eyes.

"Girl, what's wrong?" she asked.

Gianna tried to smile. "Long story, but you need to hear it." She stood up and grabbed her lunch bag. "Let's eat in the teacher's room so Brandon can hear this, too."

Tracy narrowed her eyes. "Uh, ok."

Inside the lunchroom, Gianna, Tracy, and Brandon sat at a small round table in the back corner.

"So, what's going on?" Tracy asked.

Gianna folded her hands on the table. "Well, Danny received a fantastic job opportunity in New Jersey."

Tracy sat there, mouth open and speechless.

"Good for him," Brandon said. He bit into his sandwich, then swallowed hard. "But wait. Not so good for my family. I'll have to find another practitioner."

Tracy blinked. "Wow, that's wonderful news, I guess." She sipped her water. "When are you moving?"

"January," Gianna said.

Tracy rested her hand on her stomach. "Oh, you'll miss my baby's birth," she said, dropping her lashes.

"I'm sorry, but we can always visit. Two hours away isn't too far." Gianna opened her hands, palms up. "But, hey, a lot can happen in a New York minute—like if our placed doesn't sell..."

"How do you feel about moving?" Tracy asked.

Gianna shrugged her shoulders. "I don't know, but this could turn into a partnership for Danny. Please, don't say anything just yet. I haven't told Mr. Sterling."

"I won't," Brandon said. "Good luck."

Tracy nodded. "Everything will work out."

After school, Gianna joined the crowded sidewalks and walked home. The crisp, cool air helped clear her head. She was tired of thinking.

The only downfall to walking was the alluring aroma from street vendor carts. She smelled spicy sausage, barbecue wings, and buttery popcorn, among many other treats. *This walk home is hazardous to my waistline.* She craved something sweet and couldn't resist temptation. Before she realized what she was doing, she'd handed over a ten-dollar bill in exchange for a bag of kettle corn.

When she reached the condo complex, she noticed Danny's truck in his parking space. *What's he doing at home already?* She entered the building and rode the elevator to the second floor. When she arrived at their front door, she dug through her purse for her keys, but before she found them, the door opened.

"Oh, thanks," she said, repositioning her purse and satchel straps on her shoulder.

Danny's face split into a wide grin. "Living dangerously, are you?" He pointed to the bag of kettle corn. "Watch that stuff. It's addicting."

"I know. It ruined me last time," she said. She stepped inside the foyer. "What're you doing home?"

"Dr. Collins offered to take my shift at the hospital since I worked all weekend."

"Wonderful." She lifted her nose to the delicious aroma of chicken. "Mmm, is that dinner?"

Danny nodded. A thoughtful smile curved his mouth. He took her hand and led her to the table.

"What's going on?" she asked.

As soon as she saw the red candles and the assortment of red, white, and pink rose petals scattered on the dining room table, she covered her mouth in awe.

"Dinner for two," he said, pulling out a chair for her.

"Oh, Danny! You are such a romantic. Thank you."

"This is my way of making up for ruining last night."

"Aww, but you didn't. Last night was fantastic."

Danny's eyes caught and held hers. "I love you."

"I love you, too."

He captured her mouth in a kiss that spilled through her soul. When he lifted his lips from hers, he left her hungry for more.

"Here." He picked up a fork and knife. "You've got to try this," he said, feeding her the first bite.

"Mmm," she said, tasting it. The chicken was moist, not rubbery. "You'd make an awesome chef."

"Thank you," he said.

"If dinner is this good, I can't wait for dessert."

Danny chuckled. "We're having kettle corn."

She looked at him with amused wonder. "I'm looking forward to it."

As Gianna and Danny enjoyed their supper, they discussed their day.

"Did you talk to your boss?" she asked.

"Nope. She's in California."

"What? You're joking, right?"

Danny shook his head. "Dr. Collins and Dr. Browne said she's overstressed, so she combined a business trip with some R&R. She'll be back in two weeks."

"It must be nice," Gianna retorted in cold sarcasm. "What'd they say about your resignation?"

"What're they going to say? They won't stand in the way of progress." Danny shrugged his shoulders. "They're both sorry to hear it but told me I have plenty of time to reconsider. We're going to meet when Dr. Stetson returns."

"Would you reconsider? I mean, what if we can't sell this place?"

"Our realtor said our home shows well. He's confident we'll get multiple offers. Hopefully, we'll hear positive feedback after the open house on Sunday."

"Oh." Gianna felt an instant, squeezing hurt. "Can we take a drive to New Jersey this weekend?"

Danny exhaled. "I can't. I'm on call again." He ran his fingers through his hair. "We can go the following weekend."

"Ok," she sighed.

Danny rubbed her arm. "Hey, I'm trying." He gave her a smile as intimate as a kiss.

"I know," she said.

The weekend came and went, and it was Monday evening. Gianna was home cooking supper when Danny walked through the door. An easy smile played at the corners of his mouth. She hadn't seen him that happy in weeks. She found it impossible not to return his charming smile. "A good day, I take it?" she asked.

His huge grin left her in suspense. Without saying a word, he set down his laptop bag, hung up his hat, and removed his jacket. He took her hand and led her to the couch.

"What's going on?" she asked, eagerly.

"We received an offer on the house!"

Gianna's jaw dropped, and she stared at him. A cold shiver slithered up her spine. "So, tell me."

"They offered our asking price with a generous moving allowance." A pleased smile remained on his handsome face.

"Yeah, right," she said, frowning in disbelief.

"They did!" He held up his index finger. "But...there is *one* stipulation."

"There always is."

"They want to close November twenty-fourth."

"What? That's ridiculous!" she shrieked. She took a deep breath and said, "No way! That's not even six weeks."

"Hey, I'm out of a job come January. How do I know if, or when, I'll get another offer?"

"But you said the realtor expected multiple offers. Can't we just wait? Where are we going to live in December?"

Danny took Gianna's hand. "Nothing says we must stay in New York. I'll tell Kimberly to stick it. Steve said his in-laws have a one-bedroom efficiency apartment for rent above their barn. It's small but remodeled. This way, if it doesn't work out, we're not locked into another mortgage."

"Oh, well, if that's not positive thinking."

"Babe, I'm trying to be cautious. I don't want to pay two mortgages," he said.

"I understand," she said, lowering her eyes.

But she didn't. This was not how she envisioned their move. She imagined several weekend drives to the country, exploring the area and looking for the *perfect* house. She didn't want to be rushed and dumped into someone's barn rental.

"Hey," Danny said, lifting her chin. "If we like the area, we'll build our dream home."

Gianna nodded. "I guess."

She walked into the kitchen and studied the calendar that hung on the refrigerator. A twinge of disappointment stirred through her. "I guess we're not going home for Thanksgiving as planned."

Danny sprang from the couch. "I'm sorry, not this year." He wrapped his arms around her waist to soften the blow. "Hey," he said, kissing the top of her head. "How about we go in December? We can celebrate Christmas with our families. Dr. Ross isn't opening his practice until January."

Gianna gazed into Danny's strong-willed, beautiful blue eyes. She mussed his hair and replied, "You're always so sure about everything."

"Don't worry. It'll be great. I promise."

"Fine. Call the Realtor and accept the offer. I'll type up my resignation and give it to Mr. Sterling tomorrow."

Danny chuckled. "Don't sound so sad."

"I am...but I'm not. I need a change."

She was tired of revising the curriculum, tired of the grand expectations of demanding parents, and tired of the negative attitudes from several of her students. Teaching was no longer exciting. It was stressful and sometimes depressing. Although she knew other schools would have their own issues, she hoped they would be of a different nature.

Tuesday morning, Gianna arrived at school a little earlier than usual so she could turn in her resignation. Only a handful of colleagues were in the building at the time, and the corridors were quiet. The only sound was her heels clicking on the tile floor, which rattled her nerves even more. Meeting with Mr. Sterling again was as intimidating as the day she was hired. *I hope this goes well.*

She stopped a few feet from his office and straightened the neckline of her blouse and smoothed out her skirt. She took a deep, unsteady breath and gave his door a knock.

"Yes?" Mr. Sterling's deep muffled voice called out.

Gianna managed to turn the doorknob with her trembling hand. "Good morning, sir," she said in an unsteady voice.

"Good morning, Gianna," he said in his usual friendly, chipper voice. He motioned for her to take a seat. "What can I do for you?"

She sat down and folded her hands in her lap. "Uh, Mr. Sterling, I need to resign my position, effective November twenty-first. My husband received a job offer in New Jersey."

Mr. Sterling's cheerful smile vanished, replaced by a disappointed frown. He removed his glasses and said, "I'm so sorry you need to leave, but I understand."

"I really appreciate that, sir, and the opportunities you provided me."

"You've worked hard, especially redeveloping the curriculum. You should be proud." He formed a steeple with his hands and held them to his lips. "You know, Gianna, most people would have walked away. Your dedication and determination are commendable."

"Thank you, sir."

Mr. Sterling gave her hand a gentle squeeze and held it briefly. "It has been a pleasure, Gianna, and I wish you well." His eyes held steady. "And if you need a letter of recommendation, I'd be happy to write one."

"Yes, please, and thank you."

Gianna returned to her classroom and dropped into her desk chair. She nodded compulsively. *Wow, that went better than I expected.* She scanned the room and tears blinded her eyes. *I wanted this job so badly. Oh, how I bickered with Daddy for his blessing to move here, and now I'm letting it all go.* A crazy web of conflicting desires trapped her. She closed her eyes and let out a deep breath. *Oh, God, please help me stay strong. I need to do this for Danny.*

Chapter Twelve

Dan parked his truck in his spot. *Ah, finally home.* He released the seat belt, grabbed his laptop, and hopped out. The cool dampness in the air touched his face. *Smells like rain coming.* He gazed up at the sky. Dark gray clouds threatened a storm. *I hope Gianna took a cab home.* He hurried along the sidewalk toward his end unit. Just as he reached the covered porch, tiny drops began to fall.

The lobby door opened, and Troy stepped out. "Hey, cowboy! How're you doing?"

"What's up, neighbor?" Dan asked. He pointed at Troy's uniform. "I thought your shift ends at three."

"Not today, my friend. I'm working a double. I'm on break now...waiting to see Tracy before I leave."

"Oh. I'm through for the day." Dan sat down on the top step, hunched over, with his arms resting on his thighs. "I have to pack for a three-day seminar."

Troy dropped down beside him. "Oh, fun."

"It should be. It's at a resort in the Catskills. Gianna's going to love it."

Troy smacked his lips. "A second honeymoon! Enjoy, cowboy."

Dan tried to suppress his smile by clearing his throat.

A taxi pulled up to the curb and two umbrellas emerged from the back seat into the depressing drizzle. Troy jerked to his feet and rushed down the steps to assist Tracy.

Dan followed. "Hey, baby," he said, greeting Gianna.

Just as he gave her a kiss, the sky let loose. He squeezed in underneath her umbrella and ran for cover.

"Did you get my text?" he asked.

"Huh, what text?" she asked as she fumbled through her purse for her cell phone.

"About my conference." Dan held the door open for her. "You requested the rest of the week off, right?"

Gianna's eyes widened in alarm. "Oh, Danny! I'm so sorry. I forgot."

Dan's enthusiasm deflated like a balloon. He smiled bitterly at her, then glanced at Troy.

"Alrighty then," Troy said, rubbing his stubbly chin. "Good luck there, cowboy." He pointed at the door and said, "Duty calls." He kissed Tracy goodbye and left.

Tracy put her hand on Gianna's shoulder. "I'll be home if you need to talk."

"Thanks," Gianna muttered.

Dan shook his head regretfully. *I can't be mad. I put her through enough emotional hell these last few weeks.* He flipped his wrist in a gesture of dismissal. "Forget it; it's ok."

"No, it's not!" Gianna said with both hands on her hips. "You told me months ago. I dropped the ball."

Dan tipped his head, motioning her to the lounge chairs by the garden fountain. He sat down, leaned back, and closed his eyes. The babbling sounds of the water trickling into the stone-filled basin calmed his tense body. *I really wanted this for both of us.*

He looked at Gianna and reached for her hands. "Can you just call and ask?"

She exhaled with agitation. "I can't. I just resigned today. It wouldn't be right."

Dan blew out his breath.

Gianna threw her hands out, palms up. "What would I do there anyway? You'll be in the seminar all day."

"They have a spa, mini-golf, even horseback riding."

"But I'd want to do those things with you."

"We'll have dinners and evenings together."

"But, Danny, this is business." She reached up and raked her fingers through his hair, sweeping the wet strands away from his forehead. "It wouldn't be the same."

Dan pleaded, "Listen. The last seminar ends at noon on Friday. Steve's brother is going to meet us there to do a little hiking and camping. You can ride up with him."

Gianna shook her head. "School isn't over till three, and I'm chaperoning the middle school Halloween party."

"How about I ask him to wait until school is out?"

"That's too late. Besides, I don't even know Dr. Ross's brother. It'd be weird." She reached up and traced the hard angles of his face with her soft hands. "Look, this trip would be a perfect guys' weekend. Besides, I don't feel up to the great outdoors."

Dan dropped his head and stared at his empty hands. *She clearly doesn't want to go.* He looked at her and nodded. "Ok. I promise, after Sunday Mass, we'll take a drive to New Jersey."

Gianna smiled. "Thank you." She leaned in and kissed him. "You'll have more fun without me, anyway."

Dan laughed. "I doubt that."

Early the next morning, Dan loaded his suitcase and camping gear into Steve's Jeep. He gazed up at the bright blue sky. "Couldn't ask for better weather."

"Supposed to be nice through Saturday," Steve said. He pointed at his watch. "Hey, uh, time to hit the road."

"Right. Let me just say good-bye to Gianna. Would you like to come in for a cup of coffee before we leave?"

"No, thanks. I've got a mug in the console."

"Ok. I'll be right back."

Dan opened the door to his suite. The crispy aroma of toast wafted through the air. "Hey, can I get a coffee with a bagel to go?" he shouted across the living room. He poked his head into the kitchen and gave Gianna a witty smile.

"Sure. Does Dr. Ross want anything?" she asked.

"No, no," Dan said, waving his hands. "I was just kidding. I need to get going." He walked to the counter and held up the papers he'd set out earlier. "Here's the address and phone number of the resort."

"Ok. What's the seminar about?" Gianna asked, gliding her warm, smooth hands up and down his back with unanticipated tenderness.

Dan's brain faltered under her expert touch. "Uh, 'Emergencies in Primary Care.' Fascinating, huh?"

Gianna batted her lashes at him. "No. Not really."

"Oh, c'mon. It's good stuff, like life-threatening allergies, dangerous rashes, neurological disorders…"

"Ok, ok," she said, covering her ears.

Dan laughed. "I love watching you cringe." He refocused on his papers. "Here's our itinerary, a map of the trail, and the campsite we're staying at Friday night."

Gianna put her left hand on her hip. "I'm impressed, but are you sure you packed everything? Extra clothes, your new boots, food, water—"

"Whoa there, baby. Of course, I have everything."

She slanted him a wary look. "Are you sure?" She walked across the kitchen and unplugged his cell phone from the charger.

Dang! I'll never hear the end of it. "I was going to get it," he said, tugging at his collar. "Besides, there probably isn't a signal in the woods anyway."

Gianna rolled her eyes. "Men!"

"Relax." He put his hands on her shoulders. "I have everything. Steve's brother, Rob, is bringing the perishables on Friday."

"Fine. If you say so," she said.

Dan reached into his jeans pocket, pulled out his keys, and placed them in her hands. "I'll leave you my truck."

"Danny, I haven't driven a manual shift since Matt taught me to drive his Mustang."

"Babe, you can drive my stick shift anytime."

Gianna's face turned crimson. "Oh, stop!" she said, playfully swatting his shoulder.

"What? Get your mind out of the gutter, girl." He wrapped his arm around her. "Seriously, if you need my truck, it's here. I've got to go. Steve's waiting," he said, walking her to the front door. "And remember, don't answer the door."

"Not even for trick-or-treaters?"

"Ok. Just don't let the little goblins eat you up."

"In that case, don't let the grizzlies attack you."

"There aren't any grizzly bears where we're going," he said, grabbing the doorknob. *Only black bears, but you don't need to know that.* He turned around and took Gianna's hands in his. "I'm going to miss you." He gently touched her face and glided his fingertips over her sweet lips. "I love you."

Gianna tearfully embraced him. "I love you, too. Be safe and have fun."

"I will." He lowered his mouth to hers, eager to taste and feel her tongue stroking his. His body burned with an innocent desire. "See you late Saturday," he whispered, reluctantly pulling away.

Chapter Thirteen

ater that morning, Gianna caught a breather during her prep period. She sat down at her desk and glanced at her cell phone. *Fiddlesticks! I missed Danny's call.* She called her voice mail and listened.

"Hey, babe. We made it here with no speeding tickets. I only have a few minutes, but wow! I'm standing on the balcony outside my room. The view is spectacular. There's a lake surrounded by colorful trees. And the mountains...they're magnificent." He paused. "Ah, and the fresh, brisk air...for the briefest moment, I thought I was back in Montana. Baby, I wish you were here with me. Listen, I'm headed to my seminar now, but I'll call you tonight. Love you."

Goose bumps tickled Gianna's arms just hearing his voice. His enthusiasm made her smile. *I love you, too, sweetheart.*

She hoped he would find the seminar enlightening, and more importantly, find himself compatible with Dr. Ross. Afterall, come January, he would be his new boss.

Gianna bowed her head and prayed. *God, please let this work out according to your will. Thank you. Amen.*

That evening, Gianna had a dinner date with a can of soup. As she sat down to eat, her cell phone rang. *That's got to be Danny!* She quickly hopped off the stool and hurried into the living room to grab her phone.

"Hi, Danny," she said, crashing on the couch. "How was your day?"

"It's me," Jessica said, laughing.

"Oops! Sorry, Jess, but I thought you—"

"I know. Don't worry, chickadee. Dan will call."

Gianna sighed. "Life is so crazy. So much to do, so little time. After I eat, I'm going to start packing."

"I'll talk to Matt. In a week or so, we can fly out and help," Jessica said, eagerly.

"Oh, Jess, that's really kind, but save your personal days. You'll want them after your baby is born."

"Aww, but I want to help. I wasn't there for you when you lost—"

"Jess, it's ok. I'm ok. Sometimes terrible things happen, but I think with this move, we're on the direct path to something better. It's all good."

"I guess. I'm just glad to hear you smile."

"I'm fine, really."

"Ok, then." There was a sudden note of high excitement in Jessica's voice. "I'm having a gender reveal party Thanksgiving weekend. We're combining it with our first anniversary celebration. It'll be so much fun. I can't wait to see you."

"Uh, Jess, didn't Mom tell you? We can't come home. We have our closing. I'm so sorry."

"Oh," Jessica said, knocking her tone down a notch. "I think...Matt did mention it. Dumb pregnancy brain," she joked.

"But we'll be home for Christmas," Gianna said.

"I can't wait. I miss you."

"Miss you, too, Jess. Take care."

Gianna returned to the kitchen and reheated her soup. Just then, her cell phone rang again. It was her mother.

"Mom, hi!"

"How are you, honey?"

"Hungry!" Gianna said, rubbing her growling stomach. "Excuse me while I slurp my soup."

"Ok," Mom said, laughing. "Uh, aren't you supposed to be on a business trip with Daniel?"

"Yeah, but he was ending it with an overnight camping trip, and I really didn't want to go."

"But honey, you used to love going camping."

"I was just a kid then, Mom, and we stayed at a campground. The guys are roughing it this trip, and I prefer indoor plumbing. Besides, I'd be the only female there."

Mom laughed. "I understand. Listen, I'll let you finish eating. Take care of yourself."

"You, too. Love you, Mom."

After Gianna downed her soup, she went into the living room and grabbed the bundle of cardboard boxes Danny had brought home. As she assembled a few boxes, she scanned the room. *Where do I begin?* She stood up and walked over to the fireplace. Displayed on the mantel was the unity candle from their church ceremony and several Precious Moments figurines. Unshed tears burned her eyes. *I love these, and I hate that I must pack them away.* She carefully removed, dusted, and bubble wrapped them, then placed them in a box and continued un-decorating the living room. When she finished packing up all the knick-knacks and picture frames, she crashed on the couch. *This place looks depressing.*

She picked up her cell phone as it rang.

"Danny?" she answered.

"Hey, sorry it's late. Steve insisted on going bowling. I whipped his butt."

Gianna laughed. "I guess you never told him you were the bowling champion back in Montana."

"Nope. But tomorrow, I should just stamp my forehead, big loser. Steve's dragging me out to the golf course. He wants to prepare me for when we move to New Jersey. It's mandatory to play golf with the pharmaceutical reps," he said with a chuckle.

"Aw. You'll have fun."

"I'd rather go fishing."

Gianna laughed. "Don't I know it."

"So how was your day?" he asked.

"Fine. I just finished packing up the living room, but this place looks so blah. It's sad."

"I'm sure, but we'll make new memories. Just keep thinking about your dream house and having a horse stable in your backyard," Danny said, his voice, smooth and insistent.

"Yeah, I'll keep dreaming. Maybe when we win the lottery," she said, laughing.

"I'm serious, babe."

"Ok, Danny. But listen. I'm tired. I'll talk to you tomorrow."

"Ok. Love you."

"Love you, too. Goodnight."

Friday afternoon couldn't have come soon enough. Gianna roamed the crowded gymnasium, chaperoning the students at the PTA-sponsored Halloween party. The blaring music and shouting voices made her head pound like a dribbling basketball. She pressed both her hands over her weary eyes. *I wish this day were over already.* She snaked her way past a dancing cat, a witch, and an alien to the refreshment table. She picked up a plastic cup and scooped out some punch. Suddenly, someone shoved her into the table, nearly spilling the punch down the front of her flannel shirt. She gasped. *For the love of Pete.* She looked over her shoulder and saw Batman chasing the Joker.

"Zack and Trevor," Brandon shouted.

Gianna sighed. *Go figure, those two.* As she blotted the tablecloth with a paper napkin, a firm hand touched the small of her back. She turned to find Brandon standing there in his white striped uniform and cap, holding a baseball cap.

"Sorry about that, cowgirl," he said.

Gianna frowned. "What did *you* do?"

"I chased them out from behind the bleachers."

"With the bat?"

Brandon laughed. "No, that's just part of my costume." He shook his head. "Somehow, I think I should've dressed as a referee. Those two are a handful."

"That, they are," Gianna agreed. She glanced around the gym. "Now where did they go?"

"With Mr. Sterling. Let him deal with them."

Gianna picked up her drink and snatched a pretzel. She tilted her head in a nod, then carefully paved her way to the closest exit. She leaned against the wall and closed her eyes.

"Hey, are you ok?" he asked.

"Uh-huh," she quickly uttered. She sipped her punch. The sweet fruity taste quenched her thirst but did nothing for her headache. She watched the youths bop up and down with their arms swaying back and forth to the beat of the music. "If only I had their energy," she said.

"Yeah, tell me about it," Brandon said with a yawn. "My son is up every three hours. At least my wife gets to nap with him during the day."

Gianna nodded. *Sleepless nights—if only I could be so blessed.*

"Oh, wow!" Brandon said, pointing across the room.

Gianna looked up and spotted Tracy, dressed as a construction worker with a neon pink hard hat, waddling around the perimeter of the gym. As Tracy drew nearer, Gianna noticed her t-shirt. It depicted a bright yellow caution sign that read, Bump in the Road.

"Howdy, girlfriend," Tracy said.

"You look so adorable," Gianna said.

"Thank you, but I feel like a dump truck."

"Excuse me," Brandon said before exiting the gym. Seconds later, he returned with two folding chairs. "Here you are, ladies." He opened the chairs and motioned for them to sit down.

"Thanks," Gianna and Tracy said.

Brandon lifted his chin toward the crowd. "Oh well, back to center field. Catch you later."

"See ya," Gianna said. She gazed down at her boots. She felt drained, hollow, and lifeless. *Time cannot go any slower.*

Tracy touched her shoulder. "Girlfriend, you look whipped. What's going on?"

"I am. I haven't slept the past two nights."

"Missing Dan, are you?"

"Well, yeah, but I've had nightmares, too."

"Aww, girlfriend." Tracy narrowed her eyes, and her tone turned serious. "Please don't tell me it's Chad."

"No, nothing like that." Gianna swallowed hard. "Wednesday night, I dreamed I was camping, and when I crawled into the sleeping bag, I was greeted by a rattlesnake."

Tracy flung her hand to her chest. "Oh, crud! I would've been so out of there." She laughed. "Girl, you have some imagination."

Gianna gave Tracy a tired smile. "I know, but it gets worse. Last night, I dreamed Danny was mauled by a bear."

"Oh, sweetie, don't!" Tracy said, grabbing her hand. "You're going to drive yourself crazy thinking like that." Her amber eyes brimmed with concern. "Listen, Troy's working a double tonight. Let's have a girls' night in. We'll order pizza and hand out candy to the trick-or-treaters. What do you say?"

"I'd love to. Besides, I don't think I can handle another lonely night or stand to pack another box for that matter."

"Aw, girl. I'll cheer you up."

Chapter Fourteen

Dan and Steve arrived at the Echo Hill trailhead. "We're not the only ones taking advantage of this glorious fall day," Dan said, noticing the eight vehicles already parked in the tiny gravel lot.

"Nope." Steve scanned the parking area. "But I don't see Rob's pick-up truck yet."

Dan looked at his watch. "That's ok. We're early."

Steve opened his door. "I'm going to register us at the entrance while we wait for him."

"Ok." Dan hopped out of the Jeep, stretched his legs, and took a deep breath. The fresh air relaxed his whole being. He rubbed his hands together. *This is going to be great.* He turned to grab his backpack out of the truck when he heard the crunching sound of loose gravel and thumping music behind him. A maroon Dodge pickup truck with tinted windows pulled in. *That must be Steve's brother.*

The truck parked in the spot next to Steve's Jeep. A young man with brown hair slicked back into a ponytail jumped out. "Stay," he said to his dog.

The dog leaped from the back seat to the front and obediently sat down behind the wheel.

The man turned and held out his hand. "You must be Dan. I'm Rob, Steve's brother." His clean-shaven face gleamed with a youthful luster.

"Nice to meet you," Dan said, shaking his firm hand.

"Same here," Rob said. "Oh, and this is Denim. He'll be hiking with us." The blue merle Border Collie sat patiently, tongue hanging out of his mouth and tail wagging. Rob turned and signaled to Denim. The dog jumped out and sat by his side.

Rob looked up at the clear blue sky. "Man, it's freaking hot today." He wiped his sweaty forehead with his sleeve and then removed his camo jacket, exposing his toned biceps and an American flag tattoo.

Just then, Steve returned to the truck. "Hey, little bro," he said, patting Rob's shoulder. "It's good to see you." He crouched to meet Denim. "Hey, buddy." Denim wagged his tail and gave him a big wet slurp on the lips.

Rob grabbed his gear out of his truck bed and handed the tent to Steve. "Here, you carry this. My pack is loaded with food and cooking supplies."

Steve gave a forced smile and a tense nod of compliance. "Thanks." He walked to his Jeep and grabbed his backpack. "Where am I going to put this?"

Dan showed Steve how to pack the tent and strap the poles to his backpack. "That should do it."

"Ok, thanks," Steve said.

Dan pulled a bandana out of his backpack and tied it around his head. "I'm ready."

"Awesome!" Rob said. "Now let's get our rears in gear." He signaled his dog and Denim eagerly heeled.

The trail from the parking lot looked like a dark door to a mine. As the men reached the entrance, Denim ran ahead. Dan dawdled behind, looking around and admiring nature. The autumn leaves were at the peak of their splendor. The unseasonably warm, moist air brought out the pine scent of the fallen pinecones, the musty smell of decaying leaves, and the damp clay earth. As they walked along the path, Denim ran ahead. He would stop, then double back, attempting to herd everyone together.

Not far into their hike, Dan discovered paw prints in the mud. "Check this out...coyote prints." He took pictures with his phone. *Gianna would love to see this.*

"Let's just hope the coyote is long gone," Steve said, anxiously.

Dan laughed. "Oh, c'mon."

About a mile and a half into their hike, Denim stopped short and froze. His ears perked, and he emitted a low, threatening snarl. Dan, Steve, and Rob paused and listened. There was a rustling sound in the brush a few hundred feet to the left of them.

"Shh, easy boy," Rob whispered.

Dan reached into his pocket and pulled out his bear mace. Steve looked at him. Vivid fear flashed in his eyes.

"It's just a precaution," Dan said.

As the cracking and snapping of tree branches grew louder, five deer scrambled into view, crossing the trail, then leaping back into the woods.

Steve slapped his chest and gasped, "It's only deer."

Rob turned around and let out a raucous laugh. "Relax, bro," he said. He shook his head and cussed under his breath as he continued along the trail.

Dan put away his spray.

Steve looked over his shoulder, warily. "You'd better keep that bear spray out."

"Nervous?" Dan asked. "I thought you said you were an experienced hiker."

"No, I'm an experienced *camper* at a fully loaded RV site."

Dan raised his eyebrows. "What about Rob?"

Steve glanced at his brother, who was walking ahead with Denim. "Heck, he'd scare a bear. Four years in the military search and rescue."

"Oh, so that explains his tough-guy image and his blue streak of cursing."

"Yeah, my little bro is a bit rough around the edges, but he's a good guy to have around."

Dan nodded. "Understood."

About a quarter mile ahead, Denim stopped again and sniffed the ground. Rob looked down at his dog's find and pointed. "Bear scat." He searched the surrounding area. "All clear," he shouted.

Four miles in from their hike, they reached the campsite at Boulder Lake. "Absolutely breathtaking," Steve said, taking in the scenery in every direction.

Dan gazed at the sparkling lake and observed a flock of ducks' water-ski to a halt. In the distance, he heard a woodpecker beating its head to make a living. *This is great!* He took a deep breath and filled his lungs with fresh mountain air. It felt like he was back in Montana. *I'm really going to enjoy this outing.*

He scanned the campsite and noticed three other tents pitched on the opposite side of the lake. Boisterous voices perked up behind him, and minutes later, a group of young people emerged from another trail.

Dan turned to Steve and Rob and said, "Looks like we're not the only ones camping on Halloween."

"I'll share the space as long as they're not carrying machetes," Rob joked.

Steve gave his little brother a cold stare. "Just pick a spot before the sun goes down."

Dan grinned at the two bantering then wandered around the campsite to search for a decent sized clearing away from the creaking limbs of bare trees.

"Hey, Steve, how 'bout we set up camp here?"

Steve nodded approvingly. "Perfect."

Rob dropped his pack. "I'll go scrounge around for firewood."

"Fine," Steve said. "We'll pitch the tents."

Twenty minutes later, a couple hundred feet from the lake, Dan and Steve had the two tents assembled. Dan's two-man dome tent looked simplistic next to the monstrous four-man tent that Rob had brought.

Steve stepped back and admired their hard work. "Gee, we could've gotten away with just using Rob's tent."

Dan tossed his hand in the air. "Nah. Too close for comfort. I prefer to stay on a professional level."

Steve laughed. "Shoot, you can forget that. With my crazy brother on this trip, you can throw professionalism off the mountain."

Dan shook his head. *Oh, boy! What did I get myself into? Gianna should be glad she didn't come on this trip.*

Dan and Steve unpacked three portable chairs and set them up at the fire pit, which was a safe distance away from the tents. They sat down and waited for Rob to return.

Minutes later, Denim returned, tripping over a huge stick that he had fetched. Not far behind, Rob schlepped in carrying a bundle of firewood.

"It's about time," Steve teased. "I'm starved."

Rob dropped the wood and flipped Steve the bird. "You don't have to wait for me, bro." He let loose a string of profanity that turned the air blue. "Get off your *bleeping* lazy *bleep* and get the camping stove. You know how to *bleeping* cook. You don't need me to *bleeping* do everything!"

"Lighten up, bro, I was just kidding," Steve said, swatting at the gnats. He stood up from his chair and returned with the propane stove.

Dan laughed a single bark, taken aback by the brothers' curtness toward one another. They were like oil and water, not how he imagined the two brothers should act. He thought about Gianna's brother, Matt. He was the closest he had to a brother, and they never argued like that.

Dan pinched his bottom lip. Rob seemed madder than a cut snake. What could he do to appease him? He stood up and asked, "Rob, can I help you start a fire?"

"No, I got it. But if you want, you can get the food out. There's chicken, burgers, hot dogs, and beans." He pointed at his gunmetal backpack leaning up against the tree.

"Sure," Dan said.

"Hey Dan, you know my bro and I are just playing, right?" Rob asked.

Dan turned and gave a careless shrug. "Yeah, sure."

As he crouched to gather the food from the pack, he eyed Rob from a distance, curiously and cautiously. He certainly had a colorful vocabulary and a ruthless attitude. All at once, the back of his neck prickled. *And I suggested to Gianna to ride up with him. What was I thinking?*

"Bring the grill grate, too," Steve called out.

"Got it," Dan said.

The men shared the task of cooking. They finished eating just before dark settled in. Afterward, they sat under the night sky and listened to the subtle crackling and whistling sound of the fire, roasting marshmallows, and making s'mores.

Rob sipped his beer, belched, and then wiped his mouth with his sleeve. "Want one, Dan?"

"No, thanks. I have water."

Rob pointed up at the clear dark sky. "Hey, check out the moon."

The gentle beams of the crescent moon lit the area with a mystical silence.

"Kind of creepy," Steve said.

"Yeah, bro, you better watch out for things that go bump in the night," Rob said, gravely.

Dan chuckled at Rob. "You're a piece of work."

"He's a piece of something, but I don't know if work is the right word," Steve quipped, flinging his empty water bottle at his brother.

Dan rubbed his forehead. *Dang, these two!* He sat back in his chair and closed his eyes. He listened to the faint winds playing chase. He glanced down at Denim, who seemed content lying next to the fire, ears down and tail tucked between his legs.

The dog prompted a pleasant memory from his youth, when his parents had given him a tri-color border collie named, Angel. Every day, Angel had waited impatiently at the front door for him to return home from school. When the bus dropped him off, she'd spin in circles, barking and wagging her tail. She'd jump up on the door to open it and greet him with friendly kisses. She'd play fetch with him every day after school until sundown. The two were inseparable.

Dan smiled at the past. Warmth coursed through his body just thinking about his faithful friend. He glanced at Rob and asked, "So, how old is Denim?"

Denim's ears perked up and his eyes popped open.

"Two," Rob said. He leaned forward and stoked the fire. "My girlfriend gave him to me when I returned home from the military."

"Smart dog," Dan said. "I had one like him when I was six. Her name was Angel."

Rob settled back in his chair and crossed his arms. "I trained Denim myself," he said, proudly.

Dan nodded. "Very impressive."

"He didn't tell you?" Steve asked. "He's a professional service dog trainer." He nudged Rob's arm. "Golden Retrievers and German Shepherds, right?"

"Yeah," Rob uttered as he idly poked at the fire.

"Sounds like a rewarding job," Dan said.

"It is." Rob's voice was rich with emotion. "My heart melts when I see a dog bond with someone in need." He reached over the side of his chair to where his dog was resting. "You're my buddy, right?" he asked his dog.

Denim jumped up and gave Rob a wet kiss.

"That's my boy," he said, hugging Denim.

The excited cries from Denim stirred Dan's memory again. Angel had been his best friend. She had always been there, in the good times and bad.

He recalled how she had comforted him, especially after his parents' tragic death. She had snuggled with him every night as they slumbered in front of the warm fireplace. *I miss you, girl.* He shuddered inwardly thinking about Angel. He wasn't there for her when she passed away. He had been away at college when Joe called him with the sad news about his beloved dog.

Tears came to his eyes, distorting the memory into a hazy blur. He wiped his eyes, then rose to his feet. "I'm going to bed now."

"You ok?" Steve asked. "It's not even nine yet."

"Yeah, just beat."

"Ok, good night."

"See you in the morning," Rob said.

Dan crawled into his tent and zipped it closed. He pulled off his hiking boots and massaged his sore feet. *These darn boots still aren't broken in yet.*

He reached for his cell phone. It was fully charged, but only had one signal bar. He tried calling Gianna anyway.

She answered in a broken voice. "Hi...Dan—ny."

"Hey, baby. I can barely hear you. I miss you."

"I can't hear—"

The call was lost.

"Dang," he grumbled, hitting the redial button.

Gianna answered. "Danny, can you hear me?"

"Yeah."

"I'm spending...night...Tracy and—"

The call was dropped again. *Seriously?* Dan rubbed his tired eyes. *Maybe texting works.*

Babe, text me back if you get this.

Minutes later, his phone beeped.

Got it! I miss you, Danny.

After texting back and forth a few more times, Dan shut his phone off to preserve the battery. He slithered into his cozy, warm sleeping bag and lay flat on his back with one arm under his head. He gazed upward through his tent skylight into the star-strewn heavens. As a shooting star burned its way across the sky, a strange sensation journeyed him back to his youth when he had wished for a sibling. A bittersweet tear welled in his eyes. More than anything, he wanted a family of his own. He closed his eyes tightly and thought about Gianna. *I wish for us to have a baby.*

Drowsiness began to steal over him. Quickly, he drifted to sleep, but it wasn't long before he wrestled a wicked nightmare.

"Babe, I'm home," he called.

He opened the front door. A gloomy, dead fog greeted him like a creepy, gray cat.

"Babe? Are you there?" he called.

His lonely voice echoed through the empty house. The presence of evil swarmed him, sending a tingling shiver up his back. When he flipped on the light, a vampire holding Gianna captive jumped out and flashed his bloodshot eyes and huge fangs at him.

Gianna screamed, "Danny, help!"

Terror jumped down his throat. "Let her go, Chad!"

Ravenously, Chad bit into Gianna's neck.

"Nooo!" Dan yelled.

Dan's terrible nightmare shattered into the gaping darkness. He sat up, shaken like never before. Fear had placed its icy finger on his heart. *What a horrible nightmare!*

He lay back down, yearning to escape into an undisturbed slumber. But instead, he listened to the lonely rustle of the night wind and wondered what time it was. He rolled over and searched the cold, hard ground for his flashlight. When he found it, he discovered it was only eleven thirty.

Gradually, his heavy eyes gave in to sleep, but shortly thereafter, he awakened when a furious rumble of thunder rolled in. The wind groaned louder, and a light sprinkle pattered the tent. *Oh, man! The forecast didn't call for rain.* After the rain eased up, he dozed off.

Hours later, he stirred, shivering from the cold. He grabbed an extra flannel shirt out of his backpack and pulled it on. Again, he lay awake listening to the eerie, gloomy sound of the tree branches creaking in the wind. He was too tired to sleep.

Chilled to drowsiness, Dan finally zonked out. He slept like a dead man until a pungent, musky odor irritated his lungs. *What the—are you kidding me?* He sat up and rubbed his burning eyes. Something had spooked a skunk, and with any luck, it wasn't Denim. He ran his hands through his hair. *Ugh! And I looked forward to sleeping in the great outdoors.*

He yawned. He reached for his flashlight and checked the time. It was four twenty. He lay back down and closed his eyes. He buried his nose into his sleeping bag, trying to mask the skunk stink. With a little hope, he'd be able to snooze a bit longer before dawn.

Chapter Fifteen

Daybreak arrived. Dan woke to the lingering skunk stench and two miserable crows squawking at one another. As he rolled up his sleeping bag, pots and pans clanked outside his tent. He unzipped the door flap part way and poked his head out into the pitilessly raw air. Rob was out there preparing breakfast.

Dan stepped out of his tent. The ground crunched underneath his feet. Last night's freezing rain left a frost, and although the sun shimmered through the gray clouds, it was still chilly.

"Morning," Dan said, rubbing his hands together. "How'd you sleep?"

"Like a baby," Rob said.

"Lucky you." Dan crouched next to the campfire. "I was freezing...must've dropped into the mid-thirties last night."

"Well, I had Denim to keep me warm," Rob said.

"And your brother."

"Hell no! All he did was snore and babble in his sleep," Rob said.

"Oh, so that's what that noise was. Maybe he was the one who scared the skunk," Dan said, laughing. He looked around the camp. "Where's Steve now?"

Rob grabbed a frying pan. "He went 10-100."

Dan nodded. "I need to take a walk myself." As he stepped away from the campfire, something clicked in his mind. He stopped midstride and turned around. "You know, it finally dawned on me why my wife didn't want to go camping."

"Can you blame her?" Rob asked. He lit the propane stove then scrambled a half dozen eggs. "I mean, seriously. Think about it. She's in a toasty, warm home. Why the *bleep* would she want to spend a night sitting around a campfire with three guys telling stupid jokes, eating beans, and gassing it up? Get with it, man."

Dan shook his head and laughed. "Yeah, I suppose you're right." He took a couple of steps forward and mumbled, "But I miss her."

After breakfast, Dan, Steve, and Rob plotted their hike to Blue Sky Mountain.

Dan studied the map. "Pinecone Trail is relatively smooth ground all the way up."

"I like the sound of that," Steve said.

"Ok." Rob cleared his throat. "But what if we kick it up a notch and venture onto this path?" He pointed to a red-marked trail and followed it with his finger. "It's shorter."

Dan gave him a sideways glance. "That's Demon's Trail. It's an intense climb, almost a thousand feet a mile."

"Are you nuts, bro?" Steve asked.

"I like a challenge," Rob said, rolling up his sleeves. "C'mon. It's only a small section of the trail."

"Fine." Steve agreed, but his voice held a hint of regret.

Rob gave him a high five. "Awesome, bro!"

Dan rolled his eyes. "Ok. Let's go then."

The men packed up camp at Boulder Lake and followed Pinecone Trail northeast through a mixed forest of hemlocks and deciduous trees. The rising sun burned away the chilly morning and softened the mud beneath their feet. Along the way, they passed a cave, crossed a shallow stream, and later trudged through a muddy hollow. The hike seemed effortless until they reached a fork in the road. A wooden signpost gave them their trail options.

"Demon's Trail." Rob pointed left. "This way."

Dan took a deep breath. He rolled his eyes at Steve then followed Rob and Denim through the heavily tree-rooted terrain. Not long into the hike, the trail turned into a steep, strenuous climb up a narrow, rocky hillside. Ninety minutes later, they reached the peak and decided it was a suitable time to break for lunch.

"Well, that was invigorating," Dan said, sipping his water. His throat felt as coarse as sandpaper.

Sweat broke out on Steve's forehead like dew. "I've spent too many days behind a desk," he huffed.

"You're just old, big bro," Rob snickered.

Steve fired daggers at Rob as though he was going to deck him. "Watch your tongue, boy. Even at forty-two, I can take you."

Rob curled his upper lip and uttered, "Yeah, ok." He reached into his backpack for a dog bowl and filled it with water. Denim leaped forward and drank it bone dry.

Dan set down his backpack and stretched. He inhaled the crisp scents of the mountain air. The cool, sharp wind felt refreshing against his sweaty face. *Man, it's hot!* He removed his flannel shirt, leaving on the t-shirt he wore underneath, then parked himself on a rock and unzipped his pants legs, converting them into shorts. *Ah, much better.* He adjusted the bandana on his head. The back of his neck burned from the heat of the sun beating down on him. The temperature must've climbed into the mid-seventies. Nonetheless, it turned out to be a perfect day to hike.

He reached inside his pack and grabbed his binoculars for a clearer, more vivid look at God's exquisite art. *Wow! What a view.* The surrounding mountains stretched out into the endless blue sky. The vibrant red, orange, and yellow treetops swept from the mountaintop down to the glistening lake below. *Gianna would love this.* He took out his cell phone and snapped a couple pictures then texted her.

Babe check out the view—3,000 feet up.

"Lunchtime," Rob bellowed. He unzipped the top storage area of his pack and pulled out three sub sandwiches, handing one each to Dan and Steve. "Eat up! Last decent meal until we hit civilization." He reached inside his pack again. "Want a beer?"

Dan shook his head. "No, thanks. I have water."

Rob handed a bottle to Steve, but he waved him off. "No, bro. I'm already dehydrated, plus I value my coordination."

"Get real. It's celebration time! We mastered Demon's Trail," Rob said, proudly. "It's all downhill from here."

Steve cocked his head sideways. "We only sampled that trail, and that was enough, thank you." He glanced at his watch. "It's noon. We must get back to the trailhead by four thirty."

"Right. I told Gianna I'd be home no later than seven," Dan said. He pulled the map out of his shirt pocket and studied it. "River Rock Trail is a two-mile trek along a flat ridge leading to a bridge that crosses Celestial Falls. From there, it's only three miles back to the trailhead."

"Correct," Rob said, peering over Dan's shoulder.

"Flat ridge…I like the sound of that," Steve said, with a mouth full of food.

"Well, it's not all flat. It's a long, gradual descent," Dan responded. "We'll rest at the waterfall."

After their brief lunch break, the men headed west on River Rock Trail. Dan lagged a short distance, appreciating the sights and sounds of nature. Just before he entered the shady, tree-lined path, he caught a glimpse of a timber rattlesnake sunbathing on a flat rock. He quickly snapped a picture, planning to share it with Steve *after* they were well on their way home.

As he followed the green trail markers down the leaf covered, rutted dirt path, a soft breeze blew through the half-naked trees, cooling his backside. The twitter of birds and the shrill buzz of insects filled the afternoon air. He listened contentedly to nature's music, but the sudden rustle of leaves and twitching branches caught his attention. He stopped and looked, finding a squirrel busy stashing his earnings for the winter.

Just up ahead, Steve stopped and pointed his trembling finger at a wooden sign: WARNING! High Bear Encounter. He turned to Dan and whispered, "Do you have your mace ready?"

"Chill, bud," Dan said, loudly. "You want the bears to know you're coming. Besides, tailwind is in our favor." He put his hand on Steve's shoulder, peered ahead at Rob and Denim, and said jokingly, "Let them be our bear bait."

Steve's mouth quirked with a smile. "Funny."

"Seriously though, you have a higher chance of getting struck by lightning than being attacked by a bear."

"I suppose you're right," Steve said, adjusting his backpack. "Come on. Let's catch up."

About one and a half miles into the hike, the air grew thick with moisture. Last night's rain made the rich, dark soil mushy underfoot. With each step, Dan's boots sank into the mud. It was like walking through a rainforest. His t-shirt was plastered to his torso by sweat, reminding him of his thirst to shower. As he grew closer to a clearing in the trees, the tranquil gushing sound of water vibrated the air. An instant calming sensation flowed through his body.

When he turned the bend, he saw Rob and Denim waiting at the entrance to Reflection's Bridge.

"We made it," Dan said.

"Piece of cake," Rob replied.

"Ah, finally," Steve puffed. He took an unsteady step forward, and then slid his backpack off his slumping posture.

"You alright?" Dan asked.

"Yeah," Steve exhaled. "It's nice to stop and smell the roses once in a while."

Dan patted Steve's shoulder. "You did good."

"What time you got, bro?" Rob asked.

"One thirty," Steve answered.

"Cool. We'll take a breather on the other side," Rob said. He stepped up on the first plank of the footbridge leading to Celestial Falls. "C'mon. Let's check out this double-tiered waterfall."

"Hey, uh, be careful," Dan said, pointing to the metal sign: CAUTION! Bridge may be slippery.

"No sweat," Rob said.

Rob, Denim, and Steve proceeded with care. Dan adjusted his backpack, then followed suit, ambling across the wet, slick bridge. He stopped midway and looked up at the exquisite one-hundred-eighty-foot upper waterfall.

He closed his eyes, took a deep cleansing breath, and tilted his head back. The cool, misty spray, pure and clear, touched his face like angel's tears. *This is heaven. Thank you, Lord, for this glorious day.*

He submerged himself in a profound reverie of tranquility. The constant rush of white water spilling off the mountain, towering above the rocks below, rejuvenated his tired body.

"Hey, Dan! What the *bleep* are you doing?" Rob's obscene voice bellowed from across the bridge.

Dan quivered. His sense of euphoria plummeted.

"Yo, dude, c'mon," Rob shouted.

Attentive to reality, Dan shouted, "I'll be there in a minute." He gazed down at the mystic pool below. The sun's rays captured the eighty-foot lower falls, creating a vivid, full-circle rainbow. *Oh, wow!* He whipped out his phone and took a picture.

Afterward, he strolled to the other side of the bridge to a fenced-in concrete cul-de-sac. There was a park bench where Rob and Steve were sitting, and Denim was chewing on a dog toy.

Dan sat down. An inexplicable feeling of peace and satisfaction enveloped him. "That was exhilarating."

"Dude, you're drenched," Rob said, scooting over to the edge of the bench. He stared; his mouth partly opened in a kind of loose grin.

"Oh, but it was worth it," Dan said, peeling off his t-shirt. He wrung it out, leaving a puddle on the ground. "I could've used a soap bar, though."

Steve stared at him. "Aren't you cold?"

"No. Not yet," Dan said, untying his bandana.

Steve raised an eyebrow. "Ok then." He stood up and wandered toward the bridge railing, bypassing a half-dozen safety warning signs. "Gorgeous views," he hollered back.

"Yep, but just be careful," Dan shouted. He reached inside his backpack and removed a plastic bag storing his clean clothes.

"Hey, I hope you didn't soak the map," Rob said.

"Nope, it's right here," Dan said, patting the dry Velcro pouch where the map was safely stored.

After Dan changed into a dry set of clothes, he refilled his canteen with fresh water from a natural spring. He glanced up and observed Rob playing tug-a-war with Denim.

Rob leaned forward and kissed his dog. He looked up at Dan and grinned, his face beet red. "I know. You think I'm *bleeping* crazy, right?"

Dan smiled. "No."

Rob sat down on the bench. He glanced up at the falls and sighed. "Perfect!"

"Yeah, it is."

"But, Dan, you don't understand," Rob said. "Four months ago, I was supposed to propose to my girlfriend here."

"So, what happened? You two broke up?"

Rob took a deep breath. "I had it all planned out. I bought the ring, wrote a song, and practiced it on my guitar." He dropped his head and clasped his hands together tightly. "The day before, Masie and I were at the park playing Frisbee with Denim. I flung it too hard, and it landed across the parking lot underneath a white van. Denim chased after it but stopped at the sidewalk.

"Masie offered to get the Frisbee for him. After she retrieved it, she stepped away from the van. At the same time, a texting lunatic in a car from hell hopped a curb. Denim barked, but Masie didn't react in time. The car hit her. It's a miracle she's alive."

A sudden chill hit Dan's core. "How bad?"

Rob swallowed hard. "Masie suffered a concussion, some broken bones, and lost her lower left leg."

"I'm so sorry, man," Dan said.

"She's a fighter, though. She's making real progress."

"That's great news."

"Yep," Rob said. "Masie insisted I go on this trip. She told me not to worry about her and to have fun." He nodded. "One day I'm going to get her here, and I'm going to ask her to marry me."

"Well, don't wait. Life's too short," Dan said. "There are many other romantic places at which you can propose."

Chapter Sixteen

The men left Celestial Falls and followed the green-marked trail about an eighth of a mile before reaching a three-way intersection. There was a color-coded sign labeling the trail options. Underneath it was a warning: Heavy brush, slippery conditions, and steep drop-offs beyond this point. Proceed with caution.

"Now which way?" Rob asked, pointing to the wooden trail sign. "Green, blue, or yellow?"

"Stay on the green path," Steve said.

"I don't think so," Dan said. "That looks like a bushwhack trail."

"I got a compass," Rob said, reaching into his pack.

Dan exhaled. "I know you're adventurous, but do you really feel up to getting scraped and jabbed by thorn bushes? Besides, it'd be too rough on Denim."

"Dude, you're right," Rob agreed.

Dan opened his map and studied it. He confirmed that the green trail required bushwhacking. The blue trail went north, up the mountain, ten miles away from their parking lot. The yellow trail went south, down the mountain, then ran east for three miles, leading back to the trailhead.

"Ok." Dan pointed to their current location on the map. "Here we are, and here's the trailhead. Look for a yellow marker."

Rob quickly scanned the area. "There isn't one." He looked down and shuffled the leaves with his boots.

Steve tossed him a worried look. "Maybe we should just head back the way we came."

"We'd never make it back by dark," Dan said. He looked at the wooden sign again. The arrow for the yellow trail pointed left. "So that means it must lead somewhere down...there." He pointed at the cliff.

"Yeah right, Sherlock," Rob said. "But where? All I see is wet rocks, brush, and trees."

Dan caught a glimpse of Denim circling and sniffing the ground. "What's he doing?" he asked.

Rob turned and questioned his dog. "Whatcha got, boy?" Denim pawed at the ivy-choked oak tree until he uncovered a yellow trail marker. He picked it up with his mouth and carried it back to Rob, dropping it at his feet. Rob's eyes lit up. "Ha! It must've fallen off the tree."

Dan grinned. "Good job, Denim." He knelt and praised him.

"What a brilliant dog," Steve said.

Rob clapped his hands. "Cool! Let's go."

"Whoa there," Dan said, pointing. "That's the trail?"

They stood at the top of the escarpment overlooking a giant, curved staircase of tiered rocks, layered with moss, tree roots, and vines. A pebbled brook chattered alongside the trail, dropping off midway into a mini waterslide.

"Yep, that's it," Rob said, pointing downward. "See? There's another yellow marker."

"Yeah, I do, and I also see the ledge," Dan said.

Steve sighed. "Let's just take it slow."

Denim wagged his tail. He lowered himself to a crouch and lifted his front paw. Gingerly, he took a step, and then another. From there, he leaped halfway down the trail.

"Dude, look at him go," Rob said, excitedly. "Stay, boy," he hollered.

Denim obeyed on command. Rob ventured down the steep rock steps and waited alongside his dog.

"Ok. Who's next?" Rob yelled.

Dan gestured to Steve. "After you."

"Thanks," Steve said, reluctantly. He stepped down vigilantly, grasping tree branches along the way.

Dan teetered between wanting to go and not wanting to go. Although he wasn't afraid of heights, a flicker of apprehension coursed through him. He waited for Steve to reach the ledge where Rob and Denim were waiting. He took a deep breath and tried to relax. *I can do this.*

"Your turn, Dan," Rob called up.

Dan swallowed hard. "I'm coming."

"It's not as bad as Demon's Trail," Steve shouted. "Just stay to the inside, along the trees."

"Ok," Dan shouted. Uncertainty made his voice shaky.

He clutched a tree branch and warily stepped down onto the first rock. *Not too bad.* He slowly took a few more steps, careful not to slip on the algae coated rocks. He gazed down at Steve and Rob, then back up at the mountain. A warning voice whispered in his head, *Watch the vines.* Ivy tendrils intertwined with tree roots and zigzagged across the path like a trip wire. With each step, he became increasingly uneasy.

Rob yelled, "You got it!"

"Uh-huh," Dan said. His muscles tightened in readiness. *Only another twenty feet, and I'll be at the ledge.*

The next step was a little steeper. As Dan lowered himself, the sole of his boot slipped off the wet, rounded rock face. *Oh, fudge!* A spasm of fright tore through him as he fell backward, landing on his rigid backpack and the brutal, rocky terrain. "Ah, ow," he groaned.

"Dan!" Rob and Steve yelled.

Dan skated down the trail, his backpack acting like a sled. He dug his boots into the ground, trying to grab anything that would give him a hand. But at the speed he was sliding, it was impossible to navigate the curve in the trail. Off the ledge he went.

For the split second he was airborne, he was running on high-octane terror. A paralyzing moment of insight hit him. *This is it. I'm going to die.*

As his body dropped, it collided with trees and brush. His right ankle became wedged between two branches, jerking his body sideways. An awful snapping sound drove through him like a knife. He hit the ground like a flattened bug against a windshield.

He lay there on his left side, motionless and numb, with his face resting on the cool, damp earth. He felt the sun's warm rays on his back, and he heard the white noise of the waterfall close by.

Slowly, he opened his eyes. *I'm ok. I'm alive!* He coughed. There was violent throbbing in his chest and his head pounded. His mind screamed out in pain. *God, help me!*

"Dan, Dan!" Familiar muted voices echoed in the distance. "Dude, talk to me. We're coming, friend."

Dan tried to comprehend what he was hearing. He struggled to answer. "I'm here." He felt cries of frustration at the back of his throat. *They can't hear me. They're never going to find me.*

Every breath he took, and every beat of his pulse rocked his whole being. He lifted his head off the ground, and his face seared with pain. He reached up and touched his forehead. It was soaking wet with blood. *Oh, this is bad.* His right arm stung, and blood oozed everywhere. He looked at his forearm. It had a deep laceration that needed stitches.

I must get up. He tried to push himself up with his arms, but a monstrous bolt of pain jabbed his side. *Ah, my ribs.* He dropped back down in the soft mud.

He gasped as sharp, excruciating pain plunged deeply through his lower extremities. He tilted his head to his chin to scope out the damage. Blood-covered leaves surrounded his deformed right leg, and he could see his tibia sticking out of his skin above his ankle. *Dear God, this is serious.* He relaxed his head and closed his eyes. *Oh, God have mercy on me. I'm never going to get out of here alive.*

"Dan, answer me," Rob hollered. "We're coming for you, dude."

Dan moaned through the endless waves of pain. He opened his eyes when a cold, wet nose touched his burning cheek. He turned his head. Denim sat by his side whimpering and pawing at his shoulder.

"Dan don't move. Stay still!" Rob shouted. "Steve, I found him! He's in a clearing next to the falls." Rob called to his dog, "Easy, Denim." Denim cocked his head, obedient to his master. "Good boy." Rob carefully hopped through the thicket and knelt beside Dan. "Hang on. We're going to get you out of here."

Dan bit his lower lip, trying to stifle a moan.

Rob shouted to Steve. "Hurry up, bro."

"I'm here. I'm here," Steve said, his voice trembling. "Grab the tent poles so I can splint his leg."

While Rob unpacked the tent pieces, Steve dug through his backpack for his medical kit to check Dan's vitals.

"Blood pressure's slightly elevated," Steve said. "Look, little bro. I got this. Please, go for help."

Rob reached into his pocket and whipped out his cell phone. "No freaking service. Ok, I'm gone."

"Wait, don't go," Dan uttered. "Splint my leg and help me up."

"Dude, you're not going anywhere without a chopper," Rob said, his voice firm and final.

Steve touched Dan's shoulder. "Try to relax."

"Get my phone. Call Gianna. Tell her...I...messed up, and I'm...sorry," he mumbled.

"Shh, ok," Steve answered calmly.

Rob bolted toward the creek, where he found Dan's backpack. He searched the pocket and pulled out the phone. "I need the code," he shouted.

Dan stammered. "Uh, zero, seven...twenty-six."

Steve shouted at Rob. "Just go, little bro."

"I am," Rob yelled. "Denim, come!"

Denim sat beside Dan and whimpered. He lay down and rested his head on his side.

"Denim, come!" Rob called again.

Denim stood up and waited; his tail signaled indecision.

"Let's go, boy!" Rob shouted, his voice tense.

Denim leaped forward and took off with Rob.

Dan rested, half-swooning, while Steve tended his wounds, rinsing them gently with water.

"Dang!" Gut-wrenching pain burned through him like a blowtorch. "Ow! Are you trying to finish me off?"

"I'm sorry, but you know the drill," Steve said.

"Yeah, well, I prefer being the doctor."

"I hate to break this to you, but I didn't exactly expect our medical conference on *Emergencies in Primary Care* to end in a test, either."

"Hey, well, I'm praying this isn't my final exam," Dan quipped. He clamped his jaw, trying to block the pain.

"Hang on to your sense of humor, and you'll pull through this just fine," Steve said.

Hours passed. Dark storm clouds drifted in like some evil miasma from hell. Dan lay still in the bitter wind. The smell of electricity was in the air. "This isn't good," Dan said in a choked voice. Thunder sent involuntary shivers down his spine. "What time is it?"

"Almost five," Steve said. He turned and stoked the fire. "Are you warm enough?" He tucked in Dan's sleeping bag. "Can I get you anything?"

"I'm thirsty," Dan uttered. The metallic taste of blood lay stagnant in his mouth.

"You know if I could, I'd give you water."

"Uh-huh. That's the downside to being a doctor; I know too much." With a small catch of breath, he asked, "Can you find my Bible?"

"What? Oh, sure," Steve said. He searched through Dan's backpack and pulled out his Bible and a flashlight. "Anything in particular you want me to read?"

"Ezekiel 1:28, please," Dan said.

Steve turned the pages and started reading. "'Like the bow which appears in the clouds on a rainy day was the splendor that surrounded him. Such was the vision of likeness of the glory of the Lord.'"

"Thank you," Dan whispered. He swallowed hard, then uttered, "Earlier, on the bridge, I saw a full-circle rainbow. I had never seen one before. It was surreal." He coughed, and then took a sudden, sharp intake of breath.

"Dan, you ok?"

"Yeah, just cold." His body shivered, his head pounded, and his vision began to swim. "It's getting dark," he uttered, then closed his eyes.

"Dan, stay with me," Steve yelled.

Dan flicked open his eyes when he felt the squeeze from the blood pressure cuff. Suddenly, he heard voices and dogs barking in the distance, and the crunching of fallen leaves underfoot. "Can we go home now?"

"Very soon, my friend," Steve said.

Dan gave a pained sigh. "But I promised Gianna I'd take her to New Jersey tomorrow."

"Ok. Hang onto that thought," Steve said, patting his hand. "Help just arrived." He stood up and shouted, "Over here!"

"How's he doing?" a male paramedic asked.

"He's stable, and I've got his injuries immobilized. But he's lost a lot of blood, and I'm concerned with his distended abdomen."

Dan felt a gentle hand on his shoulder. He opened his eyes and saw a redhead looking over him. Her pretty face came in and out of focus.

"Hi, I'm Paige and this is Este. What's your name?"

"Doctor Dan Christiansen," he muttered.

"Ah, you're a doctor. So, you know I must ask you a million questions. How are you feeling?"

"Like the day after the night before," Dan uttered.

Paige laughed. "Have you had any alcohol?"

"No, and no meds, no allergies, and no food since noon," Dan answered forthrightly.

Paige glanced at Steve. "Wow, he's on the ball."

"Yeah, his sense of humor has been a big help, too."

"Dan, do you know where you are, and what happened this afternoon?" Paige asked.

"I'm at the rodeo, and I was gored by a bull."

Este smiled and glanced at Steve. "Are you sure you haven't given him any pain meds?" He patted Dan's shoulder. "Seriously, Dan, do you remember going hiking and falling off a cliff?"

Dan gazed at the paramedics. "Uh-huh."

"Dan, we're now going to place a cervical collar around your neck. Then we're going to transfer you to a backboard," Paige said. "So, relax, luv."

Dan swallowed hard and squeezed his eyes shut.

"On the count of three," Este said.

Steve counted, "One...two...three."

"Ow," Dan shouted. Excruciating pain exploded all over his body; his eyes burned with tears.

"We're sorry, luv. We're going to get you out of here," Paige said. Her voice was low, but full of intensity.

"Let's get a line in him," Este said.

"I'm on it," Paige replied. "Hold still, luv."

Suddenly, Dan breathed more rapidly. He felt his consciousness zoning out. Voices around him faded in and out. He uttered, "Gianna—"

"Dan, are you ok?" Paige asked. She examined his pupils. "His eyes have a slightly unfocused stare. Check his vitals!"

"BP, 90/50; heartrate, 170; temp, 96.6," Este said.

"He's having difficulty breathing," Paige shouted.

"He's in hypovolemic shock!" Steve shouted. "Raise his feet. Dan, talk to me."

"We need to intubate," Este said.

Dan mumbled disjointedly and then passed out. He entered a dream-like state, and scenes of his life flashed before him. The colors were so vivid, so real. He felt such an intense love that he didn't want to leave.

A recognizable, disembodied female voice spoke to him. "Daniel, my dear son. Your father and I love you and are proud of your accomplishments, but you must turn back."

The inner child came out of him. "Mom, I'm tired and broken, and there's no pain here."

"You have so much more life left in you."

"But I miss you and Dad. I need you guys. We can be a family again."

"No, son, you have a new family now. Recall Genesis 2:24– 'That is why a man leaves his father and mother and clings to his wife, and two of them become one body.' You and Gianna have created a life together."

A strong, bright light appeared, and a strident and righteous voice spoke. "Daniel, it is not your time; I have plans for you still."

Dan felt himself disturbingly pulled back into semi consciousness. He heard helicopter blades overhead. People were talking to him and calling his name.

"Dan, can you hear me?" Este asked.

"Dan, squeeze my hand," Paige said.

He moaned. The screaming pain would not subside. He forced his eyes open; everything around him was blurry.

"We've got a pulse," Paige said.

"He's stabilizing!" Este added.

"Oh, thank God," Steve exhaled.

"Ok, help me secure him," Este shouted over the noise of the helicopter. "C'mon, let's go! Storm's coming."

Paige radioed to the chopper team. "Patient stabilized. Prepare to winch." She turned and leaned into Dan. "Ok, luv. You're going to take a little ride. In just a minute, Tom will be descending on a winch line. He'll take care of you."

As the helicopter hovered overhead, Dan dwelled on what Paige said. An awful, disquieting feeling hit him. He was going to be airborne again. The thought struck him like a Mac truck. A superior voice spoke to his heart again. *Son, be not afraid. I will protect you and make you new again.*

A rescue man dressed in a fluorescent yellow jumpsuit greeted him. "Hi Dan, I'm Tom." He wrapped him in a rescue bag and secured him to the hoist. "Relax and enjoy the ride." Tom attached himself to the harness and signaled his partner.

Dan felt his senses spin and soar as the helicopter lifted him up. *I've been saved. Thank you, Lord.*

Chapter Seventeen

Gianna lifted the lid on the Crock-Pot and spooned out a sample. The tender stew meat melted in her mouth. "Mmm, delicious." She turned away from the counter and called out to Tracy, who was in the living room taping boxes shut. "Want a taste?"

"No, thanks. I'll wait till we all sit down."

Gianna glanced at the microwave clock. It was five thirty. "You sure? Danny won't be home until seven."

"Yeah, I can wait."

Gianna tapped her fingers on the counter. "Hmm, I haven't had any texts from him since lunchtime." She placed her finger on her lips. *What did I do with my phone?* It wasn't on the charger. "Tracy, is my phone in there?"

"I'll check," she said. She searched the living room. "It's not on the coffee table, end tables, or any of the stacked boxes. I hope I didn't accidentally pack it."

"Maybe I left it in the bedroom," Gianna said as she wandered down the hallway. Her steps slowed as she pondered. *Wait, it wouldn't be in there. I slept at Tracy's last night.* She leaned against the bedroom doorway, closed her eyes, and backtracked her day. *Where the heck is it?* Just then, the washing machine played a tune, indicating the cycle had finished.

Oh no, I didn't. She quickly turned down the hallway to the laundry closet. She opened the washer and pulled out the wet clothes. When she grabbed her pajama pants, there was something clunky inside the pocket. She reached inside and pulled out her waterlogged cell phone. "Oh, horse manure!" she shouted.

"Did you find it?" Tracy asked.

"Yep. I washed it."

Gianna carried her phone to the kitchen, took it apart, and placed it in a bag of rice. "No wonder I haven't heard from him all day." She sat down at the counter and cradled her head in her hands. "How can I be so stupid?"

"It happens. I dunked mine in the toilet once."

"Danny's going to be furious with me."

"Nah, your husband has the patience of a saint."

Unexpectedly, the doorbell rang. Gianna glanced at the clock. It was five fifty. It was too early for Troy to be home. She shrugged her shoulders then hopped off the stool to answer the door. "Troy, hi! You're early."

His expression was grave and his dark eyes solemn.

"What's wrong? Why the sour face?" she asked.

Tracy waddled into the living room. "Honey, why're you still in uniform?"

"I'm on overtime," he said, then looked at Gianna and asked, "Where's your phone?"

"Oh, that." Gianna brought her hand to mouth admitting her mistake. "I, uh, inadvertently ran it through the washing machine." She motioned Troy inside. "Have a seat. Danny will be home soon."

Troy put one arm around Tracy and his other around Gianna and guided them to the sofa.

"What's going on?" Gianna asked, sitting down in the recliner. She clasped her hands tightly in her lap.

Troy's mouth dipped into a deeper frown. He cleared his throat and said, "Gianna, Dan had an accident."

A fluttery feeling tingled in her body. She blinked and then focused her gaze. "What? When...how bad?"

"This afternoon," Troy said, shaking his head. "A rescue team had to fly him to a trauma center. He's in critical condition."

Gianna's core went stone cold. A dizzying, spinning queasiness seized her. "Excuse me." She covered her mouth and rushed down the hallway to the bathroom.

For the next few minutes, she gripped the toilet bowl like a drunken sailor. She retched painfully and spasmodically. After her stomach settled, she sat on the cold tile floor and cried. *Oh, God, why?*

There was a soft knock at the door. "Gianna, sweetie, may I come in?" Tracy asked.

"Just a minute," Gianna sniffled. She brushed her teeth and washed her face. After blotting her face with the hand towel, she glanced into the mirror. She watched the tears rise in her eyes. *Please, God, tell me he's going to be ok.* She took a deep breath, and slowly opened the door. "I'm sorry," she said, wiping her eyes.

Tracy hugged her. "We're here for you."

"But it's one bad thing after another," Gianna said, wiping her tears. "How does Troy know this?"

"Come," Tracy said, taking her hand. "Let's sit down in the living room. Troy will tell us what he knows."

Gianna nodded and followed her back to the couch where Troy was waiting.

Troy cleared his throat. "I was finishing my shift when Vickie, our dispatcher, received a call from Greene County police stating that there was an accident, and they needed to find the next of kin. Vickie recognized Dan's address as my neighbor and asked if I wanted to take the case."

"Was it a car accident?" Tracy asked.

"I don't know," Troy said.

"Where is Dr. Ross and his brother?" Gianna asked.

"I don't know, Gianna. Vickie did say that someone named Rob was trying to reach you, but your phone went right to voice mail," he said.

"Rob," Gianna mumbled. The name rang a bell. "That's Dr. Ross's brother." She stood up and wandered around the living room aimlessly, her tears close to resurfacing. "Ok," she uttered, rushing into the kitchen.

She shuffled through Danny's itinerary. "I don't have Dr. Ross or Rob's number." She glanced at the wooden rack on the wall and grabbed Danny's truck keys. "Whatever! It doesn't matter. I'm so out of here."

"You're not driving, girlfriend," Tracy said, taking away the keys. "Go pack an overnight bag."

Gianna halted, trying to comprehend what Tracy was suggesting. She quickly realized she was in no condition to drive. "Ok," she said and hurried down the hallway to her bedroom. As she packed, she paused to catch her breath. Her fears were stronger than ever. Tears streamed down her cheeks. *What exactly happened? What does critical mean? Will he survive?* Twitching spasms of panic rose. *Hold it together, girl.*

Gianna carried her duffel bag to the kitchen, where Tracy was cleaning up what was supposed to have been a special supper.

"I put your stew in the fridge and washed out the Crock-Pot," Tracy said.

"Thanks," Gianna uttered. "I...think I'm ready."

"Ok, sweetie," Tracy said. She looked at Troy and asked, "Ready to go?"

"Yes." He pulled a folded-up piece of paper out of his uniform pocket. "The trauma center is nearly two hours from here."

Gianna peered up at the kitchen clock. It was almost six thirty. She squeezed her eyes in agony. *I won't get there until after eight.* "Ok. Please, let's go."

Troy escorted Tracy and Gianna out to his unmarked patrol car. As Gianna settled into the back seat for the long, tense ride, Troy and Tracy discussed the shortest route. Gianna only half listened as she struggled with her own private thoughts. *Danny, wait for me. I'm coming to you.*

"Maybe I should call the hospital," she said.

"No, you should call your family first," Tracy said, passing her cell phone over the back of the seat.

"I guess," Gianna said, taking the phone. She suddenly realized she didn't have Dr. Kendall's number. She ran her fingers through her hair. "Ugh! I am so lost without my own phone." Emotional chaos chipped away at her sanity. "I'll call my mother."

The phone rang only half a ring before her mother answered. Gianna jumped right in. "Mom, it's me on Tracy's phone."

"Oh, honey, thank God. Where've you been?"

"Home. I drowned my phone." The beginning of tears stung her eyes. "Listen, Troy just told me Danny—"

"Yes, someone named Rob called Dr. and Mrs. Kendall. Dad's driving them to the airport now. But I've been worried sick about you. No one knew where you were."

"I'm ok. But do you know what happened?"

"Um, he fell," Mom said, calmly.

"I don't have Dr. and Mrs. Kendall's number. Please text it to this phone so I can call them."

"Ok, honey," Mom said.

"Listen, Troy's driving me to the hospital now. I'll call you when I know something. Love you."

Gianna ended the call. She looked up at Troy and Tracy. "Mom said it was a hiking accident. Maybe it isn't that bad."

"We're praying, sweetie," Tracy said.

Tracy's phone beeped with the text from Mom.

"Oh, good! Dr. Kendall's number," Gianna said.

Quickly, she called the number, but it rang once and disconnected. "They must be in flight. I'm calling the hospital."

The call immediately connected to an automated operator. After several frustrating minutes of pushing buttons, she was transferred to the trauma unit. The receptionist answered and placed her on hold.

Gianna sighed. "This is ridiculous."

"I know, sweetie. Hang in there," Tracy said.

After ten minutes in limbo, the receptionist returned. "I'm sorry to keep you holding. How may I help you?"

"I'm calling to check on my husband's condition. His name is Daniel Christiansen."

"Hold just a moment."

"Ok," Gianna sighed.

"Miss? Dr. Murphy is in surgery now."

"Ok. Is there a nurse I can speak to?"

"No, I'm sorry. Can you call back in an hour?"

Gianna sighed. "No. My husband was with two friends—Steve Ross and Rob Ross. Can you tell me if they're there?"

"Sorry. I don't have that information."

"I mean, are they in the waiting room?"

"I wouldn't know. I can have a nurse call you when one is available," the receptionist said.

"Forget it. I'll be there as soon as I can." Gianna ended the call and muttered, "This can't be happening."

"Honey, we're almost there," Troy said, exiting the highway. "The GPS shows fifteen minutes."

"Ok," Gianna said, rubbing her forehead. Her nerves trembled. The two-hour drive to the trauma center seemed like an eternity. She gazed out the window at the soundless lightning flickering against the dark sky. *I hate this weather. All I need now is a downpour.*

Only minutes later, heavy rain mixed with hail pounded the car's roof. Gianna sighed. *Unreal.* She rested her head against the seat and closed her eyes. Her mind drifted back to Tuesday afternoon, when she had discussed the medical conference with Danny.

"Danny, this trip would be a perfect guys' weekend. You'll have more fun without me."

"I doubt it," he had told her.

Gianna gulped hard. Hot tears rolled down her cheeks. *I should've gone with him. My job wasn't that important.*

Chapter Eighteen

Mountain View University Trauma Center's horizontal glass structure sparkled in the night sky like a boundless sea of twinkling lights. Evergreens lined the bluestone-tiled driveway that led to the main entrance.

Gianna gasped. *Wow! I hope the intricacies of the building's exterior represent the high level of care that Danny's receiving.*

Troy pulled underneath the carport where valet service awaited them. He rolled down the window and said to the attendant, "I'll park it myself." He peered up at the rearview mirror and said, "Gianna, we'll meet you inside."

"Ok," she said, opening the car door.

Like a woman on a mission, she rushed through the automated sliding glass doors straight to the front desk.

"Excuse me," Gianna said. "I was told that my husband had an accident and he's here."

A harried woman peered up from her computer. Her lips tightened in irritation. "Patient's name?"

"Daniel Christiansen."

"Ok, have a seat in the waiting room. Someone will speak with you in a moment."

"Please, how is he? I tried calling—"

"I'm sorry, miss, but you'll need to speak with his doctor." She pointed with her pen. "Please, take a seat."

Gianna blinked at the icy authority in the clerk's tone. "I understand. Thank you," she said. But she didn't, not in the least. This was an emergency, and no one was telling her anything. She turned away from the counter and bumped into a rugged man with a devilish, handsome face. "Pardon me, sir," she said.

"Hey, are you Mrs. Christiansen?" the man asked.

Gianna flinched at the tone of his voice. The man looked vaguely familiar to her, but she couldn't recall where she may have seen him before. Quickly, she glanced over her shoulder for Troy and Tracy, and then answered him distrustfully. "And you are?"

"I'm Rob Ross. I've been trying to call you."

Gianna stared at him with her mouth hanging open. He looked just like Dr. Ross, only younger, with long slicked-back hair.

"Oh! You're Dr. Ross's brother. I...my phone..." Her voice broke with emotion. "How's Danny?"

"Not sure. I just got here myself."

"Where's Doctor Ross?"

Rob scanned the room. "Uh, Steve is...somewhere." He touched her elbow lightly and urged her along. "C'mon. Let's wait in here," he said, leading her into the moderately noisy waiting room.

Clusters of people were gathered everywhere. Some looked critically ill, and others were cocked over sideways, sleeping. Pungent perfumes and sweaty body odor clogged the air, causing Gianna's stomach to feel even more queasy.

After finding a vacant row of seats near the vending machines, Gianna sat down. "So, what happened?"

Before Rob could answer, Steve entered through the heavy doors from the trauma unit. Gianna rose from her chair as if propelled by an explosive force.

"Dr. Ross!" she called.

Steve's eyes met hers in a direct and concerned way. "Oh, Gianna! Thank God, Rob found you."

"Where is he? How is he? No one is telling me anything," she said in a tremulous voice.

Steve braced her arms and looked at her intently. He spoke with a calm certainty that stopped her cold. "Your husband's in excellent hands. Come with me. We'll talk upstairs in the OR waiting room."

Gianna nodded. *Thank God. Now maybe I'll get some answers.* She turned and saw Troy and Tracy rushing in. "Oh, you're here. This is Dr. Ross and his brother, Rob," she said, introducing them. "Danny's in surgery."

Unlike the noisy, stuffy ER, the OR waiting room was quiet and smelled fresh, with a mild scent of cleaning detergents. Soothing color tones and marble accents embellished the room's interior. Leather couches, chairs, and an entertainment-style television welcomed them inside.

Gianna lowered herself onto the soft supple couch next to Tracy and Troy. Although her fragile nerves coiled in the pit of her stomach, she faced Steve and Rob squarely without flinching. "So, what happened?"

Steve leaned forward and rested his elbows on his thighs. He drew in a quivering breath and said, "We were only three miles from the trailhead when your husband slipped and skated on his back, like twenty feet, down an eroded trail. And then he fell thirty feet off a ledge."

Gianna closed her eyes. Images of his traumatic accident ricocheted in her mind. *Oh, God! His pain must be intense.* She blinked back the tears, trying to ignore the ache that resided in her heart.

Rob's voice quavered. "After Steve and I safely descended the trail, we looped around to where he'd landed. Luckily, my dog found him. He was in a clearing next to the waterfall."

"How bad?" she asked.

"He was talking to me," Rob said. He shook his head and smiled. "He wanted us to help him up so he could walk out. I told him that he wasn't going anywhere with his broken leg."

"Oh, a broken leg? That's all?" A tiny spark of hope whispered in her brain. *So, a little surgery, and he'll be fine.*

"Gianna," Steve said. The lines of his face etched with deep concern. "He's busted up badly. There's a possibility he may have a spinal injury. I do know he has abdominal distention, from internal bleeding. During the rescue, he started going into shock."

A sickening feeling churned in her stomach. "What does that mean? Is he going to live?"

Steve's shoulders slumped in despair. "They managed to stabilize him for emergency surgery. We'll have to wait."

"And pray," Gianna said.

She stood up and gazed out the window at the pouring rain slapping against the glass. A fork of lightning split across the dark sky, causing the hair on her arms to stand on end. She took a nervous step backward. *God, as if Danny's accident isn't enough. Please make this storm go away.* She plopped back down on the couch. *I just want him to hold me. I want to be able to touch his stubble-roughened jaw again.* She tried to blink back the moisture, but her warm tears trickled down her cheeks just like the rain on the windowpane.

Gianna looked up at Steve and asked, "Did you ride with him in the helicopter?"

"No, I stayed with the police and K9 unit while they did a full investigation. Afterward, I drove to my parents' house to shower, which is fortunately only five minutes from here."

"Oh," she said. That explained his sharp appearance and fresh scent of soap and aftershave.

"Bro, didn't they check you out?" Rob asked.

"Huh? No, I'm not hurt. But the police deemed that trail dangerous and closed it indefinitely," Steve said.

"Dude, at the trailhead, the police *bleeping* searched me, asked me if I was *bleeping* drunk, then sent me to the ambulance to get checked out. When the police saw my ID and realized I was military, they told me to go home and take care of my dog." He raised his hands in mock surrender. "What the *bleep* was that about?" he asked.

Gianna caught a glimpse of Troy rolling his eyes. She looked back at Rob. *Jumping Jehoshaphat! He has a trashy mouth. I can't believe Danny wanted me to ride up here with him. What was he thinking?* She shifted her position on the couch, trying to get comfortable, then rubbed her tired eyes. *It's going to be a long night.*

Outside the OR waiting room, there was a faint humming sound from the automated doors swinging open. A pair of sneakers squeaked along the tile floor, and moments later, a surgeon dressed in green scrubs entered the room. He briefly scanned the area and stopped when his eyes met Gianna's. He pulled down his face mask, leaving it to dangle around his neck.

"Are you Mrs. Christiansen?"

"Yes," she said, anxiously rising to her feet.

"I'm Dr. Murphy. We found the cause of his bleeding and have it under control."

"What was it?"

"A kidney injury caused by fractured ribs. We had to repair a torn blood vessel."

Gianna swallowed past the knot of emotion lodged in her throat. "How serious is he?"

"Mrs. Christiansen," Dr. Murphy sighed. "Your husband fell from a great height and was nearly dead when he got here. Not only does he have internal injuries caused by broken ribs, but also fractures to his ankles and legs, along with several cuts and bruises from colliding with rocks, trees, and brush."

"Will he recover?"

"Most likely, but he'll need extensive rehab," Dr. Murphy said. He stared up at the ceiling briefly, then returned a mystified gaze. "An angel must've been watching over him. There's no way to explain how he escaped a serious head or spinal injury with a fall from that height."

"What?"

"His CT scan showed no trauma to his head, and an MRI ruled out a spinal injury."

Gianna sighed, relief pouring out of her. "Oh, thank God. When can I see him?"

"My surgical team is still in there setting his right leg. He sustained a compound fracture to his tibia."

"Ok," she said, not really comprehending the severity of the injury.

Dr. Murphy placed his hands on her shoulders. "Look, he's going to be in surgery for a couple more hours. May I suggest you all go home and get some sleep? If his condition changes, I will call you."

"But I live two hours away."

Dr. Murphy pointed to the front desk. "Talk to Sherry. She can place you in a family suite." He looked over his shoulder. "Excuse me. I must get back in there."

"Thank you, Doctor."

"You bet," he said, before leaving the room.

Gianna turned to her friends. "I really appreciate all you've done for me, but you don't need to stay."

"We can't leave you here," Tracy said.

"Why not? I have nothing to go home to."

"Oh, sweetie," Tracy said, taking her hand.

"It's ok. Please, you need your rest," Gianna said.

"And so do you."

"I'll be fine, really," Gianna said.

Tracy sighed. "Ok, but—"

"If you need anything," Troy interjected, "even if it's the middle of the night, you call us, ok?"

Gianna nodded. "Thank you both, so much."

"Hey," Steve said, looking at Troy and Tracy. "No worries. I'm staying here tonight, and I can drive her back to the city tomorrow."

"No, Dr. Ross. Please, I'll be fine," Gianna said.

"Nonsense. I'm working tomorrow night anyway, so it won't be a problem."

"But to stay here tonight is crazy," Gianna said.

"I'm living here temporarily with my parents."

"Huh?" she asked.

"My wife and I sold our condo in August and had a house built in New Jersey. Barb and the kids moved in already, but I'm still here for three more weeks."

"Oh," Gianna said.

"Also, I have Dan's camping gear in my Jeep. I can drop it off at your place before I head to work."

"Fine." Gianna expelled a long, tired breath. She sank back into the lounge chair, barely able to keep her eyes opened. Just as her mind soared into the clouds, Rob's gruff voice hurled her back into reality.

"Man, it's freaking hot in here," he grumbled.

Gianna's eyes popped open. *Boy, this guy's something.* She didn't know what exactly, but he certainly was entertaining. His demeanor intrigued her more than it should have. But even if she wasn't married, his macho image was not her type.

Rob rolled up his sleeves and revealed his bulging muscles and patriotic tattoo. He stood up and prowled the room like a caged animal. "Oh, that reminds me." He reached into his pocket and pulled out a cell phone. "This is for you," he said, handing her Danny's cell phone.

"Thank you," she said, bouncing up in her chair. "I unintentionally washed mine. That's why I never got your call." She powered it on and opened Danny's pictures to view them. "Oh, wow! These are beautiful, but...yuck, not this one." She showed Steve and Rob a picture of a rattlesnake sunbathing on a rock.

"Oof, no thanks," Steve said, curling his lips in disgust. He scooted back in his chair. "I'm glad I didn't see that thing when we were there." He shook his finger. "You know what? I bet Dan purposely took that picture to show me. He knows I hate snakes."

Rob's mouth twitched into a wide, wry grin. "Dude, that's so cool. Wish I saw it." His raw amusement broke the tension of the moment, making Gianna smile. When he noticed her, he tapped her under the chin. "Hey, is that a smile, I see?"

"Nope," she mumbled, ducking her head to hide her embarrassment.

"Look at you, girl, blushing! You know, it's ok to laugh. If you don't, then I'm not doing my job to lighten up a dire situation."

Gianna looked at him with a tiny smile before her eyes filled with tears again.

"That's better," Rob said. "Except for the tears." His thumb gently wiped her cheek. "Dan wouldn't want to see you crying either." He stood up and said, "I'm heading out now, but I'd feel better if I knew you were ok."

"I'm fine, but I'm not leaving."

"Hon," Steve said. "You need your sleep. After surgery, Dan will be in PACU recovering, and they don't allow visitors there, anyway."

Gianna sighed. "You're right." She grabbed her overnight bag. "I'll see if I can get a family suite."

"Call me if you need anything—my number is in Dan's phone," he said.

She nodded. "Ok, thanks. See you in the morning."

Gianna gave the receptionist the cell phone number and requested a sleep room. While she waited, she texted her mother about Danny's status. She learned that Dr. and Mrs. Kendall's flight had landed, and they were staying in a hotel overnight.

She texted her mother back. Thanks, Mom. Love you.

Gianna searched through Danny's sent text messages. She had received all but the last one at two o'clock. It was a picture of a full-circle rainbow with an attached message. Gianna, sometimes we may see life as cruel and unsympathetic, but God's vision from Heaven is quite different from how we see it here on earth. Hold onto your faith, and I'll be home soon. I can't wait to feel you in my arms again. I love you, babe.

She drew in a bolstering breath and grasped her crucifix necklace. *God, it's as if he knew. Please watch over him. Amen.*

Chapter Nineteen

Gianna was so exhausted that she collapsed on the bed like a shoddy umbrella in a storm. *Oh, Danny, please be ok.* She allowed herself a moment of reflection, visualizing him when she had last seen him, standing in the doorway like a tough cowboy, wearing his signature black jeans and black shirt that fit his muscular body like a second skin.

She recalled his nervous, wrinkled brow that twitched when he cautioned her not to answer the door to strangers. His need to keep her safe surpassed any conceivable dangers he was up against. That morning, Gianna could've imagined a hundred things that might go wrong, but never this.

She remembered their last good-bye, how the warmth of his breath caressed her cheek and how his tight embrace protected her. That moment was as vivid as if Danny were lying there right next to her now. All she wanted was to touch him and feel his strong body against hers.

The clock ticked away the time. As Gianna drifted to sleep, negative details of Danny's condition plagued her dreams, causing her to toss and turn so much that she tangled the sheets. *I'm sorry, Mrs. Christiansen, but your husband didn't make it,* she dreamed the doctor said.

Gianna opened her eyes and gasped for air. *It's just a bad dream...a bad dream.* "Danny, wake up," she cried. She reached across the cold mattress and encountered not Danny's warm body, but an empty space.

She sat up and wiped the sweat off her forehead. As the vibrancy of her nightmare faded, she pulled the covers back up and laid her head back down on her pillow. She gazed up at the tiled ceiling, remembering that she wasn't home. *Oh, my Danny, please be ok.* She glanced at her cell phone. *Good, no calls.* She shoved the ugly thoughts to the back of her head.

Wide awake now, she kicked off the covers. As she stumbled out of bed to the shower, a dizzy and sick feeling brewed in her empty stomach. *I've got to eat something. I've got to stay strong and help Danny through this.*

After breakfast, she headed to the ICU. She stopped at the front desk and waited patiently while the unit coordinator rushed around faxing orders and filing charts.

"Can I help you?" the clerk asked.

"Yes, I'm here to see—"

"Excuse me a moment," the clerk said, answering the ringing phone. When the call ended, she sighed, "I'm sorry; how may I help you?"

"What room is Daniel Christiansen in?"

"Miss, visiting hours aren't until nine." Her response was curt, delivered in a cool, distant tone. She pointed to the sign on the door.

Gianna checked the time on her phone. It was only eight twenty. "Sorry, my mistake. I'll just wait downstairs in the chapel." As she turned to leave, a female voice with a southern accent called out to her.

"Excuse me, darling. Are you Mrs. Christiansen?"

Gianna turned sharply to the voice behind her. "Yes, I am," she said.

A middle-aged woman wearing a white lab coat introduced herself. "I'm Dr. Holly Burke. I'm responsible for your husband's care while he's here."

Gianna exhaled heavily. "How is he?"

"Stable and comfortable. Pain medications do wonders."

"Is he awake?"

"Yes, your husband's been asking for you all night." Her mouth curled into a confident smile. "I don't think he'll rest until he sees you."

"May I see him now?"

"Yes but hang on. I have something for you." Dr. Burke stepped behind the nurses' station and returned with a Ziploc bag containing Danny's wedding band and his cross necklace. "For safety reasons, we always remove jewelry prior to surgery."

Gianna nodded. "Thank you." She took the bag and looked inside. Her heart swelled at the sight of his ring.

"Follow me," Dr. Burke said, pointing down the hallway. "He's in room 207."

They stopped at the last door on the left at the end of the wing. Dr. Burke touched Gianna's forearm and gave her a warning look she couldn't miss.

"Now, Mrs. Christiansen, let me prepare you. Not only has he suffered internal injuries, but he has also endured extensive scrapes, bruises, and tissue swelling."

The doctor's words closed like a fist around Gianna's heart. "I understand," she said in a low, trembling voice.

Gianna took a few steps inside the room. The sharp smell of antiseptic permeated the air. When she saw his lifeless-looking body lying there attached to tubes, wires, and beeping machines, she faltered as if she had been gut punched and had the wind knocked out of her.

"Mrs. Christiansen?" Dr. Burke reached for her arm and guided her to a chair right outside the room. "Are you all right?" she asked, crouching beside her.

Gianna tried to find the words to explain how she felt. "I...can't...he..." Sobs crumbled her composure.

"I know. The medical equipment can seem overwhelming and intimidating, but I assure you, he's comfortable and well cared for," Dr. Burke said in a strong, steady voice.

"But it's hard for me to see him with his eyes closed and unresponsive, like he's...dead," she cried.

"Darling, what's your first name?"

"Gianna," she sniffled.

"Ok, Gianna, please listen to me." Dr. Burke grasped her hands. "Look at me. Your husband's alive. He's coherent, and his prognosis is good. But you need to stay positive for his sake. He *can* hear you. Ok?"

Gianna exhaled a long breath and quieted her sobs. She dug through her bag for a tissue and dabbed her eyes.

"Ok, I can do this."

"I know you can," Dr. Burke said, rising to her feet. She opened the door and squirted hand sanitizer into her palm. "Follow me."

Gianna slowly approached Danny's bedside. When she saw him up close, she threw her hand over her mouth to fight the nausea that climbed up her throat. He was hardly recognizable, his gorgeous face bruised and swollen. He looked so vulnerable, so fragile. His forehead was wrapped in a sweatband-style bandage and his right arm covered with gauze from his wrist to his shoulder. Both of his legs, including his ankles, were in casts.

Gianna tossed Dr. Burke an uncertain look. "Last night, Dr. Murphy mentioned fractured ribs, too. Is that correct?"

"Yes," Dr. Burke said, consulting Danny's chart. "He fractured four ribs, numbers eight through eleven, causing damage to his right kidney."

Gianna took a deep breath against the panic.

Dr. Burke put down the clipboard and patted Danny's hand. "Dan, your wife is here."

Danny moaned. Through half-closed lids, he fixed his gaze on Gianna. "Babe," he uttered through the oxygen mask.

"I'm here, Danny." She held his hand and leaned forward. "Hang in there. I love you," she whispered.

"I'm sorry...for ruining...your life," he mumbled. His eyes slipped closed then darted restlessly under his lids.

Gianna squeezed his hand. "No, no, Danny. That's not true." She looked at Dr. Burke. "Is he—"

"He's fine," she whispered. "He'll sleep now, knowing that you're here." She patted her hand. "I'll be back later to check on him."

"Thank you." Gianna pulled a chair alongside Danny's bed and sat down. She took his hand and placed it over her heart. "I'm here, Danny. I won't leave you."

She combed her fingers through his matted hair, gently sweeping strands away from his bandaged forehead. She caressed his bruised, swollen cheek down to his stubbly jaw. "I'm so sorry this happened to you, sweetheart. If only I'd been there...just maybe..." She closed her eyes. It hurt too much to look at him. *Lord, please take care of him. I fully trust you. Amen.*

She reached inside her duffel bag and took out a small box containing a set of hand-cut crystal rosary beads that her mother had given her on her wedding day. Her mother had said Nonna prayed to Our Lady every night for peace when Nonno was in the war. *Oh, Nonna, thank you for this blessed gift.* She bowed her head and prayed the rosary until her words slurred from weariness.

"Gianna?" Steve whispered, patting her hand.

She rubbed the sleep out of her eyes. "Oh, Dr. Ross, good morning," she yawned.

A concerned frown revealed his worry. "Gianna, are you feeling ok?"

"Yeah, just tired."

Steve narrowed his assessing gaze even more. "You don't look well." He put his hand to her forehead. "Your temperature seems normal."

"I'm fine. I just haven't been sleeping well, and I've been busy packing boxes."

"Dan did mention that, but I think you need to slow down and take care of yourself."

"I can't slow down. We close in four weeks."

"Call your Realtor tomorrow. Under these circumstances, you may be able to delay the closing."

Gianna threw her hands out, palms up. "What's that going to do?" She glanced at Danny, then back at Steve. She lowered her voice to a confidential murmur. "He's a mess. He'll need months to recover."

Steve gripped her hands firmly and solidly, giving her the notion that everything was under control. "I understand, but my in-laws have a studio apartment available. Rob and I will help you move."

"I don't know. Danny can't work anytime soon."

"Listen," Steve said. "I've seen cases where patients walk with crutches as early as six weeks. But no matter how long it takes, the job offer is still open. The important thing is you get some rest." He stood up. "Can I get you anything?"

"No, but thanks."

"Ok." Steve walked to the door and stopped. He pivoted on his feet. "Oh, Rob can't come today. His girlfriend isn't feeling well."

"Ok," Gianna said. *I can't handle his high-strung attitude today anyway.*

She nestled herself into a recliner as close as she could to Danny's side. It wasn't long before the beeping rhythm of his heart monitor lured her back to sleep.

Gianna stirred. The familiar sweet scent of perfume tickled her nose. Bits and pieces of conversation hummed around her.

"Hi, I'm Evelyn Kendall, and this is my husband, Joe. We're Daniel's godparents."

"I'm Steve Ross. Nice to meet you both."

"Likewise," Joe said.

Shoes shuffled across the floor, then a firm, but gentle hand rubbed her forearm. "Gianna, dear," Joe whispered.

She wiped away the last traces of sleep, then stretched her arms. "Dr. and Mrs. Kendall," she yawned. She eased herself out of the chair and hugged them. "Thank you for coming."

"We would've been here sooner, but we stopped at a church to attend Mass," Joe said.

"It was a lovely ceremony," Evelyn said. She centered her gaze on Gianna. "How are you doing, dear? You don't look well."

Gianna crossed her arms in front of her. *Boy, I must be a sight.* "I'm ok." She glanced over her shoulder at Danny. "I'm just worried."

"How is he?" Evelyn asked in her meek voice. She removed her sweater, then ambled to Danny's bedside. Her delicate fingers combed his tangled hair. "Oh, my dear Daniel." Her expression filled with uneasy worry. "What're all these wires and tubes for? He looks like someone's science experiment."

Joe wrapped his arm around his wife. He pointed as he explained. "That's a chest tube. It removes air, blood, and fluid from his lungs. This one is a Hemovac drain, which removes fluid around his incision. And those wires are for the EKG to monitor his heart rhythms."

Evelyn's voice became weak and shaky. "Oh, the poor dear. He must be so uncomfortable."

"Darling, with the dosage of pain medication they're giving him, trust me, he's feeling pretty good."

Steve nodded. "You know it."

Evelyn turned away slowly. She sat down in the chair and clutched her sweater in her lap. "Oh my, Daniel was always such a show-off."

"He was?" Gianna asked.

"Yes, especially with that motorcycle."

"Darling, he was careful," Joe said.

Evelyn shook her head. "He always bragged about escaping a near collision with an elk or a moose. Scared the daylights out of me every time he went out on that thing."

Gianna smiled, recalling the time Danny took her out on his bike. He was overly cautious.

Evelyn looked at Gianna. "And Daniel and your brother were always double trouble. Remember when they were caught drag racing with those hooligans, the Parker boys?"

"I remember hearing about that," Gianna said. "Matt got a ticket for reckless driving, and ooh, my parents tanned his hide." She tried to suppress a laugh. "They took away the keys to his Mustang for a month."

"The boys learned a lot that night. I know guilt rolled through Daniel like hot lava for a long time after that," Evelyn said.

"It sure did," Joe replied. "He realized the consequences of racing could've been as lethal as drunk driving."

Gianna dropped her head. There was no changing the past, but at least Danny learned from a drunk's grave decision and grew up to be a responsible adult.

Or did he? Doubt crept in to destroy her trust in him. *Did he fail to wear his new hiking boots?* She looked up at him and pressed her hand to her lips. *No. Dr. Ross said it was a deteriorated trail. Oh, Danny, I know what happened yesterday wasn't your fault.* Her mind continued to toil with his accident, causing her to miss the live conversation that encircled her.

"That's where Daniel met Sadie," Evelyn said.

"Wait, what?" Gianna asked. Her mind suddenly became alive and attentive. "Who's Sadie?"

"A gal he met at the drive-in diner," Evelyn said.

A wave of possessiveness rushed through Gianna. "I never heard of her."

"Probably because you were only thirteen," Joe said.

Evelyn put her hands to her cheeks. "My goodness, Gianna! She pestered him constantly with phone calls. I never much cared for her." Evelyn folded her hands together in prayer. "Thank heavens, it only lasted a month."

"What happened?"

"Daniel left for college," Evelyn said.

Joe winked at Gianna. "Sadie wasn't his type."

"She was too pushy," Evelyn added. She flipped her wrist. "No bother, it was a long time ago."

Gianna's heart turned over at the thought of him dating another girl. It didn't matter how long ago it was. Jealousy still tugged at her heartstrings.

The afternoon slipped away. Steve stood up and said, "Gianna, I hate to break this up, but I have to leave." He looked at Joe and Evelyn. "I have on-call hours tonight."

"Oh, I know all about that," Joe said. He rubbed Gianna's shoulder. "He'll be fine, dear."

"May I have a moment alone with him?" she asked.

"Certainly," Joe said, taking Evelyn's hand.

Danny opened his bleary eyes.

"Daniel," Evelyn called. "You're awake!"

"How're you feeling, son," Joe asked.

Danny's eyes settled on Joe and Evelyn. "Whoa, how'd I get to Montana?"

"Daniel, you caused quite a stir," Evelyn said.

A sly twinkle sparked in his eyes. "If I knew this was what it took to get you two to visit me in New York, I would've fallen off a cliff a lot sooner."

"Oh, you!" Evelyn said.

"If you weren't beaten up enough already, I'd knock you out myself," Joe said, shaking his fist at him.

Danny mumbled, "Thanks for flying out here."

"We love you, dear," Evelyn said, hugging him.

"Love you, too," Danny said. His eyes shifted to Steve. "Hey, friend. I owe you one."

"Yeah, well, I need you around, partner," Steve said. He turned and guided Gianna toward the bed. "We'll wait downstairs for you."

"Thanks," she said, not taking her gaze off Danny. "Those must be some heavy meds they're giving you."

"I'm feeling rather good at the moment," he uttered, "but I must be a sight."

"Yes, the best one I saw today."

"I messed up big time," he said.

"So, you have a few dents and scratches."

"Only a few? Trade me in for a newer model."

"Never! Besides, you're not totaled yet."

Danny squeezed her hand. "I love you."

"Love you, too." A tear dropped down her cheek, followed by another, then another.

"Don't cry," he said, wiping her tears with his finger.

"But I don't want to leave you."

"It's ok," Danny said. He swept her hair off her tear-saturated face. "You have my truck keys. I'll see you in the morning."

Gianna nodded. "I'm riding back with Joe and Evelyn. They have a rental car."

Danny squeezed her hand. "Hey, I'm sorry I broke my promise to take you to Jersey today."

"It's ok. You had other plans."

Chapter Twenty

Over the next five days, Gianna stayed overnight with Danny's godparents at the trauma center's family suite. During the day, she remained at Danny's bedside. Friends and colleagues of his visited to help raise his spirits, and in turn, his condition improved.

Dr. Burke removed the chest tube, wound drains, and transferred him out of ICU to the Med/Surg floor. Although Danny was still bedridden, a physical therapist began working with him, teaching him light strengthening exercises.

"You're doing so well, sweetheart," Gianna told him.

"But I need to get out of this bed," he said.

Evelyn patted his hand. "You'll be walking in no time."

"Yes, son, you'll get strong quick," Joe said.

Danny's eyes focused on Gianna. "As soon as I'm out of here, Dr. Murphy's going to set me up with PT services. And...I'm going to be present for the home settlement."

"Uh-huh," Gianna said. Determined not to give away her doubts, she looked away. *He's not going to make the closing. I'm going to have to contact our real estate attorney. Time* was dwindling, and stark reality struck her full force. *He has a long road ahead of him.*

"You ok?" he asked.

Gianna looked up at him and said, "Yeah, just tired." She looked at Joe. "We should probably get going if you want to make your flight."

Joe glanced at his watch and nodded. "Yeah, it's time," he said, pulling on his sports coat.

Evelyn pulled her sweater on over her paisley dress, then leaned over and hugged Danny. "You take care, dear. We love you."

"I'm sorry we have to go," Joe said. "But I must get back to my patients. I can't burden my nurse practitioner with my caseload."

Evelyn looked at Joe. "Maybe I should stay."

"No, it's ok," Danny said. "I understand."

"You take care, son," Joe said.

"You, too. And don't worry; I'll be home for Christmas," Danny said with complete confidence.

Gianna smiled at his comment, not wanting to discourage him. "And I'll see you in the morning, Danny."

"Hey," he said, waving her forward. "I love you."

She leaned in and hugged him. His hand skimmed down her back, and his warm touch awakened an aching hunger deep within her. "I love you, too," she said.

"Promise me something?" A bittersweet crest of emotion filled his voice. "Promise me you'll go home and take time for yourself. You need your rest."

"I will," she whispered and feather-touched his lips with a kiss.

Joe and Evelyn drove Gianna back home to the city. After a long, painful goodbye, they left for the airport. Afterward, Gianna curled up on the couch. She called her parents to update them on Danny's condition and to let them know that Joe and Evelyn's flight was on schedule.

"Aw, honey, you must be exhausted," Mom said.

"Yeah. It's been a long week."

"Dad and I are trying to book a flight to visit."

"Oh, Mom! There's no need to. Danny's stable. He's even talking about being transferred to a rehab center."

"Honey, we want to be there for you."

"Thanks. I really appreciate that, but I'm fine. Besides, I know Daddy's busy with the ranch."

Mom sighed. "Ok, but honey, you call us if anything changes. We love you."

"I will. Love you, too, Mom."

Gianna lowered her tired, achy body into the warm, sudsy bathtub. She leaned back and closed her eyes. *God, I need you. It's been a long week, but I thank you for giving Danny strength. I know you're going to see him through this, but I also know it's going to be a rough road.* She swallowed hard, trying to keep her emotions intact. *God, we settle on this place in only three weeks. Where're we going to live? Please give me a sign. Thanks. Amen.*

After her bath, she changed into her flannel pajamas and climbed into bed. She pulled the covers up and snuggled in for another lonely night. She rolled to her side and hugged her pillow. *Oh, Danny. I miss you.* Tears moistened her eyes. *He should be here with me.* She sobbed until fatigue did her in.

Hours later, she awoke to the howling wind whipping between the tall buildings. She sat up and looked out her bedroom window. A gray, hazy fog hung low in the air. Only the neighboring apartments, streetlights, and car headlights lit the dark morning.

She squinted at the clock. It was only an hour until sunup, and she was still so tired. She scanned her dark, empty room. A cold draft chilled her lonely, fragile heart. She lay back down and pulled the warm quilt over her head.

It was six o'clock, and the house was quiet. Usually, she'd rise to the sound of the shower or the aroma of coffee brewing in the kitchen.

She thought about the day ahead, the miserable two-hour commute back to the trauma center and having to drive Danny's truck for the first time. She recalled what Matthew had told her. *Once you learn to drive a stick, you never forget.* She held the crucifix that hung around her neck. *God, please don't let me wreck Danny's truck.*

She sighed. *Good times are yet to come.* She threw the blankets back and rolled to the edge of the bed. When her bare feet met the cold hardwood floor, she gasped. *Uh, how I wish I could crawl back under those covers.* She took a step forward and a familiar dizziness swept over her, causing her to sway. "Whoa, this isn't good." She eased herself back down on the bed and held her head. The last time she felt like that was when... *Oh, no! I can't be.* Her thoughts dived into a whirlpool of emotions. *But I'm late. My period was due last week.* She groaned. The possibility of another pregnancy made her blood run cold. *No, no, not now.*

She steadied herself and ambled her way to the bathroom. She opened the medicine cabinet and mumbled, "Where did Danny put those pregnancy tests?" After pausing a moment to think, she opened the bottom drawer of the sink cabinet. "Here they are," she said, picking up the box.

She ripped open the plastic wrapping with her trembling hand and stared at the label. *Now how does this work?* She read the instructions. *The result window will show a plus or minus.*

Gianna took the test, capped the tip, and then set it flat on the sink counter. *Do I really want to know?*

She sat down on the edge of the tub and cupped her hands over her face. *I'm afraid to know the truth.* She reached for the test stick and looked at it. Gooseflesh rippled up her back. A faint plus sign appeared in the result window. *Oh, no, no, please, no. Not now.* She stared at the pink positive sign, hoping the vertical line would fade away, making it negative, but as time lapsed, it became more prominent.

She sucked in a shallow breath and looked away. Her emotions were a grab bag of fear, anxiety, and hopelessness. *Oh, God, I can't go through this again, not alone.* Tears of dread fell. *This is not how we planned this. I was supposed to take this test with him here so we could share this intimate moment together.* She shook her head. There was no long gaze, no meaningful embrace, no joy, only despair.

A pang of remorse shot through her. *I brought this on that evening after we argued about Kimberly.* She shook her head again. *I'm not ready for this responsibility, not with Danny in his current condition. I just can't.*

She threw her hands wide and peered upward at the ceiling. "Why now, God? I know I should be grateful for your blessing, especially after my miscarriage, but it's not the right time. Please forgive me for not appreciating your precious gift. Amen."

Gianna grabbed the truck keys, her purse, and her hospital bag. As she ventured out to Danny's truck, an unwelcome tension flounced through her body. *Please God, don't let me crash.*

Two hours later, she arrived safely at the trauma center without missing gears, stalling out, or smashing the truck. *Thank you, God, for getting me here in one piece.*

As she moseyed into the hospital lobby, her mind shifted back to her newly discovered pregnancy. *Will my baby be healthy? I've been eating so poorly, and all this stress is killing me. I pray I don't lose this one, too.* Her stomach tumbled at the possibility. *I must keep this secret until I'm sure it's viable.*

Before turning the corner toward the elevators, Gianna passed a gift shop and noticed an adorable teddy bear displayed in the window. Extreme joy awakened her.

Danny's going to be so thrilled when I tell him we're expecting. The thought of his reaction washed away her doubts.

She browsed around the quaint boutique, then picked up the cuddly white bear she had seen in the window. It wore a t-shirt that had tiny footprints on it. It read, Could be pink, could be blue, all we know is we are due. The bear had elastic around its paw, enabling it to hold a positive pregnancy test. It was too cute not to have.

Gianna toted her mint green gift bag up to the Med/Surg floor. When she reached the unit, several doctors dressed in scrubs were congregating around the nurses' station. She recognized the physician with the braided bun as Dr. Burke. When their eyes connected, a cold chill skirted up her spine. *This can't be good.*

Dr. Burke excused herself from the group and approached Gianna, her expression etched with unease.

"Mrs. Christiansen, may I have a word with you?"

"Certainly," Gianna said.

"Let's talk in here, where's it's private."

Dr. Burke led her into a room the size of a closet that barely fit four chairs. When she sat down, her heart crawled up to her throat. "What's going on?"

"Your husband suffered a complication."

"What?"

"The compound fracture he sustained in his lower right leg is infected."

"But he was doing so well. Where is he now?"

"He's in surgery. Dr. Murphy had to go back in and clean out the wound."

"Surgery again? It's that serious?"

"It could be if the infection spreads to the bone."

"And what if it does?"

"Let's cross that bridge when and IF we get to it."

"Please, I need to know the worst-case scenario."

Dr. Burke sighed. "IF the infection worsens, they'll have to amputate." She rubbed Gianna's forearm. "But I'm confident that we caught it early enough."

Gianna squeezed her eyes shut, struggling to fight back hot tears. *For the love of Pete. Does the bad news ever end?* She opened her eyes, allowing the tears to slip down her cheeks.

"And just last night I thought I saw the light at the end of the tunnel." She dropped her head and mumbled, "Clearly, it was the headlight of an oncoming train."

"Aw, hang in there, Gianna," Dr. Burke said, patting her hand. "I know this is difficult. Would it be easier for you if I called his family?"

"No, thank you. I think I should do it. But please, let me know as soon as he..." Emotion caused her voice to waver. "I'll wait in the chapel."

"Ok, darling. I'll send someone for you."

Gianna found her way downstairs to the chapel. As she stepped inside the room, her eyes united with a portrait of Jesus hanging on the wall. *If only He could lift this burden off my shoulders.*

With the last of her strength gone, she dropped to her knees. Her eyes journeyed up to His face, and she cried, "Why, Lord? Why did this happen? Danny was getting better. I trusted you." She buried her face in her hands as sobs wracked her body. *I can't take it anymore.*

A soft hand touched her shoulder. She took a deep breath and turned around. "Tracy?" She swept aside her tangled emotions and gave her a hug. "What're you...?"

"Troy and I couldn't let you be here alone."

"Thank you," Gianna said, drying her tears. She looked over her shoulder. "Where's Troy?"

"Getting coffee," Tracy said.

"How did you know I was here?"

"Dr. Burke told us," Tracy said, sitting beside her. "How're you holding up?"

Gianna shook her head. "I...well, you know." She stared up at the ceiling, trying to hold back her tears. "I'm going to have to tell Dr. Ross that we can't move to New Jersey. I need to beg Mr. Sterling for my job back."

"What? Why?"

"I need to work."

Tracy opened her hands, palms up. "What're you going to do, break the contract on the condo?"

"No, I can't afford to keep it on my salary alone. We'll live in a hotel or something."

"But Steve offered you a place to live. He told you that he'd hold a position for Dan, too."

"Yes, but for how long? Danny's a train wreck."

Tracy grabbed Gianna's hands. "Your only job is to stay strong for him. He'll mend."

Gianna spoke in a noncommittal voice, not wishing to encourage false hope. "But you don't know that for sure. They may have to amputate his leg."

Tracy hugged her. "Let's pray together."

"That's all I've been doing."

"Aw, girlfriend, don't lose your faith."

After lunch, Gianna paced the floor in the OR waiting room. Her stomach was in knots, but she didn't know if it was nerves or her pregnancy.

"Girlfriend, you're going to make yourself sick. Please sit down," Tracy pleaded.

"I can't. I have to know what's going on."

Troy put his arm around her. "Relax, girl. Dan is in good hands."

Gianna heard the double doors outside the waiting room swing open. She rushed to the doorway and saw Dr. Murphy walking toward her.

"Mrs. Christiansen, the procedure went well. We irrigated the wound and took a tissue sample. It'll be sent to the lab so we can find out what kind of bacteria we're dealing with."

"So, he's going to be ok?"

"In time, with the correct antibiotics. We moved him to ICU. I'll take you to him."

Dr. Murphy's words released the knot in Gianna's stomach. "Ok, thank you," she exhaled.

In ICU, Danny lay comatose, connected to beeping monitors, wires, and tubes. She pulled a chair up next to him and held his hand. "I'm here, Danny."

Troy stood at the foot of the bed. "Hey, cowboy. It's about time you get back up in the saddle. I miss you, man."

Tracy patted Danny's arm. "We're praying for you," she said, blotting her red-rimmed eyes with a tissue.

It was late afternoon when Troy and Tracy left the hospital. Although Gianna's worn body screamed for rest, she refused to leave Danny's bedside. She curled up in the lounge chair with a pillow and blanket. *God, I've never seen anyone so weak. Please heal his broken body. I can't go on without him. Amen.*

About to nod off, an unfamiliar hand touched her shoulder. When she lifted her head, she saw a model-perfect, sun-kissed, red-haired woman dressed in a green designer suit and heels, holding an overstuffed Vermont Teddy Bear and three helium balloons.

"Mrs. Christiansen?"

Gianna narrowed her eyes. "Yes?"

"I'm Dr. Stetson, your husband's boss."

Sandy Beach! Cuss words were not part of Gianna's vocabulary, but anger raked over her like hot coals, and using an alternative phrase felt soothing. *So, you're the evil shrew that coerced him out of a job.* She swallowed with difficulty, then found her polite voice. "Hi, Dr. Stetson."

"Please, call me Kim," she said, approaching Danny's bedside. "How's he doing?"

"He has an infection."

"I'm so sorry."

I don't need your pity, and I don't need you here. Gianna raised her head and answered civilly, "Thanks."

Dr. Stetson gave Danny a long, admiring gaze. She turned to Gianna and gripped her arm, giving her the impression of controlled strength. "Dan's a fighter. Believe me; he'll pull through."

Gianna nodded. "Sure."

There was a brief, unpleasant silence as Dr. Stetson continued to study him with her hungry eyes. She turned to Gianna and said, "I...um...only heard about his accident yesterday, or I would've been here sooner. I've been in San Francisco for the past two weeks at a medical conference."

Sunbathing your hide, I'm sure. Gianna felt her Italian temper flare but worked hard to keep it in check. "I know. Dr. Browne and Dr. Collins visited already."

"Again, I'm sorry," Dr. Stetson said. "This must be hard on you. Can I get you anything?"

Yeah, a miracle. "No," Gianna said, but thank you."

Dr. Stetson sat down beside her.

"Listen, Gianna. Dan left his resignation on my desk, but I never had a chance to discuss it with him. I don't know what he told you, but before I left, he and I had a business disagreement." She inhaled deeply. "I was wrong, and he called me on it. Because of him, I'm declining the state's funding to perform abortions."

"What? What changed your mind?" Gianna asked.

"I took what Dan said to heart, and after some soul searching of my own, I realized life begins at conception. I would be lying to myself if I said pregnancy was only a *potential* life. Who am I to deny a human life? I'm not God."

"But Danny said you signed the lease to expand the office. What're you going to do now?"

"I'm going to propose that we specialize in high-risk pregnancies. After all, that would help save a life, not destroy it," Dr. Stetson said.

She stood up and gazed once more at Danny's broken body. She cupped her hand over his and looked back at Gianna. "Take good care of him. I need him back at the office." She walked toward the door and stopped. "I envy you. You have an honest, faithful husband, and he loves you." She flashed her superior grin before leaving the room.

Yeah, I know he loves me. Gianna rested her hand on her stomach. She turned to Danny and caressed his arm.

"Please, Danny, I need you here with me."

Chapter Twenty-One

After a restful night's sleep, Gianna refused to let a moment of doubt steal away her peace of mind. She grabbed her gift bag and headed back to the hospital with complete optimism that Danny gained consciousness overnight.

As the elevator doors glided open, an authoritative, no-nonsense voice broadcasted over the paging system.

"Dr. Wynn, ICU, Room 201."

The words wove like silken threads around Gianna's heart. *Oh, mercy! That's Danny's room.*

She hurried to the ICU. When the unit doors swung open, she noticed an extreme rollercoaster-like energy inside the usually calm wing. Physicians were shouting medical jargon while nurses were scrambling in and out of room 201.

As Gianna passed the nurses' station, the unit coordinator called out, "Miss, this is a restricted area."

"But my husband...what's happening?"

"Please, you need to wait in here," the woman said, pointing to the little room across the hall. "I'll send someone in shortly to speak with you."

Seriously? Gianna turned into the closet-sized waiting room and sat down. Her head pounded from the war of emotions that swamped her. *What went wrong now?* All her hope dissipated like smoke in a soft, gentle breeze. *Please God, I need answers.*

After waiting for what seemed like an eternity, the door opened, and Dr. Burke entered the tiny room.

"Mrs. Christiansen?"

Gianna ejected herself out of the chair. "Doctor, please tell me what's going on."

"Ok," she responded, placing her hands on Gianna's shoulders to calm her. "Last night, your husband spiked a fever, which is an indication that the infection isn't responding to the antibiotics."

Gianna threw her hand to her mouth. "Does this mean you have to amputate?"

"No, but the lab identified the bacteria sample. We need to try an alternative antibiotic to resolve the infection."

"Ok, so..."

"Dr. Wynn, our infection control specialist, will scrub in with Dr. Murphy. They'll flush out the wound again and insert an antibiotic bead treatment."

Gianna rubbed away the goose bumps on her arms.

"So, he needs another surgery?" she asked.

"Correct, but I'm certain this will be effective."

"May I see him?"

"Yes, briefly. They're prepping him now."

"Ok."

Gianna picked up her belongings and followed Dr. Burke down the hallway to Danny's room.

Dr. Burke poked her head inside. "Patient's wife is here. Give her a moment alone, please," she said.

Gianna entered the room. The moment she saw Danny's unresponsive, bruise-streaked body, her heart sank to her feet. She stroked his cold, clammy skin. "Danny, I'm here." She leaned in and listened to his quick and shallow breathing. "Hang in there, sweetheart. I'm praying for you." She gently kissed his cheek, then stepped aside while the surgical team entered and wheeled him away.

Gianna rode the elevator down to the first floor. When the doors glided open, Steve was standing there.

"Oh, Dr. Ross, you're here," she said, tears pricking her eyes. "They're taking Danny back into surgery again."

Steve lowered his eyes and said, "I'm so sorry." He wrapped his arm around her shoulder and gave her a fatherly hug. "What happened?"

Gianna sniffled. "Can we talk where it's private?"

"Certainly. Let's sit in the visitors' cafeteria."

She nodded in agreement.

Steve found a tiny square table tucked in a corner. He pulled a chair out for Gianna and gestured to her to sit while he bought breakfast. "May I get you anything?" he asked.

"No, thank you. I'm not hungry."

Gianna rested her elbow on the table with her chin in her palm. She looked out the floor-to-ceiling window that overlooked the courtyard. The morning sun barely shone through the overcast sky, giving her the impression of a miserable day to come.

Steve returned to the table with a full-blown breakfast tray for two. He presented a plate of scrambled eggs and pancakes topped with fresh fruit, along with a bottle of orange juice and a pint of milk.

"Eat up," he said.

The aroma of eggs alone made Gianna queasy. She looked at Steve and gently pushed the plate aside. "I can't. This is too much," she said.

"But you need to eat something."

She smiled at him. "Thank you." She took a sip of orange juice, then updated him on Danny's condition. "Dr. Burke believes this procedure will work, but—"

"Think positively," he said, placing his coffee cup down on the table. "Did you update his folks?"

"Uh-huh, yesterday. But Dr. Kendall can't leave his medical practice, and Mrs. Kendall is fighting a bad head cold. So, my brother Matt and his wife Jessica are flying in this morning."

"Good, good. I look forward to meeting them."

Gianna nodded. She dropped her head and fiddled with the straw wrapper on the table. "Um," she stammered. She peered up at him. "Dr. Stetson stopped by yesterday. Did you know she's planning to specialize in high-risk pregnancies?"

"I heard that rumor," Steve said.

"She's holding Danny's position for him."

"I guess that's good news," Steve said, sighing. He picked up his fork and waved it. "Listen, you don't need to make a decision right away. This is something you and Dan should discuss together."

"I suppose," she said, rubbing her tired eyes.

"Gianna, are you getting enough sleep?"

"Yeah, I'm fine." She turned and focused on the sleet that pelted the windowpane. "I'm worried about Danny."

"I know, but in the interim, you can't let yourself starve." He pointed to her plate. "Aren't you going to eat?"

She dropped her head and picked imaginary lint off her sweater. "I can't."

Steve sighed. "Dan's going to be fine."

"It's not that." She rolled her tongue over her lips and looked up at him. "I'm pregnant."

Gianna stood outside the chapel entrance with her hands folded primly in front of her. "Thank you for breakfast, Steve," she said.

Steve patted her shoulder. "Hey, I'm glad you finally ate something."

"I hope I can keep it down."

"You'll be fine. Just eat small meals."

Silence fell briefly as Gianna gazed around the empty hallway. "I, um..." She reached for Steve's hands, then met his compassionate eyes. "Let me say thank you."

"But you already have."

Gianna smiled easily. "Just let me say it again. Thank you for being here for Danny and me. You've gone way beyond a loyal friend. Thank you."

Steve squeezed her hands. "My pleasure."

"But it's not only that," she said, blotting the tears that bordered her eyelids. "I mean, you know, what I just told you in the cafeteria." She gazed down and rested her hand on her abdomen.

"Oh, Gianna," Steve said. A wide smile tipped the corners of his mouth. "Dan's going to be thrilled."

She took a long breath. "I know."

"But are you ok with it?" he asked.

She peered up at him. "Steve, I'm afraid. I'm afraid I might lose this baby, too. I just found out, so please, don't tell anyone."

"I understand." He put his fingers to his lips and mimicked a zipper closing. "Patient-doctor confidentiality. And in the meantime, I'll fill that script for your prenatal vitamins."

"Thank you. I really appreciate it."

"You're welcome," Steve said, glancing up at the hall clock. "I should head upstairs to the waiting room before Rob shows up."

A warning look spread across his face.

Having met Steve's brother, Gianna couldn't help but smile back at his comment. "Ok. I'll see you later."

The chapel was unoccupied, but the air felt warm and welcoming with Jesus's presence. Gianna found her way to the first pew and knelt. As she gazed up at the large wooden cross, she felt small and hopeless, flawed, and overwhelmed.

I'm here, Lord. I need you. I've tried to do everything right, but I'm losing my faith. I'm scared for Danny and for the welfare of our unborn child. I can't do this alone. Please, give me something to believe in. Amen.

She stood up and wandered the room, pausing in front of a table that cradled the Holy Bible. She skimmed her hand over the textured leather cover, then opened it to a random page.

Jeremiah 29:11: 'For I know well the plans I have in mind for you, says the Lord, plans for your welfare, not for woe! Plans to give you a future full of hope.'

Gianna looked up at the statue of Jesus with flowing, meek eyes and whispered, "Amen."

Suddenly, voices in the hallway filtered through the open door, jarring her out of prayer. She turned and saw Jessica standing in the entrance with her hands folded gracefully in front of her small baby bump. She was fashionably dressed, as always, wearing black slacks and a super cute maternity blouse.

Jessica's green eyes filled with tears. "I thought I'd find you here," she said.

"Oh, Jess," Gianna sniffled. She gave her a hug. "Let me look at you." Her short strawberry blonde hair was tucked behind her ears, with several wisps framing her oval face. "You're letting your layers grow out."

"Yep, I need an easy-to-do mommy style."

"It's shaping out nicely," Gianna said. She clasped her hands together and exhaled. "Thank you for coming."

"No problem. That's what best friends are for."

Something in Jessica's tone touched a tender spot in Gianna's heart. "Oh, how I missed you."

"Aw, I missed you, too," Jessica said, hugging her tighter. She reached for Gianna's hand and led her into the first pew. "How're you doing?"

"I..." Tears threatened to rob Gianna of control. "I don't get it. Why does Danny have to suffer? What did he ever do wrong to deserve this?"

"It's divine intervention," Jessica said.

"What do you mean?"

"God has a better plan for him."

"But he's in pain. How can that be better?"

Jessica leaned in and spoke with total confidence. "God allows suffering when He has a greater blessing for us." She touched Gianna's hand. "Look." She picked up a Bible in the pew's bookrack. She flipped through the pages until she found Romans 8:28. "Listen to this. 'We know that all things work for good for those who love God, who are called according to his purpose.'" She closed the book and placed it back in the rack. "Think about it."

Jessica left the chapel while Gianna stayed behind and organized her scattered thoughts. *Somehow, Danny survived.* Realization drifted slowly. *God must not be done with him yet.* She knelt and prayed. *Lord, I know you are actively working in our lives. Whatever happens, I trust you. Amen.*

Gianna returned to the ICU waiting room, where Jessica and Steve were sitting. "Where's Matt?"

"At the vending machine...uh, no, right behind you," Jessica said.

A strong hand settled on her shoulder. She whirled around to find herself standing up against her stocky brother.

"Hey, sis," Matthew said. He opened his arms and gave her a huge bear hug.

Gianna clung to him as if he were her lifeline to Danny. "Thank you. It means so much to me to have you here."

"I'm glad to be here, too, although I wish it were under better circumstances," he said.

"Me, too," she sniffled.

Matthew gently set her down. "So, how're you doing?" he asked, stuffing his hands into his pockets.

"Well, I'm as strong as I can be," she said, half laughing. She rolled her eyes. *Whom am I kidding?*

Matthew curled his arm around her. "Don't fret, sis. This is only temporary. He'll get better." He flashed his all-knowing big brother grin, then escorted her to a chair in the lounge area.

Just like my brother, always so positive. She slouched in the chair and closed her eyes, letting her mind wander back in time to when she was ten and had gone water rafting with her family. *What a beautiful day,* she recalled. The warm sun had glistened on the river, but halfway through the day, the sky had turned black, and thunder exploded overhead. She remembered frantically paddling to the river edge to get off the water, then squatting with her arms wrapped around her knees, desperately trying to shelter herself from the wicked lightning. Tension had vibrated each nerve ending in her body. *We're going to die.* She had glanced at her brother Matthew. *Everything's going to be ok,* he had told her. And sure enough, he was right. Shortly thereafter, the rafting crew rescued them from the woods. But the incident had left a burning imprint on her.

"Mrs. Christiansen," Dr. Murphy called to her.

Gianna pushed all thoughts aside and turned to Danny's surgeon. "Yes, how is he?"

"The procedure went well; however, he had a slight dip in his blood pressure, so we moved him back to ICU," Dr. Murphy said.

"What does that mean?"

Dr. Murphy's eyes narrowed in warning. "We need to monitor him for symptoms of sepsis."

Gianna was confused and more than a little nervous.

"For how long? When will you know?"

"We took a blood culture, but the results from the lab take over twenty-four hours."

"Can I see him now?"

"Certainly, but understand, he's still heavily sedated. Follow me," Dr. Murphy said.

Gianna turned on her clunky boot heel and grabbed her brother's wrist. "Let's go."

Gianna opened the door to Danny's room. *Here we are again.* It was the same old scene, just a different day. The distinct smell of iodoform saturated the air. The only sound in the room came from the heart monitor beeping to the beat of his heart, slow and steady.

He looked the same, still comatose. Wires were fixed to his chest, and tubes protruded from his body. The only improvement was that the swelling in his face had lessened, and his bruises had changed from a reddish purple to a bluish green.

"Oh, heavens!" Jessica said, stopping short in the middle of the room. The blood siphoned from her face as she was obviously caught off guard by Danny's critical condition. Her tear-glistened eyes shifted from him to Gianna. "I'm so, so sorry."

"I know. It's ok. He's getting better," Gianna said calmly, even though her confidence was as fragile as his condition.

When Matthew caught sight of Danny, he swallowed hard, then urgently stepped forward to his bedside. He stood there in silence with a look of such profound sadness.

"Dan, it's me, Matt. Can you hear me?" His voice broke in huskiness. "Hey, did you forget?" he asked, nudging his arm. "You promised me last year you were going to show me around that crazy city you call home." A muscle flicked in his jaw. "Come on, man. I'm here. You have a family who loves and needs you. So, jump back into the driver seat and give it another go." He chuckled lightly. "Heck, I'll even give you the keys to my Mustang."

Matthew took a deep breath, leaned forward, and whispered in a weakened voice, "Dan, you can't do this to us, buddy. It's not your time...I pray it's not your time." He glanced at Gianna, then quickly looked away.

Gianna felt the water rise in her eyes. *Oh, Matt, please don't think that.* She stepped forward and hugged him. "Matt, he's going to be fine." She looked over her brother's shoulder at Steve for reassurance.

Steve nodded and quickly changed the subject. "So, Matt, how long have you and Dan been friends?"

"Since preschool," Matthew said, wiping his eyes. He pulled a chair up next to the bed and sat down. He looked at Danny and said, "Yeah, we go way back. Right, bud? Good times." He let out a short laugh. "Remember the treehouse, Dan?"

"Oh, no," Gianna said, covering her face with her hands. "Please, not this story."

Matthew lifted a finger to stifle her. He looked at Steve and said, "We, uh, built this nifty treehouse. You know, the perfect hang-out in the woods away from *everyone*."

"Gotcha," Steve said.

"Well, Gianna followed us around like a lost puppy."

"I did not," she retorted. She crossed her arms over her chest and stared at the floor. *He always warps the truth.*

"You did," Matthew said. "You were a pest."

His slightly mocking smile irritated her.

"Well, Mom told you to keep an eye on me so she could put Mark down for a nap," Gianna said.

"Where was I in all this?" Jessica asked.

"At Disney with your parents," Gianna grumbled.

"So, anyway," Matthew continued. "We built this treehouse..."

Gianna pursed her lips tightly. *It was just a stupid shack.*

"Dan and I thought it was cool to climb up and jump off," Matthew said with an eye roll. He nudged Gianna's arm and gave her a twisted grin. "Remember when we dared you to jump?"

"Yeah, and I did. I landed hard and scraped my hands and knees."

Matthew snickered. "Yeah, you started crying."

"Well, it hurt," she said. "Besides, you ditched me."

"You were a whiny brat," he said.

Gianna shoved an elbow in his ribs. "I was not!" She turned to Jessica and Steve. "I was like seven." She leaned forward and caressed Danny's forearm. "Danny didn't think I was a pest. He even carried me inside the house, cleaned my scrapes, and bandaged them for me."

Matthew crossed his arms against his broad chest. "Dan was a softy back then."

"Put a sock in it, Matt," Gianna snapped. "Like being a diesel mechanic is so manly? You're so full of yourself."

"Yep," Matthew said, smugly. He swung his left leg over his right knee and clasped his hands behind his neck. "Dan didn't feel sorry for you that day. He just didn't want to get in trouble."

Gianna shot daggers at her brother. "You're a bully!"

Matthew leaned forward in his chair and rested his elbows on his knees. "Sis, I'm just teasing. You know I love you."

She glared up at him, still hot. He batted his puppy dog eyes at her, causing her heart to melt. *Oh, I can't be mad at you.* She smiled softly. "I love you, too, bro."

Steve laughed. "You two are too much, squabbling over something that happened a hundred years ago. Funny, my brother and I aren't any better. Wait till you meet him."

Only minutes later, the door opened abruptly, and Rob whipped through the curtain, voice first. "Dude, did you hear that lady two doors down moaning like she was possessed?"

"Speak of the devil," Steve uttered.

Matthew whispered, "He certainly has a knack for making an entrance."

"Yeah, he sure does." Steve patted his forehead with a handkerchief. "Uh, little bro." He put his finger to his lips. "Pipe down. You're in a hospital."

"Oh, right, sorry," Rob said. He walked boldly forward and stood with his legs apart, in a warrior's stance. "I'm so psyched. I took Masie to dinner last night, and she said yes!"

"Congratulations, bro!" Steve said. He turned to Matthew and Jessica. "Meet my brother, Rob."

"Hi," Matthew said, shaking his hand.

Jessica pinned a polite smile on her face. "Hi."

Rob strode across the room toward Gianna and eased down into a squat beside her. "Hey, honey. How're you doing today?"

"Fine," she mumbled. She tried to smile, but it fell flat. She was in no mood to deal with his colorful charm.

"Chin up," he said. He glanced at Dan. "He's going to get better."

"Oh my!" Jessica said, obviously trying to diffuse an awkward situation. "Look at the time. No wonder this baby is kicking up a storm. I missed lunch."

"That's my cue," Matthew said, standing up. He walked toward Jessica and placed his hand on her baby bump. "Know of any good places 'round here to eat?" he asked.

"No," Gianna said, "but you all go on and explore." She massaged her bloated stomach. "I'm not hungry."

"Sis, just come with us. My treat," Matthew said, helping Jessica out of the chair.

Rob piped in. "You should go." He smoothed his hand over Gianna's cheek like it had a will of its own. "Don't worry, baby. I'll sit with Dan."

Gianna jerked her head away. "Baby? Only Danny calls me that!" She forcefully quelled the urge to slap him. "Who do you think you are?" She drew her knees up to her chest. "I'm not leaving my husband."

Rob leaned into her and braced his arms against the back of the chair. His muscles bunched beneath the thick cotton of his shirt. He glared at her, and she could feel the heat sizzling in his brown eyes.

"You're going even if I have to pick you up and throw you over my shoulder in a fireman's hold," he said.

"Cool it, bro," Steve called out.

Unimpressed, Gianna shrugged her shoulders. She palmed his chest to push him away. When he stepped back, she halfheartedly rose to her feet.

"Atta girl," Rob said.

She gave him a cold stare, refusing to let his cocky attitude intimidate her. She turned toward Danny and gently kissed his cheek. "I love you. I'll hurry back."

She grabbed her purse and joined the others waiting at the door.

Jessica took her hand and gave her a half smile. "Dan will be fine," she said.

Steve touched Gianna's shoulder. "I'm sorry my brother was such a butthead in there. He means well, but he can be pushy."

Gianna dismissed him with a careless wave.

"Heck," Matt said. "I thought I was going to have to deck him one."

"Matt, I can take care of myself," she snapped.

Matthew cut her a sharp look that dared her to uphold her words. "Seriously, sis?"

"Let's just go so I can get back," she demanded.

After lunch, Gianna returned to the hospital with Steve, Matthew, and Jessica. As they walked past the gift shop, Jessica asked if they could go inside for a moment.

"Not at all, my love," Matthew said.

The flowery fragrance outside the store's entrance provoked Gianna's senses, reminding her of the surprise baby gift she hadn't given Danny. She rested her hand on her delicate tummy. *I can't go back there.* "Uh, I'll meet you all upstairs."

"Me, too," Steve said. He put his arm on Gianna's shoulder. "Are you ok?"

"Yeah, I just want to get back to Danny."

When she reached the ICU doors, Steve excused himself to the vending machine for a cup of coffee.

The door to Danny's room was ajar. As Gianna stepped inside, she heard Rob's booming voice behind the curtain. Captivated, she paused and listened.

"I wish you could *bleeping* hear me, man. You have too much going for you to give up now. C'mon, dude. You have a freaking gorgeous wife who loves you, and I can't stand to see her cry anymore. You know, I almost had to carry her to the truck just to get her to go out to lunch with her brother and his wife. She wants you, so don't leave her hanging. She needs you. This world has too many jackasses like me who would love to have her. So, wake up already and start living. You've got too much to lose."

Gianna fought a sudden urge to weep. *Wow! Rob has a sensitive soul hidden beneath his bad boy exterior.* As she digested his words, a firm hand touched her shoulder. She gasped, then whirled around. "Oh, Steve, it's you."

"You all right?" he asked.

"Yeah. I, uh, was just heading in."

Steve slid the curtain aside. "How's it going, bro?"

Rob shook his head. "A nurse checked in half a dozen times, but no change in his status."

As Rob finished his sentence, Danny moaned. He raised his right trembling hand to his face, and his unsteady fingers pulled off his oxygen mask. His eyelids fluttered open, but his blue eyes had a flat and faraway look to them.

When he recognized the faces around him, tears formed in the corners of his eyes. His lips quivered. "I should've stayed on the green trail," he muttered.

Rob roared, "Dude, you're awake!"

Danny slowly raised his hand and pointed to Rob. His words became clear. "Too many jackasses? Is that the best you can do?"

Rob threw his head back, clapped his hands, and cackled. "Oh, man! You heard me?" He shook his head and said, "Dude, you scared the hell out of us."

Danny held his arm steady, curled his fingers, and gave Rob a fist pump. "I have to protect my interests from snakes like you." His groggy looking eyes struggled to scan the room. "Where's my girl?"

Rob's bold gaze signaled Gianna to Danny's bedside.

"I'll let the nurse know he's awake," Rob said.

Gianna sat beside Danny and grabbed his hand. "I'm right here, sweetheart," she cried.

A smile touched his lips. "No more tears, ok? I need you to be strong for both of us and our baby."

Gianna's mouth dropped open. *How did he know?* Her pregnancy was an unspoken secret. She turned sharply to Steve, who looked as thunderstruck as she felt. She turned back to Danny, locking her gaze with his. "How'd you..."

"Mom told me," he mumbled.

"What? I never told Evelyn."

"Not Evelyn." An indefinable emotion sparked to life in his blue eyes. "Mom told me," he repeated.

A tingling sensation raised the hair on her arms. *What is he saying? I never told my mother.* She gave Steve a baffled look, and he returned the same puzzled expression.

Gianna's mind sank into a light trance, trying to comprehend the significance of Danny's words. But when the curtain slid open and Dr. Burke and two nurses entered the room, she hurled her dizzied senses aside.

"Dan, how are you feeling?" Dr. Burke asked.

"Like I need to get out of this bed."

"Ok, darling, we're trying to make that happen. With pain management and rehab, you'll be walking in six to twelve weeks."

"No, ma'am, it has to be sooner," he muttered.

"Sweetheart, relax," Gianna interjected.

Dr. Burke smiled politely at her, then turned back to Danny. "Tell me your pain level now."

"A four, but this oxygen mask has to go."

"Ok," Dr. Burke said. "Let's get you comfortable." She turned to the sink and washed her hands. "Gianna, we need to take his vitals, change his dressings, and administer meds. You can show your guests to the gift shop or get a bite to eat."

"Um, sure," Gianna said, unable to drag her gaze off Danny. *I don't want to leave you again.* She caressed his unshaven jaw and whispered, "I love you."

Dr. Burke touched her shoulder. "Don't worry. We'll take good care of him."

Gianna wandered into a sitting area across from the main elevators. She leaned up against the wall and chewed on her lower lip. *How did Danny know?* The question hammered at her. *It's impossible.* She paced the floor while her inner voice prodded for answers. *I never told Mom about my pregnancy.*

"Yo, girl, chill!" Rob called out. He sat sprawled out in a chair with his leg dangling over the arm. "You're going to wear out the floor."

Gianna stopped midstride and took a deep breath. She glanced at Steve, who waved her toward a chair.

"Relax," he said. "Dan's over the hump."

"I know, but I can't stop thinking about what he said."

"What's that?" Rob asked.

"Oh, uh..." Quickly, she broke eye contact and stared down at her boots. "He, uh, said something that doesn't make any sense."

"Huh?" Rob rubbed the base of his neck. The expression on his face shadowed with suspicion. "Well, uh, you know the doctors have him pumped with all kinds of meds. Who knows what he's thinking."

"No, it's not like that. It's what he said. There's no way he could've known."

"Known what?" Rob asked.

Steve leaned forward in his chair. "Hey, bro, aren't you supposed to be going to dinner with Masie and her parents?"

Rob clicked his phone to check the time. "Oh, frig. I've got to go. Catch you guys later."

After Rob turned the corner, Gianna said, "Gee, I almost let the cat out of the bag."

Steve nodded. "I was thinking, maybe Dan saw your gift bag."

Gianna shook her head. "I had it tucked away in my duffel bag, waiting for the right moment."

Steve blew out his cheeks. "I don't know then. Medically, I have no explanation."

Gianna shrugged her shoulders. "C'mon. Let's find Matt and Jessica."

Chapter Twenty-Two

As the bed inclined to a sitting position, Dan gripped the rails, laughing bitterly as blistering pain pierced through him. Although in extreme discomfort, he was determined to fight past it.

"How does this feel?" Dr. Burke asked.

"Good," he said, gritting his teeth. "My neck and shoulders feel much better."

Dr. Burke handed him the remote. "Here. You can readjust your position should you feel discomfort. I'll check in on you in a little bit."

"Thanks, doc," he said, expelling a long, tired breath. He rested his head back on the pillow and closed his eyes, trying to ignore the ache that throbbed through his body.

When the curtain skated across the track, Dan lifted his head from the pillow. "Hey, baby," he said as Gianna whisked through the opening.

"Sweetheart, you're sitting up!" Her face radiated with joy. "How do you feel?"

"Just dandy; that is, as long as I don't move." He looked beyond her at the closed curtain. "Where's your posse?"

"They'll be here shortly," she said.

Dan patted the mattress. "Come, sit with me."

Gianna stood motionless in the middle of the room.

"But I don't want to hurt you."

"Nah. I already did that."

She laughed, then cautiously approached the bed.

"It's ok. Hop up," he said.

Gianna eased herself onto the bed beside him. Her nearness, the sweet scent of her perfume, and the heat of her body filled his pores, even the air he breathed. He cradled her face in his hands and closed his eyes, cherishing the silky feel of her soft skin. "I'm so sorry I put you through hell with all this."

"Danny, stop!" She held his hands firmly. "I love you, and we're in this together."

He gazed at her gorgeous brown eyes, noticing the purple shadows that had settled beneath them. "Babe, I'm worried about you." He stroked the dark circles under her eyes with the pads of his thumbs. "You need to rest."

"I'm fine," she insisted. "Besides, this isn't about me."

Touché. "I'm getting better, and if my blood culture comes back normal, doc is transferring me to rehab."

"Really?" Her voice perked up. "That's great!"

"Yeah, it is. I'll be able to attend the settlement in three weeks, even if it's in a wheelchair."

"Danny, about the move—"

"Shh, don't worry. Everything is happening the way it's supposed to." He placed his left hand on her belly and rubbed it. He loved knowing that they created the life growing inside her.

Gianna cupped her hand over his and studied him with her solemn eyes. "How'd you know?"

"Know what?"

"About my pregnancy. I never told my mom."

Dan swallowed hard, trying to manage a feasible answer. He didn't want to frighten her with details of his encounter with death. "Um, lucky guess?" he joked.

"Danny, this isn't funny," she said, looking at him with unflinching directness. "Tell me how you knew."

"I'm sorry," he said.

"Dr. Murphy told me..." her voice cracked, and tears streamed down her pale cheeks. "You almost died."

A heavy weight settled on Dan's chest. *She knows. I'm going to have to tell her the truth.* But he didn't want to burden her with more distress. "Don't cry," he whispered. He kissed the salty tears from her cheeks. He then took her hands and spoke in a calm, steady voice. "I did die, and I talked to my mother."

Gianna's eyes embraced his. "What're you saying?"

Dan inhaled deeply. Searing pain lanced through his ribs and stars exploded before his eyes. He tried desperately to keep it together, but a moan slipped from his lips. "Oh, God!"

"What?" she asked, leaping off the bed.

"It hurts to breathe." He pushed the down arrow on the remote control to lower the bed to a more tolerable position. He closed his eyes and waited for the pain to settle.

"Danny, you ok?"

"Yeah. Come here."

"But I..."

"It's ok," he panted.

Carefully, she sat down on the edge of the bed.

The urge to hold her, touch her, and taste her overrode his good sense. "Lie next to me."

She lowered herself onto her left side, leaving a gap between them.

"Come closer to me so I can feel you."

Gianna inched in.

"That's my girl," he whispered.

She caressed his face. "So, tell me."

"All right," he breathed. He closed his eyes, allowing the smoky images of his horrendous accident to resurface. "I was lying there in awful pain, shivering in the damp mud. Steve was talking to me while the medics worked. I felt tingly and weak, and then everything went dark. I heard people yelling at me, but I didn't care. I was suddenly buoyant, full of life. It was so peaceful, like a dream, but it was real. The colors were so vibrant. I can't describe it."

Gianna's eyes seized his, tears welling slowly from beneath her long lashes. "Oh, Danny," she cried, gripping his hand tighter.

"Babe, I heard my mother's voice. I felt pure love, and I was no longer in pain. I didn't want to leave, but Mom told me I couldn't stay."

His heart thumped madly as he watched Gianna's expression become more remote. "I was confused. I wanted to come back to you, but I was afraid to feel the pain again." He choked back his tears. "My mom reminded me of Genesis 2:24."

Gianna paraphrased the verse. "A man leaves his parents, joins his wife, and they become one."

"Yes. That's when I realized what my mother was trying to tell me. You and I created a life together. God spoke to me and told me that it wasn't my time. Next thing I remember was descending back into my broken body and feeling extreme pain again."

Gianna looked up at him, her eyes reddened from tears. "I'm so sorry you had to suffer like that."

"No, no, don't be. I've been blessed with a second chance to be with you. I love you." He touched her belly and massaged it. "And I love our unborn baby."

A tiny smile slipped across her tear-soaked face.

"You'd better, because I couldn't go on without you."

"I'm not going anywhere."

Gianna wiped her tears. "I have something for you."

She slid off the bed and handed him a gift bag.

He smiled. "What's this?"

She motioned with her eyes. "Just look inside."

Dan inclined the bed just enough to be comfortable in a semi-sitting position. He dipped his hand inside the bag, making his way through the crinkly tissue paper until his fingers felt something soft and fluffy. "Oh, babe, you shouldn't have," he said, pulling out a white teddy bear. He noticed the positive pregnancy test in its paw. "Aw, look at that. Clever."

"Check out its shirt," she said, pointing to it.

"Could be pink, could be blue, all we know is we are due." Dan smiled. Excitement fueled his soul. "Thank you." He drew a ragged breath and settled his mouth on her lips, kissing her softly and unhurriedly.

Footsteps squeaked across the floor and the curtain whipped open. In came Steve, Matthew, and Jessica.

"Hey, is this a private party, or can anybody crash?" Matthew called out.

Dan pulled his gaze from Gianna and locked them on his best friend. "What in Sam's Hill are you doing here?"

"Shoot, I can't let you go anywhere," Matthew said.

Gianna whispered in Dan's ear. "I'll be right back."

She hopped off the bed and grabbed Jessica's arm.

"Ok, I'll still be here," he said, watching the two leave the room. "So, Matt. How long are you staying?"

He shrugged his shoulders. "However long you need me. Pop gave me extended time away from the ranch to help you and Gianna get moved."

"I appreciate that, but I need a bigger favor."

"What's that?" he asked.

"Keep an eye on your sister."

Matthew gave a slight headshake. "Huh? What's wrong with her?"

"She's pregnant," Dan said, holding up the little bear she gave him. "I'm concerned that she's not taking care of herself."

Steve chimed in. "Don't worry. She and I spoke about it in length. I'll see to her care."

"Thanks, doc," Dan said.

"Congratulations, bro," Matthew said, giving Dan a fist pump. "As for looking after Gianna, I guess I'm up for the challenge."

Dan chuckled. "Thanks, and good luck with that."

Matthew pointed to the three balloons and the Vermont Teddy Bear perched on the windowsill. "Did Gianna give you those, too?"

Dan shifted his eyes toward the get-well gift. *Where did those come from?* He looked at Matthew and gave a loose-muscled shrug. "I don't know."

Steve cleared his throat. "They're from Kimberly."

"Kimberly?" A tingling sensation swept up the back of his neck and across his face. "When in tarnation was she here?"

"A few days ago," Steve said.

"Man, I must've been out of it."

Matthew gave a crooked grin that hinted at a hidden wild side. "Who's Kimberly?"

Dan chuckled with a dry, cynical sound. "My boss."

"Oh," Matthew said. The tips of his ears turned bright red. "Sorry. I've only ever heard you refer to your boss as Dr. Stetson."

"She wants you back," Steve said.

"What are you talking about?"

"Kimberly turned down state funding. She told your wife that she's holding your position, so if you decide to stay, I'll understand," Steve said.

Dan dragged his hand through his tousled hair. "You've got to be kidding me." He clenched his jaw tightly. *Dang that witch for being so arrogant, making me feel insignificant and passé.* He turned toward the large bear and had a sudden urge to pitch it across the room. "Forget it, man," he shouted. "She can keep my resignation."

"Ok, ok," Steve said, motioning him to calm down. "No worries. Discuss it with Gianna, and whatever you decide, let me know." He stood up. "I've got to head out now."

"All right, but on your way out, take that bear and balloons and drop them off in pediatrics."

"C'mon, don't think about it anymore. You're going to get your blood pressure up," Steve said.

"I won't if you get that thing out of here!"

"Ok. I'm on it," Steve said, gathering up the bear and balloons. "Just relax."

"Thank you."

Matthew sat forward in his chair and scrubbed his hand across his chin. "Man, Kimberly really knows how to rattle your cage."

Dan gave him an icy stare and pointed his finger at him. "Don't get me started, pal."

"For Pete's sake, what did she do to you?"

"Nothing." He turned his face, hoping the dim lighting in the room would hide his raw, chafed emotions. *Ooh, that Kimberly really burns my butt.* She left his mind in turmoil and his heart in an uproar. *Dang you, woman. I sold my home because of you. I nearly lost Gianna, twice, because of you.* He took a deep, painful breath and closed his eyes, but Kimberly's seductive lure prowled in the shadows of his mind. He recalled the first time she had attempted to ruin his relationship with Gianna.

Dan had stood outside the doorway to Kimberly's office, the air charged with tension. He wondered what he had done wrong again. He knocked on the slightly ajar door and asked, "You wanted to speak with me?"

"Yes. Close the door and have a seat."

"What can I do for you, Dr. Stetson?" he asked as he lowered himself into the chair in front of her desk.

"There's a leadership conference I'd like you to attend with me next week, in Florida."

Dan sighed. "Dr. Stetson, it's bad timing."

She pranced around to the front of her desk and modeled against it in a provocative fashion.

"Dan, this is your opportunity to go places, to move up in the world. You want to be part owner of this clinic someday, don't you?" she asked.

"No thanks," he shouted.

She leaned forward, enticing him with a glimpse of her cleavage. "Loosen up, Dan," she whispered as she adjusted his tie. She reached for his left hand and held it up. "Besides, I don't see a ring."

Heat curled inside him, threatening his control. He yanked his hand back. "You know I'm getting married in two weeks."

"Come on, honey. Live it up. These are your final days of being a bachelor." Her hands began to stray downward toward places that didn't need attention. "We'll have a fun time; I guarantee it."

Dan pounded his fist on the desk, then exploded from the chair. "Never going to happen," he shouted and thundered out the door.

With a shake of his head, Dan banished the memory. He dropped his gaze to Gianna's little bear that he held tightly in his hands and focused on her positive pregnancy test. *Perfect. At least the second time Kimberly interfered resulted in a happy ending.* He flexed his fingers and soothed them over the fluffy, soft bear to release the tension in him. He lifted his eyes to the ceiling. *Thank you, God.*

Matthew spoke up. "Talk to me, bud. We've been friends for a long time. I know when you're hurting."

Dan set the bear down on the bed tray. *Matt's right.* He looked at him and sighed, "Kimberly can't accept no for an answer."

"Maybe she doesn't want you to have any regrets."

"It's not that at all." Dan rubbed his aching head. "Back in July, she called me into her office and asked me to accompany her to a conference in Florida. She put on her flirtatious moves and told me we could celebrate my final bachelor days together."

"Get serious," Matthew said.

"I am. I walked out on her."

"Did you ever tell Gianna?"

"Are you kidding? Our relationship was already strained because of Chad."

"Oh, right. That schmuck caused enough turmoil. And with my sister being the jealous type, I can see why you never told her."

"Yep. The past can stay in the past. I don't need to stir up any more grief. Kimberly's done enough of that already."

"Oh, like that little sticky note she left in your jacket pocket for Gianna to find?"

"Let's not go there again. Gianna flipped out on me. I thought we were done."

"Can you blame her?" Matthew asked.

"No," Dan mumbled, lowering his eyes. "Kimberly purposely made me look like a two-timer." Dan shook his head. "She's had it in for me ever since I was hired."

"Why'd you say that?" he asked.

"She had asked me out. I told her I wanted to keep our relationship on a professional level."

Matthew tapped his chin. "Oh, right. I forgot you told me that. And you said she didn't take it well."

"No. She purposely scheduled me for every holiday except Thanksgiving last year, and that's only because of your wedding."

Matthew flipped his wrist. "So, she's a little vindictive."

"A little? When I announced my engagement, I overheard her tell my colleague, 'Oh, what a waste.'"

"Ok, so she's bitter and jealous, too."

"Well, she needs to get over it."

"I can see why you don't want to go back."

"Exactly. She's determined to ruin my marriage."

"You think?" Matthew asked.

Dan swallowed hard.

"Then I guess your mind is made up," Matthew said.

"Yep, I'll let Steve know next time I see him."

Dan rested his head against the pillow and closed his eyes. He imagined driving his pickup truck along a rutted dirt road with the windows rolled down, listening to country music. *Yes! I can just feel the warm breeze blowing in my face. Ah! And the air, smelling like a freshly plowed field. Yep, I'm so sure. Good times to come, good times.*

The hushed sound of happy voices and giggles reached Dan's ears. He opened his eyes and saw Gianna and Jessica sliding the curtain open. "Hey, did you two get lost?"

"No, we took a long walk outside," Gianna said.

"How was it?"

"Cold," Jessica said, shivering.

"It's not as nice as last Saturday," Gianna said.

Dan groaned. "Tell me about it. Last weekend, I was standing on a footbridge overlooking a magnificent waterfall." He lifted his head from the pillow. "Oh, babe, I saw this beautiful full-circle rainbow."

"I know. I saw your pictures."

"Oh, you got that text I sent you?"

"Not exactly. Rob gave me your phone." She stared at the floor and mumbled, "I drowned mine."

Dan laughed bitterly as blinding pain swept through him. "It's ok, we'll get you a new one."

Chapter Twenty-Three

Dan moaned. The pain hit him as sharp as a steel-toed kick in the ribs. Getting out of bed for the first time in three weeks was harder than he imagined. "I can't do this," he grunted as Patrice, his physical therapist, guided him into a wheelchair.

"You're doing fine, Daniel," she said.

"Yeah, sure, as long as I don't move." He exhaled as he settled into the chair.

"Oh, come on. You'll get there," Patrice encouraged. "Look, you have full use of your arms now." She adjusted his footrest. "How about giving this thing a whirl? See if you can wheel yourself to the doorway."

Dan peered across the room, analyzing the task at hand. "I'm willing to give it a try. Anything is better than being stuck in that bed."

"That's what I want to hear," she said. She turned and walked toward the doorway. "Ok, whenever you're ready, give it a spin."

Dan gripped the push-rim and rolled himself forward. Burning pain surged through his midsection. "Man, this hurts," he grumbled. When he reached the doorway, he panted, "Thank God that's over with."

"Well done," Patrice said.

"Great, can I get out of here now?"

"Hold your horses, cowboy. Dr. Murphy's working on it. He's arranging your transfer to rehab. Once you're comfortable with self-care, they'll discharge you home."

Dan nodded. "Fair enough." He reached up and rubbed his prickly jaw. "Do you think they'd let me shave and shower before I leave?"

"Let me check with your nurse."

While Dan waited, he practiced wheeling himself around the room. The more he navigated the chair, the less painful it became. *Heck, now I know how old man Hill felt in this clunky thing. The poor guy crashed into everything. I guess it didn't help that he was practically blind.*

Within a few minutes, there was a light knock at the door. Lily, a sweet nurse-in-training, who Dan had mistaken earlier for a candy-striper, entered the room. She stood there like a statue with her hands clasped tightly in front of her. "Uh, Dr. Christiansen, right?" she asked, her voice hardly above a whisper.

"Yes, ma'am, but you can call me Dan."

"Uh, your nurse Beth sent me in. You wanted to shower?" Lily asked. Her cheeks flushed something fierce, and she quickly broke eye contact. Her combination of politeness and bashfulness grabbed his attention.

"Yes, but I'd like to shave first."

"Oh, right," she said. Her eyes scanned the room, then settled back on him. "Ok." She stepped inside the bathroom and turned on the light. She mumbled something, then stepped out. "I'll...uh...be right back with some hand towels."

Dan smiled kindly, and after she left, he shook his head. *Poor thing. She floundered in her confusion like a duck in a pond. But she'll learn the ropes eventually.*

He maneuvered his wheelchair through the bathroom doorway and parked it in front of the sink counter. He caught a glimpse of his reflection in the mirror and wondered who that stranger was staring back at him. Seeing himself for the first time after his accident was dreadful. *Geez, Gianna never told me how awful I look.* He touched his unkempt jaw. *Dang, doesn't anyone know how to sculpt a manicured scruff? I look like a grizzly bear.*

He shifted his eyes up to the healing laceration on his forehead and glided his fingertip over the wound. He flinched at the sting. *Ooh, that's going to leave a scar.* He played with his hair and gave himself a few wispy bangs to hide the damage.

"I'm back," Lily said, carrying an armful of personal care items and some towels. As she attempted to set them down on the counter, she dropped the tiny tube of toothpaste. "I'm so sorry, sir." She reached down to pick it up and dropped the plastic disposable razor. "Doctor, I'm so, so sorry."

Dan couldn't help but feel responsible for her jittery disposition. In his profession, it wasn't unusual for a nurse to feel intimidated by a physician. He gently placed his hand on her forearm and said, "Hey, it's ok. I'll take it from here."

Lily stared at him tongue-tied, obviously stunned by his cool, calm persona. "Oh, very well. Thank you." She stumbled backward into the wall. "Uh, when you're ready to shower, pull the call cord, and I'll come back to assist you." She turned and hurried out of the bathroom.

"Thank you," he called out, not knowing if she heard him. *Shoot, what'd I do to that girl? She was jumpier than a frog in heavy traffic. Am I that scary looking?*

He gazed at himself in the mirror and raised his eyebrows. *Now if only I could have the same negative impact on Kimberly.* He twisted his mouth, then reached for the soap and razor.

After Dan finished shaving, he pulled the call cord. Minutes later, Lily returned with Beth.

"Hey, handsome," Beth said, greeting him with her bubbly personality. "Sorry I missed you earlier, but I was in the middle of a procedure with another patient."

"No problem, ma'am. You left me in good hands," he said, winking at Lily.

Lily returned an appreciative smile. "Thanks."

"Ok," Beth said, clasping her hands together. "Now, are you sure you don't want a sponge bath?"

"No, thank you. I don't want to seem ungrateful, but I need to step up and start caring for myself."

"Very well," she said. She eyed the supplies on the sink counter and grabbed the waterproof sleeves. "We need to put these on your casts to keep them dry."

As Beth prepped him, Dan swallowed his pride. *Really? Has it come to this?* Reliability and responsibility had always been his strong points. *I'm a doctor. I treat patients and deliver babies.* It felt degrading to him to have to rely on someone else to assist him with personal care. *This just isn't right. I shouldn't be here.*

"Ok, Dan. Now use your upper body and shift your bottom to the edge of the wheelchair."

"I can do this," he said, optimistically. He grasped the chair arms and slid forward.

"You got it," she said. She signaled Lily, and together, they lifted him out of the chair. "Now use the shower bars to lower yourself onto the shower seat."

Dan grabbed the bars and eased himself down onto the bench. He wailed. White hot bolts of pain came welling up. After the pain settled, he panted, "I'm good. It's all good."

"You sure?" Beth asked. "Maybe we need to ask Dr. Murphy to adjust your pain meds."

"I'm o.k.," he huffed. He attempted to unsnap his gown, but as he twisted, pain dug into his ribs and tore at his confidence. "Forget it. I can't do this."

"Ok. Let me help you."

He sighed, then leaned forward to allow Beth to untie his gown. He could hardly force himself to make eye contact. "Thank you," he uttered.

"It's Ok. That's what I'm here for," she said, carefully removing his gown.

"Being a physician, you'd think I'd be conditioned."

"Don't worry about it. We're all human," she said.

Beth turned on the water and adjusted the temperature. "How does this feel?" she asked, spraying some water on his arm.

"Good."

Dan tilted his head back and closed his eyes. The flowing hot water soothed his body but did nothing to drown the pain.

Lord, I'm so weak. Please, help me get through this. I can't do this alone. I know it is not your intent to take me this far and then leave me. Please, heal my broken body and my soul so that I may fulfill your will, whatever that may be. Amen.

Late that afternoon, Dan arrived at the inpatient rehab facility in the city. It was an old stone building built in the 1930s that had been recently renovated.

Carly, his new nurse, gave him a tour of the facilities, then transported him to his room. "Here we are," she said, wheeling him inside.

"Thanks," Dan said.

The mild lemony scent of furniture polish greeted him at the door, giving him the notion that the room was just cleaned. He scanned the soft green space. Both beds were made up neatly with ivory coverlets.

"Do I have a roommate?" he asked.

"Not yet. Very rarely is a bed ever vacant," Carly said. She wheeled him to the second bed, parking him in front of the window. "Most likely you'll have a roommate by the end of the week."

"Fine, as long as he doesn't snore," Dan joked.

"Could be worse." Carly laughed. "I'm sure you know that coming from your profession, doctor."

"Absolutely."

She handed him the TV remote. "Make yourself at home. Dinner will be served in the dining area at five."

"Thanks, ma'am."

Dan channel surfed, but there was nothing entertaining on. He clicked the TV off and spun his wheelchair around to face the window. He reached for the rod and managed to open the blinds with ease. *Oh, man! What a view.* Directly in front of him was an ugly, tall, windowless building, and five stories below was a parking lot filled with garbage trucks. *Thank God it's November. I can just imagine the rancid stink in July. I won't miss this when we move.*

Dan swiveled his wheelchair toward his bed. He reached for his pillow but dropped it on the floor. *Smart move, genius. Now how am I going to pick it up?*

"Oh, Danny! You're out of bed."

Startled by Gianna's voice, he turned to find her standing in the doorway with her mouth hanging open.

"Yeah, how about it? Like my new set of wheels?"

"Uh-huh," she cried. "I couldn't wait for this day."

"Shh, don't cry. I told you I'd get better."

"I can't help it. I'm so happy for you." She stepped into the room and laid her purse down on the table. "Here, let me help you with that." She picked up the pillow and propped it behind him. "How's that?"

"Much better, thank you," he said.

Gianna lowered herself into a chair. "This looks like a decent place," she said, bobbing her head in approval.

Dan gave a careless shrug. "Yeah, I guess so."

"Well, at least you're back home in the city."

"Yeah, I suppose." He stared out the window at the ugly, crime-ridden neighborhood. *What drew me here, I'll never know.*

He looked at Gianna. Her petite frame held surprising strength. "So, how's my girl feeling today?" he asked.

Gianna rubbed her stomach. "Pretty good, that is until I walked here. With all the raw fumes and fried grease, I nearly tossed my cookies."

Dan sighed. "Please, whatever you do, just don't eat anything from those food vendors."

"Believe me. There's no chance of that."

"So, how'd yesterday go?"

"Fine," she mumbled. She dropped her gaze and stared at her empty hands. "All our stuff's in storage, thanks to Matt, Troy, Steve, and Rob."

Dan heard the disappointment in her voice and felt her frustration, too. *I should've been there. It was my responsibility to move us.* "How can I ever thank them?" he asked.

"You can't. I tried by taking everyone out to dinner."

"Oh, that was a nice idea."

"Not really. They refused to let me pay. They all dropped twenties on the table. Matt handed me the cash and told me to keep it. He footed the entire bill himself."

"What?" Dan asked. Quickly he looked away to hide his emotions. *That's crazy.* He swiped a tear with his thumb, then met her gaze. "Well, I'm going to have to yell at all of them when I get out of here."

Gianna reached for his hand. "Let's pray." She bowed her head. "Father, thank you for blessing us with our special friends and family. We are forever grateful for the love and kindness they have shown us during this challenging time. Please guide them and protect them in all that they do. Amen."

"Amen," Dan said. He leaned his head back against his pillow and closed his eyes. It suddenly dawned on him that Thanksgiving was Thursday. He lifted his head from the pillow and said, "I'm so sorry."

"For what?" she asked.

For wrecking your life. "For us not being on the flight home to Montana with Matt and Jessica."

"It's ok," she said.

"No, it's not. I broke my promise to you."

"Danny, stop!" she pleaded. "We've been over this before." She held his hands firmly and said, "I'm thankful you're alive and we're together. That's all that matters."

"No, you deserve more." Guilt hit him like a freight train. "I pushed you into selling our home. I should've listened to you and not jumped on the first offer."

"Danny—"

"Let me finish." He raised his hand in a gesture to silence her. He lifted his eyes to the ceiling. *God, help me fix this.* He looked at Gianna and took her hand. "Listen, I will accept Kimberly's offer. We'll back out of the contract."

"No, it's ok." She smoothed her delicate fingers up and down his forearm. "Steve's a great guy." Her warm gaze touched him with hope. "This is your opportunity to a partnership with him. Don't throw it away. I believe this is God's will for us."

Dan sighed. "Is the settlement still on for Friday?"

"Yes," she answered firmly.

Dan dropped his fist down on the armrest. "Dang, I need to get out of here. I need to be there."

"Well, you can't."

He folded his arms across his chest. "Are you sure you're ok with this?"

"Yes, sweetheart," she said, standing up. She walked behind his chair and massaged his shoulders. "You granted me power of attorney. I've got this. Besides, Troy's coming with me."

"He is? Ok, good."

"Relax, Danny." She leaned forward and kissed him. "Everything's going to work out."

Gianna accompanied Dan to the community dining room for supper and visited him late into the evening. With the help of his nurse, she assisted him with personal care, then afterward, nestled him into bed.

"I should get going," she said, tucking in his blankets. "Troy and Tracy invited me to stay at their place," she said.

Dan blinked back his tears thinking about his generous friends. "Please, thank them for me."

"I will."

"And, babe, make sure you take a cab home."

"Sure, ok," she said, pulling on her coat.

"Babe, I'm serious. And next time, use my truck."

Gianna sat down on the edge of the bed. "I'll be fine," she said, stroking his cheek. "It's early yet and there are plenty people out and about."

"I worry about you," he said.

"Relax," she said, leaning into him. "I love you." She brushed his lips with soft, teasing kisses, then rubbed her mouth against his throat. While running her warm, smooth hand over his chest, she peered up at him with her soft, brown eyes. "I miss you."

Desire raced through him like fire chasing dried leaves. A low moan of pleasure slipped past his lips. "I miss you, too." He paused to tame his rapid breathing and heartbeat, then uttered, "But I'm not well enough for this."

Gianna stilled her caressing hand on his chest. "Oh, right. I'm sorry." She sat upright. "I should go."

He took her hand. "No, please don't." A pang of longing shot through him. "Stay with me tonight."

"Are you sure?"

He nodded. "Lie next to me."

A soft smile eased the somberness of her face. She removed her coat and draped it over the chair, then eased herself down on the bed and cuddled deep into his embrace. When her arms closed around him, he almost felt like he was back home.

He kissed the top of her head and closed his eyes. As he drifted off to sleep, his cell phone rang. *Dang.* He reached for it on the end table and answered it.

"Hello?" he muttered.

"Dan?"

"Troy? Is everything ok?"

"Is Gianna with you?"

"Yeah, she fell asleep."

"Ok. I was checking to see if she needs a ride home."

"No. She's staying here with me tonight, but I thank you for opening your home to her."

"No problem, cowboy. Good night."

Chapter Twenty-Four

The week flew by, and Thanksgiving came and went. It was noon on Friday, and Dan had just returned to his room after an intense therapy session. "Glad that's over with," he huffed.

"You're doing fantastic," Birdie, his therapist, said, pulling the door open.

Dan smelled the delicious aroma of an open-faced turkey sandwich wafting through the air. Quickly, he gripped the push-rim of his chair and wheeled himself toward the table, where his meal awaited him.

"Look at you go," she said. "Just one week of PT and you're whipping that thing around like Dale Earnhardt driving a race car."

Dan laughed. "I worked up an appetite."

"Oh, is that what it is?" she asked, putting her hand on her hip. "Keep up your superior driving and you'll be discharged to outpatient rehab by the end of next week."

Dan nodded. "I'm ready!"

"I like your enthusiasm, but we have to get you balancing on your feet first," she said. She touched his shoulder. "Eat your lunch, and I'll make a call to your orthopedist to find out when you can start bearing weight on those fractures."

"Thank you," he said.

"No problem," Birdie said before leaving the room.

Dan bowed his head and prayed.

Heavenly Father, thank you for the many blessings that you poured over me despite my foolish mistakes. Thank you for your endless love. Guide me in all that I do so that I may follow your will. Please have mercy on me and protect my family. Amen.

Later that afternoon, Dan lay in his bed reflecting on his rehab progress. *I made it this far. God willing, I'll be out of here in another week.* He clenched his bottom lip between his teeth, pondering where they were going to live. *I guess it doesn't matter as long as we're together.*

"What a day," he yawned. As he dozed off, a knock at the door jarred him awake. "Come in," he uttered.

Gianna entered the room.

"Oh, hey, baby. How'd the closing go this morning?"

"Fine," she muttered.

Her brown eyes were filled with sadness, tearing his heart to pieces. "You ok?" he asked, sensing she'd be a mixed bag of emotions. "Was it hard handing over the keys?"

"Nope," she said, tossing her purse onto the table. She sat at the foot of the bed with her shoulders hunched and her elbows resting on her knees. "I'm over it. I shed all my tears the night I carried out the last box."

Dan sighed. "Thank you for doing this for me and for staying so strong. Things *are* going to get better."

Gianna shook her head. "The medical bills are pouring in."

"Oh, man!" He tightened his fists. "They don't even wait for the bed to get cold. How bad?"

She reached into her purse and pulled out a stack of envelopes. She handed them to him, one by one. "Here's one for the helicopter rescue, the ER, OR, ICU, radiology, and anesthesiology."

Dan lifted an eyebrow. "Is that all?"

"Aren't these enough?"

"Oh, there'll be more. Don't be surprised if you see one from housekeeping," he joked. He pushed up on his elbows while she positioned two pillows underneath him. "Thanks," he said. He studied the bills carefully, then ran his hand through his hair. "No big deal. My insurance will cover a good portion of these."

"You sure? I don't understand insurance."

Dan handed the bills back to her. "Whatever isn't covered, we'll have to pay out of the sale of our home."

"What?! We need that money for a down payment on another house. Where're we going to live?"

"We might have to rent awhile," he said.

Gianna tossed him a helpless female look that he couldn't resist. He held her chin in his hand.

"I'm really sorry."

"It's not your fault," she said.

"Yeah, it is. I was clumsy."

"Danny, don't," she said, peering into his eyes. "It could've happened to anyone." She leaned in and kissed his lips. "You're healing. That's what's important."

"Yeah, sure," he mumbled.

He turned and looked out the window at the darkness. He hated watching her unravel before him. *I'm a useless husband. No matter what I do, I can't seem to get it right. She can do better without me.*

"Sweetheart, look at me," she pleaded. "Don't shut down on me. I love you."

He met her gaze. "I love you, too." He rubbed her belly. "And I love you, little one."

Dan's cell phone vibrated its way across the table. Gianna clicked her tongue against her teeth. "Oh, now what?" she asked, reaching for it.

"What is it?" Dan asked.

"A text from Troy. He wants me to meet him at the hospital. Tracy's in labor." She looked up at him, her face as pale as a ghost. "She's only thirty-two weeks."

Dan propped himself up in the bed despite the discomfort he felt in his ribs. His brain shifted into doctor mode, contemplating the many causes of preterm labor and the complications that could occur with early delivery. *This isn't good, but I'm not Tracy's OB, and I can't worry Gianna either.* He reached for Gianna's hand and said, "Ok, listen to me. I know this may seem scary, but Tracy is under the best of care. I know her physician, and he's highly qualified."

Gianna nodded, then handed him the phone. "I'll let you know what happens."

"Ok. Call me even if it's the middle of the night."
She leaned in and kissed him. "I love you."
"Love you, too."

Hours later, Dan was awakened by Gianna's call.
"Hey, babe. How's Tracy?"
"She's fine. The doctor was able to stop her labor, but he put her on strict bed rest."
"Ok, good."
"Um, Troy gave me the key to his place so I can stay there. He's staying with her tonight at the hospital, but he's working the weekend, so Tracy wants me to stay with her. Is that ok with you?"
"Yeah, sure. You know where to find me."
"Thanks. Love you, Danny."
"Love you, too." He placed his phone down on the table and sighed. *Man, I wish there was something that I could do.* He cupped his hands over his face and prayed. *Oh, Lord, I know I've been calling on you more often than usual lately. But please help our dear friends, Troy and Tracy. Give them peace as they go through this pregnancy. Please protect the life of their little one, and help it grow as close to full term as possible. Amen.*

It was Sunday afternoon. After another intense therapy session, Dan returned to his room. "Man, I'm whipped."
"You worked hard," Birdie said.
Dan covered his mouth to suppress his yawn. "I can't remember the last time I felt this tired."
Birdie put her hand on her hip. "Really?"

"Ok, scratch that. I can. It was during my residency."
"Rest up. I'll see you in the morning," she said.
"Ok, thanks."

Exhausted, Dan drifted off to dreamland, back in time to when he was ten. He had been playing fetch in his backyard with his dog, Angel. They had played for hours, but she never tuckered out. To get her to quit, he dropped to the ground and played dead. Angel pounced on him. She buried her wet nose in his face and licked him until he *woke up.* "Ok, ok, girl," he had said, giggling and rolling around on the grass with his hands covering his face.

Dan's dream ended abruptly when he was awakened by a cold, wet nose nudging the side of his head and a paw scratching at his shoulder.

"What the?" he grumbled.

He opened his eyes and saw Denim sitting beside him, panting. He scooched into a sitting position and saw Rob sitting in the rocker with his leg swung over the tabletop.

"Man, I thought I was dreaming," he said.

"I don't know about that, but you were snoring," Rob said, laughing.

"So, what's up?"

"Denim works here on Sundays as a therapy dog, so we thought we'd stop by and sign your cast."

"Funny," Dan said with a dry laugh.

"I'm not trying to be funny. You survived Demon's Trail. I should be asking you for your autograph."

"Get the heck out of here," Dan said. "That wasn't even Demon's Trail."

"Ok, Demon's Cliff." Rob walked toward the window. "Hey, uh, crappy view outside your room."

Dan held his side, trying hard not to laugh at Rob's warped sense of humor. "Yeah, tell me about it. I can't wait to get out of here."

"When's that happening?"

"Not until my fractures are healed enough to bear weight on them...and when I can care for myself."

"Oh, that sucks."

"Yep, and Gianna can't lift me because—"

The tapping sound of high heels in the corridor disrupted Dan's thought process, and Kimberly's sudden appearance startled him.

"What're you doing here?" he asked her.

"I came to see you," she said.

"Why? You have my resignation."

"We need to talk," she said, resting her fisted hands on the flair of her hips. She glared at Rob. "In private, please."

Rob's gaze followed her tall feminine frame up and down. "Is that a hint?" he asked. He pointed to the door. "I was just leaving." He stepped away from the window. As he walked past her, he leaned in and inhaled her sweet scent. "Go easy on him, sugar," he whispered, then signaled Denim, "Come, boy."

Kimberly frowned at her displeasure. "*Who* was that?"

"Dr. Ross's younger brother."

She raised her eyebrows. "Steve has a brother?" She turned and lingered her gaze on the doorway. "Maybe I see a vague resemblance." She rubbed her hands together. "Anyway, let's get down to business."

"Kimberly, I told you. I won't participate in abortions."

"Didn't your wife tell you? I declined state funding."

"Yeah, she told me."

"I'm expanding the practice so we can specialize in high-risk pregnancies."

"Do you expect me to believe your cock and bull story after you shot down my moral beliefs? Whatever happened to 'a woman's right to choose,' huh?"

"I've changed," she said.

Dan laughed with sarcasm. "Really? Well, that's good for the unborn babies, but it's too late for me. I'm leaving the city."

"Dan, don't. We can work through this." She leaned forward and brushed her fingers over his collar and the ends of his hair. "Your patients are going to miss you. I'm going to miss you."

He swallowed harshly at the touch of her hand on his skin. He jerked his head sideways. "Stop! Enough already."

"What?" Kimberly asked. "I'm offering you a percentage of ownership in the practice."

"Don't you get it? I sold my home because of you."

"So what? Buy another one. With my proposal you can afford so much more." Determination oozed from her with every word. "I'll make it worth your while."

The stubborn burn in her eyes infuriated him. He glared at her with smoldering intensity.

"Save it, Kimberly! I'm moving to the country where I belong."

Chapter Twenty-Five

Gianna sat in the corner of the waiting room next to the Christmas tree. "Ok, I'll see you when you get here," she said, ending the call. She clutched Tracy's phone tightly. *Hurry, Troy.* She leaned forward in the rocking chair. *Please God, help the doctor stop Tracy's contractions.*

She rose to her feet and wandered across the quiet waiting room to the window. Light December snow fell onto the bustling city streets. *My word! Doesn't anyone stay home in inclement weather anymore?* Although the forecast only predicted a dusting, an inch or more of snow covered the parked cars in the hospital lot.

She turned away from the window. A hot, wavering sensation came over her and the room began to spin. *Ooh, I've got to sit down.* She held onto the back of the couch and ambled her way to the other side. She sat down and leaned forward, putting her head to her knees. *I'd better eat something.* She reached into her bag and took out a granola bar and a bottle of water.

After she ate, she leaned back on the couch and closed her weary eyes. Sleep was within arm's length.

"Gianna!" Troy rushed into the waiting room.

His startling voice sent a rush of adrenaline through her, pushing her to her feet. "Thank God you're here."

"How's Tracy?" he asked.

Gianna shook her head. "They sent me out here."

"Let's go," he insisted. He took her hand and hurried her down the corridor toward Tracy's room.

A nurse greeted them at the doorway. "Good you're here, Mr. Evans. They're prepping your wife for a C-section."

"Can't they stop the contractions?" he asked.

"The baby is showing signs of distress."

Gianna was hit with a nauseating wave. "Oh, no!"

"Can I see her?" he asked.

"Yes, but let's get you changed into scrubs, first."

Gianna placed her hand on Troy's shoulder. "You go on. I'll wait in the waiting room."

The once-quiet waiting room was now filled with a noisy crowd of bubbly faces huddling around a new dad showing off pictures of his newborn.

Gianna smiled graciously. "Congratulations."

She squeezed her way past the group of excited visitors and settled back down in the rocker next to the tree. She rocked back and forth while she waited, anticipating Troy's happy announcement. *Please, God, please let Tracy and her baby be ok. Amen.*

She focused on the multicolored twinkling lights, becoming mesmerized by their joyful dance. It wasn't long before exhaustion took over, pushing out all her worries and fears. She dozed off, and what seemed like only seconds later, she woke to a gentle tap on her shoulder.

"Gianna, wake up," Troy said.

She blinked away at the last bits of sleep.

"Good news?" she asked.

A huge smile ripped across his face. "It's a girl! Trinity Noelle Evans. Three pounds, fourteen ounces, seventeen inches long."

Gianna's spirits soared. "Aw, congratulations!" She reached for Troy's hand. "So, mom and baby are ok?"

"Tracy's fine. They're finishing up her surgery now. Trinity's having a little difficulty breathing on her own, so they moved her to the NICU for monitoring. She'll have to stay there until she gets stronger."

"Oh, she will. She'll grow fast."

It was noon on Thursday. The taxi pulled up to the main entrance of the rehab center, and Gianna handed the driver a twenty. "Thank you, sir." *The fare was worth every dollar.*

She opened the door and exited the car, then watched the taxi pull out into the nonstop, horn-honking traffic. *My goodness! Get over yourselves, people. And Danny wonders why I won't drive his truck through this crazy city, let alone hunt for a parking space. Lord knows I can't parallel park. For all I care, his truck can sit in the lot until he can drive it again.*

"Gianna, Gianna, wait up!"

She turned to Steve's lively voice calling out her name.

"Steve, what're you still doing here?" Gianna asked. "I thought you left last Wednesday."

"I did. I spent Thanksgiving in New Jersey with my wife and family, then came back here Friday night to cover the weekend on-call shift at the hospital."

"But I thought you were done," she said.

Steve's face turned a rosy red, but not from the bitter cold weather. "Well, yeah, I did, but I...uh...felt sorry for Kimberly," he babbled. "You know, being short-staffed without Dan or me there."

"Uh-huh," Gianna said. She smiled wryly. "Kimberly gave you the guilt trip, did she?"

"Well, you know, it's Christmas. I did it for the patients," Steve said.

"It's Advent, actually. People forget that and jump right into Christmas."

"True. Anyway, I'm still here." He put his finger to his chin. "You know, it's about time you come in for your appointment."

"Does this mean bloodwork?"

Steve nodded. "It's routine."

Gianna took a step backward.

"Now, you're not nervous, are you?" he asked.

"A little bit. I don't like needles."

"You'll be fine," he said. He wrapped his arm around her, "C'mon. Let's visit Dan."

"Ok." She glanced at her watch. "He should be finished with his PT session by now."

"How's he been doing?"

"Um, better. I haven't seen him in a few days, but I spoke to him last night. He complained about his sore ribs and how his leg casts are causing intense itching."

Steve chuckled. "Sounds like he's getting better."

Gianna tapped on the slightly ajar door to Danny's room. "Hello?" she called out.

"Just a moment," a man with a raspy voice answered.

The squeak-thumping sound of crutches grew louder before the door swung open. A disheveled man with a broken leg, hunched over on his crutches, stood there in the doorway. He reeked of body odor and cheap cologne.

"Hello, doll," the man said. He glanced at Steve then back at Gianna. "What can I do for you two?"

Gianna stuttered, "I'm, uh, looking for my husband, Danny. Is he here?"

"Nope. He went to therapy."

Gianna glanced at the time. "Still?"

"Yep, um, some woman doctor was here earlier."

Gianna looked over her shoulder at Steve then glanced back at the man and said, "Thank you."

She hurried down the corridor toward the elevator.

"Where's the fire?" Steve asked, huffing as he tried to keep her pace. "Are you ok?"

She pinched her nose. "If I don't get fresh air, I'm going to puke. Danny didn't mention that his new roommate bathed himself in bathroom polo."

Gianna stopped at the elevator and pressed the button.

"I didn't know he had a roommate," Steve said.

"Yeah, since Monday, but I hadn't met him yet."

Gianna pulled the double doors open to the fitness room, but Danny wasn't there. No one was there, or so she thought. A heavy thud from a closing door thundered across the gym. Seconds later, Birdie emerged carrying some dumbbells.

"Oh, hi, Gianna," Birdie called. "If you're looking for your husband, he's in the lounge." She pointed at the door. "It's down the hall and to your left."

"Ok, thanks." She turned on her heel and said to Steve, "At least he's becoming more mobile."

"I told you. It just takes time," he said. He took her hand and said, "Let's go."

Gianna and Steve entered the festively decorated lounge. Silver and gold garland with white lights adorned the windows and doors. A wreath with a red velvet ribbon hung above the stone fireplace where Danny was sitting in his wheelchair talking on his cell phone.

"Yes. My orthopedist is sending my medical records," he said. He flipped the page on his notepad. "My first outpatient appointment is on the eighteenth."

Gianna touched Steve's shoulder and spoke in an eager whisper, "Oh, he's being discharged! Now we can finally move on with our lives!"

Her bubble of excitement quickly burst when she felt the stares of onlookers. She glanced over her shoulder at a group of seniors sitting at a card table. She smiled and gave them a tiny wave. They smiled in return, then resumed their game.

Gianna turned her attention to Steve. "Sometime after Danny is discharged, do you think you can take us to New Jersey? You know, show us the town, your new practice, introduce us to your family?"

Steve's response to her question was delayed.

"Uh, sure," he said, unbuttoning his coat. "But first, let's see if Dan feels up to it."

Gianna nodded and set her gaze on Danny's handsome face. He looked so much better. The bruises on his face and arms were healed. His left leg was now in an air cast, but his right leg, which had the compound fracture and the bad infection, still had the plaster cast.

She bowed her head and prayed. *Thank you, Lord, for healing him and giving him the strength to carry on.*

She looked up again at Danny. When their eyes met, he winked at her.

"Ok, doc. See you soon," Danny said. When he ended his call, he waved them over.

Gianna greeted him with a hug and kiss. "I missed you."

"Not anymore, babe. You're going to get sick of me," he said with a satisfied smile. "I'm out of here tomorrow."

"That's great news," Steve said, shaking his hand. "So, how do you feel?"

"Much better," Danny said, looking down at his legs. "I can put some weight on my left leg, but I can't say much for this one." He patted his right thigh. "I really busted it up bad. It's going to be weeks before I can stand on it."

Steve nodded with confidence. "You'll get there." He glanced at Gianna, then back to Danny. "Hey, uh, how do you feel about taking a drive this week to meet my family and check out the area?"

Danny smiled and shook his head. "I...uh..." He looked down at the floor and sighed. "This was a tough decision." He lifted his gaze to Steve. "I thank you for your offer, but I can't move to New Jersey."

Gianna's stomach fluttered. *What?* She opened her mouth, but the words would not come.

"I'm so sorry, Steve," he said.

"No, no. Don't be. Things change. Life happens. Kimberly has given you a fantastic opportunity, way more than I can offer. I understand that you can't pass it up."

"Wait, what?" Gianna felt like a curve ball that had kept going in circles. "But you said Kimberly—"

"Babe, forget Kimberly," Danny said with a broad smile. "My time here in the Big Apple is up. We're going home."

Chapter Twenty-Six

Gianna took the window seat next to Danny in the bulkhead and watched the other passengers trudge down the aisle with their carry-on bags and children in tow. *Oh my!* A family with seven active boys and one more on the way just boarded the flight. The children were dressed in red and green candy cane print pajamas. They all wore Santa hats, each with their names printed in glitter.

"This flight must be the holiday travelers' special," Gianna whispered.

Danny chuckled. "That'll be us in a couple of years."

She patted his hand. "Oh, please, let me get through this pregnancy first, and then we'll talk about it."

The parents stopped in the aisle and steered their clan into the rows across from Gianna and Danny, completely filling that section of seating. *Oh, no!* Gianna rubbed her temples. *Oh, please don't be noisy. I need sleep.*

The obviously pregnant mother quickly settled her children into their seats, then handed out teddy bears and blankets with fluidity and calmness to her four youngest. "Now, boys," she said, "Please remember to be respectful of those around you."

The father closed the overhead compartment and turned to the three oldest boys. He pointed his finger and said, "I expect good behavior. No goofing around."

One little inquisitive boy of about the age of five stared at Danny. "Hey, mister. What happened to you?"

"Thomas!" the mother said. "Mind your manners." She looked at Danny and said, "I'm so sorry, sir."

"It's ok, ma'am," Danny said. He smiled at the boy. "I fell and broke both my legs."

"Does it hurt?" the boy asked.

"It did at first, but it's getting much better."

"Oh," the boy said, his stare still glued on Danny.

"Hey, I like your PJs and your hat," Danny said. "Are you one of Santa's elves?" he teased.

The little boy giggled. "No, silly. The elves are busy working in the toy shop."

Danny chuckled. He glanced at the mother and said, "I reckon I need to brush up on my elf trivia."

Another little boy about the age of four chimed in. "We're going to see Santa at the North Pole."

"Really? That's sounds like fun," Danny said.

"We're going to ride on his sleigh, but you can't go because you broke your leg."

Danny grimaced in good humor.

"Samuel, don't say that. It'll make him feel bad," Tommy, the five-year-old, said.

Danny coughed to cover up his laugh. "It's ok. I prefer sitting in front of a warm fireplace enjoying my hot cocoa."

Gianna smiled. She loved watching the animation in Danny's eyes as he interacted with the boys. She rested her hand on her stomach. *He's going to be a wonderful father.*

"Final and immediate boarding call," the flight attendant announced over the loudspeaker.

Gianna looked at the door. A last-minute couple boarded the plane carrying a newborn. *Aw, so precious.* As the parents settled into their seats, the tiny baby squeaked and grunted. His soft coos tugged at her heartstrings, taking her mind back to yesterday, when she had visited baby Trinity one last time. Sadness squeezed the breath from her lungs. *I'm going to miss watching her grow up.*

She rested her head against the seat and closed her eyes, recalling her painful good-byes to Troy and Tracy. The conversation was still so alive in her head.

"I'll miss you so much," she had told Tracy.

"Don't be saying that, girlfriend, because we'll be seeing you this summer," Tracy had said.

Gianna opened her eyes. Unshed tears caused her vision to waver. *Summertime is so far away.*

"Hey, you ok?" Danny asked, rubbing her forearm.

His soft touch comforted her fragile emotions.

"I can't stop thinking about leaving Troy and Tracy."

Danny lowered his head. "I know. It was tough, but it's not like we're never going to see them again."

"I really hope they can visit us this summer."

"Me, too."

Gianna turned toward the window and gazed into the night sky at the blurred lights that trailed alongside the ascending plane. Life was about to change again.

She always knew the time would come when she'd return home but had no idea her heart would ache so much. She blinked away her warm tears. She hated goodbyes.

Danny brushed his fingers along her cheek. "Hey, you're not having regrets, are you? We talked about this."

"No. I know, but it's hard leaving the past behind."

"Nothing says you can't take the memories with you." He reached for her hand and placed it on his heart. "The friendships we've made here will always be with us."

"I know, but I just need some time."

"Time is good," he said, soothing her hand with his. "Listen, we have an incredible future ahead of us, filled with hope and love. Give it a chance to happen."

Gianna clenched her bottom lip between her teeth. *He's right. It's a new beginning for us, a new baby, a new home, and hopefully, a less stressful job for him.*

She bowed her head and prayed. *Dear Lord, thank you for the opportunity to attend college here in New York and for allowing me to explore my independence and find out who I'm supposed to be. Along this journey, you've led me to some wonderful friends, whom I shall miss dearly, but if Montana's where I'm supposed to be, then I reckon it's time for me to go. Our families are there, so we shall be, too. I place my trust in you, Lord, and feel secure by your direction. Amen.*

A sense of peace washed away her reservations. She pulled the armrest up and leaned on Danny's shoulder.

Tipping her head up, she looked into his eyes. "I'm ready to go home."

Danny's handsome face broke into a smile. "It's going to be awesome, babe. And it'll feel more like home when the moving truck arrives next week. I promise, when I get back on my feet, literally," he chuckled, "I'm going to buy you your dream house."

"Oh, Danny! That's not what's important."

"Yeah, it is. It's my job to provide for my family. Besides, this little guy," he said, resting his hand on her abdomen, "is going to need a nursery."

"Or little girl," she said.

"Right."

Gianna sat upright in her seat. "Let's not rush the house hunt though. Mom and Dad said we can stay in the guest room until we're financially comfortable."

"Well, I don't want to overstay our welcome."

"Are you kidding me? Mom and Dad are thrilled to have us. You should've heard Mom's jubilant cries when I told her we were moving back home."

"Are you sure it's not just because of their grandbaby?"

Gianna giggled. "Maybe a little."

"If you remember, they weren't too thrilled with us raising a baby in the city," he said.

"I know, but they did open their home to us for as long as we need. I don't want to rush and fall into debt."

"We won't. My medical bills are paid off, and there's still a decent down payment left to buy a house. Besides, the cost of living is much cheaper in Montana."

Apprehension wormed its way down Gianna's back. *Danny always has the answers.* She tilted her head up at the curved ceiling. *God, I know Danny has never steered us wrong, but I'm still concerned. Please help me trust his judgment. Amen.*

Danny's hand covered hers and his eyes steadied on her face. "Don't worry, I'll be back to work by April, if not sooner."

"I believe you." She took an easy breath and then gave him a playful grin. "You're like the little engine that could."

He chuckled. "Yep, that's me." His expression grew serious. "I love you." His warm breath fanned her face seconds before his lips touched hers.

Hours later, the plane landed. Gianna toted their two carry-on bags over her shoulders alongside Danny as he wheeled himself through the moderately crowded airport.

He parked his wheelchair next to a bench inside the arrivals waiting area. "We'll wait for Matt, here," he said.

"Does he know our flight was delayed?"

"Yeah, I texted him during our layover in Denver."

"Oh, ok."

Gianna watched the sliding glass doors open and close continuously as a river of changing faces came and went. Among the rush of foot traffic, she witnessed anticipated homecomings and a few dreadful farewells.

The glass doors glided open again, and another scattered bunch of people entered. *Still no Matthew.* She looked the other way toward the escalator. A bright orange hunter's cap caught her eye. It was her brother dressed in denim jeans and a beige arctic quilt coat. When their eyes met, he flaunted his huge grin and opened his arms to her.

"Oh, Matt!" she said, leaping to her feet. "Look at you, dressed like you're venturing out into the tundra."

"It's like fifteen degrees outside," he said, hugging her. "Are you going to be warm enough wearing that lightweight jacket?"

"The truck has heat, right?" she asked.

"Of course," he said. He urged her along. "C'mon. Let's help Dan so we can get out of here."

"Ok, ok," she said, shaking her head at his hastiness. *Yep, that's my brother Matt, always in a hurry.*

After forty minutes of traveling on the desolate highway, Matthew steered the truck toward the exit ramp leading to a neighboring city. Danny tapped on the side window. "Babe, there's the hospital I'll be working at."

Gianna looked out her side window and caught sight of the bright-red emergency sign that glowed above the carport section of the well-lit, four-story steel building. It seemed quiet for a hospital. The parking lot was empty, and four ambulances were parked side by side in the garage area.

"Will you be busy enough?" she asked.

"Sure. It won't be as busy as New York City, but there will be spurts of activity. Matter of fact, Doc Kendall told me the chief medical officer is eager to meet me."

"I'm not surprised, considering your experience."

Gianna leaned back in her seat. She had no doubt that Danny's interview would be a Sunday picnic. He was confident in his skills, empathetic, and personable. What was for them not to like? Her only concern was whether he could adjust to a slower pace. He worked insane hours in New York and working in a rural setting was going to be a huge change for him. She hoped he wouldn't be bored.

Matthew turned the corner onto their parents' road. The asphalt was black under the night sky, and the reflectors marking mailboxes and neighbors' driveways gleamed under the headlights. Gianna sighed, thankful that her brother was driving. Had it been her, she would've hit the brakes half a dozen times trying to decipher the reflectors from the glowing eyes of deer grazing at the edge of the road.

As he cautiously navigated the last sharp bend along the mile-long road, Gianna's heartbeat sped up with tremendous anticipation. She was home.

The SUV made a left turn at the break in the evergreens. The driveway opened to an idyllic scene from a Christmas card. *Oh wow!* The spectacular view astounded her. "Look at that!"

A string of white icicle lights glistened along both levels of the center-hall colonial home. Colored lights danced in and out of the rows of shrubs that bordered the wraparound porch. An illuminated nativity scene embellished the front lawn, and candy cane markers gave a lustrous glow to the sidewalk leading to the red foil-wrapped entry door.

"John and Luke did it all," Matthew said.

"No way!" Gianna said in awe.

"Yep, and they used colored lights just for you."

"Really?"

Gianna hopped out of the warm truck into the freezing cold, her breath now a puff of moist steam. *This is amazing!* She stood there, taking in the holiday cheer. She couldn't figure out whether the decorations or her brothers' efforts surprised her more. *Mom and Dad weren't kidding when they said the twins grew up.*

While Matthew assisted Danny back into the wheelchair, Gianna grabbed the overnight bags from the truck. As she turned to head up the sidewalk, the front door opened, and her brother Mark stepped out onto the porch wearing red flannel pajamas.

"Hey, sis, let me help you with that," he said, leaping down the steps in his slippers.

"Thanks, but I got it. If you can help Matt get Danny up the steps, that'd be great."

"Ok, no problem," Mark said. As he passed her on the sidewalk, he touched her shoulder. "Welcome home."

"Thanks. It's so good to be home."

She opened the front door and was greeted by her parents, the twins, and Jessica.

"Welcome home!" they said.

"Aw! You guys didn't have to wait up for us."

"Nonsense, honey," her mom said. Her voice became rich with emotion. "We've been planning your homecoming all week."

Gianna swept a few fine strands of hair out of her tear-moistened eyes. "Mom, you didn't have to go to all this trouble."

"Bella, save your breath," Dad said. He kissed her cheek, then went outside to assist Danny.

Luke took her carry-on bags. "We'll put these in your room," he said, gesturing to John to help.

As Gianna unbuttoned her coat, she peered into the formal living room. The crackling fireplace occupied the room's center, visible through to the family room where she could see the huge ten-foot Christmas tree trimmed with colored lights.

"Dr. and Mrs. Kendall aren't here?"

Jessica took her coat. "No. Joe had an emergency at the hospital, so Evelyn said she'd see you tomorrow."

"I understand."

Jessica put her arm around her. "Join me in the dining room. Mom has a huge spread for all of us."

Gianna rolled her eyes. "Mom outdid herself again."

"You know it," Jessica said.

Gianna shook her head. She couldn't remember a time her mother passed up an opportunity to entertain. She loved being in the kitchen creating new meals to serve the family. She was an awesome cook. Rarely did she make something inedible.

Gianna followed Jessica down the hallway to the kitchen where the delicious smell of Italian cooking greeted her. "Oh, Mom!"

"I have everything under control, honey," she said, removing a casserole dish from the oven.

"I don't doubt it," Gianna said, scanning the orderly kitchen. "Can I help?"

"No, no. You two take a seat in the dining room," she said shoeing them away with an oven mitt.

Gianna blinked in surprise. "Ok."

Inside the dining room, the massive oak table displayed a tray of crostini pizza, sausage roll twists with tomato dip, and a platter of finger sandwiches. *Unbelievable.* Gianna shifted her eyes to the matching oak buffet hutch. A red crocheted doily adorned its surface, enhanced by a glass plate with assorted homemade Christmas cookies, pumpkin pie, and apple pie.

She nudged Jessica's arm. "I can see I'm going to struggle with my weight living here."

"Tell me about it," Jessica said. "I'm already seven pounds over what I should be, and I'm not due till' April."

Gianna gave her a sideways glance. "I hope my knucklehead brother didn't remind you of that either."

"No. On the contrary, he keeps telling me how beautiful I look and encourages me to eat more." Jessica held her belly. "I can't see my feet now."

"Oh my!" Gianna dropped her head. *I'm going to have to watch my diet living here.* She looked up at the doorway when her rowdy twin brothers raced into the room.

"Hey, sis, your BETTER half finally made it inside," Luke said, cackling.

Luke shoved John into the back wall, nearly knocking him into the desserts. John clunked him upside the head.

"Watch it, dork!" he said, pushing him back.

Gianna rolled her eyes. *Matured? Not so much.*

Their mom scurried into the dining room. "They're coming in now!" she said.

Danny wheeled in and parked himself next to Gianna. "Well, I made it," he said, proudly. He looked up at the feast on the table, his eyes wide with surprise. "Whoa, Mom! You went above and beyond."

"Oh, Daniel!" she said, stepping forward to give him a hug. "Welcome home, son!"

"Thank you."

Dad walked in from the kitchen, carrying a bottle of wine. "I wish Joe and Evelyn could've joined us tonight."

He poured the wine and handed a glass to his wife, Mark, Matthew, and Danny. He then poured grape juice and handed a glass to Jessica, Gianna, and the twins.

Danny whispered in Gianna's ear. "I'll trade you."

"I know you would if you could," she whispered back.

She beamed inside, knowing Danny's best-kept secret. Not even Matthew knew he didn't drink. Why he never told him was beyond her. Perhaps as a teenager, with all the underage partying that had gone on, it was too embarrassing to admit. Or maybe it was just too tragic for him to talk about. Whatever Danny's reasons were for being discreet, it was his business. She knew the pain of losing his parents still lurked inside his heart.

Gianna's father held up his glass. "To my Bella and Dan, welcome home! Wishing you both health, success, and happiness always. We love you!"

Glasses clinked and everyone drank to the toast. Gianna smiled at Danny as she watched him fake a sip.

"To our future," she said.

"To our future," he replied, giving her a kiss.

Chapter Twenty-Seven

Gianna lay in bed, her brain still groggy from last night's pleasant dream. She was someplace tropical, relaxing in the warm sand with Danny, watching the tide come in, but the intimate details of her dream were fading faster than she could recall them.

She blinked her eyes open to reality. The window blinds were slightly parted, allowing her a glimpse of the overcast sky and swirling snow flurries. *Fiddlesticks!* The weather certainly wasn't anything like in her dream. *But it is winter.*

Regardless, she was safely home in her parents' first-floor guestroom, sleeping beside her loving husband for the first time since he had his accident.

A strange satisfying thought came to mind. The last time she had slept in her parents' home was the night before her wedding. Since then, the room had been painted a garden sage, and the carpet was replaced with hand-scraped hardwood floors. The attached bathroom was remodeled with a walk-in stone shower.

Gianna rolled to her right side and levered herself up on her elbow. She traced the shape of Danny's stubbly jaw with her fingertip. "Good morning, sleepyhead."

Danny groaned. "Is it morning already?"

"Uh-huh. Didn't you sleep well?" she asked.

"Not really. I feel like I just went to bed."

"It does seem that way, doesn't it?" She glanced at the alarm clock on the bedside table. "Well, we slept six hours."

"I'm still tired, and I have PT at noon."

"I can keep you up," she said, playfully.

"And how're you going to do that?"

"Like this," she whispered. She sprinkled tiny kisses along his scarred forehead, then trailed her fingers down the slope of his wide chest.

Danny halted her straying hand. "Babe, I can't. The meds...they ruin the moment."

She lowered her eyelids and sighed. "I understand." She did, but for once she didn't have morning sickness and hoped by now, he would have reached a turning point in his recovery. She peered up at him. "I miss us."

"Babe, I miss us, too." He skimmed his fingers up and down her arm. "But I need to get stronger before we can go there. I'm sorry."

Gianna curled her bottom lip down in a pout. "I know, but I'm afraid when that happens, my belly will be the size of a basketball, and you won't want me."

"Of course, I'll still want you; I love you." He toyed with the thin strap of her lace gown, letting it loosely dangle on her shoulder. He slid his hand up beneath the hem and pulled it over her head. "Lie next to me."

She settled her head on his chest and listened to his heart thump strong and steady under her ear. As he held her tightly against him, the warmth of his bare torso touching her skin made her pulse trip. A rush of desire rippled through her like a tidal wave.

"I love you," she whispered.

"I love you, too."

He turned and brushed his firm, moist lips back and forth over hers. His tongue nudged at her mouth, and she parted her lips, eager for the taste and feel of his tongue stroking hers. He made love to her mouth, letting her know how he would make love to her body if he could.

She moaned with pleasure. His touch filled her with emotions and sensations she hadn't felt in what seemed like an eternity. "Thank you for loving me," she breathed.

"Thank you for being patient with me." He ran his hand up and down the length of her back, resting it on her hip. "Just think, in a few short months, we'll have a newborn, and these quiet moments will be history."

His words halted her brain. Life was about to change again, but it was a good change. She lifted her head off his chest and whispered, "I'm ready to be a mother."

He swept a few strands of her silky brown hair out of her eyes. "And you're going to be wonderful at it."

She smiled. "And you're going to make a great dad."

"I can't wait, but I'll admit I'm going to miss these intimate moments we have now."

"Me, too." She shifted in his arms, then inched her torso on top of him. Her skin tingled as she pressed against his chest. She inched forward and captured his mouth in another kiss, pushing reality to the deepest corners of her mind.

All at once, outside their bedroom, commotion and chaos came like a bolt from the blue.

Danny broke their kiss. "What the?" he uttered, turning his head toward the door.

Within seconds, John barreled in like a bull in a China shop. Gianna slid off Danny and frantically wrestled with a tangle of blankets, striving to hide her blushes. With the covers pulled taut around her, she hollered, "Don't you know how to knock?"

John stood there like a bump on a log. Embarrassment whipped color into his cheeks. He spun around and shouted at Luke, "You idiot," shoving him into the wall.

"Me?" Luke hollered back, pushing John further into the room. "You're the dummy who opened the door."

"Never mind! Now quit the horseplay," she yelled.

"Horseplay?" John asked, raising his eyebrows. He snickered. "You're the one rolling in the sack."

"Excuse me? We were just talking," she snapped.

"Let it go, babe," Danny said in a calm voice.

"Yeah, sure you were," John said, cackling.

"Don't you two have school?" she asked.

"Delayed opening," Luke fired back.

"Ok," Danny said. "What do you boys want?"

"Brunch is ready," John said.

"Fine! Now go away," Gianna said.

"Wait!" Luke shouted. "Matt wants to know if Dan needs help getting out of bed."

"Tell him to give me fifteen," Danny said.

"Ok," Luke said. When he turned to leave, John blocked the doorway. "Move out of the way, dork," he said, tackling him into the hallway.

"Shut the door and scram!" Gianna shouted.

The door slammed closed, and seconds later, the ruckus drifted down the hall.

Gianna dropped her head back against the pillow. "This is crazy! I feel like a little girl caught with her hand in the cookie jar."

Danny laughed, mocking the absurdity of the situation.

"Well, that's what happens when you don't lock the door," he said.

"Oh, and somehow this is my fault?"

"Come on, baby. We're talking about your brothers. Taunting you is their specialty. They miss you."

Gianna rolled her eyes. "Oh, puh-leeze. I'm going into town this afternoon to meet with a Realtor."

"But we just got here. What happened to all that stuff about saving money and not rushing the house hunt?"

Danny's gentle reminder of her words may as well have roared in her ear. "Fine!" she grumbled. She rolled to the edge of the bed and grabbed her robe. "I'm going to take a shower."

Danny chuckled. "Remember to lock the door."

Chapter Twenty-Eight

After Dan's physical therapy session, Matthew drove him past the town square. The parking lot was packed with vehicles. Even in the bitter cold and light snow, the quaint village had its own bustling style and distinct aromas. Shoppers strolled from store to store. Outdoor holiday music blared from the gazebo where Santa greeted children. The noise and animation of the town warmed Dan's heart. *I am so glad we decided to move back here.*

Matthew turned the corner onto Main Street and parked diagonally in a space directly in front of Dr. Kendall's medical practice. "Now, how's that for door-to-door service?"

"Perfect, Matt. Thanks for driving me here."

"No problem."

Dan gazed up at the stucco building. It had gotten a facelift since the last time he was there. A subtle yellow replaced the dingy brown color, and a new stone veneer added texture and style to the building's face. *What an enormous difference from six months ago.* He caught sight of the wooden sign: Joseph Kendall, MD, Family Medicine and OB. Underneath it, a banner read: Joining us soon, Daniel Christiansen, MD.

Goose bumps pricked his arms. "Hey, look at that," he said, pointing to the sign. "Doc Kendall's already advertising my services."

Matthew laughed. "He's told half the town already."

"Seriously?"

"Yeah. He's thrilled you came home."

Dan smiled. He'd finally found a place where he felt needed. "It's good to be home, bro."

Matthew pushed Dan's wheelchair up the ramp and into the empty waiting room. "Where's all the patients?" Matthew asked.

"Joe closes at two on Thursdays. But he's here— in his office," Dan said.

The thud of a door shutting from a back room echoed down the hall. Seconds later, the tapping sound of leather dress shoes against the vinyl floor grew louder.

"I thought I heard voices," Joe said, entering the waiting room. "Hello, Matthew," he said, shaking his hand. "Welcome home, son," he said, patting Dan's shoulder.

"Thank you. It's good to be home."

Dan scanned the newly remodeled waiting room. Landscape artwork accentuated the nurturing green walls. Cushioned chairs were arranged to allow patients a degree of privacy. Soft nature sounds played in the background, adding to the room's ambience.

"This place looks fantastic," Dan said.

"Thank you," Joe said. "My intention is to keep the patients relaxed and stress-free." He pointed to the kiddie corner. "So, what do you think of the play area?"

Dan swiveled his chair toward a partitioned wall made of acrylic glass. Inside were toys, games, and a television. It had a clear view from the adult waiting area, allowing parents to watch their children play.

"That's really cool," Dan said.

Joe sat in a chair across from Dan and Matthew and rearranged the magazines strewn all over the coffee table.

"So, how's therapy treating you?" Joe asked.

"Brutal," Dan said, staring down at his legs.

"Oh, come on," Matthew replied. He patted Dan on the back, then looked at Joe and said, "Don't let his pathetic puss fool you. He's making terrific progress."

"I can see that," Joe said.

Dan gave Matthew a frown of discord. "Right, if you call losing your balance on crutches and falling flat on your face progress."

"You tripped," Matt said. "So what? It happens."

Joe palmed Dan's shoulder. "Son, I know it's not easy, but you've come a long way from being bedridden."

"Yeah, I guess," Dan mumbled. Frustrated by his stumble in therapy, spasms of doubt erupted within him. *What if I never walk again? What if I can't provide for my family?*

"Don't fret, son," Joe said. "You'll be running this practice in no time."

The certainty in Joe's voice twisted Dan's gut.

"What? What're you talking about?"

"I think it's time I slow down a bit," Joe said.

"Is everything ok?"

"Oh, sure," Joe said, tossing his hand. "Evelyn wants us to spend more quality time together. You know, do a little traveling before we get too old."

The idea wove an unsettling path through Dan's consciousness. *I hope nothing is seriously wrong.* Since he hadn't lived home for the last twelve years, he wasn't apprised of any underlying health issues his godparents may have developed.

Dan narrowed his eyes to Joe. "But you're certain everything's ok, right?"

"Yes, yes," Joe answered, his voice, full of buoyancy. He stood up and walked across the room to the water cooler. As he filled a paper cup, he asked, "How's Gianna been feeling?"

Dan nodded. "Pretty good—not too moody."

Matthew laughed. "Are you kidding? She almost took my head off this morning after I sent my twin bros into your room."

"If I was more mobile, I would've helped her."

Joe tried hard to keep from laughing at Matt and Dan's jabs. Quickly, he changed the subject. "Has Gianna decided on a provider yet?"

"No, not yet. She's not a fan of doctors or hospitals."

"Then why did she marry you?" Matthew asked, taunting him with a little more humor.

"It's because of the whole Chad incident."

"Oh, right." Matthew rubbed his scruffy chin. "I keep forgetting how that cockroach messed her up."

Dan let out a heavy sigh. "I wish I could assure her a comfortable pregnancy, but I can't."

"Would she consider seeing a midwife?" Joe asked.

Dan shrugged. "I think she'd be open to the idea. She does talk about the possibility of a home birth."

"There's a midwifery group next door that's been consulting with me," Joe said. He reached behind the reception desk and picked up a business card. "Here's their information," he said, handing Dan the card. "It's time Gianna sees someone."

"Will do, thanks."

Later that evening, when Dan arrived home at the Stefano residence, the house was dark except for the outdoor Christmas lights display. Everyone had gone to bed early. The only sound inside was Dan's wheelchair rumbling down the hallway to the guest bedroom suite.

Jingle bells tied to the doorknob broke the silence when Gianna opened the door. She rubbed her tired eyes, "I thought I heard voices. Did you and Matt have a fun time out?"

"Yeah, we did," Dan said. "I never realized how much I missed home until I tasted Evelyn's scrumptious chicken and dumpling casserole."

Gianna smiled. "Another one of your favorite dishes." She grabbed the handles on the wheelchair. Before pushing him inside, she leaned forward and kissed him. "I have great news!"

"You found us a house."

"Nope," she said, closing the door. "I got a job!"

"That's awesome, babe!"

"While you were at PT, I met with the school district. They offered me a substitute teaching position. It's not permanent, but it's something...right?"

Dan nodded. "That's fantastic. Congratulations!"

Gianna sat on the bed. "I won't be able to start until the paperwork is processed; hopefully by then, my morning sickness will ease up."

"Let's hope so," he said.

He wheeled his chair as close to the bed as he could and locked the brakes. Using his upper body strength, he pushed himself up onto his feet. After catching his breath, he maneuvered his body to the edge of the bed.

"Oh, Danny! Look at you." Joy lit up her face.

Dan smiled at his own accomplishment. "I'm trying more than ever."

"I know," she said, touching his face.

"I'm going to start working with Dr. Kendall."

"What?" she asked.

"Every day, after my therapy sessions, Matt's going to drop me off there. I can assist Joe with medical consults."

Gianna's eyebrows shot up. "Really? That's great!"

"Yeah, it is, and when I'm stronger, I can start seeing patients full time."

"Just don't overdo it."

"I won't." He placed his hand over her belly. "So, how're you feeling?"

"Bloated. Even my pajama pants are snug." Puzzled, she threw her hands out. "And, what's with this morning sickness ALL day? I mean, I guess I should be grateful that I feel pregnant, but Jess said she never had it this bad."

"No two pregnancies are alike." He turned and took her hand in his. "It's time to see a physician."

Gianna looked down at her stomach. "Yeah, I know, but unless you're going to be my doctor, I'd prefer to use a midwife."

Dan shook his head. "It's my turn to be the supportive husband." He reached into his pocket and pulled out the midwifery card that Joe gave him. "Here, I want you to call them tomorrow."

"Ok."

She stood up and walked across the room to the desk. As she reached to pin the card to the bulletin board, her shirt lifted, exposing her protruding waistline.

Dan loved seeing her blossom with their child. "How many weeks are you?" he asked.

She looked over her shoulder and said, "Ten."

Dan held her steady gaze then quickly looked away, catching a glimpse of her cell phone. "Hey, you have a voice mail message from Steve."

"I do?"

She walked toward the nightstand and picked up her phone. She turned on the speaker and played the recorded message.

"Hello, Gianna. It's Steve. Uh, Dr. Ross. I hope you're settling in at your parents' house. I'm calling you regarding the results of your lab work. Everything looks good; however, your HCG levels are slightly elevated. I don't know if you chose a provider yet, but maybe you can have Dan recheck them. Have him call me. Take care."

Gianna stared at Dan, tension tightening the delicate features of her face. "What does that mean?"

"Your dates could be off."

"No," she said, adamantly. "Don't you remember that night...after we argued over Kimberly's note?"

A tide of hot blood crawled up his neck. "How could I forget?" He thought about it. Their lovemaking that night hadn't been that intimate since their honeymoon. He reached for her hand and smiled. "You're probably right about the dates."

"But something's wrong. Am I right?" she asked.

The intensity of her look pounded him until he had to look away. "Not necessarily. But..." he didn't want to insult her. "You do seem further along."

Gianna threw her hands up in defense. "I swear I haven't eaten any of Mom's Christmas cookies."

Dan maintained his no-nonsense manner. "I want to do an ultrasound tomorrow."

Gianna's joking smile fell flat. "Why? What's wrong?"

"Nothing. An ultrasound will confirm our due date and give us accurate measurements. Also, we'll be able to hear our baby's heartbeat."

"But you're sure everything's ok, right?"

Dan held her hands. "Don't worry. God has our back."

Chapter Twenty-Nine

Gianna opened the coat closet in the foyer and took out her winter fleece. As she buttoned it up, she noticed how snug it already felt. It was a good thing her baby was due in July.

She sat down on the bottom step and pulled on her boots. She recalled Jessica telling her the other night about how she could no longer see her feet. Gianna suspected one day she'd have the same issue but hoped it would be summertime. At least then, she could wear flipflops.

"Honey," Mom called from upstairs. "Make sure you wear a scarf. It's very cold outside. We don't need you getting sick."

"I got one, Mom," Gianna said, springing to her feet. She wrapped the scarf around her neck. "Are you sure you don't want to go with us?"

"No, honey. This is a special time for you and Daniel. Besides, I have some last-minute Christmas errands to do."

The front door opened, and a sudden gust of arctic air blew in along with Matthew.

Whoa, Mom isn't kidding. It's freezing out there.

Matthew kicked the snow off his boots. "The truck's warming up. Dan's waiting for you. You ready?"

"Yep," Gianna said. "I'll see you later, Mom!"

"Good luck, honey."

Dr. Kendall held the door open as Gianna wheeled Danny into the cozy, warm waiting room. After a welcome home hug and a brief discussion, Joe escorted her and Danny to the dimly lit ultrasound exam room. He handed Gianna a gown and said, "Lisa will be in shortly. Since I asked her to come in before hours, I bribed her with hot coffee and a donut."

Danny laughed. "If that's how you sweet-talk your employees, then I'm in trouble."

"Well, now you know my secret," Joe said. He gave a wink and closed the door.

Gianna couldn't see the humor in their conversation. She was too consumed with the significance of the situation. What if something was wrong? *I can't handle another miscarriage.* She sat down on the bench and pulled off her boots. As she undressed, she continued to debate with herself. *Everything will be ok. I made it to the ten-week mark. That's two weeks further than my last pregnancy.* She took a deep breath to try calming herself, but the fear of another miscarriage still haunted her.

"You ok?" Danny asked.

"No," she said as she pulled on the gown. "I'm terrified. It's like I'm expecting the worst to happen. For instance, every time I use the bathroom, I'm afraid I'm going to see blood. And when I'm feeling good, then I think something must be wrong because I don't feel pregnant."

"Babe, I understand. The fear is real, but that's why we're here, to validate a healthy pregnancy."

"But even if I get past this first trimester hump, there's always going to be that feeling of anxiety, and it's going to stay with me until the day I hold our baby."

"Come here," he said, inviting her into his arms. She eased herself onto his lap and nestled her face into the warmth of his neck. He kissed her cheek and whispered, "Have faith. God is in control."

"I'm trying," she mumbled into his neck.

There was a soft knock at the door, and it opened part way, letting a stream of light pour in. A petite woman dressed in navy blue scrubs, stood in the doorway chatting to a nurse. She gave a one shoulder shrug and said, "I'll help any way I can." Then she turned and entered the room. "Good morning," she said, shaking Gianna's hand. "I'm Lisa, and I'll be performing your ultrasound this morning."

"Nice to meet you," Gianna said. She carefully slid off Danny's lap and boosted herself up on the exam table.

"Dr. Christiansen, it's so nice to finally meet you," Lisa said, shaking his hand. "Dr. Kendall has told me so much about you that I feel like I already know you."

Danny grinned, flashing his undiluted charm. "Just how much did he tell you?"

Lisa blinked, clearly thrown off by his sarcastic remark. Quickly, she retorted, "No, no! It's all good."

Danny's mouth lifted into a crooked smirk. "Well, if he should mention anything about my teenage years, just know his memory isn't all that great."

Lisa let out a short laugh and shook her head.

Danny's witticism broke the tension Gianna was feeling, allowing her to leap right into the conversation.

"And Lisa, if you do hear anything juicy, be sure to let me in on it."

"You got it," Lisa said.

Danny pinched the bridge of his nose and closed his eyes. "Somehow, I think I'm going to regret saying that."

Gianna leaned forward and patted his shoulder. "You really put your foot in your mouth this time."

"Ok," Lisa said, rubbing her hands together. "Perhaps we should get started."

"Good idea," Danny said.

"All right." Lisa placed a privacy sheet over Gianna's lap, then tapped on the keyboard a few more times. "Ok."

Gianna inhaled deeply. *Here we go again.* She clasped her hands tightly together and rested them on her chest, and positioned her head so she could have a clear view of the gray, fuzzy monitor. *I'm ready.* But as the intruding probe glided inside her, she tensed up.

"Relax, babe," Danny said, cupping his warm, gentle hand over hers.

"I'm trying," she breathed.

With awakened curiosity, she raised her left arm and propped her head up so she could get a better view of the monitor. The screen no longer looked like a TV that lost its satellite signal. A clear image of her baby appeared. She felt sudden peace and contentment. "Aw! So tiny." She tilted her head and peered up at Danny. His expression was carefully neutral, completely unreadable. A twinge of panic pinched her heart. *Oh, no! What does he know?*

"There's your baby," Lisa said, pointing to the monitor. She turned up the volume on the console. "And here's the heartbeat."

The whoosh-whoosh sound brought tears to Gianna's eyes. "Oh, Danny! That's our baby!"

Danny smiled with anticipatory delight. His eyes danced with joy. "It sure is. And what a strong heartbeat!"

"The heart rate is one forty-seven," Lisa said, typing away. "Now, just a minute; let me take some measurements."

Gianna turned her head and lingered her gaze on Danny's handsome face. His confident expression washed away her concerns.

"I can't believe that's our baby," she said.

Danny pushed up and braced himself on the wheelchair's arms. "We did it," he whispered. He grazed her lips once, then twice with tender kisses.

"Doctor, you didn't mention multiples," Lisa said.

"What?" Gianna asked, her voice high and squeaky. She lifted her head to view the screen, then looked back at Danny. Slowly, his sharp-witted smile emerged.

"I didn't know for sure," he said to Lisa, his voice remaining calm and cool. He looked back at Gianna and said, "Your increased morning sickness, your moodiness, your snug pajama pants, and the elevated HCG levels—it all adds up."

"Oh, it added up all right," Lisa said. "There's clearly two in here." She pointed to the screen. "Here's baby A and here's baby B. Baby B must've been hiding earlier."

"Wait!" Gianna said. "So, Danny, you knew last night and didn't tell me?"

"I didn't want to worry you."

"Oh, my stars!" She fanned her sweaty face with her hand, trying to cool her emotions. "No wonder I'm so sick and so huge. Oh, but it's sooo worth it!"

Lisa smiled. "Here's baby B. Its heart rate is one fifty-one," she said, turning up the volume.

"So, both babies are ok, right?" Gianna asked.

"Yes. Baby A is measuring ten weeks, and Baby B is measuring nine weeks, two days," Lisa said.

"Oh, thank God," Gianna sighed. "Ok, so...twins. Now this changes everything. I mean, now I can't see a midwife or have a home delivery, right?"

"You're young and healthy," Danny said, squeezing her hand. "But you're considered high-risk carrying twins. If you want a midwife, she can co-manage your care with Dr. Kendall."

"Ok, but what about a home birth?"

Danny twisted his mouth and sighed. "Maybe. We'll have to see how your pregnancy progresses. Honestly, I'd prefer the hospital setting. It's a safer option."

Gianna nodded. "Ok. I trust you." She turned back to the monitor. "Wow! I still can't believe this!"

"Do twins run in your family?" Lisa asked.

"My youngest brothers are twins," Gianna said. She lifted her head to Danny and joked, "This is my mother's fault! Oh, they'd better not be brats like Luke and John. Hopefully, they're girls. Can you tell if they're identical?"

Danny looked at the monitor. "I see two placentas and two separate sacs. They're fraternal."

Gianna sniffled and dabbed her eyes with a tissue. "This is crazy awesome!" She laughed in disbelief. "Twins. We're having twins!"

That evening, Gianna's sore, tired feet thanked her when she finally sat down at the large rectangular table for twelve that she and Danny reserved at Jack-n-Jill's Bar and Grill. Her feet were killing her from their afternoon shopping excursion.

She sat back in her chair and let out a huge breath.

"What an eventful day!" she said.

"Yeah, it was," Danny said. He sipped his water. "I can't wait to see your parents' reactions when we tell them our news."

"Me nether. I'm sure Evelyn will be surprised, too."

Gianna laced her fingers together and rested them in her lap, waiting patiently for their families to arrive. She peered out the thick frosted window. A fine, white powdery snow fell from the heavens and swirled around the streets. Fortunately, the weather hadn't deterred people from enjoying the holiday festivities. There were plenty of folks going about their daily activities.

"Excuse me, miss." A waiter with a deep, masculine voice startled her. "May I bring you something to drink while you're waiting for your guests?"

Gianna turned away from the snow squalls and answered, "Yes. I'd like a hot chocolate, please."

"And for you, sir?" he asked Danny.

"I'll have a cup of coffee, thanks."

"Ok. I'll be right back with those."

"You ok?" Danny asked Gianna.

"Aside from being a little dazed, yeah."

She looked toward the front entrance of the restaurant and shifted her gaze from face to face as the hostess seated incoming patrons. *They should be here any moment.*

Just as she predicted, Dr. and Mrs. Kendall strolled in holding hands like two teenagers in love. As soon as Evelyn made eye contact with Gianna, she upped her pace toward the table, tugging Joe behind.

Evelyn hugged Gianna. "It's so good to see you, dear."

Gianna replied with a sincere smile. "Good to be here."

Evelyn removed her handmade knitted hat and matching scarf, then took Gianna's hands. "Oh, and congratulations! Joe told me the exciting news. We'll help you and Daniel any way we can."

"Yes, whatever you need, just let us know," Joe said.

Gianna nodded appreciatively. "Thanks. Your help really means a lot to me." She reached for the ultrasound pictures on the table. "Here's baby A and this is baby B," she said, handing her the photos.

"Aw, how precious. Oh, you're going to have twice the cuddles and twice the fun!" Evelyn said. She handed back the pictures, then settled in at the table.

Gianna smiled uneasily as nerves danced in her stomach. Cuddles and fun didn't exactly register in her mind when she thought about raising twins. It was more like fear and chaos. *What if I'm a terrible mother?*

Gianna's parents, her four brothers, and Jessica arrived, redirecting her negative thoughts to happy ones. "Hey, guys!" she said, springing out of her chair. "Thank you all for coming."

After everybody hugged and said hello, they all drifted around the table, choosing their seats. At once, Luke reached across the table and grabbed the breadbasket.

"Ooh, I'm hungry," he roared. He nudged John. "Give me the garlic-oil dip."

"Yuck, gross!" John blurted out. "Everyone knows that sends you right to the toilet."

Mom shot the twins a harsh look, but Dad took it to a higher level. "Boys!" he said in a low, firm voice. "Where's your manners? People are dining."

Gianna ducked her head. *Why did I invite the twins to dinner?* Fortunately, the place wasn't crowded yet, and no one seemed to have noticed her brothers' disgusting manners.

As Dad continued to lecture the boys, Mom fought the urge to squirm from the twins' humiliating behavior. She turned to Gianna, trying to refocus the attention on a positive topic. "So, how'd everything go?" she asked.

"Perfect!" Gianna said, handing her mother the ultrasound pictures.

Dan chimed in. "Actually, a little *two* perfect."

Mom gleamed at the first picture, then shuffled through the next few, only to stop and compare them carefully.

"Oh, my!" Mom gasped, putting her hand to her chest. "Is this what I think it is?"

Danny's mouth broke into a huge grin. "Yep."

"What? What did I miss?" Dad asked, joining the discussion. He leaned in toward his wife. "What're we looking at?"

"Your daughter's ultrasound pictures," she said. Happy tears filled her eyes. "There's *two* in there! It's a double blessing!"

"Huh?" Dad asked. For several surprised seconds, his expression went slack, as if her words did not register. But Luke caught on. He made puffy cheeks at Gianna, thinking his humor was appropriate.

John snorted. "Sis, you're going to look huge!"

Dad cast the boys a dirty look, then gave Gianna and Danny his attention. "Congrats, Bella and Dan. I hope you're having girls."

"Vincenzo!" Mom said, elbowing him in the side.

"What?" he asked. "I'm sorry, Arianna." He stood up and hugged Gianna. "You're going to be a wonderful mother, just like your momma." He patted Danny's shoulder. "You're both going to make wonderful parents!"

"Thanks, Daddy," Gianna said.

"Thanks, Pop," Danny said.

Matthew picked up one of the ultrasound pictures and studied it. "Twins? Really?" He rubbed an eyelid. "Was this planned?"

Danny's one eyebrow shot up and the other lowered. He laced his words with sarcasm. "Uh, sure, Matt. I've always been an overachiever."

Jessica smacked Matthew upside the head and poked fun at him. "'Was this planned?'" Dumbfounded over his absurd question, she stared at him briefly. "Duh, honey. How do you plan twins?" She shook her head, then stood up and squeezed her way around the table to Gianna. She hugged her and said, "You are twice blessed. Congratulations, chickadee!"

"Thank you, Jess."

Mark raised his glass to make a toast and said, "To Dan and Gianna. Congratulations to you both, and God bless."

Chapter Thirty

February blew in, and the groundhog saw his shadow. *Great! Another six weeks of winter.* That notion froze in Gianna's brain all day. It had been a hard winter and she was ready for spring.

She stood in the doorway of the kindergarten classroom and supervised her fifteen highly active students as they scrambled back and forth from their tables to the garbage, throwing away their scraps of construction paper.

"When you're finished cleaning your space, you may go to the cubbies and pack up for the day."

A little blonde girl with braids held up her version of Montana's groundhog, Bitterroot Bill. "Can I take my groundhog home?" she asked in a squeaky voice.

Gianna put a finger to her lips and raised her hand to remind the girl of the classroom rules. "Yes, Emma."

A gentle hand tugged at Gianna's blouse. A sweet little redheaded boy with freckles peered up at her. "Miz Chris..." his timid voice trailed off.

"Yes, Timmy," she answered.

"The zipper is stuck," he uttered.

Gianna squatted down to his level and carefully unjammed the zipper from his coat fabric. "There you go, sweetie."

"Mrs. Christiansen, Mrs. Christiansen!" a little girl called out in a panic. She approached Gianna with a troubled look on her face. "I can't find my other mitten," she cried.

"Ok, ok, Chloe," Gianna said, searching the girl's floor space. "Did you check your pockets?"

"It's not there."

"How about your backpack?"

Chloe went back to her table and dug through her backpack.

Meanwhile, another little boy stomped toward Gianna. He looked up at her with puppy dog eyes. "My boots feel funny," he said with a pout.

Gianna peered down at the boy's feet and smiled. "That's because they're on the wrong feet, Nicky."

He giggled. "Silly me."

"Try again, honey."

"Mrs. Christiansen," another little girl called out. She wiggled in place, with her legs crossed. "I really have to go potty," she whined.

Gianna felt light perspiration on her arms and face. *Oy vey! If I can't manage a classroom of kindergarteners, how am I going to handle newborn twins?*

"Ok, Kayla," she said, pointing to the classroom bathroom. "Go," she said.

Chloe held up her mitten and squealed, "I found it!"

"Good detective work," Gianna said.

Chloe giggled. "It was stuck in my sleeve."

"It was playing hide and seek with you," Gianna said.

When the children finished packing up, they sat down at their assigned tables and waited anxiously for Gianna's cue. "I like the way Nicky, Olivia, and Noah are sitting so nicely. Your table may line up."

As the three children quietly lined up, the others straightened their postures and waited patiently to be called. Gianna thanked them for being good listeners, then asked the remaining four tables to line up.

"Timmy, you are our line leader. Would you show our friends how to walk in a straight line, keeping your hands to yourself?"

Timmy nodded politely.

When the dismissal bell rang, Gianna led her class in a single file down the hallway to the front lobby. "Enjoy the rest of your afternoon, boys and girls," she said as she waved good-bye.

Back in the classroom, Gianna sat down at the desk and rubbed her weary eyes. *Phew! I don't know how kindergarten teachers do it every day.*

She had been subbing on and off for several weeks now, but mostly with fourth and fifth graders. They were old enough to work independently, but young enough to have a clean sense of humor. The younger students were like little sponges, eager to learn, but rambunctious, which tired her out more easily. But they were fun, and she was grateful for the experience to sample each grade level.

Gianna straightened up the classroom, then reviewed the teacher's plans for tomorrow's health lesson on self-esteem. The instructions were to write the words, I LOVE ME on the white board, and then draw a sample flower with colored petals to represent positive characteristics. The children were then to recreate the flower design on paper. *This sounds like a fun project.*

At the whiteboard, she uncapped a dry erase marker. The fruity odor triggered a memory sending her mind back to the very first day she taught middle school in the city. She had written POSITIVE ATTRIBUTES on the whiteboard and asked her students to list theirs. One of her eighth-grade boys had decided to challenge her authority by pointing to his groin and asking her if it counted as a positive attribute. Gianna's cheeks had burned with embarrassment, but she knew she had to react quickly if she wanted to gain their respect.

My stars! I was mortified. Gianna still felt an echo of humiliation thinking about that day. She shook her head and laughed at the memory. For some reason, that teen's mischievous behavior suddenly seemed funny.

Reminiscing, she realized just how much she enjoyed the challenge of teaching middle school. Her teaching style and personality seemed to fit in better with the older students. They were more independent, and they grasped the material easier.

Gianna sighed. *I miss my seventh and eighth graders.*

Exhausted from a harried day, Gianna crashed on the oversized sectional sofa in the sunken family room. As she closed her heavy eyes, her thoughts blurred while bizarre images flashed through her mind. Slowly, her muscles relaxed, and her body sank deeper into the couch as she drifted off to sleep.

"Oh, you're home," Mom said, jolting her awake.

"Huh? Yeah," Gianna mumbled, rubbing her eyes.

"I'm sorry, honey. I didn't know you were asleep."

"It's ok, Mom."

Awake now, she smelled the comforting aroma of roast chicken and stuffing. She pushed herself to an upright position. "I'll help you with dinner."

"No, no," Mom said, sitting down beside her. "The bird's done and is cooling on top of the stove. I'm just waiting for the guys to come in."

Gianna stretched her arms into the air. "Oh."

"How was kindergarten?" Mom asked.

Gianna shook her head. "After a day like I had, I'm convinced I'm going to fail at juggling twins. I don't know how you did it."

"Teamwork. You have a supportive husband, and we're all here to help. You're not alone."

"Thanks, Mom."

"No worries," she said, kissing her on the forehead. "You rest up. I'll call you when it's time to eat."

Gianna settled back onto the couch and closed her eyes. Quickly, her thoughts went fuzzy, and she slipped back into dreamland. A clack, shuffle, clack, shuffle sound disturbed her. She let out a snort, then drifted back to sleep.

"Hey, Sleeping Beauty, wake up," Danny muttered against her lips. "Supper's ready."

His familiar moist lips and minty breath roused her. She moaned, then forced her eyes open. "I thought I heard your walker but didn't know if I was dreaming."

"Nope. I'm right here," he said. He lifted her hand and held it in his lap. "How was your day?"

"Wild. Those kids wiped me out like a tidal wave."

Danny laughed. "No more kindergarten for you."

"Wrong. I must go back tomorrow."

Danny frowned. "Tell Mrs. Dodson that you can only teach third grade and up."

"Sweetheart, I'll take whatever assignment I can get while I can still work. Besides, we need the money."

"Why don't you let me worry about that?"

"We need a second vehicle."

"No, we don't. I carpool with Joe; you use my truck."

"I hate driving your truck. Besides, if I get any bigger, I won't fit behind the wheel."

Danny laughed. "Then we won't need the second vehicle."

"Ha, Ha. Funny. Seriously, Danny, in a few weeks, you'll be driving again, and you'll need your truck back to fulfill your hospital obligations."

"I get that, babe, but take it easy. Rome wasn't built in a day."

Chapter Thirty-One

April finally arrived. The bare tree branches of winter gave way to budding green leaves. Birds were chirping and tulips were blooming. Spring was in the air, and spring break was in session.

On her first day off from work, Gianna enjoyed a morning of pampering at the salon. Afterward, she and Jessica indulged in lunch at the Chuck Wagon.

"Enjoy ladies," the waitress said, serving their meals.

"Thanks," Gianna replied. She looked at Jessica's plate of spicy hot wings in disbelief. "You're not really going to eat that, are you?"

Jessica blew out a breath and ruffled a blonde strand of hair on her forehead. "Well, since the foot massage didn't work, I'll try anything to induce labor," she said.

Gianna threw her hand out, palm up. "So, you're three days past your due date. Big deal. Danny said that very few babies are ever born on their actual due date."

"Yes, but I thought I'd have this baby before Easter."

"First time babies rarely come early."

"But I'm *so* over this pregnancy. I'm tired and uncomfortable. I want my body back."

"But Baby Stefano is warm and cozy in there."

Jessica dropped her chicken wing down on her plate and wiped her greasy hands on her napkin. "No," she snapped. "My baby girl has a cute nursery that Matt and I spent weeks designing and preparing for her. Her new home has a light pink blanket that took me seven months to crochet. So, don't give me that nonsense about my womb being a comfortable place for her."

Whoa! I just struck a nerve. Gianna reached across the table and took Jessica's hand. "I'm sorry, Jess. All I'm saying is that you're not going to be pregnant forever."

"Really? I had no idea!" Jessica retorted. "Just wait. You're only halfway there, and you're delivering twins."

Gianna glanced down at her blossoming belly. She was twenty-five weeks along, and her babies were kicking up a storm. She was cherishing every minute of her second trimester and couldn't relate to how miserable Jessica was feeling.

Jessica exhaled heavily. "I'm sorry, Gianna. I overreacted." She grabbed a tissue. "It's the hormones."

Gianna gave an empathetic smile. "I know the waiting has got to be frustrating at this point."

"It is. Every day that passes, I feel more anxious about giving birth. What if something goes wrong?"

"Aw, Jess. Try to stay positive and relax."

"I'm trying," Jessica said. "Besides, we're so ready." She sipped her lemon water. "Look at you. You're carrying twins. Aren't you nervous?"

"Listen, Jess, this is a new experience for both of us. Neither of us know how we're going to feel during labor, not until we're in the moment, so there's no point in freaking out over it now."

Jessica fell silent briefly, then perked up. "You're right. Let's eat, then go shopping."

"Sounds good to me."

After lunch, Gianna and Jessica walked around the town square. The warm air smelled like flowers and sunshine. It was a lovely spring day to be outside.

They circled the pond in the courtyard once, then Jessica stopped short.

Gianna gulped in a quick breath. "What's wrong?"

"Nothing."

"Then why'd you stop?"

Jessica pointed to a chalkboard easel sign: Sweet Dreams Baby Boutique. "Let's check it out."

The black and white wooden rocking horse displayed in the store's window sparked Gianna's interest, but the thought of not having a nursery to design dissuaded her.

"No, thanks."

"Why not?" Jessica asked, sounding annoyed.

"Because I don't have a place to put anything."

"But you're still going to need a crib...or two. There's enough space in your parents' guest room to set one up."

"Another time." Gianna put her arm around Jessica and giggled. "And here I thought you stopped because you were having a contraction."

On their way back to Jessica's car, Gianna noticed the weather-beaten clapboard building on the corner of Main and Elm. The creaking signboard hanging from the porch identified the place as Forever Home Realty.

"Ooh, let's go in," Gianna said, excitedly. "Someone from the school highly recommended this place."

"Fine. I need to make a pit stop anyway," Jessica said.

The door chimed as they entered the foyer. A young woman with a gleaming mane of jet-black hair streaked with fire-engine-red highlights and a milky-white complexion stepped in from the back room, along with the lingering remnants of musty cigarette smoke. She adjusted the neckline of her hippie-style sheer blouse then smoothed the front pleats on her white capris.

"Afternoon, ladies. How may I assist you today?"

Caught off guard by the woman's annoyingly adenoidal voice, Gianna stuttered. "I, uh, just recently moved back here from New York, and I'm looking to buy a four-bedroom house in the area."

"That's so fabulous!" the giddy woman replied. She clasped her hands together, jingling the wad of silver bracelets that dangled on her wrists. "I'm Sadie Delbeck, and I'll be *happy* to help you find the perfect home."

"Thank you," Gianna said.

Sadie gaped at Jessica. "Girlie, you look like you're going to pop!"

Jessica laughed to cover her annoyance. "I feel like I am. Thanks for noticing my misery."

"No problem," Sadie said, oblivious to her own rudeness. She waved them forward. "Take a seat in the conference room and make yourselves comfortable. I'll meet you in there right after I grab some paperwork."

She turned toward the doorway and nearly tripped when her left heel snagged the throw rug in the hallway.

Jessica whispered, "I don't like her. Let's go before she comes back."

Gianna touched Jessica's forearm. "I know she seems a bit tactless, but please, I want to see what houses are available on the market."

Jessica sighed. "Fine. I'll put up with her...for you, but first, I'm going to the ladies' room."

As Jessica walked past Gianna, she pinched her nose to mimic Sadie's voice and rude comment. "'Girlie, you look like you're going to pop!'"

Gianna stifled a giggle. "Shush, Jess, she'll hear you!"

Jessica laughed, then waddled off.

Gianna pulled out a deep-cushioned high-back office chair and settled in at the mahogany conference table. She gazed at the sunshine-yellow walls. They were tastefully decorated with framed photos of real estate properties, both historic and modern.

She liked one picture of a Cape Cod-style home that was encircled by a white picket fence. A huge oak tree shaded the postage stamp sized front yard. *A modest home like that would be perfect...in town and close to Danny's work.*

A few minutes later, Sadie returned to the table with some paperwork to fill out. "Ok, first, let me tell you that I've been in this business full time for ten years. As your agent, I will identify your wants, needs, and preferences. I am most certain that I will find you your ideal home within five to ten showings."

Gianna nodded. "Ok, sounds good."

"Now, let's start off with your name."

"It's Gianna Christiansen."

Sadie held her pen against her lips. "Hmm, I once dated someone, Dan Christiansen. Any relation to you?"

Gianna stared silently at Sadie. *Oh crud! Just my luck to find the Sadie that Mrs. Kendall mentioned. Why me?* Jealousy ripped away her outer calm, causing her to respond defensively. "Danny's *my* husband."

A sly smile cracked Sadie's face. "Oh, my, my! What a small world it is."

Jessica waddled back to her chair in the middle of the conversation. Gianna took it as an opportunity to change the subject. "Uh, Sadie, this is Jessica, my sister-in-law."

Sadie smiled at Jessica. "Oh, so are you Dan's sister?"

"Huh?" Jessica tossed Gianna a puzzled look. "No, I'm married to her brother, Matt."

Sadie tapped her pen on the table. "Matt? Did he once own a classic Mustang and hang out with Dan on cruise night at the diner?"

Jessica nodded her head slowly. "Y-e-a-h, years ago."

"Aw, he was a hunk, too," Sadie said.

Jessica's eyes grew big and wide. "Ok then! Can you show us some houses now?"

Sadie didn't answer. It was as if her attention disappeared down some endless corridor of the past. A past that included Danny, and the thought devoured Gianna's confidence.

Emotions played out on Sadie's face. "When I was seventeen, I was a carhop at Clay's Drive-In Diner. Every Friday night was cruise night. Dan and Matt were always there in their classic Mustang. They'd spend time together in the parking lot till closing. After my shift ended, I'd join them." She moistened her blood-red lips, then smiled deviously. "Good times."

The green-eyed monster prodded Gianna for details. "So then, why'd you two break up?"

"He left for college, and we lost touch," Sadie said.

"Oh, well, that happens." *Now, let's keep it that way.*

"It was a long time ago," Sadie added.

"Thirteen years to be exact," Gianna muttered.

Jessica sat forward in her chair, eager to keep the pot boiling. "So, Sadie, are you married?"

"No, but I was engaged twice. I guess you can say I'm still looking for Mr. Right."

"Well, you won't find him in your past," Jessica said.

Gianna kicked Jessica's foot, trying to discourage her from continuing the personal chat. Aiming to leave the past behind and eager to get back on topic, she said, "I have a preapproval letter from the bank."

"Oh, yes. I'll need that," Sadie said.

While Gianna retrieved the document from her phone, Sadie handed her another paper. "This is a buyer's home questionnaire. If you check off your preferences, it'll help me get a better idea of what you're looking for."

"Ok, great," Gianna said.

Sadie folded her hands and rested them on the table. "So, what's Dan up to these days?"

I'm sure that's not a question on the form. Gianna looked up and answered her. "Busy working. Did I mention he's off the market?" She dropped her head and massaged her active belly. "And we're eagerly expecting."

"Oh! You're pregnant, too?"

Gianna smiled with contentment. "Due in July."

"Really? You look big enough to have twins."

"That's because I am."

"You are? Oh, well, you don't look *that* big."

"Thanks." *I think, assuming that was a compliment.* Gianna had never met anyone as completely in-your-face honest.

Sadie handed her another form. "This is your copy of the buyer representation agreement." She then took the house questionnaire form that Gianna had completed and said, "I'll be right back. I'm going to print out some listings that meet your criteria."

"Terrific," Gianna said. *Now we're getting somewhere.*

The moment Sadie left the room, Jessica asked Gianna in a loud whisper, "Why'd you kick me before?"

"You were asking her questions as if she was your best friend. Keep it professional."

Jessica sneered. "Jealous, are you?"

"I am not!" Gianna said, folding her arms across her chest. She lifted her chin and said, "That's ridiculous."

Jessica placed her hand on Gianna's forearm. "Chickadee, believe me when I say there's no competition. Whatever she was to Dan is now history. Trust me."

Gianna exhaled. "You're right. How silly of me to get anxious over the past." She swallowed her brief surge of jealousy. "I'm here to find my dream house."

"Yes, you are," Jessica said.

Sadie returned with a stack of papers. "Ok, here are a few listings in town like you requested, but they're a little pricey. Look them over, and let me know which homes interest you, then I can schedule a showing over the weekend."

Gianna nodded. "I will. Thanks."

"Do you have any fixer uppers?" Jessica asked.

"Yes. There's a house two blocks from here that's going on the market tomorrow," Sadie said. She looked at Gianna. "I could show it to you today if you're interested. It needs a little TLC, but it's way below your price point."

"Well, I don't know—" Gianna said.

"Sure!" Jessica intervened.

"Fabulous! Let me make a quick phone call," Sadie said before dashing out of the room.

"Jess! We don't have time for a fixer upper."

"Sure, we do. We can remodel anything."

"What do you mean, *we?*"

"You saw my house. Matt did an awesome job."

"Seriously, Jess? All he did was paint the walls. Your dad and his contractors did all the work."

"And they'll help you, too."

Gianna rolled her eyes. "Yeah, for a pretty penny."

Jessica's father was a home builder. His company had erected an entire second floor over the tiny ranch she and Matthew bought last year.

Gianna shook her head. "I don't have time for a renovation project. Besides, Danny won't go with it. You should've seen the dilapidated studio apartment I wanted to rent in New York."

Jessica frowned. "Oh, puhleez! It wasn't the apartment that concerned him. It was you living there alone like an orphaned calf with hungry wolves nipping at your heels."

Gianna gave her head a little shake. "Where do you come up with this stuff?"

"It's true! Dan said it."

Gianna rubbed her forehead. "Whatever."

Sadie pulled her jasmine green Subaru alongside the curb in front of the faded gray bungalow with the boarded-up picture window. The front yard looked like a jungle, and the gravel driveway was overgrown with weeds and undesirable plants.

"This is it?" Gianna asked as she shuffled through her papers trying to pair up the listing of the house.

"Yes, but try to keep an open mind," Sadie said.

"Open mind? Oh, come on. Just look at this place. The knee-high weeds took over the property."

Jessica patted her shoulder. "That's no biggie. One quick mow of the lawn and—"

"What lawn? It's all weeds."

"Oh, Gianna! Look at the bright side," Jessica said.

"I don't think there is a bright side."

"Sure, there is," Jessica said. "You wanted in-town living, and this is only two blocks from Dan's practice."

Gianna sighed. "You're right. Let's check it out." She opened the car door and uttered, "That is, if we can find the front door."

They traipsed their way through the overgrown sidewalk. Gnats and mosquitos swarmed their heads.

"Oh, gross!" Gianna griped, swatting at them.

"Careful you don't trip," Sadie said as she climbed the crumbling porch steps. She unlocked the door and pushed it open. "After you, ladies."

At once, Gianna caught a musty whiff of mildew. Cautiously, she stepped inside and did a quick scan of the small, empty living room. Cobwebs hung in every crack and corner, handprints smudged the dreary dirty walls, and mold covered the baseboards. *Yuck! Should I even be in here?*

"This isn't bad," Jessica said as she walked across the creaky, worn wood floor. "I mean, it's rough, but with a little elbow grease, it could be really cute and cozy."

"Exactly, Jessica," Sadie agreed. "Gianna, you need to look beyond the grimy surface."

Jessica pointed to a door. "What's this?"

"Probably a coat closet," Sadie said.

"Oh." Jessica turned the doorknob and opened the door. She screamed, "Oh, my heavens!" and slammed it closed. She threw her hand to her chest and gasped, "Don't look in there!"

"Why?" Gianna asked, her curiosity now piqued. She cautiously opened the closet door and encountered a life-sized grim reaper Halloween decoration staring back at her. Annoyed, she stepped backward and placed her hands on her hips. "Really, Jess?"

"That thing scared me!" Jessica screeched.

Gianna rolled her eyes. "Apparently not enough to trigger your labor."

"Ok, ladies," Sadie said. "Shall we continue the tour?" She led them toward the back of the house. "These next two doors on the right are the bedrooms."

There was nothing unusual about the rooms. They were both tiny with shallow closets. One room had a fist hole punched through the plaster wall. The second room had an entire wall of Crayola artwork; once a kid's room.

"Only two bedrooms? I really need three," Gianna said.

"We can build up," Jessica suggested.

Gianna sighed. She saw Jessica's positive vision of the place but really didn't want to live through a renovation project with newborn twins. "Who do you think I am, Wonder Woman?"

Sadie opened the next door. "Here is the bathroom."

"Only one bathroom," Gianna uttered.

She poked her head inside the doorway. The walls were done in mini pink tiles, and the grout was stained black. The matching fiberglass tub was cracked and had been repaired with masking tape. A dark ring of filth encircled the toilet.

"It's a total gut job," Gianna said.

"Yes, but you can make it your own," Sadie said, before leading them into the dining room.

"Good golly! Check out the flower power wallpaper from the seventies," Jessica said with enthusiasm.

"Enough already," Gianna griped. *Meeting Danny's ex-girlfriend was enough blast from the past for one day.*

She peered out the sliding glass door. The backyard was a junkyard, too, cluttered with a collection of rusted-out lawnmowers and littered with a broken tube television, two mattresses, and an old refrigerator.

"And lastly, the kitchen," Sadie said, pointing to the left. "This, too, can easily be updated."

Gianna stepped away from the glass door and went as far as the arched entryway before stopping. The kitchen looked like a nightmare from a horror flick. Damaged cabinets that barely hung on the walls had been splattered with who knows what. Grimy, dated appliances forming the U-shaped layout rendered the space unusable.

Gianna sighed. *Another complete gut job.* She turned to Jessica and Sadie. "I think this house may be way over our heads."

"But it's way below your budget," Sadie said. "You can hire someone to do the work for you."

"And don't forget, you don't have to offer asking price either," Jessica said.

"Fine. Let me bring Danny back to see it."

"Not a problem," Sadie said.

The second Gianna agreed to keep the house as a contender, something tickled her left foot. She peered down at her open toe sandals and spotted a black carpenter ant crawling on her. She screeched, "Eww! Get it off me!"

She shook her foot, knocking the ant off. It was then that she glanced up at the sink counter and noticed the ant and cockroach infestation, and her natural fear of bugs kicked in. "Forget it! I'm so out of here." She turned and fled for the front door.

Gianna stood by Sadie's car and itched while Sadie locked up the house. *Ick! I hate bugs. Never again do I listen to Jessica about buying a fixer upper.*

Jessica met up with her at the car. "I'm sorry, Gianna. I never thought this house would need so much attention."

Sadie unlocked the car door. "When I get back to the office, I'm going call the listing realtor and let them know about the infestation problem."

"Good, I wouldn't want anyone else to waste their time looking at this one," Gianna said with bitter humor.

"Keep your head up, Gianna. I will find you what you're looking for," Sadie said with overconfidence.

"Un-huh," Gianna mumbled. *You have nine more cracks at it if you're as good as you say you are.*

"Would you consider expanding your search?" Sadie asked. "You'll get more bang for your buck."

Gianna shrugged her shoulders. "I guess so."

"Ok, then. I'll e-mail you some listings tonight and we can set up some showings on Sunday."

"Ok, thanks."

Gianna exhaled heavily when Jessica pulled the car into her parents' driveway. "There's no place like home, even if it's Mom and Dad's house."

"Don't worry, sweetie. As quirky as Sadie is, I'm certain she'll find you your dream home."

"So, she claims."

Gianna opened the car door. The light breeze blew a strong odor of cattle and fresh manure in her direction.

Yep, I'm home. She stepped out of the car, then followed the stone path that led to the pasture between the barn and the house. She propped her foot up on the lower fence rail and watched a herd of cattle chomp on some hay.

She turned to Jessica. "I love it here. It's so peaceful; but, unfortunately, I can't live with my parents forever."

Jessica sighed. "You won't, especially if you're open to looking on the outskirts of town."

Gianna gazed at the calf that greeted her. "But I wanted the convenience of living in town...for Danny."

Jessica touched Gianna's shoulder. "I know, but Dan seems to be adjusting well to living rurally again."

Gianna sighed. "I guess so."

Jessica shielded her eyes from the sun and peered at the far pasture, where her father-in-law and Matthew were rounding up cattle. She rubbed her belly and joked, "You watch. Those two will be baling hay before this baby is born."

"No way! The first cut won't be for another few weeks. You'll be delivered before then," Gianna said.

"I sure hope so."

Gianna stepped away from the fence. "I'll see you later."

She traipsed up the path to the barn. When she slid the double doors open, the clean smell of fresh hay, sweet grain, and cedar shavings invited her inside.

She walked past the office and the tack room, then stopped at the third door. She opened it and flipped on the light. The once-tidy storeroom was now filled with all of her and Danny's household possessions.

She spotted the deep-buttoned plush upholstered recliner that once cradled her beside the gas fireplace in their living room. She sat in it, but the chair lost its coziness being wrapped snugly in heavy-duty plastic.

She closed her eyes and imagined sitting in a rocking chair, nursing her newborns in their gender-neutral nursery. She opened her eyes and gazed down at her growing belly. "I can't wait to meet you both."

She pushed to her feet and exited the storeroom. She continued down the barn aisle, stopping at the tenth stall, home of her horse, Gemma. The stealthy, sixteen-year-old Bay stood with his head down, munching on the stray strands of hay that had fallen from his now-empty hay rack.

"Hey, boy. Don't they feed you?"

"You're joking, right? Look at him!" a gruff voice bellowed from inside the tack room.

Startled, Gianna turned and saw Brody, her dad's hired help, perched against the doorway, wearing leather chaps and spurs.

"He's too fat," Brody said, carrying a bridle slung over his broad left shoulder. "This big guy doesn't get nearly as much exercise as he did before you moved away."

"Well, I'm back now for good."

"I heard."

Gianna opened the top half of the stall door. Gemma stuck his head out and nuzzled her face. "You know I'd ride you if I could," she said, patting his neck.

Brody gave her a thorough once-over with his stern brown eyes. "Sorry, can't let you do that. Strict orders from Dan."

Gianna frowned. "Oh, please! I know better than to ride in my condition."

"Hey, I'm just saying…if I saddled up a horse for you, your husband would brand my hide."

Gianna laughed. She knew he was teasing, but not completely. She recalled how furious Danny had been the time she rode Gemma after her calamity with Chad.

Brody adjusted the tack that was draped over his shoulder. "Well, I've got to get back to work." He tipped his cowboy hat and winked. "See you around."

"See ya," Gianna said. She turned her attention back to Gemma. She noticed the clumps of dried mud and who knows what on his coat. "Have you been rolling in the pasture again?" She shook her head. "Boy, you're filthy."

She glanced across the aisle at the wash stall. "It's probably not a good idea to give you a bath, but nothing says I can't brush you out." She picked up the grooming caddy from the wooden storage unit just outside the stall. "First, I need to cross tie you in the aisle."

"Don't even think about it," Danny shouted from the front barn entrance. Brusquely, he strode in. The rhythmic thunk-tap of his leather boots against the concrete floor were disrupted by sporadic shuffles from his limp.

"I was only going to brush him out," she said.

"What if something spooks him and you get kicked?"

Gianna dropped her gaze. It was too painful to think about the consequences.

"Hey," Danny said, lifting her chin. "I know you want to spend time with Gemma, but it's not worth the risk."

Gianna sighed. "You're right. If something did happen, I could never live with myself."

Danny hugged her, rubbing his cheek against the top of her head. "I'll help you wash him tomorrow."

She smiled appreciatively. "Thanks."

"No problem."

Together, Gianna and Danny left the barn. As they strolled back to the driveway, Danny wrapped his arm around her. With an amused twitch of his mouth, he said, "I heard you found a house for us with lots of potential."

"Ha, ha! And did Jessica tell you the grim reaper lives in the coat closet?"

"Yeah, she did," he said, laughing.

"And did she tell you who our realtor is?"

Danny's happy-go-lucky expression quickly crumbled. "Babe," he exhaled. He encircled her waist with his strong hands and embraced her eyes with his. "Sadie and I were nothing more than friends."

"Really?" Gianna asked. "Because she made it sound a tad more serious than that."

"Absolutely not. She was never my type."

"Ok. I believe you."

"Hey, chickadee," Jessica shouted, yanking Gianna away from her conversation with Danny.

Gianna looked up at Jessica rocking peacefully on the porch swing. "Yeah?" she asked.

"Come, sit a spell," Jessica said.

"Ok, we're coming," Gianna said. She took Danny's hand, and together, climbed the porch steps. "Where's your other half?" she asked Jessica.

"In the shower."

"Oh."

"Have you two decided on a location?" Jessica asked.

"Gee, I don't know," Gianna said. She pitched Danny a stumped look. "We didn't even discuss it."

"Babe, it's ok. We can house hunt outside of town."

"What? But I thought you wanted convenience."

"No. Part of the reason I moved back here was for some elbow room. When Steve, Rob, and I went camping, I realized then how much I missed the quiet, wide-open space." He nodded contently. "I missed this."

The front door opened, and Matthew stepped out with a t-shirt half on over his head. "Mom says supper's ready."

"Good. I'm starved," Gianna said.

"Not me, but I'll join you all," Jessica said. She leaned forward in the rocking chair but struggled to stand up.

"Let me help you," Matthew said, sprinting across the porch in his bare feet.

"Ow! "No, wait," she moaned. She leaned back into the chair and squeezed her eyes shut.

"Jess, what's wrong?" Danny asked.

A tiny shrug lifted Jessica's petite shoulders. She opened her eyes and let out a slow, controlled breath. "I'm fine. It's just another Braxton Hicks contraction."

"You sure? They're not usually painful," Danny said.

"No, just uncomfortable," she said.

"I wouldn't be surprised if you have that baby tomorrow," Danny said.

"Let's hope so," Jessica replied.

Chapter Thirty-Two

Dan opened the bedroom door looking for Gianna. He poked his head inside the doorway and called her. "Babe, you in here?"

"I'm in the closet," she answered.

"What're you doing in there?"

"I'm looking for something suitable to wear."

"What's wrong with what you wore to church?"

"That dress was...uh, too...traditional."

Dan rolled his eyes. *Why did I ask such a trivial question?* The powder-blue maxi dress looked striking on her beautiful pregnant body.

He stepped into the room and spotted the white bi-fold doors ajar. Gianna stood there, her backside to him, wearing only a bra and panties, shuffling through a section of outfits.

A rush of desire clawed and clutched at his insides. He wrapped his arms around her expanding waistline and pressed himself tightly against her back. "I like what you're wearing now," he whispered.

"Oh, Danny, stop!"

He felt her insecurities as she squirmed in his arms.

"What?" he asked, locking his gaze on her. "Can't I hold you? I love you."

"I love you, too, but..." With a sigh, she settled in his arms with her cheek against his chest.

"But what?" he asked. He held her chin in his hand and tilted her face upward. "What's wrong? Talk to me."

"I can't measure up," she said.

Dan raised his eyebrows. "You can try wearing heels, but I'm still taller than you."

Annoyed by his humor, she clicked her tongue against her teeth. "Funny. I mean...Sadie. She's tall, slender, and generously gifted up top."

"So what? I'm buying a house, not her." He took Gianna's hand and placed it on his heart. "You're my everything...petite and curvy, with muscle and grace."

"Really?" she asked, her voice tainted with doubt. "Can you honestly say you're not the least bit interested in seeing her after all these years?"

"I was *never* interested in Sadie. She did absolutely nothing for me. Why everyone thinks I dated her is beyond me." He stroked Gianna's cheekbones with his thumbs. "You're my best friend. And you're incredibly sexy, even more so carrying *our* twins."

His flattery whipped color into her soft cheeks.

"Aw, Danny, stop!"

"What? It's true." He took her hand and led her to their bed. "It's you I want," he whispered, before pressing his lips to hers.

Careful not to lose his balance, Dan grabbed his jeans off the floor and jammed one leg in and then the other.

"What time are we supposed to meet Sadie?"

"At one," Gianna answered from the bathroom.

He quickly pulled on his blue plaid dress shirt and buttoned it. "We should get going. Are we meeting her at the office?"

"No. The house on Bison Road."

Gianna stepped out of the bathroom wearing a dusty-rose, figure-hugging dress that defined her blooming baby bump.

Dan drifted his gaze over her, his body heating up with fresh urgency. "Wow! Look at you."

"You like?" she asked, posing like a model.

"Oh, yeah." He caressed her cheek and cherished its tender warmth. "You look gorgeous, as always."

Gianna blushed. "Oh, Danny!" She grabbed his hand. "C'mon, or we're going to be late."

Dan stopped his truck at the corner of Elk Street and Bobcat. Across the quiet intersection was Bear Creek Estates, a new housing development.

"Sadie's showing us a house in there?" he asked.

"Yeah. Go straight, then make the first left on Bison."

"What's the house number?"

"Nine."

Dan turned left on Bison. Lined up on both sides of the street were cookie-cutter houses, equally spread apart, with identical landscaping, making individual houses indistinguishable.

He noticed the number three posted on a stone pillar at the end of a driveway. "Looks like odd numbers are on your side," he said as he crept along the freshly paved road. As he pulled up to house number nine, one thought came to mind. *This isn't it.* The house had no character, the neighbors were too close, and there was no room for nature. He wanted a peaceful retreat with lots of open space, where wildlife was his closest neighbor.

"I don't know about this," he said as he parked his truck behind Sadie's car in the cobblestone driveway.

"Why? It's beautiful," Gianna said.

"Every house looks the same, and the neighbors are right there."

"And that's a bad thing? Look where we came from."

"I want something with personality."

"Personality? You mean eccentric like Sadie, or eerie like that house she showed me in town the other day."

Dan sighed. "I'll ignore the remark about Sadie. Look, forget the house in town. I want move-in-ready, but I want a house that we can put our own stamp on."

"Ok, but we're here, so let's just take a look."

"Fine," Dan said, opening his door.

When he helped Gianna out of the truck, he heard the subtle click of a storm door opening. Out of the corner of his eye, he caught sight of Sadie standing on the front porch.

Whoa! She changed. Her short, punk hairstyle had grown out long and feminine.

"Dan!" Sadie shouted.

Once again, she caught his attention. She quickly hobbled down the concrete step, then bounced along the stone sidewalk in a flirty black club dress and stiletto heels.

Gianna uttered, "She's such a fashion diva."

"Now don't throw the first stone," he said.

Gianna sighed in frustration. "Can't you see she's dressing for you? She didn't look like that the other day."

Dan shook his head to dismiss her accusation. "Babe, like I said earlier, there's no match." Not wanting her to feel threatened, he wrapped his arm snugly around her midriff.

When Sadie approached them, Dan held out his hand and offered her a handshake. "Hello, Sadie."

Sadie hesitated, clearly expecting a hug, but then accepted his firm handshake. She gave her bright-red lips a soft, sensual lick. "It's so nice to see you again, Dan. How've you been?"

Her voice seemed even more adenoidal than he remembered, triggering an unsolicited memory of their last encounter, thirteen years ago...

It had been a usual Friday night at Clay's Drive-in Diner. Dan sat in his portable folding chair behind Matt's Mustang, hanging with his best buds, talking muscle cars and horsepower.

Sadie had attempted to sneak up behind him, but her cigarette stench ratted her out. She wrapped her arms around him and said, "My shift ended."

"I noticed," Dan said, rubbing his irritated nose. He broke away from her embrace. "I thought you said you quit."

"Well, I had a few left in the pack," she retorted.

"In that case, you should've pitched them."

Sadie put her hands on her hips. "Whatever! So anyway, what about tomorrow? A bunch of us are going camping at Gray Wolf State Park. Tonya's bringing a keg, and Rick is bringing the hard stuff." She leaned into him and whispered, "You and I can share a tent together. We'll have a blast. What do you say?"

"No thanks."

"Why not? Don't be such a party pooper."

Dan shook his head. "I have plans."

"Doing what? Having tea with your parents?"

Her sneering remark cut him like a knife. What he'd give to have another moment with his parents again.

"For your information, I'll be busy packing for college," he grumbled and stormed off.

Dan shuddered as he snapped back into reality.

"Yoo-hoo!" Sadie called, waving her hand in front of his face. "Are you still with us?"

"Danny, you ok?" Gianna asked, rubbing his chest.

"Huh?" he asked.

"You were in a daze, like a time warp or something."

Was I ever? Dan blinked. "Yeah, babe, I'm fine."

Sadie shook her head. "You haven't changed a bit." She looked at Gianna. "He was always a dreamer."

Yeah, wishing I were somewhere else. Dan pulled a bandana out of his pocket and wiped the sweat off his forehead.

"So, Dan, are you still an avid hiker? Go on any exciting adventures lately?" Sadie asked.

Dan exchanged meaningful smiles with Gianna, then answered, "Yeah, last fall." *No pun intended.*

"How 'bout that time we went camping at Gray Wolf?" she asked. "We had a blast together."

"Uh, Sadie. I didn't go. Remember?"

Sadie blushed. "Oh, that's right." She toyed with her diamond necklace. "It was Jake Parker who went with me." She gave a toss of her hand. "No matter. I got so wasted that day."

Dan cleared his throat. "So, tell me about this house."

"Oh, yes, it's a new build. Three bedrooms, two baths, and a two-car attached garage." She pulled out her notes. "It's fifteen hundred square feet situated on half an acre."

"Nice," Gianna said, venturing toward the sidewalk.

"Gianna, I picked this one specifically for you, since you didn't care for the one I showed you the other day."

"Good," Gianna said. She looked over her shoulder. "Well, Danny, aren't you coming?"

"Yeah," he said, reluctantly.

He knew it. Sadie was going to get Gianna all hyped about this house that he didn't particularly like. Then they'd argue, and he'd wind up looking like a jerk. *Yep, I can already see the outcome.*

Dan stepped up onto the tiny concrete porch. *Eh, I'm not impressed. Can't even fit a chair out here.*

He entered the front door. The living room was a decent size, with a propane fireplace finished in a white herringbone tile. Weathered gray laminate flooring flowed into the kitchen and dining area.

Gianna wandered right to the kitchen. "Oh, Danny, check this out," she said, opening the builder grade white shaker cabinets.

"There's plenty of storage," Sadie said. She brushed her hand along the countertop. "What do you think of the granite and the stainless-steel appliances?"

"Nice. I can picture myself preparing meals here, and I like the open view to the living room," Gianna said.

"Dan, what do you think?" Sadie asked.

Dan shrugged, uninspired. "It's boring."

"A happy wife is a happy life," Sadie reminded him.

Dan rolled his eyes, then meandered down the hallway toward the carpeted bedrooms. He poked his head inside each one and then checked out the two bathrooms. The floorplan was too small.

He moseyed his way back to the dining room, where a set of French doors led outside to a small wooden deck. Gianna and Sadie were already out there, scoping out the fenced-in backyard.

"Danny, I really like this place," Gianna said, rushing back up the steps. "I can see us barbecuing out here; our kids playing in the yard."

Dan shook his head. "Sure, it has more green space than we had in the city, but..."

"Uh, yeah," Gianna said.

"But I think we need to see more," he said.

"I have three other properties lined up," Sadie said.

"Great, let's go," Dan said, eagerly.

After seeing a log cabin and an older farmhouse, Sadie led them to a three-story chalet on Coyote Creek Trail. The home was nestled on five acres in the foothills overlooking Ruby Valley.

"Now this is what I'm talking about," Dan said as he stood in the asphalt driveway. "A three-car garage...nice."

"Now you can get your motorcycle out of Doc Kendall's shed," Gianna said.

Dan nodded. "This is the house."

"How do you know? We haven't even seen the inside."

"I just know."

"Ok, guys," Sadie called from the front entrance of the house. "Let me show you the inside."

Dan and Gianna climbed five steps up to the wraparound cedar deck that encircled the main living level.

Sadie held the door. "This house has four bedrooms, three and a half baths, and is twenty-eight hundred square feet."

"Oh, wow!" Dan and Gianna said in unison as they stepped inside the foyer.

The main living area had an open floor plan with a massive two-story stone fireplace that separated the great room from the kitchen and dining area.

Dan wandered the living area and stopped near the French doors that opened to the backside of the deck.

"Check it out, babe!" The entire west side was a wall of windows, giving a lovely view of the wildlife outside. "I told you this is the house."

"Beautiful," Gianna said as she gazed out at the green treetops and rugged terrain. She nodded, pleased. "It certainly is picturesque here."

"Yes, it is," Sadie agreed, quickly urging them back inside to the kitchen. "So, Gianna. Can you see yourself cooking in here?"

The G-shaped custom kitchen had hickory cabinets, quartz countertops, and slate black appliances.

Gianna gazed up at the exposed wood beams, then down at the hardwood floors. "This place has a lot of wood finishes, but I really like it."

"Fantastic," Sadie said.

She showed Gianna and Dan the large pantry, a coat closet, and a powder room before leading them upstairs to the third level that opened to a balcony overlooking the main living space.

A large master bedroom with its own bath, three other generously sized bedrooms with huge closets, and another full bathroom occupied the third level.

"Whoa, you really knocked the ball out of the park with this house, Sadie," Dan said. "I'm impressed."

"I'm not finished yet," Sadie said with a head nod. "Follow me downstairs to the ground level, which has outside access to the garage and yard."

The lower level had a home theater, a wet bar, and a full bathroom.

Dan smiled. "My man cave. Babe, I'm home."

Gianna wandered over to the sliding glass doors that gave access to the backyard. "Oh, they fenced in a tiny section. This is perfect! We can sit out on the patio and watch the kids play."

"Would you like to write an offer?" Sadie asked.

"What's the asking price?" Dan asked.

"Well..." Sadie gritted her teeth. "It's thirty thousand over your budget."

Dan rubbed the back of his neck. Hearing that was like a sucker punch to the gut. *Why did you bother showing us the house then?* Frustrated, he sighed. "Sadie, I can't do it."

"The price is negotiable," she replied.

"Yeah, but what we could offer would be insulting to the homeowner," Gianna said.

"Well, I do know the homeowner is eager to sell. His job transferred him to Philadelphia just seven months after he had this house built, and he can't afford to keep it." Sadie threw out an open hand. "Make an offer. The worst he can do is reject it."

Dan ran his hand through his hair. *If only I hadn't had my accident, I could have afforded this house.* He pulled out his phone and calculated some numbers. *Well, there's always the CD I can close out, and if we share a vehicle awhile longer, then maybe...* He snapped his phone back into its case and said to Sadie, "I can go up ten thousand, but not another penny more."

Gianna's face lit up. "Listen, Danny, I can cover the closing costs."

"Fine! Let's do it then," Dan said, willingly.

When Dan and Gianna arrived home at her parents' house, her father was sitting on the front porch step.

"Hey, you two, how'd it go?" he asked.

"We put in an offer," Gianna said. "Danny will tell you the details." She hugged her father then went inside.

Dan sighed. "Let's just say if this deal goes through, I'll be working every extra on-call hour available."

Mr. Stefano smirked. "Went over budget, did you?"

"Yeah. But it's the perfect house for us."

"I see," Mr. Stefano said. He stood up and pulled his wallet out of the top pocket of his overalls. "Maybe this will help." He handed him a folded check.

"What's this?" Dan asked, opening it. "What the...? I can't accept this!"

"Take it. It's your money."

Dan stared, baffled. "What?"

"This isn't New York City, son. Why you pay me so much rent money?"

"Pop, you're too generous. Thank you."

"No, son. Thank you. You brought my stubborn daughter home."

Chapter Thirty-Three

It was a beautiful spring afternoon at Gray Wolf State Park. The sun was blazing hot, but a cool breeze off the lake softened the otherwise intense heat, and the hardy trees acted like a leafy umbrella, making the unseasonably warm temperature more bearable.

Gianna parked herself on a flat rock beside the shimmering lake and watched five ducklings stumble over one another as they tried to keep up with their mama.

So cute. She laughed, then took the last bite of her crunchy ice cream cone. "Yum! That hit the spot," she said, rubbing her hands together to knock off the crumbs.

"Yep, just what the doctor ordered," Danny said as he tossed another stone, skipping it twice across the water. "Man, it's so good to be back here. Good times."

"And many more to come," Gianna said. *I hope.* She picked up her phone. "Still no call from Sadie. I guess we didn't get the house."

"It's only been two days. If it's not meant to be, then we'll find something else."

"I know, but you loved that house," Gianna said.

Unexpectedly, both of their cell phones rang in sync.

Gianna checked her phone. "Oh, it's a group text from Matt."

It's a girl! April Lynn Stefano, 8 lbs., 12 oz., 20 in. long. Mother and baby doing fine.

"Wow! She's a big girl!" Gianna said.

"Well, your brother's a big guy."

"Poor Jess. She's so petite."

Seconds later, another text came in with pictures.

"Aw, so precious!" Gianna said. "Can we visit them?"

Danny texted Matthew back and forth.

"Tomorrow, babe. Matt says Jess isn't feeling up to any visitors."

Gianna raised her eyebrows. "What happened to her spiel about wanting everyone to celebrate her baby's birthday?"

"Births don't always go as planned."

Gianna nodded. "I certainly can respect that."

Two days later, Gianna and Danny strolled along the concrete sidewalk leading to Matthew and Jessica's front door. Perched in the garden bed was a painted wooden stork announcing the arrival of baby April. Tied to the porch railing were pink and white balloons blowing in the soft breeze.

Matthew greeted them at the door and invited them inside the living room, where Jessica was resting comfortably on the couch with their new baby girl.

"Congratulations, Jess," Danny said, hugging her.

"Thanks, Dan." She peered up at Gianna and patted the chair cushion. "Have a seat."

Danny turned and kissed Gianna. "I'll leave you two to talk. Matt and I will be in the kitchen."

Gianna nodded, then sat down beside Jessica. She gazed in awe at the tiny newborn all bundled in pink.

"Oh, Jess. She's a doll. I'm so happy for you."

Jessica rubbed her tired eyes. "Thank you."

"So, how're you feeling?"

"Exhausted and sore."

"But you did great. She's amazing," Gianna said.

Jessica reached for Gianna's hand. "Listen, I'm sorry for flipping out on you the other day at the restaurant."

"Oh, Jess. We all have our moments."

"No, really. I was so anxious about labor and..." She glanced down at her baby and shook her head. "It was nothing like I imagined. I was too exhausted to celebrate."

"I'm sorry, Jess."

"I was so miserable," Jessica said. "I threw everyone out except Matt and my midwife."

A chair scuffed across the kitchen floor and Matthew's voice bellowed, "Are you kidding me?" He entered the living room and positioned his butt on the arm of the chair. "You were beyond miserable." He looked at Gianna, then back at Danny, who was now leaning against the doorframe. "Man, she yelled at me and told me it was my fault. I honestly thought she was going to hit me."

Jessica rolled her bottom lip and whined, "I'm sorry, honey, but I was in so much pain."

Danny shook his head. "Believe me. As an OB, I've witnessed so much worse."

A wide grin spread across Matthew's face. "Tell me."

"Oh, no! Another time. I'm not going to give your sister any ammunition."

Gianna smiled, knowing her Italian temper could easily explode in a stressful situation. "Don't worry, sweetheart. I'll be nice to you."

Jessica puckered her lips at Gianna. "You're such a suck-up. You just wait. Believe me when I tell you, labor is no picnic."

"But it'll be so worth it in the end," Gianna said.

On their way home, Gianna's cell phone rang. She glanced down at the caller ID. "Ooh, it's Sadie calling!"

"It's about time," Danny said.

Gianna activated the speaker phone. "Hello?"

"Gianna, it's Sadie. I'm sorry it took me so long to get back to you. The seller's agent told me that Dan's heartfelt letter explaining his dreams for the house swayed the seller's decision. He accepted your offer and your terms."

"Oh, my stars! Really?" Gianna asked.

"That's awesome," Danny shouted.

"Congratulations!" Sadie said. "We'll be in touch."

Chapter Thirty-Four

eeks passed, and it was June. Gianna sat at the edge of her recliner unwrapping the last knick-knack from the cardboard box and placed it on the wooden shelf next to the fireplace. She sat back down and observed the open room. She sighed happily. *We're finally home.*

"Babe? Come up here a minute," Danny called.

"Coming," she said, pushing herself to her feet.

She waddled to the staircase and slowly climbed each step. *Oh, these stairs.* It was a good thing she and Danny agreed not to move in until after the babies were born. Being pregnant at thirty-four weeks with twins made climbing stairs a major challenge.

She stood in the doorway of the nursery. Double cribs, side by side against the minty green accent wall, were the focal point of the room.

"Wow, Danny! It's really coming together nicely."

Danny was lounging on the white shag area rug next to a newly assembled bouncy seat. He nodded. "It's getting there. But I still need to assemble the swings and..." he turned and eyed the pile of baby shower gifts that cluttered the other side of the room, "a whole bunch of other stuff."

Gianna laughed. "You should hire Matt. He's the baby gear expert."

"Oh, no. It's my turn," he said, proudly.

Gianna sat down in her glider chair. "I'm going to spend the afternoon writing out my thank you cards."

Danny patted her knee. "That's fine—"

His cell phone rung a distinctive tone.

"Dang! It's the hospital. I have to go."

Gianna nodded. "I know, you're on-call."

Danny stood up. "I'll drop you off at your parents."

"No, it's ok. Mom's coming over in an hour to help me tidy up the nursery."

"Ok," he said.

Gianna slid forward in her chair and stood up. A sharp pain shot down her leg like a bolt of lightning. She squeezed her eyes shut until the pain diminished. "Oh, why can't I just go into labor now?" she asked in frustration.

"Because it's too early," Danny said. "So far, you've had a textbook pregnancy, and our babies are doing fantastic, but they still need a few more weeks." Danny wrapped his arms around her. "Has your sciatica been bothering you that much?"

She nodded. "Yeah, the past couple of days."

"Well, try to take it easy. I've got to go," he said.

"I will."

Another two weeks passed. Gianna was now thirty-six weeks along in her pregnancy, and her instinct for nesting kicked in.

"Gianna! Slow down," Mom yelled. "You're going to wear yourself out."

"I'm fine," she said as she carried a laundry basket of newborn clothes into the nursery.

"Well, at least let me help you fold them," Mom said.

"I've got it," she said, sliding the wooden door aside. She took a tiny white hanger off the rod, then reached into the basket. She pulled out a yellow ducky print sleep sack. "This is going to be one huge wardrobe of yellows, greens, and whites."

"I'm sure you'll have either pink or blue or both as soon as those babies are born," Mom said.

Gianna gazed at the minty green, gender-neutral room, and pointed to the Noah's Ark themed bedding.

"I'm going to make up their cribs next."

"It's going to look adorable, honey."

Suddenly, the oven timer buzzed.

"Oh, I forgot about the lasagna," Mom said, rushing out of the nursery.

Gianna followed her mother downstairs.

"Mom, let me help."

"I've got it, honey. After this cools, I'm going to separate it into servings and freeze them."

Gianna scanned her once bare kitchen. Her mom had turned it into an Italian restaurant with dishes of sausage and peppers, chicken alfredo, meatballs, and several sides of vegetables.

"Mom, I don't mean to sound ungrateful, but you cooked enough food to last us six months."

"Trust me, honey. Caring for newborn twins, you don't want to be thinking about what to prepare for dinner."

"I suppose," she sighed.

Gianna turned to the sink and started loading the dishwasher when a familiar pang hit her. "Oh, no!"

"What's the matter?" Mom asked.

"Oh, nothing. Just another Braxton Hicks contraction."

"I thought you were going to tell me your sciatic nerve was bothering you again."

"That too, at times," she said. "I'm starting to understand how Jess felt at the end of her pregnancy."

Five minutes later, Gianna was hit with another false contraction. But this time, it was different. It started in her back and radiated to her stomach, and it was more painful than usual.

"Oh, no. There's another one," she said, nervously.

Mom put her arm around her. "Honey, why don't you sit on the couch and rest."

"Ok."

Gianna sat down and waited. "It can't be the real thing, not yet." But five minutes later, another one came, and lasted thirty seconds. She gulped. "Mom, they seem to be consistent."

"Do you want me to call your midwife?"

Gianna glanced at the clock. "No, I'll call Danny. He should be leaving the office soon." She stood up and wandered around the living room. *Where did I leave my phone?* The second she spotted it on the end table, Danny walked through the front door.

"Hey, babe. I went to your parents' house and Pop said you and Mom were here." He set down his laptop bag and said, "Hmm, what smells so delicious?"

"Danny..." Gianna sat back down on the couch and waited to ride out another contraction before talking.

Mom walked in from the kitchen, drying her hands on a towel. "I think she's in labor."

Danny's voice broke with emotion. "What? Now?" he asked, crouching down next to Gianna. "Are you having a contraction now?"

Gianna nodded. When the pain subsided, she slowly opened her eyes. "They seem to be every five minutes, lasting thirty seconds or so."

"Should we call Nina?" Mom asked.

"Not yet. I'll check her first to see if she's making any progress," Danny said.

At the hospital, Gianna settled into bed. She looked up at Danny and said, "I can't believe this is really happening."

Danny kissed her forehead. "We're going to be parents real soon," he said, excitedly.

The curtain glided across the track and Nurse Mia walked in. She hooked up the fetal heart monitors and started an IV drip. She glanced at Gianna's chart and said, "Oh, you're having twins! Do you know if they are boys, girls, both?"

"We didn't find out," Gianna said.

"Really? Most parents nowadays find out."

"Life rarely has happy surprises," Gianna said. "Besides, you can't return them if it's not what you wanted."

Mia laughed. "So true." She logged out of the computer. "You're all set. I'll check in on you in a little bit."

During the early phases of labor, Gianna walked the maternity floor, stopping regularly for contractions. As the contractions became more intense, she returned to her room and tried other techniques to ease the pain. She rocked side to side on a birthing ball while Danny stood behind her and balanced her.

She moaned. "I'm so miserable."

"But you're doing so well," he said.

"I want this to be over," she cried.

Nina, her midwife, entered the room. "Gianna, how're you holding up?" she asked.

"I'm so tired."

"Aw, I know, but Mia tells me you're making tremendous progress. You're four centimeters."

"That's it? After all these hours?"

"You're doing wonderfully, Gianna," Nina said.

"Thanks, but I think I need to lie back in bed now."

"Ok. I'd like to monitor the babies anyway," Nina said.

Danny assisted Gianna back to bed, then blotted her sweaty forehead with a cold washcloth. "You're doing beautifully, babe."

The hours passed. Gianna rested in between contractions. When a strong one ripped through her, she emitted a shriek and curled up on her side. She gripped Danny's hand and cried, "I can't do this anymore."

"You're doing great," he said.

"Ow, but it's too painful," she cried.

"Do you want the epidural?"

"Nooo!" Gianna moaned. "I have to do this naturally."

Danny shook his head. "I respect your wishes not to have intervention, but sometimes labor doesn't go as planned. It's the outcome that matters, not how you get there."

Gianna panted, "No drugs. I'm going to do this."

"I know you can," he said, caressing her back.

"Ow!" Gianna groaned at another contraction. She squeezed her eyes tight. As the pain tore through her, she tried hard to focus on a pleasant scene. She imagined vacationing on a secluded island with white sandy beaches and clear, turquoise-colored water.

"You got it, babe. Ride it out," he said.

The contraction faded away, and Gianna set aside her *happy place*. "It's over," she breathed.

"You've been at this awhile now," Nina said. "Let me check your progress."

"Fine," Gianna said, shifting her position. She hated cervical checks more than the contractions.

Nina lifted the sheet and examined her. "Oh wow! You're fully dilated. You're ready to push."

Gianna's heart hammered with surprise. "I am?"

Nina nodded. "On your next contraction..."

"Ok," Gianna panted. "Here I go again," she cried.

"Ok, baby," Danny said. "Breathe in through your nose and out through your mouth." He spoke with complete enthusiasm. "Come on, chin to your chest. You can do it!"

Gianna recalled Jessica's advice on the correct way to push. *I can do this.* She grabbed her knees, scrunched her eyes shut, and took a deep breath.

"Good, good, good," Nina said.

After twenty minutes of pushing, baby A's head crowned. "Oh, it burns," Gianna shouted.

"I know, darling," Danny said. "Baby's almost here."

After a few more pushes, the baby's head was out.

"Rest," Nina said as she suctioned the baby's airway.

"Ok, one more push," Danny shouted. "C'mon, Gianna. You got this!"

Really? Again? I'm so over this. With all her might, she gave one more push.

"It's a boy!" Nina announced. "Here he is," she said, lifting him up. She placed him down on her chest.

"Oh, my goodness!" Gianna cried. "He's so tiny."

He made a few squeaks before he started wailing.

"He sure has a healthy set of lungs," Danny said.

Gianna's bubble of happiness burst, and tears streamed down her cheeks. Her little miracle was finally here, so real and alive, and he was dependent on her. "We have a son," she cried.

Danny leaned in and kissed her. "I love you."

Nina clamped the umbilical cord and handed Danny the scissors. "Would you like to do the honors?"

Danny's face beamed with happiness. "Absolutely. In all my deliveries, I've only had one or two fathers decline the opportunity. Of course, one of those two men fainted."

After the cord was cut, Mia scooped the baby up and took him to the warming crib where she cleaned him up.

"Six pounds and nineteen inches long," she said.

Danny stood alongside the crib. It was a treasured moment to watch him bond with his son. "Hey, little man. Don't cry. I'm your daddy." The moment the baby heard him, he stopped fussing and focused on his calm, teary voice. "It's ok. I'm right here."

Gianna got caught up in the moment, and it wasn't until Nina mentioned performing a cervical check to determine baby B's position that she realized she still had another baby to deliver.

"I feel the bulging bag of water," Nina said, "Oops, I popped it. Ok, Gianna, baby B is in position. On your next contraction, give a push."

Danny returned to Gianna's bedside and assisted her into position. She took a deep breath and pushed again. After fifteen minutes, baby B was born.

"It's a girl!" Nina said, holding the baby up.

Again, Gianna's heart burst with joy. "A girl!"

Danny's gentle hands framed her face. His features softened and tears of bliss dampened his eyes. "We have a daughter! Thank you."

Mia scooped up the little girl and brought her over to the warming crib to clean her up and assess her. "She's five pounds, seven ounces, and eighteen inches long."

Afterward, Mia and another pediatric nurse bundled the twins in blankets and hats and carried them over to Gianna and Danny to bond.

Gianna gazed down at her nursing babies. *Wow! I'm a mother.* It was instant love, instant protection, instant worry.

She prayed silently. *Lord, thank you for blessing us with these little babies. We ask for your guidance to raise them according to your will and to protect them as they journey through life. Amen.*

She glanced up at Danny. "So, are you ok with the names we picked?"

He smiled. "Yep. It fits them both perfectly."

She nodded contently. "When our folks come to visit tomorrow, we can announce their grandchildren as Daniel Joseph Jr. and Alessia Rose Christiansen."

Two days later, Gianna and the twins were healthy enough to go home. However, the summer weather wasn't ideal. Heavy rain lashed the ground, leaving miniature streams flowing through the hospital parking lot.

Gianna, her babies, and a patient transport aide waited in the hospital lobby while Danny pulled his truck underneath the carport.

He clicked the car seats into the back seat and helped Gianna into the front. "Nice weather to bring our little family home in, huh?" he joked.

The transport aide laughed. "Could be worse. It could be snowing."

When Danny and Gianna arrived in the driveway of their new home, the rain stopped. A stray beam of sunlight peeked through the dark, stormy clouds.

Gianna lowered herself out of the truck into the thick, humid air. Steam writhed around her feet from the hot, wet pavement.

As she waited for Danny to unlatch the car seats from their bases, she turned and gazed out into the distance at a little dirt road that skipped off into the hills. Just over the green treetops, a vivid double rainbow presented itself in the foreground of the misty mountains.

She pointed. "Oh, wow, look! So perfect, just like our little double blessings."

Danny stood beside her with a car seat gripped tightly in each hand. He gazed in awe at the miraculous double rainbow. "There's more to it, babe."

"What do you mean?"

"God is not only shining his blessings down on us. He's reminding us that He is faithful in keeping all his promises to us in both good times and bad."

A note from the author...

To My Readers,

Thank you for reading, *In Good Times and Bad*. As a self-published author, attaining exposure to interested readers relies on word-of-mouth. Please consider writing an honest review wherever you can. Any review, positive or negative, really helps readers determine if my book is worth their attention. Your opinion really makes a difference. Thank you.

Janet

Conversation Starter: Discussion Questions

1. Why do you think the author chose the title, *In Good Times and Bad?* How does it relate to the story?

2. Which character did you identify most with and why?

3. Which character did you particularly like or dislike? Why?

4. Dan was faced with making a moral decision. What choice did he make, and how did it affect his life and Gianna's? Why did he make this choice?

5. Several characters made choices that had moral implications. Choose one character. Would you have made the same decision? Why or why not?

6. Both Gianna and Dan experienced hardships throughout the story, yet they never lost their faith. Do you feel their healing process would've been the same without religion?

7. How did Gianna mature through the duration of the novel? What events triggered her growth?

8. If you could insert yourself as a character in this book, who would you be?

9. Does the story remind you of a situation that happened in your life?

10. What was the peak event of the novel? What conflicts lead up to it and what was the resolution afterward?

11. What passages strike you as profound? Is there a scene that sums up the central dilemma of the book?

12. Was the plot engaging? Was the story a fast-paced page-turner, or did the story unfold slowly with a focus on character development?

13. Were you surprised by the plot's complications, or did you find it predictable?

14. What do you think the author was trying to accomplish? Do you think the book was written for entertainment? Was there a message, or both?

15. Did you like the book? If you have read the author's first book, *Always Faithful and True*, how does this book compare? Does this book inspire you to read more from this author?

16. If you had to describe the book in just one word, what would it be? Would you recommend it to others?